Praise for
Benjamin E. Miller

Deep Current

"A terrific blend of speculative science and adrenaline-charged action."   —*Jack Du Brul

"A fascinating premise—in Antarctic waters, a giant iceberg has been detected, moving against the stream and heading straight for Hawaii. Marines and biologists are dispatched to land on the leviathan, where they discover a young boy and his infant sister, the only survivors of a shipwreck. . . . Think *Night of the Living Dead* on an iceberg. . . . The story works on a gut level, thanks to a chilling monster and brisk pacing. . . . [An] imaginative and promising setup."   —*Publishers Weekly*

Zero Hour

"An exciting first novel."   —*Chronicle*

"Rare is the chapter that doesn't end with a gripping cliff-hanger. Miller's heroes conquer one seemingly impossible challenge after another while the world's fate hangs in the balance. Making the novel even more attractive is the abundance of real science within."   —*The Sun Chronicle* the "adrenaline-charged" novels of

SILENT ASSAULT

Benjamin E. Miller

AN ONYX BOOK

ONYX
Published by New American Library, a division of
Penguin Group (USA) Inc., 375 Hudson Street,
New York, New York 10014, USA
Penguin Group (Canada), 10 Alcorn Avenue, Toronto,
Ontario M4V 3B2, Canada (a division of Pearson Penguin Canada Inc.)
Penguin Books Ltd., 80 Strand, London WC2R 0RL, England
Penguin Ireland, 25 St. Stephen's Green, Dublin 2,
Ireland (a division of Penguin Books Ltd.)
Penguin Group (Australia), 250 Camberwell Road, Camberwell, Victoria 3124,
Australia (a division of Pearson Australia Group Pty. Ltd.)
Penguin Books India Pvt. Ltd., 11 Community Centre, Panchsheel Park,
New Delhi - 110 017, India
Penguin Group (NZ), cnr Airborne and Rosedale Roads, Albany,
Auckland 1310, New Zealand (a division of Pearson New Zealand Ltd.)
Penguin Books (South Africa) (Pty.) Ltd., 24 Sturdee Avenue,
Rosebank, Johannesburg 2196, South Africa

Penguin Books Ltd., Registered Offices:
80 Strand, London WC2R 0RL, England

First published by Onyx, an imprint of New American Library,
a division of Penguin Group (USA) Inc.

First Printing, July 2005
10 9 8 7 6 5 4 3 2 1

Copyright © Benjamin E. Miller, 2005
All rights reserved

 REGISTERED TRADEMARK—MARCA REGISTRADA

Printed in the United States of America

Without limiting the rights under copyright reserved above, no part of this
publication may be reproduced, stored in or introduced into a retrieval system, or transmitted, in any form, or by any means (electronic, mechanical,
photocopying, recording, or otherwise), without the prior written permission
of both the copyright owner and the above publisher of this book.

PUBLISHER'S NOTE
This is a work of fiction. Names, characters, places, and incidents either are
the product of the author's imagination or are used fictitiously, and any resem-
blance to actual persons, living or dead, business establishments, events, or
locales is entirely coincidental.
   The publisher does not have any control over and does not assume any
responsibility for author or third-party Web sites or their content.

If you purchased this book without a cover you should be aware that this
book is stolen property. It was reported as "unsold and destroyed" to the
publisher and neither the author nor the publisher has received any payment
for this "stripped book."

The scanning, uploading, and distribution of this book via the Internet or via
any other means without the permission of the publisher is illegal and punish-
able by law. Please purchase only authorized electronic editions, and do not
participate in or encourage electronic piracy of copyrighted materials. Your
support of the author's rights is appreciated.

For Sam

Acknowledgments

This story was brought to life by many individuals who believed in its importance. My gratitude to them will endure. HMCM(SS) Rick Wilson, USN, the most experienced submarine medic on active duty in the U.S. Navy, provided as much factual detail as restrictions on classified information would allow. Tim Printy, USN retired, contributed an inside view of the life of a modern submariner. Most of my background research was conducted at the fascinating Submarine Force Museum in Groton, Connecticut, and at the Randall Library in Stow, Massachusetts. Many thanks to the Stow librarians for their efficiency and patience with my deluge of requests. The editors who saw this project through included Ron Martirano and Dan Slater. Thanks to Ron for recognizing the potential of the original premise and to Dan for weeding out the clichés and streamlining the action. I am also grateful to my agent, Ethan Ellenberg, for his expert feedback and patience with the long process of trial and error through which ideas like this are born. The foundation of this book's success was the unwavering love and support provided by Samantha Parker and by my parents and grandparents. Last but not least, my heartfelt thanks to the brave volunteers who dive to the perilous depths, leaving comfort and safety behind to defend my freedom.

Chapter 1

Christopher Long, age ten, sat up in his rickety bunk bed, sniffing the humid Louisiana night. "Paul, are you smoking?"

Paul Treacle, one of Chris's five foster brothers, liked to sneak smokes during the night.

"It ain't me," Paul whispered above him.

Chris got out of bed and sniffed again. "Hey, guys, I think . . . I think the house might be on fire."

The boys all slept in a long, narrow attic room with one window at the north end. There was a fire escape beneath that window, as required by law, but in desperation, to stop the boys from sneaking out at night, the two elderly widows who ran the foster home had fastened the window shut by driving fourteen screws through the outside of the sash.

Paul jumped down from the upper bunk, flicking on his cigarette lighter so he could see his way to the light switch. He and Chris shook the other four boys awake. They ran barefoot to the end of the attic opposite the window, halting before the wooden door at the top of the stairs.

White smoke was pouring into the attic room through the gap atop the closed door, creeping silently across the water-stained ceiling like a living liquid.

These stairs were the only way out.

Fourteen years old, Paul was the oldest. He handed

his lighter to Chris, then reached out his right hand and grabbed the doorknob.

"Eyow!"

Paul jerked back his hand and bent over, gripping his right wrist with his left hand. "Ow, shit! Hot!"

A loud boom came from below, and the whole house shook. Chris could hear hissing and whistling like a thousand teakettles, along with the crackling of flames. Then one of the widows started screaming down below. She was shrieking the boys' names.

Chris looked down. He could see flickering orange light through the gaps between the rough-hewn floorboards.

A burning pain stabbed into the arch of his bare right foot. He jerked the foot upward and stumbled sideways.

Now his left foot was burning. Realizing the heat was coming up through the cracks between the boards, he placed his feet together at the center of one board. Then he yelled at the other boys to do the same.

He could still feel hot air blowing upward through the cracks. It smelled different from the smoke coming in around the door, more bitter and foul. It began stinging his eyes and nose.

The boys started to cough.

"What do you want to do?" Paul yelled.

Chris tried to answer, but he couldn't stop coughing.

Another of his brothers yelled, "Open it!"

Paul grabbed the heavy brass doorknob with both hands this time. Chris heard a searing sound. Then he could hear nothing but Paul screaming.

The door sprang open. Chris saw bright light and felt intense heat on his face. He was falling, twisting in the air and flailing his arms. He landed on his left side. His skid across the rough floorboards was arrested by splinters digging into his skin. He looked up and saw giant fists of flame punching into the room, surging across the ceiling.

He couldn't breathe. It felt as if the fire had somehow

gotten inside him and was burning up his chest from the inside out. He tried to say "help" but couldn't even grunt.

The other boys had also fallen. Charlie Ochone and Dan Smith were getting up. Andre Perot and Dan Bolling were lying still. Paul Treacle was on fire from head to toe. He was writhing back and forth against the end wall, slamming his head and his outstretched arms against it.

A stratum of smoke was descending from the ceiling. It looked as dense as a rising flood. It engulfed Paul's head, then his shoulders. He fell over and lay still at the base of the wall, still burning.

Charlie and Dan Smith were bleeding from the eyes and drooling pink froth. Chris swiped at the tears on his own face and saw that they were made of blood as well.

Chris knew his only chance was to get out of the attic within the next few seconds, and that the only way out was through the window that couldn't be opened.

Somehow he got to his feet and began running through the smoke. For a moment he could see nothing but the edges of the bunk beds lining the walls on both sides. Then the smoke began to clear, and he could see all the way to the far end of the long attic room.

The window wasn't there.

There was just a solid wall of vertical pine boards, like the wall above Paul's burning body at the other end. *No! It's not possible! The window has always been there! I was looking at it just a minute ago!*

Chris kept running. *Maybe I can smash through the wall if I build up enough speed.*

The attic began to elongate. The faster he ran, the longer it became. It started changing in other ways as well: The hot wooden floor became cold linoleum tile. The bunk beds looked different—now each bunk had a brown curtain hanging in front of it. Instead of flickering firelight beaming upward through cracks in the floor, the room was illuminated by cold fluorescent lights shining down from a tangle of wires and pipes beneath the ceiling.

Chris ran on, knowing he should have collapsed from suffocation by now. Suddenly he reached the end, and he saw that the wall was a steel bulkhead rather than wooden boards. There was no chance at all of smashing through, but it was too late to stop.

He slammed into the wall headfirst.

And opened his eyes with a gasp.

The bedroom was quiet except for the rain outside. His body was naked and wet with sweat. He reached for the top sheet and discovered that he'd kicked it off the bed.

In the sixteen years since the fire, Christopher Long had grown into a very big man. He was six feet four inches tall and weighed two hundred sixty pounds, most of it muscle. He did not know the identity of his biological parents, but he appeared to be a mixture of races. His eyes were a dark olive green. His skin had a Mediterranean tone, but his prominent nose looked Native American, and the thickness of his lips hinted at African genes. He'd been told more than once that he was handsome, but he did not believe it.

Soony was lying beside him, watching him in the dim light trickling in from the parking lot. She wiped sweat from his forehead with her delicate wrist. "You had that dream again?"

Chris took a long drink of water from the cup he kept by the bed. He was still catching his breath. "It's not just a dream, sweetheart."

"You dream it exactly the way it happened?"

He nodded, clasping her hand and kissing it. "Usually. This time there was a twist—the window wasn't there."

Soony's small fingers brushed across his lips. They were warm and soft, with closely trimmed nails. He kissed her fingertips until she caught her breath in the way that meant she was aroused. The sound caused a similar response in him. He still felt the unease that always lingered after the recurring memory-dream, but it wasn't strong enough to keep his libido down.

"Sounds awful," Soony said in a distracted tone.

He gazed at her. She was nude as well, lying on her side, silhouetted against the plate glass window. Rain was trickling down the windowpane, diffusing the harsh light from the parking lot lamps. He reached out to touch her lips, admiring the womanly curve of her hip and thigh.

Soony was only five one with a slender build. A second-generation Vietnamese American, she had long, straight, fine black hair. Her complexion was light and smooth.

"I also think the attic was turning into a submarine at the end," Chris said.

Soony sat up with a laugh. "Now *that's* a nightmare."

He watched her as she bounded off the bed, disappearing into the bathroom. He heard her pee and start brushing her teeth. "Good thing you don't believe in premonitions," she lisped around her toothbrush.

"Yeah, no kidding." Chris glanced at the clock. He had planned to get up at dawn, which was still an hour away.

When Soony came out of the bathroom, he went in. "My turn. Keep the bed warm."

After brushing his teeth and relieving himself, he decided to play a prank on his lover. He got down on all fours and crawled back into the bedroom, circling the bed to her side without rising high enough for her to see him. He was about to reach under the covers and grab her when he thought better of it. Instead, he growled like a tiger to warn her he was there.

She rewarded him with a fake scream, then laughed as he pounced on her. The whole bed bounced under his weight.

They locked eyes for a moment. Chris used his uncommonly thick arms to suspend himself above her. "You heard me sneaking up, didn't you?"

She nodded guiltily.

"Next time I'll be quiet as a mouse," he squeaked.

She laughed. "I'll believe that when I don't hear it."

Chris turned serious. "I can be as quiet as a mouse when I'm at sea. Sometimes we have to, for days at a stretch."

Soony smiled up at him lovingly. "I'm allowed to know that?"

"Oops!" He feigned a look of shock.

She gently swatted his bulging left triceps. "Cut it out."

He lowered himself and kissed her. When he finally came up for air, they were both breathing fast.

She held a warm palm against his cheek. "Are you sure you shouldn't go back to sleep, Chris? You don't want to be tired tonight."

"Too late now," he said.

Soony grinned, reaching between his legs. "Okay, lover. If we're going to make the most of our last day, we'd better get started."

Chapter 2

They walked down to the Delta Wharf an hour after darkness had fallen on the forested mountains west of Puget Sound. Rain was still coming down. Christopher Long was about to meet his new crew, and his fear of first impressions was unusually strong; nevertheless, he took care not to hog the umbrella.

Soony's stride was reluctant. The balance of reluctance and eagerness made Chris inclined to walk faster, but he matched her stride.

Chris had long dreaded and looked forward to this night, September twenty-second. In a few minutes, he would have to say good-bye to the woman with whom he hoped to spend the rest of his life. Then he would step through a portal into an alternate reality, an intriguing and challenging world that many men had sacrificed everything else to be a part of.

Chris was wearing work dungarees—blue jeans and a long-sleeve light blue shirt. He was also wearing a navy blue baseball cap. On its front was an embroidered silver emblem showing two scaly fish symmetrically facing the bow of a submarine. Above this symbol, which was known as the Dolphins, embroidered letters read U.S. SUBMARINE FORCE. Below the Dolphins were the words PRIDE RUNS DEEP.

Chris owned few material items. The exception was his large collection of baseball caps. They were not just souvenirs—he wore one whenever possible. At the age of twenty-six, Christopher Long was as bald as a light bulb.

Despite the rain, Soony was wearing her best dress. It was a dark chocolate brown that matched her eyes and was embroidered with tiny red roses. "I wish you didn't have to go now," she said.

Chris almost said "me too," but that would have been only half true.

"I wish you could come with me, sweetheart."

"Really?"

"No, but only because I want you to be safe."

"I'm not safe if you're not safe," she said.

"Nobody's safe right now," he replied.

While they spoke, Chris discreetly reached into his pocket to make sure the velvet box containing a modest engagement ring was still there.

When he withdrew his hand, she grabbed and squeezed it. "I wish you could at least tell me where you're going, Chris."

"Nobody knows, exactly," he replied. "The captain won't decide until after we dive. If no one on land knows our PIM, they can't give it away to a spy." PIM stood for point of intended motion, the position where a submarine was expected to be at a given time in the future.

Squinting in the glare of the wharf's powerful floodlights, Chris peered across the dark, rain-dappled water of Puget Sound, looking for his new home. He abruptly stopped walking. "There she is! The USS *Vermont*."

"My God, it's *huge*!" Soony said.

Despite her size, the nuclear-powered submarine was not easy to spot. She was surfaced alongside the wharf, but only the very top of her black cylindrical hull protruded above the water. The sinister-looking hulk stretched on until it disappeared in the rain. Instead of a ship, it looked like a gigantic pipeline through which most of the world's submarines could safely navigate without touching the sides.

Chris knew that in fact the *Vermont* was the largest

kind of submarine ever built in the West, 560 feet long and more than 42 feet in diameter, with an extra bulge along most of her top to make room for her 24 internal missile silos. If the Washington Monument were laid on its side, it would have been five feet shorter than the *Vermont*. Her submerged displacement was 18,750 tons, heavier than any but the largest battleships ever built.

Technically, the *Vermont* was an *Ohio*-class SSBN (submersible ship ballistic nuclear), but *Ohio*-class subs were commonly called Tridents because they carried Trident D-5 long-range ballistic missiles.

"Incredible," Chris whispered, still staring. He always found it scary but thrilling to recall that each Trident submarine was technically the sixth-largest nuclear power in the world. The subs' mission was strategic deterrence, the American doctrine of using nuclear weapons to prevent war. In theory, the threat of retaliation in kind would deter any nation from attacking the United States with nukes or other weapons of mass destruction. The morbid irony of deterrence was that if a Trident's crew ever had to actually launch their nuclear missiles, it would mean their mission had already failed.

"You sound all excited," Soony said, accusingly. "If I were you, I'd be scared to death."

"I am! I feel like I'm about to barf."

"I noticed you seemed kind of serious," she said, "for you."

He pinched her behind. "Don't get used to it."

A few steps later, he said, "The thing is, I figure this run is either going to salvage my crazy life or scuttle it."

By choice, Chris had begun his seven-year Navy career as a submariner, but he made some mistakes on his first run. Submariners could get away with almost anything, except mistakes. He left the Sub Force in disgrace and served on surface ships for the next five years. Hoping to get back into submarines, he went through the one-year training program to become an Independent Duty Hospital Corpsman. The Hospital Corps provided

the medics on all vessels and bases of the Navy and
Marine Corps.

The unexpected order to report for sea duty aboard
the *Vermont* had arrived only two days ago—and less
than a week after Chris had completed his medical training. He had heard that he was replacing a highly regarded and experienced corpsman who had been
diagnosed with lung cancer. There had been no time for
the usual interview process preceding the appointment
of a new corpsman, so he had never met any of the men
with whom he was about to be confined for ninety days
in the deep ocean.

Supposedly Chris had been handpicked by Barlow
Scott, captain of the *Vermont*. Captain Scott was legend-
ary for salvaging sailors with troubled records, helping
them to become the best submariners in the fleet. Their
gratitude, hard work, and loyalty toward him were
equally famous. In recent years, the *Vermont* had won
the coveted Battle E award for crew proficiency more
often than any other sub. The Navy would not have
allowed a boomer—any class of submarine armed with
nuclear ballistic missiles—to take on more than its share
of problem sailors if Captain Scott had not proven that
they could excel under his leadership. Thanks to him,
the *Vermont* was known as the sub of second chances.

Chris could hardly wait to find out what his new crew
was like. If most of them were misfits sent to Captain
Scott for reform, did that mean they would be unusually
quirky for submariners? Chris hoped they would. At sea,
his life would depend on their abilities, but living with
them would be more interesting if they weren't all
clones.

Of course, he knew submariners could be only so eccentric. Their performance had to be reliable at all times,
and mastering the 100,000 high-tech systems on a
nuclear-powered submarine was a mental challenge that
allowed for few distractions. On the other hand, all
American submariners were volunteers, and—in Chris's

opinion, at least—you had to be a little crazy to voluntarily board a ship that was designed to sink.

They stopped walking before they were within earshot of the two guards posted at the landward end of the brow—the steel gangway between the wharf and the sub's deck. The guards, Marines armed with M-16 rifles, were wearing dark, hooded rain slickers. They looked miserable as they squinted through the floodlight glare at the approaching couple. Soony glanced at them apprehensively. Until recently, civilians had not been allowed on the nuclear wharves.

Soony gripped Chris's hand and looked up at him. "How long do we have?"

He glanced at his watch. "About twenty minutes. You can leave now if you want. You're getting wet."

"Do you want me to leave now?"

"No."

"Then I'll wait. Chris, can't you just guess where they're taking you?"

He sighed. "I've heard one of the other Tridents out of Bangor is three weeks overdue to return. That should be a secret, but the rumor gets around once the wives start to panic. It could mean we've finally lost one, but no search has been laid on, so I'd say she's just waiting on station for a relief patrol. Meanwhile, the *Vermont* was scheduled to get under way a month ago, but she's been delayed for major repairs—the whole Trident fleet is getting pretty old. Now they're rushing her to sea before all of her refits are . . . anyhow, I doubt the timing is a coincidence."

"Do you know where the overdue sub is patrolling?"

"No, but her crew has probably run out of food. The Navy would never have let that happen if she was just on a routine deterrence patrol. They would have repositioned the rest of the fleet to keep all the targets covered and brought that boomer home by now."

Food was the only resource that limited how long Trident submarines could remain submerged. They produced oxygen from seawater, and their nuclear reactors could operate for twenty years without refueling.

"Couldn't they just send a ship out to reprovision the overdue sub?" Soony asked.

"Not without giving away her position. Depending on where she is, that could be even worse than aborting the patrol."

Soony's slender eyebrows squeezed together. She gripped his free hand in both of hers. "Chris, what mission could be so important that the Navy would let a starving crew operate a Trident?"

Trident submarines were the worst places imaginable for any kind of trouble among the crew. The most complex machines ever built, they cost 1.8 billion dollars apiece, plus more than 50 million dollars for each of the twenty-four D-5 missiles. Each missile was armed with eight W88 thermonuclear warheads that could be guided onto separate targets once they were lifted into space. Within half an hour after launching, they could bull's-eye a target the size of a stadium anywhere in the hemisphere surrounding the sub. Altogether, the 192 warheads on one Trident submarine packed more of an explosive punch than all of the bombs dropped in all of the wars in the history of the world.

The Trident system was truly the ultimate doomsday weapon.

Chapter 3

Waiting with Soony under the floodlights of the Delta Wharf, Chris kept an eye on the seconds ticking down until he had to board the *Vermont*. He stooped so that the umbrella would not be so high above her head that it let in the rain. She was shivering a little, but her forehead felt warm against his chin, stirring the desire he always felt at the slightest touch from her, no matter what else was on his mind.

How in the world am I going to get through a three-month run without touching her? Without even seeing or speaking to her?

She looked up with a frown. "Chris, please tell me honestly how much of a chance there is that you won't come back."

"Don't worry. Boomers never engage enemy forces," he reminded her.

The Navy considered Trident submarines too valuable to risk in combat. All missions other than nuclear deterrence were normally left to *Los Angeles*—class attack subs, which were smaller, cheaper, faster, more numerous, and equipped with better defenses than the Tridents.

"Our passive sonar is still the best in the world," Chris added, "so we can hear other subs and ships before they can hear us. And you shouldn't worry about accidents— we have procedures to deal with everything that can go wrong."

Soony's frown deepened. "You can't have procedures for *everything*."

"Sweetheart, there's always going to be danger when we dive down under a trillion tons of water with an unstable reactor full of bomb-grade uranium. Our predeparture checklist is longer than the space shuttle's. That's what operating a submarine is like—like flying into space. No matter how many times we do it, it's never routine. We're still penetrating an alien environment that's hostile as hell to us land mammals."

He stopped on the verge of mentioning that exposure to deep space would take about a minute to kill a man by suffocation, whereas the deep ocean would do it instantly by imploding his skull.

"I'm sorry," Chris said. "Damn it, I didn't mean . . . Of course we can't be prepared for everything, but that's where good old Navy ingenuity comes in—plus lots of caulk and duct tape."

Soony tried to return his smile. "Chris, I know Tridents are not supposed to do anything but hide in the ocean and stay ready to launch their missiles, but they're sending yours on some kind of special mission, aren't they?"

He nodded, smiling. Chris was amazed by how much Soony had learned about the Silent Service—the U.S. Submarine Force—during their four-month whirlwind relationship. It meant the world to him that she was curious about his other life and understood what little he was allowed to tell her. Sometimes she seemed so smart it was scary, though, especially considering that she was four years younger. Chris knew she came from a well-off and educated family, unlike him, and that she'd made better grades than he had in school.

Hesitantly, he said, "I don't know, but the commander in chief may actually be considering a preemptive nuclear strike against Iran."

Soony pushed back with a look of horror. Rain splattered on her petite eyeglasses. "I thought we were never going to use nuclear weapons again unless someone had already used them on us!"

Chris felt a pang of dread. "Don't look at me like that. It's not up to me—I'm just an E-6 corpsman." After a tense pause, he added, "The U.S. can't rely on deterrence anymore. It might have worked against the Soviets, but it won't work against crazy fanatics. And they have weapons that are almost as deadly as ours, nowadays."

Soony still looked repulsed. "So we're going to start World War Three?"

"Too late!" Chris said. "You've seen the news. Since we took over Iraq, it seems like every Muslim fundamentalist in the world has declared holy war on America. Meanwhile, we're trying to disarm all the terrorists and power-crazed dictators before they can use their new weapons of mass destruction. We're just trying to make the world a safer place for everybody, but our so-called allies are not helping at all. It's costing so much, the American economy is basically kaput for the first time since the nineteen-thirties, and our overseas forces are stretched too thin. The military is about out of money, cannon fodder, and patience."

When Soony replied, her usually warm voice was as cold as the rain. "None of that justifies a first strike with nuclear weapons."

Chris suddenly wondered whether she had seen pictures of the radiation sickness cases from Hiroshima and Nagasaki. Soony was a premedical student at the University of Washington, planning to specialize in AIDS research because a close aunt of hers was dying from the scourge. Chris had seen the horrifying photos of nuclear war victims, and he was pretty sure they would always remain fresh in his memory.

Soony was still standing back. Chris was reaching out with the umbrella to keep her covered, getting soaked as a result.

"Chris, you've said the U.S. military is just trying to

stop the proliferation of weapons of mass destruction. Won't it defeat the purpose if we use our own? Our rationale for invading other countries is already pretty damn thin. There won't be a shred of it left if we violate the principles we're supposed to be upholding. Then the other major powers won't just refuse to help; they'll band together against us."

"I know all that!" he said, glancing along the wharf. The two armed Marines still looked bored but relaxed. If they'd heard raised voices, they had probably assumed it was just a mundane lover's quarrel.

Chris lowered his voice back to its usual deep bass. As if changing the subject, he said, "What do you think most of us dread more than anything else when we're on patrol in a Trident?"

"How should I know? Being detected?"

"No."

"Colliding with another ship?"

"No."

"Making mistakes?"

"Close."

"Having to launch your missiles?"

"Yes! Not enemy torpedoes, not depth charges, not flooding or fires. Even I'm not as scared of fire on the sub. Every time an EAM comes in, we wonder until it's decoded if it's a launch order from the president. None of us want to incinerate millions of people." EAM stood for emergency action message.

Soony now looked more sad than angry. "Chris, if the *Vermont* gets an order for a first strike, will you help carry it out?"

He felt his face flush in spite of the cold air. *Does she have any idea what she's asking?* "Of course I will!" he said. "That's part of my sworn duty."

Soony winced, looking away.

For a breathless moment, Chris thought she was about to tell him their relationship was over. Even worse, she could just walk away and leave him wondering for the next three months.

He reached out and grabbed her cold wet hand. "Sweetheart, the president will not order us to launch unless it's definitely the only way to stop the Iranians from launching their missiles at us."

Israeli spies had recently discovered that Iran possessed ballistic missiles concealed within grain silos. Judging by their size, the missiles might be capable of reaching American targets. Western intelligence agencies had apparently not yet determined what kinds of warheads the missiles carried. The Iranians claimed they were merely high explosives, but arming such expensive long-range missiles with conventional warheads would have been an absurd waste. The Spear of Allah missiles were almost certainly weapons of mass destruction— nuclear, biological, or chemical.

Human intelligence reports indicated that the Iranians had not built their ICBMs just to establish a deterrent against aggression, as had the United States and the Soviet Union. A fanatical group of Islamists within the Iranian military apparently wanted to use the missiles someday in an apocalyptic jihad against the "infidels" in the West.

The president of the United States had demanded that Iran allow United Nations inspectors to confirm that their warheads did not violate the international laws against proliferation of nuclear, biological, and chemical weapons. The Iranian government had refused, and now the United States was amassing forces in the Middle East in preparation to disarm the rogue nation.

Informed Americans were almost as tense now as they had been during the Cuban missile crisis in 1962. Not since then had the commander in chief been forced to plan an invasion that might provoke massive reprisals against American civilians. The defense readiness condition of the armed forces had just escalated from DEFCON 3 to DEFCON 2.

Soony stepped closer and moved the umbrella over him, then reached up and put her arms around his neck. "Oh, Chris, I'm sorry. We shouldn't argue; not now. I'm just worried."

He hugged her and resumed breathing. "I don't blame you," he said, glancing at his watch.

Only five minutes left.

Christopher Long wanted to go to sea engaged. It would provide some reassurance that his beloved would still want him when he came home. If he came home.

He switched the umbrella to his other hand and reached into the pants pocket containing the ring case. When he started to pull it out, his clammy hand stuck to the thin lining of the pocket, forcing him to pause.

What if she says no? What would it do to my concentration during this run?

Worse yet, what if she said yes without giving it enough thought? The only thing worse than losing her now would be to get married and then find out years later that she couldn't live with a submariner. Chris knew about the horrible divorce rate in the Silent Service. It took a special kind of woman to manage alone for three months at a stretch, never knowing where her husband was, what he was doing, or when he would come home.

If I ask her now, she'll feel pressured to say yes. If I wait until I come back, and she still wants to marry me, I'll know she loves me enough to wait.

He let go of the ring case and withdrew his hand from his pocket. Soony didn't seem to notice. She was hugging him and sobbing against his thick chest.

Chris had no doubt that he wanted to marry her, that he loved her as much as any man had ever loved a woman. But that was the best reason not to take a chance on saddling her with an obligation she would later regret.

They held each other for a while. Then he kissed the

top of her head, handed her the umbrella, and broke away. "I have to go, sweetheart."

She grabbed him and squeezed his chest so hard he could barely breathe. He hadn't known she was so strong. "Chris, we haven't had enough time together!"

He felt tears rolling down his own cheeks, mixing with raindrops. "I know," he said.

She let go, and he kissed her trembling lips one last time before stepping backward toward the brow. She held on to his hand until she almost fell. "I'll be here," she said.

"I hope so, sweetheart. I love you."

"I love you too, Chris. Please come home."

Chapter 4

Captain Barlow Scott plucked the black hand microphone for the 1MC circuit from its cradle and asked
Lieutenant Commander Gene Kurlgunn, his executive
officer, to call him on the nearest sound-powered phone.
The 1MC was the *Vermont*'s public address system.

When the phone on Scott's desk let out a *whoop*,
Scott picked it up and spoke in his Down East Maine
accent. "Gene, the new corpsman is scheduled to report
in about fifteen. Come to my stateroom so we can discuss how to handle him. I'll get Steve Brady on the
speaker."

"Aye, sir," replied Kurlgunn.

Commander Steven Brady had been the captain of the
other Trident on which Christopher Long had served his
first tour of sea duty. In the U.S. Navy, "captain" was
both a rank and a role. Most commanding officers of
submarines were called "captain" by their crews, but
they actually held the lower rank of commander. Barlow
Scott was a rare exception who held the rank of captain.

Scott had a thick red mustache, bushy eyebrows, and
reddish gray hair around his bald crown. His large and
ruddy nose resembled the beak of a parrot. His dark
blue eyes were often bloodshot and watery from the allergies that tormented him whenever he was on land or
surfaced near shore. Until recently, he had kept his short
and narrow frame looking young with exercise, but he
appeared to have aged a decade in the last six months—

his posture had begun to stoop and his muscles had gone to flab.

At fifty-one, Barlow Scott was by far the oldest submarine captain in the Navy. He would not have been allowed to remain so long on a fast-attack sub, where stamina and reaction speed were crucial, but his superiors had chosen his maturity and experience over the quicker reflexes of youth for the *Vermont*'s grave deterrence mission.

Until now.

This was going to be Barlow Scott's last run. The U.S. Navy was perennially desperate for qualified submarine captains, but Scott had staved off promotion as long as he could. A desk job at fleet command would be waiting for him when the *Vermont* returned, although he had other plans.

Scott didn't really want to deal with the new corpsman tonight. Watching over new sailors while they adjusted to his crew had once been his favorite part of the job, but his heart had not been in it for the last half year. The same could be said of his other duties, which was why he now left them to the XO—the executive officer—whenever possible. He knew Kurlgunn didn't mind the extra work—responsibility was power, and Gene Kurlgunn seemed to live for power.

But Scott had agreed to take on Christopher Long and give him a chance to prove he'd shaped up, so he felt some responsibility toward the young sailor. He could have left him entirely in Kurlgunn's hands—but Scott knew that Gene Kurlgunn believed in using the same tool for every task, and that his preferred tool was browbeating.

When Kurlgunn arrived, he glanced around Scott's tiny stateroom as if checking for vermin. This was the only unkempt compartment on the sub. Books were stacked everywhere, along with exotic-food containers and empty tissue boxes.

"Have a seat," Scott said. He noticed—but didn't

care—how gingerly the XO removed a half-empty box of Thai saffron rice from the other chair before sitting on it.

As always, Kurlgunn sat as if he were about to leap up, perfectly still but not touching the back of his chair.

Gene Kurlgunn was thirty-five, much younger than Barlow Scott. His height and build were average, but his body was lean, ropy, and deceptively strong from hours of daily martial arts training. His mustache was short and black, standing out against skin that was even paler than that of most submariners. He had bullet gray eyes, thin and colorless lips, and small pointy ears that turned outward at the top. His crew-cut hair was solid black with no signs of balding.

After blowing his parrot-beak nose, Captain Scott dialed the phone. The *Vermont*'s comms were connected to landlines while she was in port.

Commander Steven Brady answered on the speakerphone.

"Steve, what can you tell us about Christopher Long?"

Brady's reply had a tongue-in-cheek tone. "Would you believe he gave up a football scholarship to the University of Louisiana to enlist in the Navy?"

Scott laughed. Kurlgunn did not. Scott wondered, not for the first time, what was wrong with his XO. If Barlow Scott could laugh at something, given the state his mind had been in lately, he figured anyone ought to be able to. Then again, he couldn't remember Kurlgunn *ever* laughing in his presence.

Brady snickered along with Scott. "I'm serious. That's what he told me."

"Somebody must have tricked him," Scott said. "No wonder he has problems. He's probably planning to shoot his recruiter."

Brady laughed. "No way. He loved it on my boat. *Loved* it. I think that's why he joined the Navy—he just wanted to live on a submarine."

"So his problem is that he's insane," Scott said, although he didn't really believe that. In fact, he thought Christopher Long sounded like a kindred spirit.

"His problem on my boat was liking it *too* much," Brady said, "and trying too hard to get along. Frankly, he could get on your nerves, poking his nose in everywhere, questioning everything. 'How do you do this? Why don't we do it that way?' I think he meant well, but . . ."

"Sounds like he didn't know his limits," Kurlgunn said.

"Immature?" Scott asked.

"Extroverted," Brady said. "Okay, I'll admit he had a juvenile streak. I'm a Raiders fan, and he was a Packers fan. When the Raiders won the Super Bowl, he stole my stateroom door and hid it down in the torpedo room. I think he might have also been involved in putting the XO's mattress in the freezer. They returned it to his rack just before he went to bed. He said it took three hours to warm up. Keep in mind, though—my XO had humiliated a new ensign that day by making fun of the spelling in a familygram he'd just received."

Familygrams were messages written to deployed submariners from their loved ones. The Navy broadcasted them semi-weekly by very low frequency (VLF) radio. They were not private, and their maximum length was fifty words. The one-way snippets were a submariner's only contact with home.

Captain Scott was more amused than scandalized by Brady's account of Christopher Long's prior misbehavior, although he shuddered to think of what might happen if one of the *Vermont's* crew dared to freeze Gene Kurlgunn's mattress. "So you kicked Long off your boat because he was a hyperactive cutup?"

"Hell, no," Brady replied. "You know that kind of stuff goes on all the time between drills, and Chris always knew when enough was enough. I decided to let him go because he fell asleep on watch. *Three times.*"

"What kind of schedule did you have him on?"

"Hey, he was on a normal eighteen-hour day. He'd been missing sleep to socialize and help a bunch of others with their chores and studying."

Regardless of his mood, Captain Scott found that a little intriguing. He knew excessive socializing was a common problem among college students, but most submariners—despite their close quarters—were technically inclined loners who would rather study or tinker with machines than shoot the bull. Furthermore, their self-discipline tended to be extraordinary for such young men.

"I think Chris was just too busy making friends," Brady said. "He didn't know you can't please everybody."

"We'll teach him that in the first week," Kurlgunn said with a slight elevation of the right side of his upper lip.

I'll bet you will, Scott thought. "Now tell us the good news, Steve. Why did you recommend I take him on?"

Commander Brady replied with conviction. "Because he really cared, and he wasn't dumb. Chris understood what he was doing wrong on my boat—he just couldn't help himself. It's been several years. Maybe he's grown up by now."

"Sounds like a troublemaker to me," Kurlgunn said. "Why didn't you just kick him out of the Navy?"

"Well, for one thing, the kid has had a pretty hard life."

"Nobody told me the U.S. Navy was a charity," Kurlgunn replied.

Scott winced but suppressed his natural urge to give the younger officer advice on his manners. Why bother? He'd be free of Kurlgunn soon enough.

Even over the tinny speakerphone, Brady sounded indignant. "Captain Scott, I really believe in this kid's potential. I've never seen a crewman work harder."

"And you swear he's really smart, Steve?"

"Absolutely, when he's awake."

Scott sighed nostalgically. Christopher Long sounded like the kind of sailor he had once gotten so much satisfaction out of leading. "Okay, thanks, Steve."

"Thank you, sir. I know it's kind of scary taking on such a young corpsman, but I'm betting Chris won't let you down."

After Scott hung up, Kurlgunn said, "Let's pray we don't have any medical problems on this run."

At sea, a hospital corpsman had all the responsibilities of a civilian physician and a surgeon combined—prescribing drugs, diagnosing illnesses, performing major operations—with only a fraction of the training and supplies that a civilian doctor could draw upon. If a submariner had a problem at sea that was more complex than a scrape or a cold, the corpsman had to figure out how to diagnose and treat it by digging through medical manuals. A submarine's sick bay, which was officially called a pharmacy, had little more equipment than an ambulance.

Breaking radio silence was prohibited for a Trident on patrol, so the corpsman could not call a doctor on land for advice, nor could the captain request a relief sub and leave his patrol area to take the victim home. If one of the crew came down with something the corpsman could not fix, the victim had to live with it for the duration of the run. If he couldn't last that long, he would die on board the sub. This draconian practice had been replaced by medical evacuations during the relatively peaceful 1990s, but it had recently been reinstituted. It was one of the many extraordinary risks submariners were expected to live with.

When his shipmates were all healthy, a corpsman could feel like a fifth wheel. But when a mishap produced human casualties, he suddenly became the most important man on the ship. Many lives and mission success could depend on his ingenuity.

*   *   *

After dismissing Kurlgunn, Captain Scott slumped in his disheveled stateroom, sipping stale ginseng tea and brooding over the conversation. He doubted that Christopher Long would cause any problems on this run. He wished he could feel the same about Gene Kurlgunn, his own goddamn XO.

Lately, Scott had felt glad that Kurlgunn had effectively taken over, in spite of their opposite command philosophies. He'd never met a man who knew more about his ship or followed Navy regulations more rigorously. And when he'd first joined the crew, Kurlgunn had acted as if he wanted to follow in Scott's footsteps, emulating his every move.

But as he settled in, the XO had become more brusque, impatient, and domineering. Scott was sure that most of the crew despised him by now. Furthermore, Scott had discovered several seemingly trivial facts about Kurlgunn that made him wonder what planet the hardnosed XO was from. For example, there was no television in Kurlgunn's home, and his two children, ages nine and twelve, were not allowed to go outside after dark. Ever. Kurlgunn claimed he had never drunk a beer, camped out, or seen *Star Wars*. He'd never heard of Dr. Seuss. And to Barlow Scott's abiding horror, Kurlgunn had not known—before Scott told him—what sport the Red Sox played.

In spite of Kurlgunn's willingness to take over the captain's duties, Barlow Scott was beginning to wish he'd never allowed the harsh and bizarrely out-of-touch XO onto his boat two years ago.

Chapter 5

As Chris marched across the rain-slick brow, a swell of excitement rolled through him. It felt like the first plunge of a roller coaster. He couldn't wait to meet his new captain and the crew. *I just hope the XO isn't a ballbuster.*

He also hoped he could live up to this crew's expectations. Field experience was a corpsman's prime asset, and he had none in submarines.

What if I screw up again?

He knew the answer to that question. He would be out of the Sub Force, permanently. To Christopher Long, that would be like coming down with an incurable disease.

When he stepped onto the *Vermont*'s topside deck, he waved to Soony one last time, and she blew him a kiss. He caught it and staggered backward under its weight, pretending to almost fall overboard. Soony was laughing and crying at the same time when he climbed down through the round, thirty-inch-diameter crew hatch.

While stepping down the vertical ladder, he had to hang his seabag from his neck. Descending into the *Vermont* was like going down a manhole into a sewer pipe.

Except it smelled better. Even on modern submarines, the air got stale after days of submergence, and it always smelled of fuel from the backup diesel engine. But when a sub was surfaced or snorkeling, the fan room kept fresh air blowing in.

As Chris descended through the forward escape trunk, he detected faint odors of lubrication grease, fried food, ozone from the high-voltage circuits, and amines from the chemical scrubbers that were used to remove carbon dioxide when the hatches were sealed. The familiar yet exotic blend of scents gave him another visceral thrill of anticipation.

He climbed down to the second of the four internal decks, then headed aft. The narrow passageways were bustling with men frantically trying to prepare the submarine for its ordered departure at 0800—eight o'clock the next morning. Like Chris, they were all wearing utility uniforms.

The sailors—that is, the enlisted crewmen—were divided into nine ranks. The bottom three ranks were all called seamen. The middle three were called petty officers. The top three were called chief petty officers, CPOs, or just chiefs. The seamen and petty officers wore blue dungarees like Chris's. The work uniforms of the chiefs and commissioned officers were khaki. There were only 15 commissioned officers in the *Vermont*'s crew of 155 men.

To avoid detection by the passive sonar of an enemy, the *Vermont* was designed to be as quiet as possible on the outside, but she was usually a noisy place on the inside, especially in port. Tonight the steel compartments echoed with footsteps, voices, and a symphony of clanging and banging tools—Chris's favorite music. In the background was the deep hum of powerful pumps and fans, a sound he found more soothing than a burbling brook.

Most of the crew were laying in provisions, including crates of frozen food, massive sacks of flour and sugar, and twelve-inch-diameter cans of vegetables. Several times Chris had to pause, detour, or squeeze past a heavily laden crewman in the narrow passageways. He also had to stoop beneath the bright fluorescent lights and the tangle of pipes, ducts, and wires that composed the overhead.

Normally the overheads would have been high enough even for a man as tall as Chris, but several of the passageways were being used to store canned goods. Plywood planks had been laid atop the cans for the crew to walk on until they ate their way down to the decks. Chris knew this practice was common on smaller submarines, but he had never heard of a Trident running out of pantry space. The *Vermont* was obviously provisioned with more than the usual 119,000 pounds of food required for a three-month run. It was the first clear sign he'd seen that this was not going to be an ordinary deterrence patrol. It made him wonder how long he would be away from Soony.

The other men stared at Chris as he passed by. Most of a Trident's crew knew their shipmates well, so they couldn't help noticing a stranger in their midst, especially one with Chris's dimensions. He introduced himself to a few of them, and he wanted to keep talking, but he didn't dare arrive late at his first meeting with the captain and the XO.

One chief shook his hand, smiled warmly, and said, "Welcome aboard, Chris. Watch out for the XO—he's a real ballbuster."

Before reporting for duty, Chris wanted to drop off some medical supplies he'd brought aboard. He made his way aft through the vast missile compartment, which occupied roughly the middle third of the long hull. The straight passageway led him along the midline of the ship between two identical rows of vertical launch tubes. The burnt orange tubes extended through all of the sub's decks from the top of the hull to the bottom. The three-stage ballistic missiles inside these twenty-four tubes were forty-four feet tall and more than seven feet in diameter.

The sick bay was a nook about the size of a walk-in

closet on the outside of missile tubes twenty-two and twenty-four. When Chris got there, he was surprised to find it occupied. Judging by the lack of insignia on the occupant's shirt, he was a seaman, the lowest of the three main enlisted ranks.

The seaman was tall and skinny with short brown hair. He looked very young. He had large ears, a large Adam's apple, patchy stubble, and acne. He didn't notice Chris at first, because he was intently drawing something with a pencil on the back of a sterile gauze package.

Chris leaned over the seaman's shoulder to look at the drawing. It was a cartoon of a submariner with a fishing rod, reeling in a shark from the open bridge atop the sail of a Trident. The sail, also known as the fairwater, was the steel tower on top of the hull that housed the periscopes and other sensor masts. The cartoon looked professional to Chris. The seaman's hands were a blur as he drew a lifelike turban atop the shark's head.

"Is that for a newspaper?" Chris asked.

The seaman lurched and dropped his pencil, then turned to face Chris. He spat out a small wad of snuff into the paper cup he'd been using as a spittoon. "Naw, I'm just doodlin'."

"Well, I wish I could draw like that. I'm Chris Long, the new corpsman." Chris reached out his huge right hand, remembering to be gentle when they shook.

"Tumor," the young seaman said with a buck-toothed smile.

"Pardon? You have a tumor?"

"You can call me Tumor," the gangly seaman clarified. "My name's Brian Cahill, but everybody on the Gold Crew calls me Tumor. I guess I'm your first patient."

Each submarine was staffed by two separate crews that rotated between runs. They were referred to as the Gold Crew and the Blue Crew.

Chris glanced at his watch. He had about ten minutes to spare. "Okay. What's the trouble, Tumor?"

"Well, I've been kind of dizzy all day, but I don't think that's related. I'm afraid"—Tumor leaned out of the sick bay and looked both ways, then stepped closer to Chris, who noticed that he had a four-alarm case of halitosis—"I'm afraid I caught something from a girl, Doc."

Chris felt a small thrill. This was the first time a crewman had called him Doc, a title that was usually bestowed on a corpsman only after he earned the crew's trust and respect.

"Some of us were at the Spirit Tender bar last night," Tumor continued, "and these three girls came in and started talking to us. Two blondes and a colored—I mean an African American—girl. They let three of us get in this huge white Cadillac they had, and they drove us up to the Pine Ridge Motel. I swear I didn't realize what them girls wanted till one of them took me to a room by ourselves and I could hear Kyle Orbison and the girl he was with through the wall, going at it like a couple of dadgone hound dogs. If I'd known they wanted sex, I wouldn't have gone up there with them— dang nymphomaniacs. I don't believe in messing with wild women, no, sir. You never know what they might be carrying."

Chris was having some trouble understanding Tumor's hillbilly accent, not to mention keeping a straight face, but he thought he got the gist. "So why did you have sex with her?"

"I didn't!" Tumor whispered.

"Then how could you have caught an STD?"

"We kissed."

"You kissed, and . . ."

Tumor blushed and put a hand over his eyes. "Dang, don't tell me. There ain't any diseases you can catch that way. I wasn't sure."

"Actually, there are," Chris said. "Including herpes simplex virus, types one and two." Venereal disease was one topic his medical training had covered in more than cursory detail.

Tumor moved his hand to cover his mouth. "Oh, no, I've got herpes! It's not fatal, right?"

"No."

Tumor's eyes grew wide, and he started to sway.

Chris grabbed his arm to steady him. "I mean, no, it's not fatal! And, no, you probably don't have herpes. I don't have the equipment to test for specific viruses or bacteria, so there's no way to tell unless symptoms show up. If you get any sores around your genitals, let me know."

Tumor let his shoulders back down, looking sheepish. "Dadgone, that was one weird night. You should have seen the cigars that girl smoked. Hand-rolled. She offered me one, but I didn't try it."

"Why not? You dip snuff."

Tumor made a disgusted face. "I didn't want to get sick like I did the one other time. . . . Anyhow, it was a good thing I didn't, 'cause I had to go sleep out in their car."

"Why?"

Tumor shuddered. "The fleas! I hate bugs. Best thing about a submarine—no bugs. One time I got stung by a whole dadgone nest of—"

"Your date had *fleas*?"

"No, no, no—the fleas were in the motel bed when we got there. Hundreds of them. Some dang redneck must have brought his hound dog in there."

Chris suddenly remembered to check his watch. "Oh, shit, I gotta go!" He grabbed the snug top of his baseball cap as if holding it on in a wind. "Say, how did you know I was coming back here just now?"

"Freud told me."

"Freud?"

"Ensign Patterson. You met him in the hallway. He's a nuke."

Nukes were the crewmen qualified to help operate the nuclear reactor.

"Don't tell Freud anything you don't want the whole dang crew to know in five minutes," Tumor advised.

"Okay, thanks. I'm late. It was a pleasure meeting you."

Chris swung out of the sick bay and jogged down the passageway between the missile tubes.

Tumor called after him. "Thanks, Doc! I'll probably be back. I tend to have a lot of problems at sea. Small stuff, mostly. Bad luck, I guess."

Chris waved over his shoulder, grinning. He liked Tumor, foul breath and all. He had a feeling he was going to have a blast on this run.

Chapter 6

To Chris's surprise, the captain's private stateroom was as cluttered and filthy as the bedroom of a stereotypical teenager. It was also pitifully small for such a large ship. Even with Scott's rack folded up against a bulkhead, there was standing room for only the three men present.

At first sight, Chris was alarmed by Captain Scott's appearance. It certainly was not what he had expected. Instead of his khaki uniform shirt, the captain was wearing a sweaty, yellowed tank-top undershirt. His reddish gray hair was unkempt and longer than the appropriate length. Purple bags protruded beneath his eyes. His red mustache was too long, and it was surrounded by a few days' stubble. The man looked as if he stank.

The captain's handshake was brief and unenthusiastic. "Welcome aboard, son. I'm Barlow Scott. This is the XO, Gene Kurlgunn."

Chris turned to face the third man in the cramped stateroom. He almost stepped away when he saw the XO glaring at him. The metallic gray irises of Kurlgunn's eyes reminded him of the end of a chrome revolver barrel.

The XO's handshake was the first one Chris had ever felt that was truly painful. He could see Kurlgunn's knuckles turn white from the effort. Chris could have crushed half the bones in the officer's hand, but he carefully restrained his strength.

"You're late," Kurlgunn said.

Chris glanced at the chronometer behind the XO. *Three minutes?* "Sorry, sir. I had to—"

"The captain and I do not have time to listen to excuses." Kurlgunn's voice was fast and loud, and it reminded Chris of snapping shears—the consonants were sharp, the vowels brief.

Captain Scott looked annoyed too, Chris noticed. Then he realized that Scott was shooting a warning glance at Kurlgunn, who looked away and briefly closed his eyes with his jaw clenched.

Perfect—my new CO and XO hate each other.

"Take off your hat," Kurlgunn ordered.

Chris winced. "Sorry, sir. I forgot." He removed his Pride Runs Deep cap, and they stared at him.

When Chris wore a baseball cap at the perfect angle, its visor cast shadows that almost looked like eyebrows. When he removed his cap, his complete lack of eyebrows became his most unusual feature.

Kurlgunn squinted suspiciously. "You're not on chemotherapy, are you?"

"No, sir. I was exposed to chemical fumes that permanently destroyed almost every hair follicle on my body, except for my eyelashes."

"I'll be a baboon's uncle," Scott said. "I've heard of a mutation that makes people completely bald, but never a chemical. What kind of chemical did it?"

"I don't know, sir. If I did, I'd be making a fortune selling cosmetics."

"When did it happen?" Kurlgunn asked.

Chris hated remembering the story. He'd learned it was best to tell it all at once and get it over with.

"When I was ten. I'd been living in a foster home in New Orleans since I was five. It was run by two older ladies who took on boys nobody else could handle. There were six of us at the time. They took good care of us but didn't have much money, so they rented out the basement and the garage and a big shed that was attached to the house. The renter was a company that paid them a lot just to store a bunch of old barrels. Well, the house caught fire one night. The barrels ruptured, and the stuff inside them mixed up and burned. I almost died from the smoke, but a firefighter saved me."

"Was anyone else hurt?" Scott asked.

"I was the only survivor, sir."

Kurlgunn was still eyeing him suspiciously. "Do you have any other injuries we should know about?"

Chris was tempted to say no, but so far he had never told even a little white fib to an officer. Lying to your superiors was the most unforgivable sin in the military. Even if you were lying to cover up a minor infraction that would have resulted in no discipline by itself, punishment for lack of candor was invariably severe.

He said, "Just a mild cough, sir. It only acts up when I'm under extreme stress."

"Very well," Kurlgunn said. "Regardless of what you may have heard, Long, the *Vermont* is not a rehab center. It's a warship of the United States Navy, and we expect every member of the crew to give us his very best at all times. No exceptions will be granted, and no irresponsible behavior will be tolerated. That includes tardiness and falling asleep on duty. Is that clear, Long?"

"Yes, sir. Sir, I know it's irregular, but may I have permission to wear this cap on the boat from now on?"

Kurlgunn said, "The uniform code states that—"

Captain Scott interrupted the XO, drawing what appeared to be another spark of hatred from him. "Of course, son. You can wear it anywhere except in the crew's mess."

Chris heard a knock behind him and turned around.

Ensign Mark Patterson, also known as Freud, was slouching in the doorway, chewing a match. He didn't look anything like Sigmund Freud, for whom Chris supposed he was nicknamed. Chris guessed his racial mix was half Caucasian and half Pacific Islander. He was short, trim, handsome, and athletic-looking, with short but thick and elaborately coiffed black hair. He smelled of cologne and looked barely old enough to be out of high school. A thick gold necklace was just visible beneath his collar. His dark tan looked out of place on a submarine—since they spent half their lives in a realm without sunlight, most submariners were pale. But Chris didn't think the tan was half as strange as the sunglasses.

Freud grinned when he saw Chris staring askance at his black secret-agent shades. "Chill, Doc. I'm not hung over. I just have sensitive eyes."

Chris nodded and tried to stop grimacing at Freud's splendid hair. He was surprised that the ensign had not asked Captain Scott for permission to enter and speak. *I'll bet this little guy is a cocky son of a gun.*

Freud handed a small package to Chris. It was wrapped in brown paper and had a crumpled red Christmas bow on top. "I was just topside, dude. Your girlfriend said she meant to give you this and forgot."

Chris felt his face flush. "She's still standing up there in the rain?"

Freud nodded. "Last I saw."

Kurlgunn snatched the gift out of Chris's hand.

Chris almost responded to the theft instinctively. He barely managed to hold his tongue and stop his hands from grabbing the present back.

Kurlgunn shook the box at Freud. "What's wrong with you, Patterson? You know better than to bring a package someone else gave you onto the boat!"

Freud cringed in the doorway. "Sorry, sir. She begged me. She already came through base security."

He turned to Chris. "She also asked me to remind you that she'll wait for you, Doc."

Chris nodded, feeling mortified.

Kurlgunn handed the box back to Freud. "Take this off the *Vermont* immediately and deliver it to the base security office. I'll expect you to be back by the time I'm done writing you up."

With a weary sigh, Captain Scott motioned for Freud to hand him the gift. Freud did so, glancing apprehensively at Kurlgunn, who stared at the captain in apparent horror from behind his back.

Scott massaged his hairy chest as if giving himself one-handed CPR. "I'll see what's in it. You gentlemen can step out if you'd like. Would you rather let Freud take it off the boat, Chris?"

Chris shook his head, hoping the gift wasn't something too personal. To his surprise, Kurlgunn did step out of the room. Freud stayed, peeking into the box as Scott opened it. He leaned so close that he obstructed Chris's view.

The gift was a homemade recording on several cassette tapes. It included an inexpensive portable player and headphones. A note on top read, "*The Three Musketeers* by Alexander Dumas, read by Soony Nguyen. I love you, Chris. Please come home. I'll be waiting."

Captain Scott smiled up at Chris, blinking rapidly. His bloodshot eyes looked even more watery than before.

Good grief, are those tears?

Scott grabbed a tissue for his runny nose and vigorously scrubbed his thick red mustache, then tossed the tissue over his shoulder. "I'll bet *The Three Musketeers* is your favorite book."

"Yes, sir."

"Wonderful gift," Scott mused. "Just wonderful. Looks like you'll have more than twenty hours of her voice. Is this the first time you've left a girl behind?"

"Yes, sir." Chris reached out for the tapes. "May I?"

"Of course." Scott slowly handed up the box but seemed reluctant to let it go. Chris tugged a little harder, and the box slipped out of the aging captain's grasp.

"I remember the first time I had to leave a girl behind," Scott said, staring into space with a nostalgic sigh. "I almost asked her to marry me before we got under way, but I decided to wait until after the run."

Chris felt his throat tighten. "What happened, sir?"

"To the girl?" Scott gave a dismissive wave. "By the

time I got home, she was engaged to a tugboat skipper. Never saw her again."

Chris backed toward the door. "Captain, I need to . . . ah . . ."

"Visit the head? Sure. Dismissed. And welcome to the Gold Crew of the *Vermont,* son."

Chris launched out of the room.

Kurlgunn grabbed his arm as he passed by. "Long, I want a complete inventory of the supplies in the sick bay on my desk by twenty-two hundred. And you'll be in your rack with the curtain drawn ten minutes after that. I'll expect you to be rested tomorrow. Is that clear?"

"Aye, sir. Inventory . . . twenty-two hundred."

Kurlgunn let go.

Chris bolted along the passageway.

"No running on the boat except during emergencies!" Kurlgunn yelled. "You're a grown man now."

A few seconds later, Chris flew up the forward escape trunk into the rain and peered across the dark water.

Soony was gone.

Chapter 7

Submariners live by an eighteen-hour day. Six hours on watch are followed by six hours for studying, chores, and free time. Then they theoretically get six hours to sleep before their next watch. On the rare occasions when they are not kept awake by drills, snoring berth mates, sexual frustration, or unfinished chores, they try to spend those precious six hours catching up on the sleep they lost on more typical nights.

Chris finished his inventory by 2100 and decided to turn in early, determined not to repeat the mistakes he'd made on Commander Brady's boat. Crew berthing was down on the third level. He found berth ten, his assigned berth, near the middle of the missile compartment on the port side, outside launch tubes eleven and thirteen. The berth's entrance was formed by the narrow gap between the two vertical tubes.

He pulled aside the heavy curtain hanging over the entrance and stepped inside. The berth was lit by a dim red night-light. Each of its three sides was lined with three racks that were stacked vertically like bunk beds— one near the floor, one at waist height, and one at shoulder height. The open space in the middle was a generous six by six feet.

Chris's assigned rack was the middle one on the right. The metal platform supporting his three-inch-thick mattress also served as the hinged lid of his shallow bunk pan, which had to hold most of his personal belongings. He lifted the lid and dumped the contents of his seabag into the bunk pan.

Several of his berth mates had recently turned in and were still whispering. Chris briefly introduced himself, then undressed. When he was down to his underwear, he glanced at his watch. *Asleep in ten minutes. No more than five minutes of talking, even if these guys get the impression that I'm a dummy or a stuck-up snob.*

He saw the other men staring at his smooth scalp. When he took off his shirt, they stared at his chest. He didn't know whether they were looking at his huge muscles or the strange baldness of his skin.

A skinny petty officer named Miguel Cervesu finally broke the ice. "So, how long are you, Long?"

Chris grinned. That one wasn't new to him. "The Navy has classified that information top secret, and you don't need to know."

They laughed. An African American named Cheever said, "Aw, Miguel won't sleep a wink tonight if you don't tell him."

Miguel blushed, and the others laughed again, including Chris.

"What happened there?" Cheever asked. Reaching from his rack, the one above Chris's, he pointed to Chris's left upper arm, where a rectangular patch of skin about the size of a postcard was upraised and whiter than normal. The mammoth scar was laced with faint blue swirls.

Chris frowned. "I erased a tattoo."

"How can you erase a tattoo?" Miguel asked.

"Lots of ways," Chris said. "I did it with a rat-tail file."

Miguel and Cheever exchanged a wary glance.

Chris had thought long and hard over the last nine years about whether to invent a different story to explain the scar. He didn't want people thinking he was a self-cutter, which he wasn't, or the kind of guy who looked for extreme ways to prove his machismo—he wasn't that either. But he also didn't want to lie.

"Must have been one ugly-ass tattoo," Cheever said. He patted Chris on the back. "My man Long going to do just fine with us."

Miguel was lying in the bottom rack on the left side. He reached out a foot and kicked the bottom rack at the rear of the berth. "Hey, Orbison. What are you doing in bed, man? You never turn in early."

"I'm feeling kind of woozy," Orbison said.

Chris's eyes were now adjusted to the dim red light. He could see that Orbison was short, flabby, and pear-shaped, with close-set eyes and blond muttonchop sideburns.

"Then how come you're grinning like you just got laid?" Miguel asked.

"Cause I did," Orbison said. "Last night. I think I'm in love."

Chris smiled. He knew the feeling. "What did you say your name is?"

The dumpy crewman continued staring up at the rack above him with an expression of rapture. "Kyle Orbison."

The name sounded familiar to Chris, but he couldn't remember from where. "What do you mean by 'woozy'?"

"I don't know," Kyle said in a dreamy voice. "Just kind of tired. Head hurts a little. Seems like my chest feels kind of funny."

Cheever laughed. "That's love. Right, Doc?"

"Maybe," Chris said. "Kyle, have you taken anything? I always carry aspirin and ibuprofen with me."

"No, thanks. I just had a wild time last night. I'll be fine tomorrow."

"Shhh, here comes Adolph," Miguel whispered.

The other sailors abruptly lay down in their racks and drew their brown privacy curtains closed. Chris did the same. Then he peeked out around his curtain, wondering who Adolph was.

Brisk footsteps approached outside the berth, then stopped. Lieutenant Commander Kurlgunn's crew-cut head poked around the curtain in the doorway. Squinting suspiciously in the dim nightlight, he made four checkmarks on a notepad. Chris surmised that the strict XO was keeping track of who was in bed.

When Kurlgunn was gone, the other sailors opened their curtains and resumed talking.

Chris kept his privacy curtain closed, but it was hard to sleep with his berth mates jabbering away and his mind spinning with curiosity about the new crew, along with fear that he would screw up this last chance or lose Soony or have to take part in a real missile launch.

Soony had promised at least three times that she would be waiting when he returned. Surely that meant she really would.

He finally drifted off with happy thoughts. *I've come to the right place. It feels like home.*

Chapter 8

The *Vermont* got under way on schedule. Chris wondered what it would be like to ride on the bridge as they navigated on the surface out of Puget Sound. He'd heard that the rain had cleared and it was a gorgeous autumn day. Unfortunately, even a massive Trident had such a tiny bridge box atop the narrow fairwater that only the top officers and a harbor pilot normally got to ride up there.

Chris didn't mind. Freud was off duty and had dropped by the sick bay to chat. He was providing juicy tips about the crew that Chris would not have wanted to miss.

Both men had changed out of their work uniforms into the baggy blue coveralls that were the standard attire of American submariners at sea. The coveralls included no metal parts that might bang against something and make a noise when an enemy was listening. They wore soft athletic shoes, which made quiet footsteps and worked wonders for crew morale.

Freud was reclining on the sick bay's examination table, his hands clasped behind his head and one knee upraised with his opposite ankle crossed over it. Chris couldn't remember ever seeing a Navy officer look so relaxed at sea, especially on a submarine setting off on a war patrol. Submariners were normally so busy with drills that they literally went for days without ever standing still, much less sitting down. But Freud looked as if he were lying on a beach, working on his already perfect suntan.

Instead of the cheap sneakers worn by most of the crew, Freud was wearing designer high-top basketball shoes that must have cost close to two hundred dollars. Chris also noticed that the athletic-looking half-Polynesian ensign was still wearing strong cologne and his dark shades, and chomping some kind of minty breath gum.

While Freud held forth, Chris bent over straight-legged with his palms on the floor.

Freud paused. "You got a cramp?"

"Just trying to postpone submarine rigor mortis," Chris said. "The only thing I don't like about subs is the lack of exercise."

Freud gave colorful descriptions of the *Vermont*'s engineer and the chief of the boat (COB), who apparently despised each other because their religious beliefs were at opposite ends of the spectrum. The COB's real name was Will Jordan, but the crew called him Oral. His nickname derived from the fact that his belief in faith healing and occasional proselytizing reminded the crew of the famous televangelist Oral Roberts. Freud also warned Chris about a notorious sonarman they called Pigpen.

Chris knew Captain Scott had a penchant for taking on the rejects from other submarine crews. The captain had supposedly harnessed their gratitude to turn them into the most formidable fighters in the fleet. But Chris was beginning to get the impression that Scott had failed to conquer all the drawbacks of his unique recruitment strategy. Chris just hoped he wouldn't end up contributing to the crew's issues.

He pulled his left foot up behind him to stretch his thigh. "What's with all the funky nicknames, sir?"

Freud laughed. Chris had noticed that the hip young ensign laughed at just about everything. "It's a tradition on the *Vermont,* I guess. You'll have one soon enough."

Oh joy. Baldy?

Freud started tapping his upraised foot to an imaginary beat. "Most of us prefer to be called by our nicknames. I think it helps us feel better about being just a gear in the machine."

"Why do they call you Freud, sir?"

Freud laughed again. "You haven't noticed? I'm sort of the *Vermont*'s unofficial psychoanalyst. If you want to know what makes any of these weirdos tick, just ask me. I've got them all figured out."

Chris glanced at his watch. *I've got to stop gabbing with Freud and find something useful to do. If Kurlgunn catches me, I'm dead meat.*

"Hey, how did Tumor get his nickname?"

Freud laughed especially hard at that. "On our last run, he kept complaining about all kinds of aches and pains, ringing ears, blurred vision . . . I told him those were the exact symptoms of a rare kind of brain tumor. He just about went bananas by the time we got home. The doc told him I was teasing, and I even admitted it, but Tumor was still convinced he was a goner."

Chris could see a kind of humor in that, but he didn't join in Freud's laughter. "How do you think Tumor passed the PRP?"

PRP stood for Personnel Reliability Program, a background check designed to flag any personnel who might be mentally unstable, so they could be excluded from positions involving the handling of nuclear weapons. The PRP probed into legal, financial, and medical records.

Freud shrugged. "His hypochondria never acts up on land."

"What do you think is the XO's problem?" Chris asked.

Freud grimaced. "He's been getting meaner and meaner lately. Some of the guys think he kicks our asses for the fun of it, but I think he just wants us to be tough, like him. And he's getting frustrated with the captain. We all are. Captain Scott is a sweet old dude, but I don't know if I'd want to follow him into battle anymore. Kurlgunn has nerves of steel, though—he'd get us through."

"Do you think Captain Scott is depressed?" Chris asked. "I noticed he seemed kind of . . . folded up."

"For a totally good reason, dude! His wife split about six months ago. Darlene. No warning; just gone. They'd been married since high school. He has a totally awesome sailboat, and they were planning to sail around the world together after he retires so he could show her all the places he's been on subs. He'd been looking forward to it for years and years. Now he says he's better off without her, but that's, like, total bullshit."

Chris kept stretching while he had a chance. "God, that sucks. I wonder if I should offer to counsel him."

After a pause, Freud lowered his shades to peek over them at Chris. "Dude . . . you do know that Barlow Scott is old enough to be your dad, and that he's the Navy's top-rated sub captain, even if he hasn't been himself lately."

"Right," Chris said, blushing. "Ridiculous."

"He was amazing before Darlene split," Freud added. "Great sense of humor, and a hell of a way with words. They say he never lost a cursing contest."

A booming announcement came over the 1MC. "Attention, all hands. This is the XO. We have emerged from the Juan de Fuca Strait and are approaching the six-hundred-fathom curve. Rig ship for dive. Rig ship for patrol quiet. That is all."

Chris chose the wording of his next question carefully. "Freud, were you handpicked by Captain Scott?"

Freud laughed. "You mean, what did I do to get committed to this seagoing loony bin? Nothing—just a few ordinary mistakes."

Chris sat down on the deck to stretch his glutes. "Are you afraid of getting sent off to a skimmer if you mess up again?"

In submariner parlance, a skimmer was a surface ship,

and surface sailors were called skimmer pukes. The surface fleet could survive with lower crew performance standards, so sailors who washed out of the Sub Force usually ended up serving on a skimmer, which paid less than serving on a submarine. According to most submariners, it also did not have half the mystique or camaraderie of the Silent Service.

Freud rolled over and peered down at Chris over his shades. "Me? Of course not. They know they couldn't keep the reactor running without *me*."

The stylish ensign appeared to be serious.

Chris was about to ask another question when a deep wet cough resounded from the passageway.

Chris jumped up.

The visitor stepped into view, and Chris recognized his blond muttonchops, close-set eyes, and pear-shaped physique. It was Kyle Orbison, Chris's berth mate who had attributed his "woozy" feeling to falling in love.

"Should I wait out here?" Orbison asked between coughs.

Freud hopped off the examination table. "Come on in, dude. I was just chilling. What's the matter with you?"

Orbison's response was another deep cough. He held a hand over his mouth and bowed a little.

Chris felt his heartbeat quicken. *My first real patient!* He started anxiously going through his mental checklist of the things he was supposed to do. "I thought you said you were going to be all better today, Kyle."

Orbison nodded. "That was the plan." His voice was hoarse and phlegmy.

Chris motioned for him to sit on the examination table.

Freud was still in the sick bay, which would have been crowded with only two men. Chris had to reach around him to get a stethoscope hanging from the overhead.

Freud stepped around to the other side of Orbison and asked, "Anything wrong besides the cough, Kyle?"

"My headache is a little worse. I've just never had a cough like this."

Chris suddenly remembered that he should put on a surgical mask to protect himself from infection, especially with a patient who was coughing. Now Freud was standing in front of the masks. "Sir, could you hand me one of those masks? You might want to put one on too if you plan to stand so close while I'm examining the patient."

Freud gave Chris one of the masks and picked up another one for himself. It was a thin square pad, white on the inside and milky green on the outside, with four slender straps attached to the corners. Freud tossed his mask back onto the pile with a grin. "Not my color."

Chris almost suspected he wasn't joking.

Since Freud had put his mask back, Chris assumed he was about to leave. When he didn't, Chris said, "Sir, could you excuse us?" The last thing he needed was to offend an officer, even a lowly ensign, on the first day of the run, but Freud was contributing to his nervousness, and that wasn't good for his patient.

Without a word, Freud stepped out of the sick bay.

Chris pulled out a printed checklist he'd made during his training and carefully completed every step twice. Despite his own nerves, he even remembered to make small talk to put the patient at ease, taking care to counteract the muffling effect of his mask by enunciating clearly.

"Are you still in love today, Kyle?"

"You bet. I can't wait to get back to Bremerton."

"You think she'll still be around?"

"Sure. She promised. We're going to go down to Vegas together."

Chris wondered why a girl Orbison had just met would promise to wait three months for him. He hoped she hadn't deliberately set up the rather unattractive petty officer to break his heart. Thanks to his own disfigurement, Chris had learned in school that there really were people who made a sport of wanton cruelty.

"Sounds like a chest cold," he finally reported to Orbison. "That's most likely, anyway. It could be just about anything."

Orbison slid off the examination table and stood for a moment, breathing hard, trying not to cough.

"Sorry there's not much I can do," Chris said. "Go spread it around so we can get it over with."

Almost every submarine run began with an epidemic of mild viral infections. The crowded quarters and recirculated air guaranteed that if one crewman came aboard with a cold, the rest of them would catch it eventually. Since these diseases were not dangerous or disabling, the standard procedure was to let them spread as swiftly as possible so the crew would build acquired immunity and return to health by the time the submarine reached its patrol area.

"Aye, aye," Orbison said.

As the patient trudged out of the sick bay, something in his expression caused Chris to feel a chill. *What if this is not just one of the usual bugs?*

Orbison let out the deepest cough yet, a gurgling eructation that sounded like a clogged drain breaking loose.

Chris grabbed one of the surgical masks. "Orbison, hold up. Put this on for now. Let's just make sure you don't have something serious before you give it to everyone."

Orbison frowned. "It's going to go around, whatever it is."

"I know," Chris said, still holding out the mask.

Orbison grimaced but tried to tie the mask on, reaching behind his head to fumble with the straps. "Ugh, this is even harder than you'd think."

Chris helped him. When they were done, Orbison glanced at himself in the mirror. "All the guys"—he paused for a phlegmy cough, gripping the mask with one hand—"all the guys are going to be scared of me."

"I know. I'm sorry." Chris handed Orbison a small packet of pills. "Take two of these aspirins with food for the headache, and come back if your cough gets worse or any new symptoms start up. Okay?"

Orbison nodded and left the sick bay. As he walked away, Chris could hear deep wet coughs echoing up and down the long missile compartment.

Chapter 9

After the *Vermont* dived to test depth in the open Pacific, all compartments were inspected and three leaks were found. One of the leaks was being simulated by the drill coordinator. The other two were real but minor. An hour later, all leaks were stopped and all systems were reported nominal, which meant they were functioning within specifications.

The four six-hour segments of a submariner's day were called the morning watch, the afternoon watch, the evening watch, and the midwatch. The evening watch was coming on, and Chris was scheduled to spend it sleeping. He had just hit his rack when Kurlgunn's sharp voice came over the 1MC. "Attention, all hands. This is the XO. Rig ship for deep submergence. Angles and dangles will commence in fifteen minutes."

Chris pulled back his privacy curtain and sat up with a groan. Angles and dangles was a series of maneuvers used to test whether all gear on board was stowed properly. If objects fell or liquids spilled, they might cause damage, danger, and noise, but it was better for that to happen now rather than later in a battle situation. Like a slow-motion roller coaster, the *Vermont* would alternately pitch up and down as much as thirty degrees during angles and dangles. A crewman trying to sleep could end up standing on his head, sliding down to the foot of his rack, or falling out onto the floor.

I hope they'll remember that they kept us up late if a few of us are groggy tomorrow.

The *Vermont*'s control room was a relatively large but equipment-packed compartment on the top level beneath the fairwater. In its port forward corner, the seated chief of the watch spoke to the officer of the deck. "Sir, all departments have reported rigged for deep submergence." That meant the crew had secured everything that might roll, spill, topple, or slide.

"Very well," said the officer of the deck. "Dive, take us to eight hundred feet at twenty degrees down bubble."

The diving officer echoed the order. "Making my depth eight hundred feet, diving at an angle of twenty degrees. Aye, sir."

Aboard submarines, every control order was supposed to be repeated back by its recipient so his commander could confirm that the order had been understood correctly.

The *Vermont* was currently cruising at periscope depth, about sixty feet below the surface. Eight hundred feet was the maximum depth to which she was officially capable of diving safely. The real depth limit of Tridents was classified.

The officer of the deck, or OOD, was the officer currently in charge of the entire sub, per the captain's orders. At present, the OOD was Lieutenant Frank Morrison, the ship's engineer, whom the crew called Eng—pronounced "inj." The ship's third in command, the engineer was responsible for overseeing everything that happened in the aft compartment, especially the watchstanders in the maneuvering room who manned the nuclear reactor.

Eng was a tall, extremely thin African American with a reputation for being a stuck-up loner who knew approximately everything. His bony head was shaved, and he wore large angular eyeglasses.

While serving as the OOD, Eng stood on the conn, the round dais surrounding the two periscopes in the middle of the control room. The conn functioned as the ship's nerve center and command post.

The *Vermont*'s steering controls were in the port forward corner of the control room. They resembled the cockpit of a jumbo jet. The "pilot" in the left seat was called the sternplanesman. He held a yoke that he could push forward to pitch the sub downward or pull back to pitch the sub upward. The yoke was attached to hydraulics that moved the stern planes, small winglike fins sticking out from the sub's tapered tail. With minor help from the fairwater planes, the stern planes controlled the sub's pitch angle during dives.

The driver on the right, sometimes called the helmsman, controlled the fairwater planes, the engine order telegraph, and the rudder. The fairwater planes were horizontal fins sticking out from the fairwater—the sail, or tower, atop the sub that had been called the conning tower in prenuclear designs. The engine order telegraph was a rotating handle used to send speed change orders back to Maneuvering.

Whereas the helmsman had to manage three control functions at once, the sternplanesman was responsible for only one. This was because a moment's inattention at the stern planes yoke could send the sub plunging past crush depth. The difference between a Trident's maximum operational depth and its theoretical crush depth was not much more than one ship's length. During a steep dive, the life of every man on board was in the sternplanesman's hands, with only seconds between smooth sailing and certain death.

Behind the sternplanesman and the helmsman sat the so-called diving officer, a watchstation that was usually performed by an enlisted man, not a commissioned officer. The diving officer's job was to micromanage the sternplanesman and helmsman like a backseat driver, allowing them to devote their attention to their control yokes. He watched the array of instruments on the ship's control panel and translated the orders from the OOD into "rudder orders," precise instructions requiring no interpretation. The diving officer also called out the depth at regular intervals during dives and ascents to make sure everyone in the control room was aware of the changing depth.

The man serving as diving officer on this watch was Master Chief Will Jordan, the COB. Chief of the boat was the highest enlisted position on a submarine. It was also the title Christopher Long aspired to have by the end of his career. Although the COB was not a commissioned officer, his effective authority approached that of the XO in the complex command structure of a submarine.

The *Vermont*'s COB was a tall, beefy, seriously overweight African American. A registered Pentecostal minister, he held weekly nondenominational prayer services on the sub. He had a double chin, jowly cheeks, and a large, bulbous nose. His lips were thick and heavy. His light brown eyes seemed unusually large, and his hair was a short afro going gray at the edges.

After repeating back the OOD's order to dive, Oral passed the order on down the chain of command to the helmsman and sternplanesman, following the cumbersome procedures used on submarines to prevent confusion. "Maintain your speed all ahead one-third, steady course two-four-two. Full dive on the fairwater planes. Sternplanesman, make the ship's dive angle twenty degrees down bubble."

The sternplanesman and helmsman repeated their orders back to Oral, then carried them out.

As the *Vermont* plunged into the abyss, all of the men who were standing leaned to remain upright. It was a nerve-wracking moment for all but the oldest hands. No amount of experience on surface vessels could mentally prepare a sailor for riding a ship that flew through the ocean like a plane with no windows, especially when it took a nosedive. Beyond about ten degrees, the new crewmen—known as nubs—tended to panic and grab something to hold on to.

The sternplanesman on this watch was Petty Officer Second Class Kyle Orbison, who was still wearing the surgical mask Chris had given him. Kyle usually enjoyed the thrill of angles and dangles. Like looking down from a precipice, it made him aware of the vertical dimension, which did not exist for skimmers. It also reminded him of the vast depth of the ocean, even though he normally couldn't feel the sub moving. Trident submarines were too massive to speed up or slow down swiftly, and far beneath the ocean surface there was no wave motion. When the sub was running deep, it was easy for submariners to feel as if they were in the basement of a building rather than a moving ship.

This time, however, Kyle Orbison *could* feel motion, or so it seemed. It felt as if the compartment were rotating to the left. But how could that be? Was the *Vermont* diving in a spiral? According to the ship's control panel in front of him, the rudder was at zero degrees.

As the dive began, the deck felt to Kyle as if it would never stop tilting—as if it might tilt all the way up and drop the crewmen onto the forward bulkheads of their compartments. He had been through many high-angle dives, but this one felt like his first. This time Kyle Orbison was not enjoying angles and dangles at all. But he knew that if he let his discomfort show, the teasing would never stop. He already felt like a branded outcast behind the green filter mask the doc had made him wear.

So he swallowed and said nothing when a wave of vertigo hit him so hard it made him nauseous.

At least Kyle was sitting down, holding the hefty stern planes yoke in both hands. He discreetly took a deep breath, hoping it would stop his head from spinning. *If I mention how bad I feel, the OOD may decide to abort angles and dangles just because I have a cold. The officers*

*won't officially blame the failed drill on me, but they'll
remember who wimped out.*

"Passing four hundred feet," announced Oral, the diving officer.

Kyle Orbison cringed when the *Vermont*'s hull gave
out a tortured groan. It was normal but still unnerving
when the reversible compression of hull plates caused
eerie noises during deep descents. By the time she
reached eight hundred feet, the *Vermont* would be at
least a foot shorter than she had been at the surface,
having shrunk by the volume of a small bedroom.

"Passing four-five-zero feet," Oral announced.

The hull groaned again, this time in two places at
once.

Kyle wished he could let go of his yoke to wipe sweat.
The tension of controlling the stern planes during a steep
dive always made him feel a little overheated, despite the
coolness of the sub's nuclear-powered air-conditioning. But
today the control room felt like a sauna. His skin was
hot and clammy all over. He could feel sweat trickling
down his jaws from his muttonchops.

Since coming on watch, Kyle had been straining not
to cough. The urge was striking him every few seconds
now. Whenever it came, he held his breath and swallowed repeatedly to help clear his throat. Despite his
best efforts, a few coughs had escaped, enough to draw
suspicious glances.

"Passing five hundred feet," Oral announced.

Kyle held the yoke firmly, with his gaze riveted to
the ship's control panel, which was packed with digital
indicators and backup analog gauges. He was holding
her steady at twenty degrees down bubble.

Glancing over his shoulder, he saw Eng—the current
OOD—step off the conn and carefully walk downhill
toward him. Eng skirted Oral and stooped beside Kyle.
The scrawny black lieutenant spoke in a low monotone.
"Orbison, are you certain you feel fit for duty?"

"Yes, sir," Kyle whispered through his mask. "The new doc said I just have a chest cold." *It's the worst damn cold I've ever had,* he thought, *but surely the corpsman knows what he's talking about.*

"Passing five-five-zero feet," Oral said.

"You're sweating," Eng whispered to Kyle. "Do you feel feverish?"

"Maybe a little, sir."

Eng straightened up and called out, "Stand by to zero the planes at six hundred feet." The planes had to be returned to level about two hundred feet before the desired depth was reached because the sub would take a while to level out and stop descending.

"Passing five-seven-five feet," Oral announced.

Kyle was feeling worse by the second. An uncanny weakness was coming over him, along with a strange sense of unease bordering on panic.

This can't be just a cold. So what the hell is it? And where did I catch it? None of the other guys seem sick. I probably picked it up on shore. When was I last around sick people? Or a big crowd?

Maybe I shouldn't try to make it through this watch after all. It would be bad to wimp out in the middle of a drill, but it would be worse to make a mistake because I'm distracted. Surely I can get through this one dive. Then I'll ask the OOD to give someone else the planes and let me grab some rack time.

Eng was still standing beside Kyle, contemplatively tapping a long bony finger against the right side of his clean-shaven head. Lowering his voice again, the emaciated lieutenant said, "When this drill is over, I want you to report back to the corpsman."

Kyle attempted to say "aye, sir," but all that came out was a low gurgle, like the last sound of a sinking ship.

He swallowed, but his trachea remained blocked.

He tried to cough but couldn't.

Glancing over his shoulder, he saw that Eng had

turned away. The tall stick figure was climbing back toward the conn.

"Passing five-nine-zero feet," Oral said.

Kyle leaned forward against his seat belt. His grip tightened on the yoke until his knuckles turned white. He tried to cough again and again, to no avail. Sweat flooded down his forehead and stung his eyes. His head felt as if it were about to explode.

"On my mark, zero the planes," Eng said.

Kyle was still maintaining twenty degrees down and still trying in vain to breathe. The bright fluorescent lights in the control room seemed to be growing dimmer. The voices seemed far away.

Kyle knew he was in trouble now. So were the rest of the crew if he failed to zero the planes in time to halt the descent above crush depth, where the *Vermont* would implode and sink to the seafloor in pieces. He had to get help, but how? If he couldn't breathe, he couldn't speak, and he certainly couldn't let go of the yoke to signal with his hands.

"Passing six hundred feet," Oral announced.

Still choking, Kyle Orbison started stomping the deck with both feet.

Everyone in the control room glanced at him. Then most of them had to return their attention to their instruments.

Eng stepped off the conn. "Orbison, what's wrong?"

The helmsman was turned sideways, staring at Kyle. "Sir, I think he's choking!"

"Secure from dive," Eng ordered.

"Securing from dive, aye," Oral said. "Helm, full rise on the fairwater planes until we level out." The ungainly COB shifted his large rear end uncomfortably in the small diving officer's chair.

Kyle started to zero the stern planes. Even now, he did not jerk abruptly on the yoke, which could have thrown the sub out of control. Instead, he pulled back gently.

I can do this! I'll stop this dive if it's the last thing I ever do!

Eng stepped downhill from the conn and pushed in front of Oral. He leaned precariously over the thick chrome railing behind the sternplanesman's chair and gripped the yoke, placing his bony hands over Kyle's. "Easy does it," he said.

The stern planes were almost level when the dissolved oxygen in Kyle Orbison's brain became so low that blind panic took over. He jerked his hands out from under Eng's. He tore off his mask, irrationally thinking it might help him breathe. He ripped loose its straps with such force that the two straps on the right side, remaining tied to each other, caught on his ear and tore the base of it before pulling free. Blood trickled down his neck as he hysterically struggled with his seat belt. He managed to unbuckle the belt and attempted to stand up, bumping Eng's bony chin with his head.

Eng lost his balance and fell against the back of Kyle's chair, instinctively hanging on to the yoke.

"Hey, watch it!" Oral said when Eng accidentally kicked him.

Eng's hands had jerked the yoke all the way back. The hydraulics responded by attempting to instantaneously rotate the stern planes. When the planes turned partially broadside to the eight-knot current slipping past the sub's tail, the effect was like that of a drag chute. The entire nineteen-thousand-ton ship shuddered and slowed, seeming to lurch backward.

The lurch was gentle, but the watchstanders in the control room were not prepared for it. Combined with the steep downward pitch angle, it was enough to throw several standing men off balance.

The quartermaster fell against his chart table just aft of the conn. Then he tumbled onto the deck. He rolled and slid forward, picking up speed on the twenty-degree slope.

The chief of the watch had risen from his seat to see

whether he could help Kyle Orbison. He saw the quartermaster coming and tried to dodge, but the quartermaster knocked his feet out from under him. Both men fetched up in a tangle of arms and legs beneath the ballast control panel; the quartermaster groaning in pain.

As soon as Eng realized he had fallen, he let go of the yoke.

At about the same time, Kyle Orbison finally managed to clear his airway by ejecting a thick wad of bloody phlegm that splattered against the digital trim gauge and slid down the ship's control panel.

Kyle sucked in a loud breath, but it was too late. Before the oxygen could reach his brain, he passed out and collapsed onto the yoke, striking his head on the edge of the backup hydraulics console separating him from the helmsman. If the sub had been level, he might have bounced off the yoke and landed on the deck. As it was, the downward pitch was still steep enough to cause his limp body to hang up on the yoke, and his weight pushed it all the way forward.

The *Vermont* shuddered again, and her pitch began to increase. Within a few seconds, it passed thirty degrees down.

"Passing nine hundred feet," Oral called out in a higher octave than usual. His protruding brown eyes were rolling back and forth between Orbison, Eng, and the instruments.

An eerie moan came from the hull, reverberating through the congested enclosure. Its source seemed to travel from the stern to the bow before it terminated with a rising squeak.

Eng struggled to get up from the increasingly steep deck, grasping at the railing behind the sternplanesman's seat, his long limbs flailing. He recognized that the immediate danger to the *Vermont* was as bad as if an enemy torpedo were homing in at close range with a good sonar lock. Maybe worse, since the present emergency was one that the crew had never trained for.

Submariner training attempted to cover rote procedures for every contingency. Under hundreds of feet of ocean, pausing to think in an emergency could be fatal. Fortunately, Eng realized this situation was actually quite similar to another hair-raising casualty that they had all practiced surviving many times. That scenario was called a jam dive.

Technically, a jam dive was when the stern planes were stuck in the full dive position due to a hydraulics failure. That was not the case now, but Kyle Orbison's body resting on the stern planes yoke had the same effect. Unless the planes could be zeroed or the *Vermont*'s forward momentum could be arrested in time, she was doomed to descend until she imploded.

"All back full!" Eng shouted. "Chief of the watch, prepare to blow the forward main ballast tank."

Blowing the ballast tanks would release compressed air into them at high speed to force the ballast water out through vents in the bottom and increase the sub's buoyancy. An emergency blow could reverse the *Vermont*'s steep descent faster than just rotating the planes, but it could also cause her to nose up, lose her ballast air through the tank-bottom vents, and sink backward. If the air remained in the tanks, it was likely to force her to the surface before the crew could regain control, possibly exposing her position to enemy surveillance.

Oral did not answer Eng's order. He seemed frozen, still sitting in the diving officer's chair with his seat belt fastened, staring at the digital depth indicator. Sweat was flooding down the ravines between his plump cheeks and his bulbous nose. His protruding eyes seemed about to pop out of their sockets as he mouthed the words "passing eleven hundred feet!"

The chief of the watch, who was responsible for controlling the sub's ballast and trim systems, was just crawling out from under his console, along with the quartermaster.

The pressure hull emitted a low growl, followed by a series of strident twangs.

Only the helmsman responded immediately to Eng's order. "All back full. Aye, sir." He reached his right hand under his console and rotated the handle of the engine order telegraph to back full. At the same time, he continued gently pulling on his yoke to rotate the fairwater planes into the full rise position. A second later, he glanced at the needle on the engine order dial that indicated the response from the men at the throttles back aft. "Sir, Maneuvering is answering the back full bell."

As the screw's rotation reversed and began braking the *Vermont*'s descent, Eng felt as if invisible hands were trying to drag him downhill. Now it seemed impossible to stand up without a handhold. The floor had become more like a wall. According to the ship's control panel, the deck's real pitch angle had reached thirty-six degrees, and decelerating at maximum reverse thrust added several more degrees of apparent pitch.

"Passing twelve hundred feet," Oral said in a cracking voice. Eng caught a glimpse of his pudgy face, which was wet with sweat. It had changed color from mahogany to weathered asphalt.

"Estimate crush depth in less than one minute!" Oral added.

Eng finally managed to get up just in time to see the captain and XO stagger down into the control room from the aft passageway. Both officers stopped behind the quartermaster's chart table, leaning on it for support, staring down the slope at Kyle Orbison's motionless form and the streak of bloody phlegm he had left on the ship's control panel. Then Captain Scott went down on the deck.

Eng thought the captain had fallen; then he realized the aging officer was deliberately sliding down the steep slope on his rear end. Kurlgunn watched him for a split

second, then followed suit. Scott somehow managed to
control his slide so that he remained upright, but Kurlgunn got twisted around sideways and ended up rolling.

Before Eng could get around the sternplanesman's
seat to grab Kyle, the captain had zoomed past him,
landed feet first against the forward bulkhead, and
jumped up beside the stern planes yoke. Barlow Scott
gripped the left hip pocket of the unconscious sailor's
coveralls with one hand. He grabbed his collar with the
other hand and heaved backward with a mighty grunt.

Kyle slid off the yoke and tumbled onto the deck,
dragging Scott down on top of him.

"Fuck a feral vacuum cleaner; that turkey's heavier
than he looks," Scott panted.

Eng slid into Kyle's seat, grabbed the stern planes
yoke, and began gently easing it backward.

Kurlgunn was just getting up with an expression of
barely contained rage. Unlike the captain, he had
landed headfirst.

"Passing one-two-five-zero feet," Oral said. "Sir, it
looks like we're going to stop above crush depth."

Captain Scott stood up and stretched his back, apparently oblivious to the fact that he was standing with one
foot on the deck and one on the forward bulkhead, with
his weight distributed evenly between them. He looked
down at Kyle Orbison, who was still unconscious, drooling bloody mucus. The diminutive captain inhaled
deeply, catching his breath. "Okay, who wants to tell me
what the goat-fucking devil just happened in here?"

Chapter 10

Chris and Tumor were in the crew's study, which was located on level three outside missile tubes fourteen and sixteen. In spite of the *Vermont*'s gyrations, they were trying to study for their next round of qualification exams. They were seated at desks, facing forward, each using one hand to support his upper body against the sub's steep pitch angle. If their hips had not been restrained by their desktops, they would have fallen forward out of their chairs.

Chris was distracted by thoughts about Soony. He already missed her, and he still worried that her feelings about nuclear weapons would come between them. She had three months to think it over without any interference from him. If she made up her mind not to date a nuclear warrior anymore, there wasn't a damn thing he could do about it.

Tumor was absently picking at his acne, apparently immersed in a book. "Gee whiz, this is the wildest angles and dangles I've ever felt."

"Me too," Chris said. "Hey, are you still dizzy today?"

"I don't think so, Doc, but my guts have been acting up."

Chris had noticed that Tumor was experiencing some flatulence in the tight confines of the crew study. "Let me know if you want some gas pills."

"Nah, I'll just worry with it."

Chris leaned sideways to see what the gangly country boy was studying so intently. He saw that Tumor was drawing frogs in the margin of his hydraulics manual. His amphibian creations were doing a trapeze act, balancing and swinging from the lines of text.

"I take it you're ready to ace your quals."

Tumor looked down at his doodles with an expression of surprise that morphed into dismay. He threw down his pencil and jammed the heels of his hands against his eyes. "Oh, Lord!"

"What?"

"I already failed once. If I fail again, I'll end up on a skimmer or back at the stupid farm."

In addition to Tumor's hillbilly accent, his speech had a slight lisp from the small wad of snuff tucked under his lower lip.

"You know, you really ought to stop chewing that stuff before you lose your jaw," Chris said.

Tumor spat in his cup with a worried grimace. "I know, dang it."

Now Chris felt bad for not minding his own business. "So . . . you grew up on a farm?"

Tumor nodded. "An apple orchard, actually, in east Tennessee. Five hundred acres. My dad wanted me to stay and work, but I said no cotton-pickin' way."

"What's so bad about it?"

"It's hot, it's boring, and you can't get away from the dang bugs. And my folks drive me crazy when I'm home. All they do is work and watch TV, and their conversations are like . . . like two people talking to themselves in the same room. My dad will say something dumb, like, 'You know, cooking shows are better than dog shows,' and two minutes later my mom will say the exact same thing, word for word, like she never heard Dad say it. And then Dad will disagree and start arguing with her!"

"Maybe you need some better study habits," Chris

said. "I know all the tricks for concentrating on dry technical stuff."

"I'll take any help I can get," Tumor said, "but you have to study too."

"I can make time."

Tumor smiled. "Okay, I'll teach you how to win at Time Warrior."

"What's that?"

"My favorite video game. Last year I had the record high score in the state of Tennessee. When we get back to Bangor, I'll show you where my name's listed on the Web. You play video games?"

Chris shook his head.

Tumor slumped. "Shoot. Me and Vince—kid I grew up with—we used to play all the time after school. But I've had a hard time finding anybody willing to play on the *Vermont.*"

"I'll play," Chris said. "I'll try about anything once."

Tumor brightened. "I bet you'll like it. Maybe it will be just like old times. I miss Vince."

"Do you visit him when you go home?"

Tumor sadly shook his head. "He was on the Metro."

Chris felt a knot cinch tight in his stomach, as he always did when the tragedy was mentioned. Islamic fundamentalists had released nerve gas in the subway of Washington, D.C., as crowds were dispersing after the Fourth of July fireworks. Almost five thousand men, women, and children had died. Like many Americans, Chris had made the mistake of sitting in front of a TV for the next three days, glued to CNN, waiting to see what would happen next. It had been three years now, but it still felt like yesterday.

"I'm sorry, Tumor. Did that have anything to do with you deciding to join the military?"

Tumor nodded darkly. "You betcha."

It occurred to Chris that he and Tumor had something unusual in common. He started to tell his new friend about the five older foster brothers he'd lost in the fire. Before he could get started, he was interrupted by an announcement on the 1MC.

"Corpsman, lay to control. Repeat, corpsman, lay to control for a medical emergency."

Chris swung out of the crew study, using his arms more than his legs. Then he scuttled down the frighteningly long and steep central passageway of the missile compartment.

I'll bet it's the captain. I thought he looked sick. Probably a heart attack. If I screw this one up, I might as well crawl into a torpedo tube and die.

The *Vermont* was swiftly returning to a level pitch. Chris was no longer running downhill by the time he bounded into the control room, where he saw several crewmen clustered around the steering controls in the port forward corner. He approached them, but even with his great height he could not see what they were doing.

"Excuse me."

The officers were talking loudly and seemed to be staring at something on the floor. When Chris realized no one had heard him, he raised his voice and said "Excuse me!" again.

This time the XO turned around, looking annoyed as usual. He gasped and tensed up when he saw Chris's hulking form standing close behind him.

"Sorry, sir. Didn't mean to scare you."

"You did not scare me, Long." Kurlgunn stepped aside and yelled, "Let him through!"

The throng parted. Chris saw that Kyle Orbison was lying on the deck, not moving except for his rapid, shallow breaths, which made a gurgling noise. Captain Scott was standing over him with a worried frown. The captain had evidently seen the exchange between Chris and Kurlgunn—he looked up at Chris and said, "There are times when a sailor should speak up, son."

"Sorry, sir. I usually do."

At first, Chris assumed Orbison had been the victim

of an accident caused by the steep dive angle. Then he looked around at the gory mess the sick sailor had made on the deck and the instrument panel, and he realized that Orbison had probably collapsed because of his illness.

Chris momentarily stopped breathing. *Oh, shit, I told him it was just a cold!*

Kurlgunn shoved him toward the victim. "Don't just stand there, Long. Do something."

Chris stooped to speak softly beside the diminutive captain's ear. "Sir, you should probably order the men to stand back. Orbison may have a communicable infection."

Scott spoke loudly. "I want all nonessential personnel to leave the control room. The rest of you return to your watchstations. COB, take us up to four hundred feet on steady course two-four-two, and get an A-ganger up here with a bucket of Betadine solution."

The A-gangers, or auxiliarymen, were enlisted handymen who performed most of the sub's maintenance and cleaning.

Chris pointed to a long red welt above Orbison's right eye. "Did he hit his head?"

"Yeah, pretty hard," the helmsman said.

"Okay, I'll get the Miller board." The Miller board was a rigid yellow plastic stretcher used for transporting victims who might have spinal injuries.

Chris started to leave. Kurlgunn grabbed his arm. "Aren't you even going to check his pulse?"

Chris stopped and looked back at the crumpled victim. He didn't want to touch him without a mask and gloves, but the XO's critical gaze changed his mind. Holding his breath, he reached down and pressed two fingers to Orbison's neck. A few seconds later he backed away and resumed breathing. "He has a strong pulse, sir. His breathing sounds congested, but he's getting enough air."

"Very well." Kurlgunn waved him off.

When Chris reached the sick bay, the first thing he did was swab Betradine scrub on the two fingers he had used to check Orbison's pulse. Then he put on a surgical mask and latex gloves, grabbed an extra mask to tie on to Orbison, and headed back to control with the yellow Miller board.

In the narrow passageway, he ran into a flabby and disheveled petty officer with thick eyeglasses and wildly frizzy blond hair. The man's mustache was long and unkempt, resembling a roll of granddaddy spiders. His body odor was unusually ripe, even for a submariner, and his uniform looked as if it had been buried and dug up a few times. Chris wondered how he had managed all that after less than two days at sea.

"You need any help, Doc?"

"Sure. You saw what happened?"

"No, but Freud told everybody already."

"What's your name?" Chris asked.

"Evram Ruleberg, sonarman. You can call me Pigpen if it's easier to remember. I'm not like pretty-boy Freud—I'm here to get a job done."

"Okay, thanks. Can you go get a mask and gloves and catch up with me?"

"No problem," Pigpen said.

Chapter 11

The available higher officers gathered in the wardroom, the private dining room where all officers were served their meals. The wardroom was between the galley and CPO berthing on level three, in the starboard forward corner of the people tank—the sub's inner pressure hull.

After drills and real emergencies, the officers met to discuss what had gone wrong. Criticism was supposed to be uninhibited. It was an event where procedures could be improved but careers could be destroyed.

As usual, Kurlgunn sat on the edge of his seat, as if he were about to pounce across the table. "This would not have happened if Orbison had told us he was so sick before the drill," he said. "Failing that, you should have seen that he wasn't fit for duty, Eng. You were the OOD."

Eng was rubbing his shaved temples with his long, bony forefingers. "Sir, I was observing him closely. I even asked if he felt fit for duty, and he answered in the affirmative. He said the new corpsman had informed him that he just had a cold. Whatever caused that . . . that *blockage* seemed to overcome him in a matter of seconds."

Kurlgunn ran a hand over his coal black burr cut, then balled it into a tight fist, flexing his ropy biceps. "So this whole fiasco was really the new corpsman's fault for misdiagnosing Orbison and failing to take him off duty."

"Freud told me he was there when the doc checked

Orbison out," said Lieutenant Matthew Covers, a tall, weathered, long-faced Texan with a brown handlebar mustache. The others usually called him Weps because he was the nuclear weapons officer. "Freud said the doc seemed kind of distracted, like he wasn't real sure what he was doing."

Freud himself was not present in the wardroom—he was back in Maneuvering, managing the reactor.

Kurlgunn shot an accusing glance at Captain Scott. "We should not have gone to sea on an op like this with a green corpsman."

Scott looked away, slumping in his chair at the head of the wardroom table. He was still wearing his sweaty tank-top undershirt. The reddish gray hair surrounding his bald crown was wet with sweat as well, despite the cool dry air.

Eng pushed his large eyeglasses up his bony nose and spoke slowly, with exaggerated emphasis, as if to a group of children. "Orbison's symptoms may have appeared the same as those of an ordinary cold at the time the doc examined him. Respiratory infections are notoriously difficult to diagnose, especially in the early stages."

"I suppose you know all about that," Kurlgunn said.

Eng nodded. "I happen to have read several books about infectious diseases."

"Good," Scott said. "The new doc will probably appreciate any help you can give him."

Eng winced slightly, then returned to his customary expression of patient disdain.

"We need to get the corpsman in here," Kurlgunn said. "Surely he's figured out what Orbison really has by now. If it's something contagious, we have to stop it from spreading."

Responding to a page from Kurlgunn, Chris arrived in the wardroom less than a minute later. He took one look at the officers' faces and knew that the winds were not blowing in his favor. He had expected as much, and he felt as if he deserved it.

This was the first time Chris had been face to face with the tall black engineer, the sub's third in command. He couldn't help staring at the black stubble that was beginning to sprout from the lieutenant's shaved scalp. It was obvious that Eng could have a full head of hair if he would let it grow. *What a waste!*

Chris noticed that Eng was skin and bones, and Freud had been right about him having a peculiar default expression. How had Freud put it? Resigned frustration? Benevolent condescension?

Eng's body language was cautious and reserved. His shaved head and quick, alert eyes made him look fiercely intelligent and austere. But his bizarre eyewear did nothing to enhance his scholarly image. The huge lenses of his glasses were almost square, and instead of the usual brown or black, the plastic frames were bright red.

No seats were available, so Chris remained standing in front of the closed door while most of the ship's officers scrutinized him.

"How's the patient?" asked Captain Scott.

"Still unconscious, sir."

"From his illness or that bump on his head?"

"From a concussion, as best I can tell."

"Did you leave him unsupervised just now?" Kurlgunn asked.

"Pigpen is watching him, sir."

"So what does he have? You'd better not tell us it's just a cold."

"That's what it looked like before, sir. I'm sorry if I was wrong."

"What do you mean, 'if'?"

"I still have no idea what he has, sir."

"*What?* You've had an hour to examine him!"

Chris felt the XO's bullet gray eyes boring into his. He looked down to avoid them. "Sir, I'm sorry. We

don't have the lab equipment to test for pathogens or
antibodies. Until he wakes up, I can't even take his
history."

"What about that . . . that *stuff* he coughed up? Can't
you tell anything from that?"

"It was abnormally viscous," Eng added. "It almost
made him choke to death."

Chris felt hot all over except for his hands, which were
freezing. He was trying to ignore the urge to take off
his hat and wipe the sweat from his scalp. Hesitantly, he
said, "I was about to search for that in the database of
symptoms. It may not tell us much. Kyle's record says
he has presented twice with dehydration on previous
runs. Some people just have a habit of not drinking
enough."

A wave of relaxing shoulders washed around the
table.

Captain Scott raised one of his bushy red and gray
eyebrows. "Are you saying he just choked on his own
phlegm because he needed a drink of water?"

"It's possible," Chris said. "I checked his blood—one
of the few things I can measure is electrolyte
concentration—and he was mildly dehydrated. I put him
on a saline IV that should have restored his fluids by
now."

"That stuff he coughed up was bloody," Kurlgunn
said. "Could dehydration cause that?"

"No, but a mild nosebleed could. Or bleeding gums."

"Wow, that's a relief," said Lieutenant Covers. "I
thought he had something serious."

Captain Scott released a weary sigh. "Maybe it's just
a cold after all."

Chris said, "I doubt that, sir. He has a moderate fever
now, and severe chest congestion. I've upgraded the
probable diagnosis to pneumonia."

"Is pneumonia contagious?" Kurlgunn asked.

"That depends on what's causing it, sir. It could be

viral, bacterial, or rickettsial. There are even fungi and protozoa that can cause pneumonia."

"Pneumonia just means infected lungs?"

"Yes, sir."

Scott said, "Give us your best guess, son."

Chris took a deep breath. *Please let me be right this time.* "Orbison's white blood cell count is elevated, sir. I'm still working on a hematocrit and a urinalysis. That's about all I can do, as far as lab procedures go. So far, everything I've seen suggests a bacterial pathogen, probably *Streptococcus pneumoniae*. If that's it, it's transmissible but not terribly contagious."

"What's your second guess?" Scott asked.

"Flu," Chris said.

"That wouldn't be so bad," said Weps. "I've had the flu."

"Tell them about the Spanish flu," Eng said to Chris.

Chris vaguely remembered something from his training about the Spanish flu pandemic, but he couldn't recall any details. Feeling embarrassed, he said, "Would you like to tell them, sir?"

"Spanish flu was an unusually virulent strain that swept the world in 1918 and 1919," Eng said. "Most influenza strains are dangerous only to the weak, the elderly, and infants. This strain preferred healthy victims in their twenties and thirties, and it caused hemorrhaging in the lungs that often drowned them within hours. In one famous case, a woman got on a bus in New York feeling fine. By the time the bus got to her stop, she was dead.

"The Spanish flu was so contagious, it infected a fifth of the world's population in less than two years. Twenty-eight percent of Americans caught it. It killed about six hundred and seventy-five thousand Americans, ten times more than the fighting in World War I, which was drawing to a close at the time. Worldwide, it killed more people in those two years than any other epidemic in history, somewhere between twenty and forty million.

"The 1918 strain probably still exists in aquatic bird species, which are the natural hosts of influenza. In 1997, a different strain of flu they called 'chicken Ebola' jumped from poultry to humans in Hong Kong. Even with modern medical care, it killed a third of its human victims. Fortunately, the Hong Kong outbreak was stamped out with quarantine before it could rage out of control. Ask any doctor—it's just a matter of time until one of those flus or a new mutant strain takes out a swath of the overcrowded human population again. We still haven't developed any drugs that can kill the influenza virus. If Orbison's infection is bacterial, we can probably combat it with antibiotics. If it's flu, however . . . we've lost the bubble, gentlemen."

Chris was wondering what they needed a corpsman for, if Eng knew as much as he sounded like he did.

Kurlgunn was staring at him. "What are you doing to stop this bug from spreading, Long?"

"Nothing yet, sir. That's the next step. We need to screen the whole crew and isolate everyone who might be sick."

Captain Scott leaned forward and looked up at Chris with a stern expression. "You'll do no such thing, young man."

"Why not, sir?"

"Because it would scare the crew to death. If they panic now, they may not survive this run."

"Sir, we need to take whatever precautions we can to isolate the sick."

Captain Scott got up with a groan and began wearily circling the table, staring at his officers. He plucked a white Kleenex from a box on the table but did not use it immediately. Instead, he waved it like a flag with each emphasized word he spoke. "Corpsman Long, what is the worst disease that could break out on a submarine?"

"I don't know, sir."

"Fear," Scott said, swishing the Kleenex in a broad arc. "It can cause paralysis like polio. It can cause insan-

ity like rabies. It can turn men to mush faster than Ebola. After ninety days underwater, a few men always get loopy, even when everything is going fine. Can you imagine how this crew would perform if they believed some killer bug was working its way through them? I can. When you're terrified all the time, you can't eat or sleep, you can't get along, and you can't concentrate. You start fighting and making mistakes. Then you stop caring whether you live or die. If the men on this boat start spending all their time wondering which one will be the next to go down, you might as well have detonated a torpedo on its rack—we're sunk either way."

Scott's audience was riveted. Chris backed against the door, awed by the depressed captain's burst of conviction.

Eng spoke up, blinking slowly as if proud of his patience. "Captain, if Orbison's infection spreads, morale is going to plummet, regardless of what we do. Perhaps we could delay the panic a few days by withholding information from the crew, but I doubt that would be wise in the long run."

Scott shook his Kleenex at Eng. "What information? Jesus Johnson, we don't even know for sure that it's an infection!" He turned to Chris, finally using the tissue to blow his parrot-beak nose and scrub his big red mustache. "Right, Long?"

"That's right, sir. It could be anything from an allergic reaction to lung cancer. My gut feeling is that it's infection, but that's based on zero experience."

Eng voiced Chris's thoughts. "Shouldn't we take precautions just in case?"

"Not yet," Scott said. "What if you deploy precautions and the bug turns out not to be real? What if it is real but your precautions don't help? Either way, you've screwed morale three ways at once for nothing."

Chris exchanged a desperate look with Eng, who was hunched over with his sticklike arms crossed on his lap.

There are times when a sailor should speak up, son.

"Captain, we have to at least check the rest of the crew for fevers and coughs. If even one other man has the same symptoms, we'll know for sure it's infectious. And I may be able to diagnose it if I can talk to a conscious patient."

Scott flopped down on his chair, looking exhausted. He winced and massaged his hairy chest but said nothing.

Chris tried to swallow. His throat had gone dry. "Captain, *please*. This may be serious, and I may be able to stop it, but only if you give me a chance."

Scott hung his head for a moment, slumping as if he were dead. Then he mumbled something that sounded like "fuck it" and looked up. "Go take their temperatures. But that's all. You try not to panic about germs, Corpsman Long, and I'll try not to panic about panic."

Chapter 12

Chris returned to the sick bay to check on Orbison, who was lying on a rack mattress on the floor, still wearing the surgical mask Chris had tied on to him in the control room. The patient remained unconscious, and he had coughed up more liquid, making wet pink stains on his mask. At least he seemed to be breathing without difficulty for the moment.

Even with Pigpen's help, the screening took three hours. They had to walk all over the sub to test crewmen who could not leave their watchstations. Despite Scott's orders to only take temperatures, Chris also listened to each man's breathing with a stethoscope.

He began with the officers in the wardroom. They all seemed eager to be screened, except Gene Kurlgunn, who left just before Chris could get to him.

Later, Chris went to Kurlgunn's stateroom and knocked on the closed door. The XO opened it and waved him in, then closed the door behind them. "I'm busy," Kurlgunn said. "Let's get this over with."

Chris took his temperature—it was normal—then asked him to remove his shirt.

"Listen through it," Kurlgunn ordered.

Chris pressed the stethoscope's chestpiece to the back of Kurlgunn's shirt. The ripples of muscle covering the XO's back felt as hard as a leather saddle. After listening for several seconds while Kurlgunn breathed deeply, Chris said, "Sir, I'm sorry; you'll have to take your shirt off."

Kurlgunn complied.

Under the harsh fluorescent light, Chris saw a large black-and-red tattoo of a yin-yang symbol with two fanged dragons circling it just above his belt. There were also several other marks on the pale skin of the XO's back, higher up, between the shoulder blades: a patchwork of broad, raised, triangular welts that looked very deep and very old.

"Wow, where'd you get these huge scars, sir?"

Kurlgunn's ropy back went rigid. His hands flexed into white fists. His small, outward-tilting ears turned red.

Chris winced and palmed the top of his baseball cap. *Shit, my mouth has done it again.*

With his back still turned to Chris, Kurlgunn said, "If you were a grown man, you wouldn't have asked me that."

"I'm sorry, sir!"

"Why did you cut that fucking tattoo off your arm? Huh?"

After a tense pause, Chris replied, "Sir, I'm sorry. I know I should mind my own business."

"Damn right. Are you done?"

"No, sir."

"Hurry up."

"Aye, sir."

A minute later, Chris reported, "Sounds clear to me, sir."

Kurlgunn hastily buttoned up his shirt. "You're the new corpsman, so I figured you would see my back sooner or later. Whatever you think you were staring at back there, it's between you and me. Is that clear?"

"Yes, sir. Of course."

"Good. Dismissed."

Chris eagerly vacated the XO's cramped stateroom.

The triangular shape of the huge scars on Kurlgunn's

back had reminded Chris of the shape of the tip of an electric clothing iron.

They found three possible fevers—none severe—and no serious chest congestion. Chris decided not to take the three men off duty, since there was no clear evidence that they had anything serious. Mild fevers could be caused by various benign conditions.

According to the crew roster, there was only one man left to test now, a seaman named Maurice Hereford.

"Where do you think he is?" Chris asked.

"Probably studying," Pigpen replied.

They set out to search the likely places—enlisted mess, crew study, exercise area. Chris tried to stay upwind of Pigpen. As they walked through the warren of equipment-lined passageways, the words Freud had used to describe the disheveled sonarman came back to him:

"Pigpen is our secret weapon, dude. If we ever have to strike and run out of missiles, we'll just send him ashore. My advice is don't sit close to him in the mess. Whatever you do, don't watch him eat. I don't think he has a phobia of soap and water. I think he's just stuck in that rebellious stage children go through. I wouldn't be surprised if he pisses in the bilges just for fun. The captain makes us put up with him because he's the best damn sonar operator in the Western Hemisphere. I swear, dude, on an under-ice patrol in the Arctic, he could hear a scuba diver let a fart off Australia."

Sonarmen were reputed to be the most eccentric of submariners. Even within the Silent Service, they were considered a breed apart, strange but elite, creatures who could see with their ears.

Chris had almost become a sonarman himself. On his first submarine run, he had been a striker, an unspecialized seaman. Strikers performed menial chores until they decided which department they'd prefer to work in; then they went back for more specialized training. Chris had decided right off that he wanted to be a sonarman, but after he had fallen asleep on watch three times, Commander Brady had advised him to become a corpsman. If a corpsman fell asleep, someone could just wake him up. If a sonarman fell asleep, the result could be a fatal collision.

Chris and Pigpen had both been scheduled to sleep during this watch, and it was almost over. Throughout the "night," Pigpen had been draining cup after cup of black coffee and running back to Shaft Alley to smoke cigarettes.

Shaft Alley, the rear of the engine room near the propeller shaft, was the *Vermont*'s designated smoking area. Smoking was allowed on American submarines because the air purifiers could remove enough of the pollution to keep the atmosphere breathable even after weeks of submergence.

"Are you having trouble staying awake?" Chris asked.

"Shit no. I'm doing fine."

"Because of all the coffee and cigarettes?"

"Are you kidding? We've been so fucking busy, I've had hardly any since we started this project."

After striking out in the crew's study on the third level, they went to the exercise area in Auxiliary Machinery Room Two, which included two treadmills and a weight bench. None of the exercisers said they had seen Maurice Hereford lately.

They headed forward.

"Why didn't you want to do that last guy?" Chris asked. At their last stop, Chris had picked one of the men they needed to examine and asked Pigpen to check the other, but Pigpen had insisted on switching patients.

"Ingersoll?" Pigpen whispered. "I'm pretty sure he's a fag."

"That bothers you?" Gay rights were not Chris's axe to grind, but he took pride in not being prejudiced.

"Shit, yeah." Pigpen took out a cigarette and put it in his mouth but didn't light it, since they were not in the smoking area.

The crude sonarman reeked of cigarettes. Chris hated any kind of smoke—the slightest whiff could make him feel panicky. But he was pretty sure that anyone but himself would consider stale cigarette smoke the least noxious note in the symphony of Pigpen's body odor.

"Worst thing about a submarine," Pigpen added. "You just know there's faggots in here checking out your ass. That's one disease I sure hope isn't catching."

Chris frowned. "If you hate being cooped up with other guys, why did you volunteer for submarines? Just to make more money?"

"Shit, no. I don't have to work. My family is loaded."

"Must be nice."

"Not really. They're all musicians."

"So?"

"I hate music."

"Why did you become a sonarman?"

"Oh, I love listening to the sea, especially the biologics. What I hate is the fucking pathetic noises human beings make."

"Did your parents want you to be a musician?"

Pigpen nodded. "My dad's a record producer, and my mom was an opera star. My little sister has her own band now. They made me try every goddamned instrument from bongos to banjos, but I couldn't play shit. None of them have a fucking clue what math and science are for."

They came to the enlisted mess. It was between mealtimes, and only two men were there. One was making himself a sandwich. The other was getting a round of drinks from the bug juice dispenser to take back to the sonar shack. Neither man could tell them where Maurice Hereford was, so they headed back to the laundry in the aft starboard corner of the missile compartment.

"I wanted to be an astronaut," Pigpen said. "I used to be crazy about space. Spent my whole life training for it, until my sophomore year at Cal Tech."

"What happened then?"

"My eyes finally got too bad. NASA won't consider candidates with vision worse than twenty over two hundred. Mine's twenty over two-twenty now. Pretty fucking ironic—I might not have gone so blind if I hadn't studied so hard. Anyhow, I dropped out and just bummed around the house for a couple of years. Then I enlisted in the Navy, and it was the best move I ever made."

"Why? You can't even see the stars from a submarine."

"So what? Astronauts only get to spend a few days up in space, but we spend half our lives down here, and flying through the deep is just as interesting. I'd like to keep doing it forever . . . unless it starts turning me queer."

"You do know that's impossible," Chris said.

"I hope so, man. The military spaceships you see in science fiction movies—what do you think those are based on? Air Force planes? NASA rockets? Not hardly. The crews, navigation, weapons systems, even the control room layout—those ships are just nuclear submarines set in outer space."

Maurice Hereford was not in the laundry.

"Shit, where haven't we looked?" Pigpen asked.

Chris said, "I don't—good grief, of course: his rack. He's probably taking a nap." Chris checked the roster for Hereford's berth and rack number. "Okay, let's head up to berth four."

On their way forward through the missile compartment, Chris said, "Pigpen, I appreciate your help today. Why did you volunteer?"

"I didn't figure anybody else would."

"Aren't you afraid of catching Orbison's bug?"

"Shit, no. I've never been sick a day in my life. Germs are my best friends."

Berth four was behind missile tubes five and seven. Chris stopped in front of the curtain hanging between the thick burnt orange tubes. An unfamiliar noise was coming from the berth, a rhythmic alternation between creaks and thumps.

He glanced at Pigpen.

Pigpen shrugged.

They entered the berth, peering through the dim red night light. Only one of the nine racks was occupied. It was Hereford's, the top rack on the left. The thick brown privacy curtain was drawn across its front.

The rhythmic noise was coming from Hereford's rack, and something behind the curtain was causing it to shake and poof out a little just before each thump. Now Chris could also hear rapid, shallow breathing.

"That better not be what it sounds like," Pigpen whispered. His tone was menacing, his expression disgusted.

Chris knew what he meant. It sounded a little like a couple having sex. Chris wondered whether Maurice Hereford had an unusually rambunctious way of masturbating.

"Maurice?" he whispered.

There was no answer, and the noisy movement behind the curtain continued.

Chris knocked on the bunk pan beneath Hereford's rack. "Hey, Maurice," he said, louder this time.

Again there was no response except the rhythmic *creak-thump-creak-thump*.

Chris suddenly felt as if he had swallowed a whole tray's worth of ice cubes. He glanced back at Pigpen, whose back was plastered against the tier of racks on the opposite side of the berth. The crude sonarman's expression had turned from disgust to horror.

"Maybe he's just listening to headphones," Chris said.

Pigpen licked his lips, leaving a residue of moisture on his scraggly blond mustache. "With the volume way up?"

"Yeah, and bopping to the music," Chris added hopefully, and he pulled back the curtain.

In the high rack lay a tall and athletic-looking Caucasian man with brown hair, crooked teeth, tattooed arms, and a hairy chest. He was prone on his back, wearing nothing but a wet pair of gray boxer shorts. He was rolling from side to side on his elbows. His skin was flushed and beaded with sweat. Sweat had run off his body and soaked his sheet. His hands were clenched into tight claws, thrust upward above his midriff as if he were prepared to fight. His neck was arched backward so that his head rested more on its top than on its back, forcing his mouth to hang open. Thick saliva was drooling down from both corners. His bloodshot eyes were rolled back in his head.

"Shit, that fucker's dying!" Pigpen said. "What are we going to do?"

"Get him back to the sick bay." Chris pulled on his latex gloves as fast as he could and started tying a surgical mask onto Hereford. "You clear the way. I'll carry him."

Chapter 13

After doing all he could for Maurice Hereford, Chris started setting up a treatment ward where the patients could be isolated to minimize the danger of spreading airborne germs to the rest of the crew. Unlike subs of the World War II era, the *Vermont*'s interior was not partitioned into several watertight compartments that could be sealed off in case of flooding. Most of the rooms were separated only by false walls that were full of holes for ventilation, wires, and pipe runs. So he couldn't just pick a compartment and shut off its air flow.

After discussing the problem with the captain and XO, Chris chose the officers' wardroom. The wardroom's walls were designed to provide privacy, so they came closer than most to being solid bulkheads. More important, no vital functions took place in the wardroom that could not be moved elsewhere without ripping out equipment.

Chris sealed every crack, seam, and hole he could find, using silicone caulk or strips of polyethylene plastic and green EB high-pressure tape. *Caulk and duct tape—Navy ingenuity.* The ironic memory brought on a pang of fear that he would never see Soony again.

Germs could still escape through the door, in the air or on people and fomites—infectious objects—leaving the room. Chris wrote a lengthy warning on the outside wall with a Magic Marker: "Put on mask and gloves before entering. Do not hold door open. Keep door sealed with tape." He placed a lidded garbage can outside the door to collect used masks and gloves, alongside a box of fresh ones. Then he fetched several packets of lithium hydroxide crystals in case they were needed to keep down the carbon dioxide level in the almost airtight room.

While Chris was still taping over holes in the walls, Freud stopped by. The stylish young ensign did not offer to help. Instead, he leisurely leaned against the door frame, grinning and chewing a match beneath his dark shades. "Dude, I heard you gave up a football scholarship to join the Navy. That's not true, is it?"

"I decided football was too dangerous," Chris said with a wry smile. He was on his hands and knees, working in a corner. Wiping sweat, he craned his neck to look back at Freud. "Actually, I didn't want to spend my life playing a game, sir."

"Oh, come on, Doc, life *is* a game! Why didn't you accept the scholarship and get an officer commission through ROTC?"

Chris returned his attention to his work, wondering whether Freud had been told that two members of the *Vermont*'s confined crew were deathly ill with what appeared to be a contagious disease. "I'm not a leader, sir. I've seen the kind of trouble being the boss can get you into. Besides, I couldn't wait to get on a submarine."

As far as Chris knew, he was telling the truth about his motives, although he'd omitted the fact that the Naval Academy and most universities probably would have rejected him if he had applied. Until his senior year of high school, his grades had been worse than mediocre in everything but math. The few universities that might have accepted him would have required him to play football, which wouldn't have left time for ROTC.

Freud chuckled. "Each to his own, dude. Why did you want to become a submariner so much? Money, travel, high-tech toys? Please don't tell me you just wanted to serve your country."

Chris frowned. "What would be wrong with that? I'm sure lots of guys volunteer for that reason."

Freud shrugged. Chris was glad he didn't seem to have taken offense at the knee-jerk response.

"To be honest, sir, I heard that submariners tend to form bonds that are stronger than blood, that the camaraderie in the Silent Service is like . . . like nothing else in the military or civilian worlds. I know it's not the noblest reason to volunteer."

"Whatever—I bet you're having second thoughts now."

Chris crawled to another corner with his roll of tape. He wondered whether taping over holes in the walls wasn't a futile waste of effort, considering how much contaminated air would escape every time they opened the door. "No way," he said. "This is not the worst trouble I've seen . . . so far."

"Yeah, I heard about the fire you almost died in," Freud said. "You must have hated living in a boys' home, though."

Chris paused his work for a moment. "Actually, those were the best years of my life. We had to work hard to help keep the place up, but there was never a dull moment with those guys."

Failing to anticipate Freud's response, Chris added, "I'm not even sure the fire was the worst thing that ever happened to me."

"Really? What could be worse than that, dude?"

Chris hesitated. Now he had a choice. He could lie, tell the truth, or take the Fifth and leave it up to Freud's imagination. He decided to stall.

"Sir, if you don't mind my asking, why did you volunteer for submarines?"

"I'm a cool guy," Freud said with a sly grin. "So I needed a cool job. Girls love the top secret and high-tech stuff, in case you haven't noticed. Especially when you tell them about the missiles. That really gets their juices flowing.''

While Freud chuckled, Chris wondered just how much he'd told the women in his life about the Tridents. Everything but the basics was classified. Recalling Soony's feelings about nuclear weapons, he wondered what kind of women Freud was talking about.

"Come on," Freud said. "What's worse than getting caught in a house fire and ending up bald?"

Chris groaned. "Actually, I'm not sure it was worse. It was just a fight back in high school."

"Ooh, a fight!" Freud crowed. "Don't tell me you got your ass kicked."

"No, I won."

"What was so bad about it, then? Well?"

Chris winced and decided to get it over with. At least if Freud was as bad a gossip as Tumor claimed, he would have to tell the tale only once.

"My first girlfriend had green hair and a ring in her nose. I couldn't afford to be picky. We were juniors in high school. Her older brother was the leader of a street gang, so I ended up hanging out with them. I didn't like any of them, not even her, but they were the only friends I had."

A tattoo of the gang's insignia was what Chris had later mutilated his left arm to remove.

"One night we were all drinking at a party, and she goes off to get another beer, and her brother says, right out of the blue, 'Chris, you can do better than that skank.' Talking about his own sister. I said, 'I love her.' I didn't know any better then. So he says, 'Do you think she loves you? Do you really think that's why she shows you off to everybody? Maybe you two do deserve each other.' So I challenged him to a fight. I was fifteen and he was twenty-two. He couldn't say no in front of his gang."

Chris stopped there, afraid the *Vermont*'s officers

would question his reliability if he told any more. That wouldn't be fair, because he was not the person now that he had been on that night. Someone else—or something—had taken control of his fists. He had fought fairly until his opponent went down, but then he hadn't stopped. By the time five other boys dragged him off, his first girlfriend's brother was very nearly dead.

All because he gave me some of the best advice I ever got. And I had to behead the messenger. Chris shook his head, trying to clear out the bad memories.

"What's the worst thing that ever happened to you, sir?"

Freud laughed. "Nothing, dude! I've been lucky since the day I was born. Nothing bad ever happens to me. Sounds like you've had a bitch of a life, though."

"No, I've been lucky too," Chris said. "I've been *damn* lucky. Ever since the fire, I've felt like my whole life is a freebie. Now I'm where I want to be, doing something important, and I have a girlfriend I really like. Even being bald isn't as bad as I get older. Both of my adoptive parents are still living, and I get along great with them. What more could a man ask for?"

Freud peered at Chris over his shades as if doubting his sanity. "Duh! A million bucks? Better yet, a *billion.*"

"I guess that would be nice," Chris said.

"When did your parents adopt you?" Freud asked.

"My dad was the firefighter who rescued me. They had tried to have a kid for fifteen years and finally gave up. I could hardly believe it when they asked me. With my background, I didn't think anybody would ever adopt me permanently."

Freud leaned over to look at his reflection in a bucket of calcium hypochlorite bleach solution that Chris planned to use periodically to clean the new sick bay's surfaces. The ensign was apparently checking his coiffure. He tucked in a few stray hairs and said, "Was it as great as you expected?"

"Well . . . it was great, but they didn't adopt any other

kids, and they both worked hard. Dad became fire chief
and Mom was a nurse. So I was alone most of the time
at home. I missed the other guys. . . . I missed them a
lot. Excuse me, sir."

Freud stepped aside while Chris started constructing
a crude gasket around the door out of silicone caulk.

"Do you still keep in touch with your parents, Doc?"

"Of course. When I'm not at sea, I call them at least
once a week. It's easy to take your parents for granted
when you inherited them, but I'll always appreciate
mine."

Chris wanted to change the subject. This conversation
was bringing on a surge of homesickness like he hadn't
felt in years. He had noticed with some surprise that
Freud's left ring finger was encircled by a thin gold band.
"Are you married, sir?"

Freud removed his shades, apparently so Chris could
see him roll his eyes. "Yeah, with one kid and one in
the oven."

"Do you have any pictures of them?"

"I think so." Freud took out his wallet and rummaged
through it. Chris noticed a raised circle on the wallet's
back that could have been caused only by a rolled condom tucked inside.

Freud held up a picture. "Here, check this out."

Chris paused his caulking just long enough to glance
at the photo. It did not contain any women or children.
It showed a huge red pickup truck with a Jet Ski in the
bed. The truck was towing a trailer with an expensive-
looking speedboat. The rig was parked in the freshly
paved driveway of a brick house with large white col-
umns on the front porch.

"All yours?"

Freud grinned proudly. "All mine. Is that a sweet
setup or what?"

Chris could hardly imagine ever owning that many big
toys. "Did you win the lottery or something?"

"Nope. I just know how to shop."

"Is your new baby due during this run?"

Freud nodded. "In a week. It's been a hard pregnancy, a lot of complications."

"Wow. I bet you hate having to leave now."

Freud shrugged.

"You won't even know how it turned out until the next familygram comes," Chris said. "Are you worried?"

"Yeah, I guess. See ya." With that, Freud swaggered down the passageway.

Chapter 14

When the wardroom was ready for patients, Chris washed his face in the head behind missile tubes twenty and twenty-two on level three. He found the wash refreshing after working all night, but its purpose was to remove the oil from his skin so tape would stick to it. After drying his face thoroughly, he put on a clean surgical mask and applied broad strips of green high-pressure tape around its edges, making an almost perfect seal. The rated particulate-filtering efficiency of the standard surgical mask was only ninety-five percent, but with the edges taped down, he figured it might catch as much as ninety-nine percent of the microscopic particles in the air. There were three kinds of sophisticated breathing apparatus on board the *Vermont,* but all of them were cumbersome enough to inhibit his functionality without providing significantly better protection than the taped surgical mask.

As he worked with the sticky tape, Chris tried to stop thinking about the upsetting memories of the fight dredged up by Freud's probing. Whenever he was reminded of the horrible experience, he couldn't help reliving it for hours.

The day after the fight, he had visited his victim in the hospital to apologize and offer reparation. The gang leader just told him to stay the hell away. Three years later, he was killed by the police in a shootout.

The fight had made Chris start planning the rest of his life. He resolved to never lose his temper again. He realized he needed a lifestyle that would force a few others—preferably people he respected—to get to know him well in spite of his disfigurement. Then they would surely realize he was a friend worth keeping.

And now, here I am! I just hope I'll get to stay.

When he finished taping his mask, he leaned on the tiny stainless steel washbasin and stared at himself in the mirror. "Now you *really* look like a freak," he muttered.

The tape was not part of any standard procedure. It was his own idea, and a dumb one for all he knew. It hurt his skin and made breathing through the mask even more difficult, and he knew his sweat would make the tape peel.

None of the guys on the Vermont *know me yet. I'm lucky none of them ran screaming or died laughing before I put this shit on—now they're going to flip out for sure. Besides, only two patients are sick, and only one is coughing. The tape is bound to be overkill.*

He lifted one huge arm to rip off the tape, then hesitated.

He dragged a deep breath through the mask, still staring at the mirror. *One way or another, I have to get back to work.*

"Hell with it," he concluded aloud, then whirled out of the head with the tape in place. *When it comes to biohazard protection, it pays to think ahead. A contagion barrier applied a second too late is worthless.*

After making himself a waterproof apron from a garbage bag, Chris carried Kyle Orbison from the pharmacy to the new sick bay. The unconscious patient was trembling and twitching as if a hundred fishhooks embedded in his flesh were tugging him in all directions. He also coughed up bright red blood twice on the way, soaking his surgical mask.

Maurice Hereford was no longer delirious, thanks to

the medication Chris had given him, but he was not fully alert. He tried to walk on his own but was unable to stand. "Why am I so weak?" he asked.

"You're sick," Chris said as he scooped the patient up.

"Sorry," Hereford said.

"It's okay." Chris gently carried him along the narrow passageway. By the time they reached the wardroom, Hereford had fallen asleep in his arms.

After the patients were settled in, Chris bathed with diluted Betadine, changed his gloves, and taped on another mask. Then he put on his dungarees while an A-ganger washed his coveralls. As he got dressed, Freud entered the washroom and stopped to stare at him. "Yo, dude, you look like something from outer space."

Freud appeared to be pondering something, fingering the gold chain beneath his collar and staring into space. He was neither using the washroom nor moving to leave it.

"Did you want something, sir?"

"Huh? Oh, yeah; the XO sent me to find you. He wants to see you in the Goat Locker ASAP."

The Goat Locker was the domain of the chief petty officers. It occupied the forward end of level three, adjacent to the wardroom. At the center was the tiny CPO lounge. Freud said the chiefs had given up the CPO lounge to the officers for the time being, since the officers could no longer meet in the wardroom.

As Chris hurried to the Goat Locker, an announcement came over the 1MC.

"Attention, all hands. This is the XO. Be aware that the ship is still rigged for patrol quiet and will remain so throughout this run. As most of you probably know from watching the news, war with Iran is imminent. You should also know that this run is not a routine deterrence patrol. I cannot reveal more about our orders at this time. All I can tell you is that this single operation is probably more vital to the future of our country than all of the *Vermont*'s previous ops combined. Millions of lives may depend on our performance in the coming weeks. That is all."

Two seamen Chris didn't know passed by him in the narrow corridor, whispering to each other. They stared at his taped mask. He listened to their whispers. One said, "If we're going to Iran, that's about fourteen thousand miles by sea. It'll take more than two weeks to get there, even at flank speed."

Nuclear subs had four standard propulsion levels: one-third, two-thirds, full, and flank. Full power drove a Trident at about twenty knots. Flank provided about thirty knots but required twice as much power from the reactor as full did.

Chris could tell by the drone of the turbines and coolant pumps—and by the distinctive vibration of the decks—that the *Vermont* had been running at flank speed since the angles and dangles drill was terminated. Wherever they were going, the officers were obviously in a hurry to get there. The noise level emitted by any submarine skyrocketed with increasing speed, so running at flank strangely contradicted the XO's orders to rig for patrol quiet.

Chris was sure they would slow down if the *Vermont* approached waters that might contain hostile forces. At one-third power, she only made about five to seven knots, but she slid through the ocean so quietly that another ship could detect her only if she approached within a few hundred yards. And that would never happen, because the *Vermont*'s sonarmen would detect the other vessel first and the *Vermont* would stealthily detour around it. As long as the *Vermont* didn't speed up and had no noisy malfunctions, the only way another submarine or skimmer could find her was if it happened to be hovering directly in her path with all its machinery shut down and not a creature stirring on board.

Chapter 15

When Chris got to the Goat Locker, he found the tiny CPO lounge packed with most of the *Vermont*'s officers. Captain Scott was sitting on a chair at one of the two tables, glumly nursing a mug that Chris had noticed he always seemed to be holding. The tall mug had fat, horizontal, red and white stripes and was shaped like a lighthouse. The whole Goat Locker reeked of his strong ginseng tea.

Chris had been awake for twenty-four hours, after sleeping no more than four, and he could feel it. Once again there were no seats available, so he had to stand in front of the door while addressing his seated audience.

The captain said, "Come in and close the door, Chris. How's Hereford doing?"

"Better, sir. I gave him acetaminophen to bring down his fever. He came out of the delirium about an hour ago and was able to answer my questions."

"Good," Kurlgunn said. "What do they have?"

"I . . . I still don't know, sir. I can't even be sure both patients have the same thing."

Kurlgunn's pupils dilated, and all of his small, hard muscles tensed up. "That's ridiculous, Long! If two men come down with a debilitating disease on the same boat at the same time, they have the same bug."

"Do they have different symptoms?" Scott asked.

"Yes, sir. Hereford's fever is much worse than Orbison's, and his chest is not congested, whereas Orbison can barely breathe."

"The same pathogen can induce different syndromes in different individuals," Eng pointed out.

Kurlgunn kept glaring at Chris. "Assuming they both have the same bug, do you still think it's bacterial pneumonia?"

Chris felt his throat tighten. *It's not fair!* he thought. *They give you one year of training and seal you up in a can with God knows what, and the senior officers expect you to know everything a real doctor would. And I'll bet a real doctor would be just as baffled, but there aren't any doctors around to tell the officers that.*

"Sir . . . I'm sorry. I just don't know. I did a Gram stain on Orbison's sputum and saw some Gram-negative bacilli, but I have no way to tell what species they are or whether they're the bugs that are making him sick. We've been trained and equipped to handle about any mechanical emergency, but this is a *biological* emergency, and"—Chris raised his big hands in a gesture of frustration—"we're totally unprepared for this kind of thing! I feel totally helpless!"

"I didn't ask how you *feel,* " Kurlgunn said. "I asked for your professional opinion."

Chris looked down to hide his anger. He wished the captain would defend him. Scott had frowned at Kurlgunn's harshness but said nothing. Apparently it would have been too much effort for the aging, heartbroken officer. "I doubt it's bacterial pneumonia, sir, because Hereford's lungs are clear. My current guess is a bad strain of flu, although flu normally causes a dry cough. It's certainly not the usual crud or one-eighties."

Crud was the generic name for the head colds that often spread through the crowded crews of deployed submarines. The one-eighties was so called because it affected its victims at both ends—its primary symptoms were vomiting and diarrhea.

Kurlgunn suddenly looked less angry and more concerned. "Have you checked all the TLDs?"

TLD stood for thermoluminescent dosimeter. A TLD was a small cumulative radiation counter that each crewman had to wear on his person at all times. Monitoring of radiation levels and crew exposures was among the corpsman's duties.

"Yes, sir," Chris said. "During the fever screening. None of the TLDs showed unusual exposure, and all compartments had normal radiation levels. Besides, the symptoms the patients have are not the symptoms of radiation sickness."

"Assuming it's infectious, do you think it will spread beyond Orbison and Hereford?" Kurlgunn asked.

A sharp ache began between Chris's eyes. *They want all the answers, and I don't have any.*

"Some of us may have it already, sir. After you get exposed to germs, they usually have to replicate in your body for several days before there's enough of them to make you sick. That's called the incubation period. But you're already infectious the whole time the germs are breeding. We could be passing the bug around to each other right here in this room."

No one spoke for several seconds. It seemed to Chris that all of the officers were concentrating on their breathing, as if listening for telltale rattles.

Kurlgunn glanced around at the others suspiciously. He clenched and released his fists a few times. The rest of him was like a statue—rigid, still, and silent. Unlike everyone else in the tightly packed lounge, he did not look scared, but his venom seemed to have momentarily dried up.

"What if no one else is incubating the bug?" Scott asked. "Does that put us in the clear?"

"It might, sir. Keeping the patients isolated in the wardroom should make it a lot harder for the infection to spread."

"But not impossible," Scott said.

"That's right, sir. Orbison and Hereford clearly have something unusual. If they were in a good hospital on land, they'd probably be put in a special ward with ultraviolet lights to keep the surfaces sterilized. The air would be processed through virus-proof HEPA filters and kept at negative internal pressure. The doctors and nurses would wear airtight biohazard suits and breathe through hoses like deep-sea divers. They would go in through an airlock and take a chemical shower to decontaminate themselves on the way out. Frankly, sir, our makeshift sick bay is a pathetic substitute for a modern biocontainment ward."

Chris was leaning against the wall, thinking seriously about sitting on the floor. When he tried to reach around and knead the small of his back, Eng stood up and said, "I have to stretch my legs. Would you like to borrow my seat, Chris?"

"Thank you, sir." Chris allowed himself to fall into the engineer's chair. He crossed his arms over his chest—a difficult feat, because his muscles got in the way. He averted his eyes from Eng's skeletal form. *Must remember: speak to Eng about his eating habits.*

"Did you find out anything at all from talking to Hereford?" Kurlgunn asked. "Like where he might have caught it?"

"I asked if he'd been around Kyle Orbison lately. He said they hadn't even seen each other since we got under way. Hereford is a nuke, so he spends most of his time back aft. Orbison is a planesman, so he's always forward. And Hereford could remember only one time that they'd been near each other recently on shore—they went to the same bar on the night before we left."

Kurlgunn's suspicious eyes narrowed to coin slots. "Which bar?"

"The Spirit Tender."

Captain Scott groaned and started massaging his hairy

chest, which was exposed as usual by his undershirt. "Jesus, half the crew must have been in there. Do you think Hereford caught it from Orbison, or vice versa?"

"Neither of them had symptoms back then," Chris said, "and they seem about equally sick now. My guess is that they both caught it from someone else, although Hereford said he couldn't remember being around anyone lately who acted sick."

Weps spoke up. "Maybe we should keep a special eye on all the guys who were at the Spirit Tender that night."

"Actually," Chris said, "I want to start screening the entire crew hourly and putting anyone who has a fever into quarantine."

"That's too much for you to do by yourself," Scott said.

"Pigpen will help me, sir. But I might need help from an officer. Some of the crew might not go for being stuck in quarantine, especially by a new corpsman who isn't even a chief."

Kurlgunn looked around the table. "I need an officer to assist the corpsman."

Even in the drab CPO lounge, all of the other officers found something riveting to gaze at besides the XO. Several seconds went by before Eng called Maneuvering on the speaker phone and said, "Freud, do you think you can handle the reactor by yourself for the next few watches?"

"Sure, of course," Freud replied.

"I will assist you," Eng said to Chris with a grave nod.

"Thank you, sir."

Captain Scott stood, and the others followed suit. Leaning wearily on his chair, the captain reached up and patted Chris on the back. "Hang in there, son. You're doing a great job."

Chris felt a flood of relief. He let out a deep yawn. "Captain, do you think we should consider heading back to Bangor or maybe calling for a medical evacuation of the patients?"

The room went silent.

Kurlgunn was staring at Chris as if he'd just loaded a torpedo backward. The right side of the XO's thin, colorless upper lip was elevated slightly. All of the other officers were looking away from Chris.

"Son, you must be exhausted," Scott said. "Considering what you've been through in the last thirty hours, we'll all pretend you didn't say that. Let Eng take over for a while, and you go grab some rack time."

Chris managed to squeeze two words through his throat. "Aye, sir."

Chapter 16

Chris lay in his rack, curtain closed, trying to sleep. The thick brown curtain made it mostly dark, but enough light was seeping through the gaps to remind him that the *Vermont* never slept, that things beyond his control were going on all around his twenty-six cubic feet of semiprivacy.

He caught a snippet of conversation through the curtain.

". . . said it was Spanish flu, the strain that killed about a zillion people during World War I. He said most of us probably have it already; we just haven't felt it yet."

"Shit, man, I feel a little queasy. What about you?"

Chris yanked back his curtain and abruptly sat upright. His forehead slammed against the roof of his rack. The thud was so loud, he was sure the COB or XO would come running to vent wrath on whoever had made it.

"What the hell?" said the sleepy voice of Cheever from the rack above.

Chris tumbled out onto the deck, holding his bald head. The pain was agonizing for a couple of seconds, then it let up enough for him to speak.

He knelt beside Miguel Cervesu, the first man he'd overheard whispering. "Who told you that?"

"Who told me what, man?"

"That it's Spanish flu, and that more men have caught it. There are only two known cases, and I don't have any idea what the bug is yet."

"Really?" Miguel said.

"Who told you?"

"Okay, man! It was Freud."

"Are you serious?"

"Well, he didn't actually say it's Spanish flu. He just said it might be, but you could tell by the way he said it that . . . you know . . . the 'might be' was in quotes."

Chris was remembering Captain Scott's speech about the worst disease that could break out on a submarine. He looked longingly at his rack, which was still warm.

Damn you, Freud!

He jogged to the captain's stateroom, holding his throbbing forehead.

The captain was supposed to be sleeping, but his light was on. "Come in," he said when Chris asked permission to enter. Chris found Captain Scott propped up on his rack with a hefty hardback on his chest. Its title was *The Voyages of Columbus*. The aging officer was wearing reading glasses and sipping ginseng tea from his lighthouse mug.

Scott glanced up, then returned his gaze to the book. "Please don't tell me some suicidal turkey just attacked you, son."

Chris gave his forehead a swipe and looked at the blood on his hand. "I just bumped my head on the top rack, sir."

"Very well. I presume that's not why you came to see me."

"No, sir. I just heard from . . . I just heard that someone has been telling the crew what I've said when I briefed you and the other officers about the patients. And he's making it sound even worse than it is."

Scott dropped the heavy book, scowling. "Who?"

Chris hesitated, leaning back to make sure no one was within earshot in the passageway. "Miguel Cervesu said it was Freud, sir."

"Jesus, sailor, speak up! You're bound to have functional lungs inside that massive chest."

Chris stepped closer. "Freud, sir."

Scott nodded understandingly and heaved a weary sigh. "Thank you, Corpsman Long. Is there anything else?"

"No, sir."

"Very well. Dismissed."

Remaining in bed, Scott called Kurlgunn into his stateroom after Chris had left. The private staterooms of the captain and XO were adjacent to each other in the port forward corner of level two, separated only by the head they shared. "Gene, it seems that Freud is spreading exaggerated rumors about the illness. Would you have a word with him?"

"My pleasure, sir."

"I'm sure," Scott said. "Make a note: After this run, we have to let him go."

"Aye, sir. I would have gotten rid of him after he blew the sanitary tanks inboard on his first run. Then he couldn't have scrammed our reactor in Guam."

Scott sighed. "Do you know what Freud did before I took him on?"

"No."

"He accidentally submerged a six-eighty-eight docked at Electric Boat, and the spray from the MBT vents soaked the whole shipyard. Shorted out the power for half a day. He seemed to think it was funny."

"He would," Kurlgunn said without humor.

Scott took a gulp of stale tea and swished it around his mouth as if washing down a sour taste. "You can't win them all, Gene."

Chapter 17

Chris dropped by the sick bay to put a Band-Aid on his bleeding forehead. A swelling had developed that made wearing his baseball cap excruciating. He put the cap on and took it off several times, trying to decide what to do. When he didn't wear a hat, he felt as if his private parts were showing. And if his head wasn't armored with at least a layer of fabric, his great height and baldness made him extra vulnerable to collisions with the overhead. This trivial injury could be the start of a vicious cycle.

He finally decided the hat was too painful and laid it aside.

Yearning for his rack, he made one more detour to check on his patients.

To his surprise, he found Oral, the chief of the boat, manning the wardroom. The graying, overweight, African American COB was slumped against a wall, snoring. His ponderous lower lip was sagging behind his thin surgical mask. When Chris shut the door, Oral woke with a snort and waved hello.

"Where did Eng and Pigpen go?" Chris whispered.

Maurice Hereford appeared to be sleeping as well, so Chris didn't want to wake him.

The big COB yawned, nearly devouring his mask. "They're doing the next round of fever screenings."

"Have they reported any results?"

"Not yet."

"How are the patients?"

"Hereford's fever is going back up. Orbison is still unconscious, and he seems to be having more trouble breathing."

"I'm going to put Orbison on supplemental oxygen," Chris said. He walked to a corner and picked up a green pressurized gas cylinder, along with some tubing and a transparent plastic respirator mask. He had been reluctant to start using the medical oxygen earlier because the six small bottles on board the *Vermont* would provide a total of only eighteen hours of pure oxygen.

After replacing Orbison's filter mask with the respirator, Chris whispered, "Thanks, COB. I didn't know you volunteered."

Oral rubbed a pudgy hand over his jowls. "I couldn't sleep . . . kept thinking about these poor souls, trapped in this can so far from their families, going to war sick. I thought some spiritual solace might help." He nodded at a stack of tool crates that was serving as a countertop. Chris saw a thick, black, worn-out Bible on top. An equally worn guitar was leaning against the crates.

"Do you sing or just play?"

"Both," Oral said.

"What kind of music?"

"Mostly hymns and old cowboy songs, and some Fats Domino. I sung to Hereford till he went to sleep."

The COB looked and sounded as if he would have a deep, soothing singing voice. Chris almost asked him for a song, then decided it might wake Hereford.

Chris plopped down with a weary groan and leaned against the wall beside Oral. He wanted to go back to bed, but how could he with both patients getting worse? "Damn it, I just wish they had symptoms that would make it obvious what this bug is."

"Why do you need to know?" Oral asked.

Chris wasn't sure how to answer that without sounding disrespectful. "Chief, I have detailed instructions on how to treat every disease known to man, but that won't help until I know which one they have."

Oral gave him a sympathetic nod. "You look like you could use some rack time, son."

"Yeah, but I'd better stay, just in case. . . ."

"You won't be much use to them if you're too tired to think. Go on. I'll get you up if anything bad happens."

"Okay. Thanks, COB."

Chris returned to berth ten. As he stepped in, Miguel Cervesu reached out from his rack, the one on the bottom left, and tossed something up to him. "Hey, man, here you go."

Chris caught the object, recognizing it because it was his. It was an orange Bic lighter with scratched-up plastic and a corroded metal top.

Chris stared at the lighter in shock for a moment. Then he put it in his pocket and swiftly bent over with his massive arms outstretched. He grabbed the chest of Miguel's shirt and dragged him out of his bunk.

"Hey, man! What the hell?" Miguel shouted.

Chris lifted him up until his dangling feet were a foot above the floor. Miguel's back was pinned against the left tier of racks.

"Don't touch my stuff!" Chris yelled.

"I just borrowed it, man! Jesus Christ! It was just lying there on your mattress." Miguel was breathing fast, looking down at the floor.

Chris lowered Miguel until he was standing on his tiptoes. "You didn't get it out of my bunk pan?"

"No, man, I swear to God."

Chris let go and stepped back, bowing a little and palming the top of his bald head. "I'm sorry. Miguel, I'm . . . I'm truly sorry. Oh shit. *Damn it.*"

Miguel straightened his shirt, glowering. "Damn thing doesn't even work. I got all the way back to Shaft Alley, and I couldn't get a spark."

"It's sixteen years old," Chris mumbled, holding back tears.

"Well, what are you carrying it around for?"

Chris hesitated. "Miguel, I'm really sorry I grabbed you like that. The next cleaning chore you get, I'll do it."

"Whatever, man. A guy your size ought to watch his temper."

Miguel returned to his rack. Chris turned in too, drawing his curtain. He knew how the lighter had gotten onto his mattress. He had undoubtedly taken it out of the toiletries case hanging above his feet during his sleep. He had done that a few times over the years, usually when he was under serious pressure.

The lighter had belonged to Paul Treacle, his oldest foster brother. It was the only object, besides his own night clothes, that Chris had saved from the fire. The irony of the fact that the defunct lighter had once been a source of flame had occurred to him, but even that had not dispelled his attachment to the pitiful heirloom.

Now Chris was too upset with himself to sleep. He put on his headphones and slipped the first of the tapes Soony had made for him into the cassette player. Her voice was sweet and cheerful. "Hi, Chris. I love you. I'll be waiting when you come home." And she started reading his favorite book.

At the sound of her voice, his eyes filled with tears.

Then he fell asleep.

Sometime later, he was briefly woken by an announcement on the 1MC. "Attention, all hands. This is the XO. We have just received an emergency action message informing us that the United States and the Islamic Republic of Iran are at war. At approximately sixteen hundred Zulu time, aircraft from the carrier *John C. Stennis* began sorties over Iran's coastal waters to establish air superiority and eliminate ground-based air defenses. That is all."

In the rack above Chris, Cheever mumbled, "Aw, man, they're starting without us."

Before exhaustion could drag him back to sleep, Chris had enough time to wonder whether there would still be a world worth returning to when the *Vermont* eventually surfaced.

Chapter 18

As long as Hereford was sleeping, there was nothing for Oral to do but watch and wait. Still sitting on the floor, he quietly took down his threadbare Bible, which he carried with him at all times when he was not on watch.

Which passage should I read? The Book of Job? Revelations?

He decided to rest his eyes instead. He already knew those two chapters so well he could almost recite them.

Oral had come to offer solace and guidance to the patients, but he doubted his ability to do so, since it seemed so hard to provide those services for himself. And he needed them. Lord, how he needed them, regardless of this strange new scourge that had apparently befallen his crew.

Oral lacked only three years of the twenty he would need to retire, and he had no idea how he would support his family after leaving the Navy, but he had finally resolved just yesterday to get out after this run. He had knelt by his rack and prayed for God to postpone Armageddon at least that long.

Judging by the news, he feared his prayers would not be answered this time.

Oral glanced at his watch. According to the instructions Chris had left, it was time to check the patients' blood pressures. He picked up the sphygmomanometer and started wrapping its pressure cuff around Orbison's right upper arm, trying to ignore the unconscious man's creepy lack of response.

He heard tape being ripped off the outside of the wardroom door. A few seconds later, Eng and Pigpen stepped in, wearing masks and gloves.

Eng froze when he saw Oral. "What are you doing here?"

"Watching over the patients," Oral said through his mask.

Eng glared at the Bible lying by Oral's feet. "Trying to win a couple of converts, no doubt."

"I offer guidance to those who seek it."

"Or those who are helpless and can't get away from you," Eng replied. "Go guide yourself, COB. Go on, get out of here." Eng stepped aside, leaving Oral a clear path to the door.

Oral glared at Eng for a moment. The two black men were eye to eye, mask to mask, although one man's weight was more than twice the other's. *This scrawny, faithless devil has no right to deny these men my spiritual services!*

But Oral knew this was not the time to argue with Eng. He grabbed his guitar and trudged toward the door.

Pigpen whispered to Eng, "Sir, the new doc needs all the help he can get!"

Eng groaned. "COB, wait."

Oral reluctantly turned around.

"Pigpen is correct." Eng looked as if he were stabbing himself in the gut. "Thank you for helping. Please stay." He raised one fist and started to say something else but managed to choke it off.

"Aye, sir," was Oral's cool response.

"We identified three men with significant fevers," Eng announced in a monotone. "Two of them are coughing."

"Oh, no," Oral said. "Who are they?"

"Jimmy Courier, Don O'Roark, and Lou Renault."

Oral knew Don and Lou as if they were his brothers.

Jimmy was a new ensign whom he had barely met. "Lord have mercy on the poor souls."

"I'm going to go ask the captain how he wants us to manage them," Eng said.

He started to open the door, then slammed it and turned around, pointing a bony forefinger at Oral's thick, flabby chest. "You just remember, COB; your job at this moment is to save lives, not souls. If you try to take advantage of these men while they are afraid of dying and start poisoning their brains with your fire-and-brimstone bullshit, I'll . . . I'll find a way to make sure this is your last run."

Make my day, Oral thought. *Godless asshole.*

Chapter 19

Chris woke an hour earlier than he had planned. He wanted to shower but didn't dare waste the time. He went to the head with a thermometer in his mouth and read the temperature after relieving himself.

Ninety-nine-point-one degrees Fahrenheit.

A little high, especially for someone who had just gotten up. Not a clear sign of infection, but a cause for concern, given the circumstances.

He quickly degreased his face and taped on another mask. The thick green tape hurt even worse today because his skin was already irritated from the day before.

He marched to the wardroom.

Five men were lying on rack mattresses in the passageway outside the makeshift sick bay, all wearing surgical masks. Some of them were coughing. The icy feeling he'd had when he first found Hereford returned to his gut.

So, it has begun.

One of the men spoke in a hoarse whisper. "Hey, you're the new doc, right?"

"Yes."

"Why do we have to lie out here? We're not that sick."

"Do you have a fever?"

"That's what Eng said, but what's the big deal? It's just the crud going around."

"Is that what you were told?"

"It's what Freud said. He said you made a mistake and thought it was some kind of special flu, then you realized it was just the crud."

Chris stared at the man in disbelief for a moment. Then he made his way to the wardroom door. The hall was so narrow that he had to straddle the prone men, carefully watching where he stepped. With his athletic coordination, it was not a difficult task, but some of the crowded victims were clearly apprehensive of his 260 pounds crashing down on them.

"Hey, it is just the crud, right?"

Chris hesitated. "I don't know."

There was no tape on the outside of the door, so he knocked. Then he leaned close and listened for the sound of tape being ripped off the inside. All he heard was the strident rasping of someone struggling to breathe. Actually, it sounded as if more than one man was suffocating.

An agitated voice spoke through the door. "Who's there?"

"Corpsman."

The tape was ripped off, and the door opened. Eng motioned him to hurry through. The emaciated lieutenant looked tired and scared behind his mask, which was taped to his face like Chris's.

Chris stepped in. The almost airtight chamber was hot and humid. It stank of iodine, sweat, and excrement.

Eng slammed the door and retaped it. Chris noticed that he had unzipped his coveralls down to his lower chest, apparently to beat the heat. He wasn't wearing a shirt beneath the coveralls, and Chris could see protruding ribs where his muscles should have been.

Two new patients had been admitted to the wardroom. With four patients altogether, the floor was now crowded. The two newcomers were sweating and coughing and looked terrified. Chris could tell by listening that the fluid in their lungs was beginning to drown them.

Eng wiped his shaved head with a damp paper towel. "Hereford and Orbison are much worse."

Chris could see that. Hereford was groaning in pain and shaking in such a way that Chris couldn't tell if it was severe chills or a mild seizure. Orbison was also trembling with chills. He was still unconscious and slightly cyanotic in spite of the supplemental oxygen flowing into the plastic mask covering his mouth and nose.

Chris stepped over to the oxygen cylinder and turned up the flow.

Eng leaned on the stack of crates to rest his spindly legs. "Orbison's blood pressure is dropping."

Chris made a decision. "I'm going to give them antibiotics."

"What kind? How do you know which drug to use if you don't know what the pathogen is?"

Chris shrugged. "I'll hit it with at least one drug from every family of antibiotics we have, and hope for the best."

"Doc, in their state, the wrong antibiotics could kill them." Paraphrasing the Hippocratic oath, Eng added, "First, do no harm."

Chris whispered in Eng's ear, noticing that the scrawny officer smelled of Listerine. "Sir, these men are dying."

"Yes," Eng whispered back, "and if they die after you've filled them with a cocktail of powerful drugs that may interact, you'll never know if that was what killed them. In the civilian world, you'd get sued for malpractice."

"I know that, sir. But from what I can see from the advancement of their condition, I'm willing to take that chance."

They stared at each other at close range over their tape-enhanced masks. Chris could see his reflection in the unusually large, square lenses of the lieutenant's red-framed eyeglasses, but he couldn't quite tell whether his own eyes looked as scared as Eng's.

Eng swallowed loudly. "Okay, let's do it. Show me how."

Chris stepped to the door. "I'll have to get the vials from the pharmacy."

"Hurry," Eng said.

Chris glanced back at Orbison's bluish face. "Damn it, I should have started the antibiotics yesterday. I would have if I'd been sure it was infection then, and if we didn't have such a short supply."

He returned a few minutes later with five boxes marked FRAGILE. Eng helped him take out the precious glass vials of antibiotic solutions. Some of the drugs had to be administered as intramuscular injections. Others were formulated for intravenous use. One by one, Chris and Eng injected the latter into the medication ports on the clear bladders of sterile saline solution flowing into the patients' veins.

When they were finished, Chris said, "We have to find a better place for the guys out in the hall."

Eng nodded. "They aren't that sick yet, so they refused to come in here."

"I don't blame them," Chris said. "Lots of things can cause a fever or cough. If any of them don't already have this bug, they're more apt to catch it in here. But we can't just leave them out there—the ones that do have it are spewing it into the recirculating air. Will you help me seal off the torpedo room? That's the only major compartment besides the wardroom where no one really has to sleep or work . . . except the crew mess, and it has too many openings."

"What if we need to launch a torpedo?"

"Sir, no Trident submarine has *ever* needed to launch a torpedo, right?"

"Right," Eng said. "We can station the torpedomen in the passageway outside, just in case. You get permission from the captain and get started. I'll come down to help you as soon as Pigpen comes back from the screening he's doing and takes over in here."

On his way out, Chris paused to stoop over one of the new patients. "Hey, did you go to the Spirit Tender bar on the night before we left Bangor?"

The man couldn't speak—he was concentrating too hard on not coughing—but he clearly shook his head.

"What about you?" Chris asked the other one.

"I already debriefed them," Eng said. "The men outside as well. Most of them did not go to the Spirit Tender that night and had not been near Orbison or Hereford for weeks."

Chris squeezed the top of his bald head. "Great. That means it's being transmitted on board for sure."

Eng nodded. "Almost certainly."

Chapter 20

The torpedo room occupied the forward end of level four, the bottom internal deck. It was a large compartment, but it could feel cramped because it was packed with tiered racks of torpedoes and missiles that were designed to be launched through the torpedo tubes.

The Mark 48 ADCAP torpedoes were green cylinders with blunt black noses. The word "warshot" was stenciled on their sides in white. They were twenty-one inches in diameter and nineteen feet long. Each ADCAP weighed 3,695 pounds, carried 650 pounds of high explosive, and cost 3.5 million dollars.

The *Vermont*'s torpedo room contained twenty-two torpedoes but only six small missiles. Tridents never engaged in combat unless attacked, and unlike torpedoes, missiles were of little use for a submarine's self-defense. They were used to attack skimmers or land targets at a distance.

Two of the missiles in the *Vermont*'s torpedo room were Harpoon antiship missiles. The other four were Tomahawk cruise missiles, which had a range of one thousand miles. Both kinds of missiles were enclosed in waterproof capsules that allowed them to rise to the surface without getting wet when launched from a torpedo tube. The Harpoons were propelled by solid rocket fuel. The Tomahawk cruise missiles had rocket boosters to lift them out of the water before their air-breathing jet engines started.

Most American Tomahawks were armed with a thousand pounds of conventional high explosive, but a few, including all four of those on the *Vermont*, had W80 tactical nuclear warheads.

When Chris got to the torpedo room, he began frantically dismantling equipment to gain access to the holes in the walls. The torpedo room was going to be at least ten times harder to seal off than the wardroom had been.

Eng pitched in soon after Chris had started. As they worked, Chris said, "Sir, I couldn't help noticing that you look a little underweight. Have you talked to a doctor about it?"

"I don't have much appetite, Doc."

"Do you know why?" Chris asked.

Eng hesitated. "Doc, do you mind if I ask you a personal question?"

"Shoot." Chris expected to have to explain his total baldness yet again.

"Do you believe in God?"

Oh, boy; this guy doesn't beat around the bush. "I have some pretty strong opinions, sir, but that's one thing I haven't made up my mind about yet."

Eng looked as if he'd just been turned down for a job. "That's too bad. At least you intend to use your mind. That's better than regurgitating asinine dogma and believing it's a sin to think."

Chris was somewhat taken aback by Eng's vehemence, even if it wasn't directed precisely at him. But it also made him curious.

"Why don't you believe in God, sir?"

Eng was breathing hard from the effort of carrying a toolbox. Chris was surprised that the stick-figure officer could lift the box at all. "Can you keep what I say to yourself?"

"Sure, as long as it doesn't affect the mission."

Eng looked angry now. "Faith in absurd fantasies is for the weak, the childish, and the ignorant . . . and for some of the con artists who prey on them by selling high-priced tickets to a nonexistent paradise in the sky. Do you really think an all-powerful supreme being is any more likely to exist than, say, Santa Claus or the Easter Bunny?"

"Sir, if God doesn't exist, why do so many people believe in him?"

Eng rolled his eyes. "Because the people they love and trust taught them to believe. If you start the brainwashing early enough, you can teach anyone to believe anything."

"Good grief, sir. You really despise religion, don't you?"

"Of course I do! Why do you think we're going to war now? After all the glorious advances of human knowledge and reason, I won't be a bit surprised if the ancient forces of ignorance and superstition rise up and destroy the world within my lifetime."

"Eng, that's only one side of it. What about all the good religion has done?"

"People should be willing to do good without having to believe they'll get a supernatural reward for it," Eng said.

"Were you always an atheist, sir?"

Eng was violently cranking a socket wrench to remove the bolts securing a torpedo control console to the floor. "No, I was reared a Christian fundamentalist. I might still be a lobotomized zombie if it weren't for the U.S. Navy. I went to college on a Navy scholarship, and the knowledge started pouring in from all directions. It didn't take me long to figure out what all religions are, from Christianity to voodoo."

"What do you think they are, sir?"

Eng's sweaty face twisted into a contemptuous snarl. "Socially sanctioned delusions that take the edge off reality permanently. You get an imaginary friend who will never die or dump you. You get to believe you'll live forever and rejoin your departed loved ones someday.

You get to believe all the random shit that happens to you has a purpose. You can feel that you've achieved a moral triumph, when all you've really done is trade in your sanity for peace of mind. Best of all, you get to feel special because your religion is true and everybody else's is false. You get all that and more, an emotional cure-all, and all you have to give up is your grip and some tithing! *What a fucking bargain!*"

Eng was trembling and breathing like a charging bull. It seemed to Chris that if the emaciated lieutenant's eyes bulged any more, they would touch the lenses of his odd-looking glasses. Eng had lifted up the socket wrench in one bony hand and was brandishing it menacingly.

"Easy there, sir!"

Chris was not afraid. He was confident that he could take the wrench away from Eng if he had to. But he wasn't sure what he should do if the irate engineer started bashing the machinery.

"Huh? Sorry, Doc." Eng put the wrench down and slumped against a torpedo rack, still panting. "Goddamn, I haven't blown up like that in years. There's something you should know, Doc—I can't stand germs. I was always sick when I was a kid, and my immune system is still pretty lame."

"Why did you volunteer to help me, then?"

"Because I know a lot about infectious diseases, possibly more than you do. If this one has a high mortality, and we fail to contain it, it's not going to matter which end of the people tank I'm at. So I concluded that my chances are best if I pitch in."

"Well, thank you. I'm uptight too. This is my first run as a corpsman, as you know."

Eng's fury seemed to be collapsing into a sad funk. His body language created the illusion that he was physically shrinking. "If you want to return the favor, don't repeat what I just said about the religious bozos. I've learned to keep my mouth shut most of the time. That's the only way to get along when you're packed in a can with a tribe of superstitious savages."

"Eng, if you don't like the crew, why have you stayed in so long? I'll bet you could make good money as a civilian engineer."

"Perhaps, but I'd have to leave my lady." Eng was kneeling to tape the gaps around a pipe run. He gently pressed a palm against the gray bulkhead and closed his eyes, bowing a little. "She's the most beautiful work of art in the world. Eight million parts. Miles of wiring. More electrical power and computing capability than a good-size city. No machine is more complex, more precise, more perfectly suited to its task. When I come on board, I feel like I'm a part of her. The last day of a run is always the saddest one."

"You're not glad to get home?"

"Why should I be? I live alone. When I'm not working, I just read or watch the news."

"Sir, you and I just met. If you usually don't talk much to the rest of the crew, why have you been so open with me?"

Eng shrugged. "You don't look like a book burner. And this damn epidemic . . . I might be running out of chances to speak my mind."

"Sir, can I ask you something *really* personal now?"

"I guess so," Eng said warily.

"Why are the frames of your glasses red?"

Eng cracked a wan smile—he had removed his mask after leaving the wardroom. "They were eighty percent off at a clearance sale."

Chapter 21

Chris and Eng were halfway through sealing up the torpedo room when a loud *whoop* made them both jump. Someone was calling on the JA circuit, the sound-powered phone system linking watchstations in the forward compartment. Eng picked up the receiver and said, "Torpedo room."

A moment later, he put the receiver down and frantically motioned for Chris to stop working. "That was Pigpen. It's Orbison."

They ran upstairs to the wardroom.

Chris got there first. In the corridor, he could hear Kyle Orbison struggling for breath on the other side of the wall. The shrieking inhalations sounded inhuman.

The men Eng had ordered to lie in the passageway were all standing up. They were whispering, staring at the wardroom door, fidgeting like zebras with a lion in their midst. One saw Chris and pointed at the door with a reproachful glower. "That is not just the goddamn crud!"

Chris barreled past them and shoved the door open, ripping loose the tape on the other side. He was already wearing a mask and gloves.

Orbison was lying faceup, awake. His close-set eyes rolled toward Chris, pleading. His back was arched, holding his broad hips above the thin mattress. His hands were squeezing the sides of the mattress, white and trembling. His face was grayish purple. The inside of his transparent oxygen mask was covered with blood.

Pigpen was standing behind Orbison, staring down. When he saw Chris, he shook his gloved hands in the air and yelled, "What should I do?"

"Turn up the oxygen," Chris shouted, loud enough for Pigpen to understand him over Orbison's rasping stridor.

Pigpen lunged toward the green gas cylinder and cranked the valve on top of it.

Orbison stopped trying to breath for a moment. He clawed the respirator off his face and grunted something that sounded like "car."

"Hey, he's trying to say something," Pigpen said.

Chris nodded, leaning over the patient's head.

He could hear the men out in the passageway loudly arguing with Eng, who was apparently trying to calm them down.

Orbison resumed trying to breathe for several seconds, then grunted the word again.

Chris looked up at Pigpen. *"Cigar?"*

"Yeah, cigar!" Pigpen came closer and spoke in Chris's ear, giving Chris a stout whiff of his ripe body odor. "He knows he's dying, and he wants a last cigar."

"He can't breathe!" Chris replied. "How could he smoke a cigar?"

Orbison tried to speak a third time, and Chris heard something catch in his throat. The sound gave Chris just enough warning to twist away and close his eyes before a geyser of blood and pink foam erupted from Orbison's mouth, shooting upward at least two feet. Chris felt warm droplets strike the back of his bald head. The fountain of infectious gore missed his face by a few inches.

Orbison's arched back collapsed. His fists opened. His eyes stared up at the overhead, unmoving. His only sound was a faint gurgle.

Chris grabbed the oxygen mask, now covered with

bloody mucus. He replaced it over Orbison's mouth and nose. The flowing oxygen bubbled out around its edges.

Orbison didn't move.

Chris checked for a pulse at his left carotid artery. After several seconds, he checked the other side of his neck. Still nothing.

"Is he dead?" Pigpen whispered.

Chris nodded, feeling sick. He was breathing through his mouth because the bloody fluid splattered around Orbison's head smelled putrid and sour. He closed his eyes and tried to recite prime numbers in his head, hoping the distraction would control his nausea. If he threw up, he would have to rip off his taped mask to avoid choking.

Maurice Hereford had silently watched throughout his shipmate's final ordeal. Now he began to weep in long gasping sobs, still staring at the bloody corpse. His tears quickly soaked the top of his surgical mask.

Chris looked over at the two newer patients. One was staring intently at Orbison and trying to stifle his own coughs. The other appeared to have slept through the whole episode.

"What are we going to do with his body?" Pigpen whispered.

"Put it in the chill box," Chris said. The chill box was the large refrigerated compartment in the galley.

"Are you serious?"

"Yes. Standard procedure."

Chris tried to wash the infectious mess off his gloves. His big hands were trembling.

There was no sink in the wardroom, so he held his hands over a garbage can and poured from a jug of dilute bleach solution that Pigpen had been using to wipe down surfaces. He wished he could use Betadine disinfectant, but they had to conserve the *Vermont*'s scant supply. Once his gloves were clean, he soaked a wad of paper towels with the weak solution and wiped his face.

As he ran the wad of wet paper towels over his bare

scalp, he felt a long-dormant but familiar discomfort in his chest. A second later, a barklike cough erupted from his lungs.

Pigpen jerked and spun around toward Chris. "Hey, you okay? You need the bucket?"

Chris shook his head, concentrating on breathing smoothly.

"That was just a cough?"

Chris nodded.

"How does your chest feel?"

"It feels fine," Chris said through his teeth. "The fire I was in did some damage to my lungs. It makes me cough like that sometimes."

"You're sure it's not the bug?"

"Did it sound like it?"

"No, it sounded dry."

"Right, so just forget about it."

Chris swallowed and made sure he wasn't about to retch or cough again, then said, "Let's dig out a body bag for Orbison and leave him in here for now. I don't want to take him past the men outside. I'll carry him to the galley after we get them moved into Purgatory and brief the officers."

"Purgatory?" Pigpen asked.

"That's what we're calling the torpedo room now. We'll keep the uncertain cases down there. When we know for sure that they have this bug, we'll move them up here to the wardroom."

"I guess that means this room is now known as Hell," Pigpen said.

Chris nodded. "You got it."

Chapter 22

Eng agreed to get the A-gangers to help him finish sealing the torpedo room while Chris reported the fatality.

In the control room, Chris found Kurlgunn in charge. The XO was standing rigidly on the conn with a squinty glower, like a brooding king about to leap down from his throne and sentence a disappointing courtier to execution.

Chris cautiously approached the conn and spoke in a low voice. "Sir, do you know where the captain is?"

"He's racked out. What do you want, Long?"

Chris glanced around. He didn't want to tell the harsh XO that he had just lost the first patient of his probably short career as a corpsman.

"Spit it out, sailor!"

"Sir, I should probably speak to you in private," Chris whispered.

Looking peeved, Kurlgunn announced, "Weps, you have the deck and the conn."

"I have the deck and the conn," Weps said. "Aye, sir."

Kurlgunn led Chris down one level to the officers' study, which was unoccupied. He pulled out a chair and said, "Have a seat."

Assuming that was an order, Chris sat.

Kurlgunn remained standing while Chris told him about Orbison's death and the new cases. As Chris spoke, the tense XO removed a stainless steel butterfly knife from his pocket. He expertly flipped it open and began paring his fingernails. Chris noticed that his nails looked as if they'd already been trimmed down to the quick.

"Seven new victims," Kurlgunn said. "Are all of them going to die?"

"I don't know, sir. With any infectious disease, there's a lot of variability in individual responses."

"Do you think Orbison might have had some condition that made him especially vulnerable?"

"I wouldn't count on it, sir."

"Okay, you can't predict the outcome for a particular individual, but what percentage of the cases do you expect to be fatal?"

"I don't know, sir."

"Goddamn it, what *do* you know? Anything?"

Chris felt his throat begin to sting. *Damn it, I must not lose my temper ever again.* He recalled the horrible scars on Kurlgunn's back, and the memory calmed his anger.

"Every pathogenic species has a different mortality rate," he explained. "The Spanish flu killed only about three percent of its victims. About thirty percent of smallpox cases were fatal. Ebola Zaire takes out ninety percent. As far as we know, AIDS kills a hundred percent, except for some people with a rare mutation in a gene called CCR5 that seems to let them harbor HIV without symptoms."

"And you still don't know what kind of germs are causing this," Kurlgunn said. "It always comes back to that."

"Exactly," Chris said.

"What are you doing to find out?"

"Nothing, sir. I've been too busy taking care of the patients."

Kurlgunn ran a hand over his dense black crew cut, then clenched it into a fist. "That's a stupid waste of time, Long. You should have someone else playing nurse while you dig into your manuals and figure out a way to identify what we're up against."

"Sir, I agree, but I'm just a corpsman. I can't order other men to abandon their normal duties and do what I tell them."

"I can," Kurlgunn said. "How many do you want?"

Chris hesitated. "I'm not sure it would be best to order healthy men to work in the sick bays, sir. It might be better to ask for volunteers."

Kurlgunn had stepped behind Chris's chair. He leaned so close that Chris could feel warm breath on his ear. "Don't ever try to tell me how to command, sailor. I know how to control the men on my boat."

Chris sat still, facing forward, wondering if Kurlgunn had forgotten that he wasn't actually the captain yet. "Aye, sir. I probably need about four or five assistants."

Kurlgunn stepped in front of Chris. He flipped his knife closed and dropped it into the right front pocket of his coveralls with a subtle flourish that looked to Chris as if it must have been practiced in front of a mirror. Then he marched to the door and back with his hands clasped behind him, flexing his tense neck muscles and pursing his thin, colorless lips. Chris noticed with a twinge of wry amusement that the way the XO's small, pointy ears protruded outward at the top reminded him of horns.

Kurlgunn finally said, "We'll do it your way, Long. If I don't keep *you* happy, we're probably all as good as dead."

Chris almost stood up. He clenched his teeth and tried to remember prime numbers. *I'm going to do my best,* he thought, *no matter how much you piss me off, you anal prick!*

"I guess ordering men to work in the sick bays *would* be kind of like ordering them to walk into the reactor compartment with the reactor running," Kurlgunn said.

Chris managed to calm down enough to grind out a

statement he had composed on his way to control. "Sir, I recommend we call COMSUBPAC to request immediate evacuation of the patients." COMSUBPAC stood for Commander Submarine Forces Pacific. "A hospital on land could probably diagnose and treat them right away. I know surfacing for a medevac would violate standard wartime procedures, and I know this is an especially important op, but we have an unprecedented situation here. We're not talking about a single man with a toothache or appendicitis. If the victims remain on board, they may give this deadly bug to the rest of us, no matter what I do to contain it."

Kurlgunn silently stared at the door. His expression was intense yet inscrutable. He was flexing his striated jaw muscles and squeezing his thin, colorless lips together, but his lead gray eyes were blank.

"What do you think, sir?"

"First we save the mission," Kurlgunn said, as if reading from a script. "Then we save the ship, then the plant, then the crew, in that order."

Chris found himself chanting along with those words, which formed one of the mantras used to indoctrinate every American submariner. The "plant" was the sub's nuclear reactor. In Western civilian society, a human life was theoretically priceless. Not so in the military. And it took a lot of lives to add up to the three-billion-dollar price tag of a loaded Trident.

"Sir, I am trying to save the mission. If too many men get sick, we won't be able to launch our missiles. I know our enemies buy their intelligence from Russian satellites. I know they probably wouldn't miss a rescue operation. But we could offload all the sick men in an hour, tops. Then we could dive, check our baffles, and clear datum before enemy forces could possibly hit us." The baffles was the cone-shaped region behind a submarine where its own hull and propeller noise blinded the directional sonar in the bow. "While we're up, we could also take on medical supplies, replacement crewmen, and a team of doctors who would know how to handle this thing."

Kurlgunn lifted the right side of his upper lip a little. "That's a charming fantasy, Long. Too bad it's logistically impossible in our present location. Even if it weren't, COMSUBPAC would never approve a medevac."

"Why not, sir? As long as we get away before—"

"An enemy attack on the *Vermont* is not the danger, Long. If it were, we'd be escorted by a pack of six-eighty-eights. We can't break radio silence, much less surface, because we can't let the enemy find out a Trident is in this part of the ocean. If they do, they could figure out what we're up to, and that would have consequences far beyond our ship."

Chris wished the XO would tell *him* what they were up to, and what part of the ocean they were in. He knew that the policy of never telling most of the crew their objective would make it easier to keep the operation secret afterward, but it seemed to him that the unity gained by bringing the whole crew in on the plan would increase their odds of success.

"Sir, if we can't call for help, I recommend we turn back. If we stay out here and the bug keeps spreading, the *Vermont* may eventually become completely disabled. Then she'll be vulnerable to accidents, collision, attack—even capture and boarding. We can tell STRATCOM as soon as we get back to a location where it's safe to call. Then they can send another Trident to take over for us while we limp on home." STRATCOM, the United States Strategic Command, was responsible for coordinating the missions of all Tridents and other nuclear weapons platforms.

Kurlgunn was starting to look irritated again. "It's too late for that. You'll have to trust me, Long—speed is almost as important as stealth on this run. It's unlikely that a replacement boomer could get to our op area in time."

Chris wondered why Kurlgunn was being so uncharacteristically patient with him. The XO could have just ordered him back to work instead of trying to explain. It seemed almost as if Kurlgunn himself was not convinced they should press on. Chris knew timid officers didn't last long in the U.S. Navy. Could Kurlgunn be defying his own judgment to avoid looking like a coward or a softie? Chris wanted to discuss the options directly with Captain Scott, but he didn't dare try to go over the XO's head.

"Sir, I know you can't tell me our orders, but please tell me one thing: Is this mission really more important than the ship and the men?"

"You need to learn your place, Long. You ask too many questions."

"Is it, sir?"

Kurlgunn's momentary lapse of viciousness came to an abrupt end. He lunged toward the door and jerked it open. "Yes, it is, Long! So you'd better get back to work. And get used to the fact that we're on our own for the rest of this run, no matter what happens."

Chapter 23

Just pretend you're warming up for a homecoming game,
Chris told himself as he followed Lieutenant Commander Kurlgunn toward the enlisted mess, where he
was supposed to brief the crew and recruit medical
volunteers.

Back in high school, Chris had loved playing football
for many reasons. He was good at it, and the uniform
completely covered his hairless skin. But perhaps the
best benefit was allowing him to step out of his usual
civilized persona. Out there on the muddy grass, he
didn't have to be constantly vigilant against showing aggression. Blocking, chasing, tackling—it all felt natural.
Ironically, putting on all that armor had signaled his subconscious that it was time to throw off its restraints and
run free for a while.

But he couldn't do that now. This felt nothing like
going into a game. It felt more like being marched to
his execution. He had a bad feeling that the crew was
going to grill him with questions he couldn't answer and
blame him for the answers they didn't like.

Even if he survived this meeting, the prospect of having to command other men like an officer was shooting
cramps of dread through his gut. His adoptive father had
hated being a fire chief because six of the men he had
led into burning buildings over the years had been killed
or maimed in the line of duty. He had warned Chris
many times that the perils of leadership outweighed its

perks, at least for a man who cared about the lives of those he was leading.

The enlisted mess was the largest open space on the sub. By the time they got there, it was packed like a popular nightclub, and nearly as noisy. Kurlgunn slammed his fist on a table and yelled, "Shut up! The doc has some things to tell you, and he doesn't have all day."

The room grew quiet. Chris looked around at the faces. Some looked angry, some confused. Many had obviously been rousted out of their racks by Kurlgunn's announcement of the meeting.

All of them looked scared.

It took him about three minutes to tell them everything he knew about the mysterious illness. Then he made the mistake of inviting questions.

"Why did you tell Kyle he just had a cold?" one asked.

Another shouted, "First you said it was Spanish flu, then just the crud, and now you don't know?"

"Freud said Kyle probably died because you gave him the wrong antibiotics," someone shouted. "Is that true?"

One sailor pointed to Chris while looking at Kurlgunn. "Sir, I heard he's fresh out of training. Why didn't they give us a doc with more experience?"

"Long was handpicked by the captain," Kurlgunn replied.

"Oh, shit; you know what that means," the sailor said, hardly lowering his voice. The men around him nodded, looking Chris up and down.

Chris had never experienced anything like this. It was even worse than he'd feared. Most submarine crews were extraordinarily cohesive and mutually supportive. He wondered if these men were heckling him because of group fear, or because he was new to the crew—or because he deserved it.

The hailstorm of questions and comments had abated. Now the men were waiting for his answers. Chris felt a twinge of the discomfort in his chest that meant the old smoke damage in his lungs was about to make him cough. *If I start coughing now, I won't be able to stop. The whole crew will think I'm infected. They'll force me to check myself into Purgatory, and I'll probably never leave.*

The audience got tired of waiting for his response. "We ought to turn back," someone said.

Another said, "They ought to take the sick men off so the rest of us don't catch it from them."

Someone shouted, "Yeah, and they should fly some real doctors out to us!"

After that, the mess became so noisy that Chris could not make out the individual statements. He glanced at Kurlgunn, who merely gestured for him to carry on.

What the hell am I supposed to say?

Chris felt paralyzed with stage fright. His mouth was dry. His tongue felt swollen. Finally, he managed to speak with his loud voice at full volume. "We can't turn back or call for help."

The babble stopped.

"Why not?" someone asked.

Chris knew it was his duty to help implement the decisions made by the officers, so he tried to convincingly repeat the arguments Kurlgunn had just given him. He doubted he could persuade his frightened audience of anything. Surely they would sense his own doubts.

To his astonishment, most of them seemed to agree by the end of his brief lecture that the *Vermont* should press on without breaking radio silence.

"How are the germs being transmitted?" asked a man wearing a blue handkerchief over his mouth and nose.

"It seems to have spread so fast, I'm guessing it's airborne," Chris said. "Most respiratory pathogens are carried in cough droplets. But our conditions are so crowded, it could be primarily spreading on surfaces, or even by skin-to-skin contact."

"What can we do to protect ourselves?" asked a

homely young man in the back, whom Chris recognized as Tumor.

"Good question," Chris said. "During the next fever screening, we'll distribute one pair of latex gloves to each crewman. Our supply is pretty short, so you'll have to reuse them and try not to tear them. From now on, you should wash your hands at every opportunity. Don't waste soap, but there will be plenty of water."

He glanced at Kurlgunn to make sure that promise could be kept. The rigid XO nodded approval.

The *Vermont* made freshwater from seawater by distillation. The freshwater tanks had a limited capacity, but with nuclear power to spare, the supply was theoretically unlimited.

"What about masks?" Tumor asked.

"We don't have enough for everyone," Chris said. "I've decided to put most of the surgical masks like the one I'm wearing on the patients. I only have a box of fifty, and they aren't reusable, so those will run out pretty fast. Vital watchstanders and volunteers working in the sick bays can use EABs when they're standing still."

An EAB—emergency air breather—was a full face mask with a hose that could be attached to an air manifold running along the sub's walls. EABs were designed for use while fighting a fire, so they drew their air from a sealed reservoir. There was an EAB on board for every crewman, but the air supply was limited. Many tasks were impossible to perform while wearing the bulky apparatus, and its user could only stray a few feet from the air manifold without disconnecting his hose and holding his breath until he found another outlet.

"For those of you who have to move around a lot, I'd recommend an NBC gas mask," Chris said. "We have fifty gas masks and enough replacement filters to last a while. Your other choice is the chemical respirators. We have fifty of those also. If this is an airborne virus that survives when the cough droplets containing it dry up into aerosols, it may get through any of the filters, so only an EAB will provide full protection. The bottom line is that we can't fully protect all one hundred fifty-four of us for the duration of this run. Whatever kind of mask you wear, you'll have to take it off to eat, drink, wash, maybe to sleep. It will be up to your commanding officer to decide if you get a mask and what kind. If you don't get one, I recommend a double layer of close-knit fabric over the mouth and nose. Check it for holes and change it every four hours or whenever it gets wet. Now, I need more volunteers. Please raise your hand if you'd be willing to help care for the patients."

Chris waited for fifteen seconds that felt like an hour. No hands went up.

He glanced at Kurlgunn in desperation.

The hard XO just shrugged. Chris thought he saw a trace of smugness in the gesture.

Chris felt as if he had already expended his life savings of nerve by facing this agitated crew. *What can I do now? Beg?*

"Okay, everybody, listen up! This emergency is no different from a fire or flood. What do you think is going to happen to you if we fail to contain it because you wouldn't pitch in? Do you think you can hide from it in the head? Three brave men are already helping me: Eng, Pigpen, and Oral. But that's not enough. If we stand together now, we may be able to stop this monster before it eats us all. If we don't, this sub may become a lifeless derelict full of corpses, the brave and the cowards alike. Now, please raise your hand if you value your life enough to help me stop this goddamn scourge while we still have a chance!"

Chris looked around the crowded mess. He was tall enough to see everyone there. No one met his eyes, and no hands went up.

Another second went by.

Still no hands.

We're doomed.

A solitary hand appeared in the back. Chris was surprised to see whose it was. *"Tumor!* Thank you. Thank you. Who else?"

"Come on, you chickens," Tumor yelled in his hillbilly accent. "If I'm willing to go in there, the rest of you got no excuse. Like Doc said, you got nothing to lose."

One by one, a forest of hands sprouted.

"Thank you!" Chris bellowed.

"Everyone who didn't volunteer can leave now," Kurlgunn ordered.

As most of the men filed out, Chris saw Captain Scott leaning against a wall in the passageway, half-hidden from view. The reclusive officer was wearing a smile that didn't seem to belong given the situation at hand. He nodded once to Chris and disappeared.

Chris addressed the volunteers. "I guess the first thing we need to do is divide into two teams for rotation. Then we—"

Eng's voice blared from the 1MC. "Corpsman, lay to the wardroom. Corpsman, lay to the wardroom. Emergency."

Chris jogged forward to the nearby wardroom. *Damn it, I'll bet it's Hereford this time.*

The passageway outside the wardroom was vacant. He assumed that meant Eng had gotten the five uncertain cases moved down to Purgatory. Hopefully they hadn't already been admitted to Hell.

When Chris entered the hot, stinking wardroom, he was surprised to see that Maurice Hereford did not seem much worse than before. The trouble was with the two new patients. One was already dead. The other was cyanotic and loudly fighting for breath. The infection had taken them even faster than it had killed Kyle Orbison.

All Chris could do was turn up the man's oxygen and watch. The third victim's death throes mimicked Orbison's, but his life did not end with a bloody paroxysm. Eleven minutes after Chris stepped into the room, the man just gradually stopped trying to breathe.

Chris recorded the time of death on a napkin that had become the wardroom's log.

"One hundred fifty-two left," Eng said.

Chapter 24

Chris put some of the new volunteers to work disinfecting every surface inside the *Vermont*. Before long, the sub's powerful air recirculators had evenly distributed the pungent aroma of Betadine iodine solution.

Chris pulled Tumor aside and said, "I heard you're the *Vermont*'s circuit technician whiz. I have a special job that needs to be done as fast as humanly possible. Are you game?"

"Yes, sir! I mean, yes." Tumor blushed, having just called another enlisted sailor "sir."

"Good. We have to rig the new sick bays for lowered pressure so air will always flow into them. I already got permission from the XO."

"How are you going to do it?" Tumor asked. "By sucking air out of the rooms? Won't the pressure equalize as soon as somebody opens a door?"

"Not if the suction is strong enough. The bug may be a virus, and I'm not sure our air filters are fine enough to trap viral particles, so all the air we suck out of the sick bays has to be vented outside the people tank. If we use the high-pressure compressors to pump it into the bottles in the ballast tanks, the air won't go to waste or cause a bubble trail—it will still be there for us to use the next time we blow the tanks to surface. We should have enough compressed reserves to keep replacing the air we pump out for a few days. What do you think?"

"I think it sounds like a dang butt-load of work," Tumor said. "Where do I come in? I don't know diddly about the air piping."

Chris said, "I think the most complicated part will be rigging a barometer to switch on the air compressor every time the pressure in the sick bays rises above a certain level."

Tumor took a can of Copenhagen from his right hip pocket and tamped a large pinch behind his lower lip. "I bet ten bucks I'll have it ready before you get the ducts rerouted."

Chris grinned. "Deal. I'll get the A-gangers to fire up their torches."

Once the construction of new air ducts was under way, Chris and Eng went to the pharmacy—the sub's original sick bay—and began digging through all the references they could find on respiratory infections. Eng ordered the cook to bring frequent snacks and set up a bucket brigade of coffee. To avoid wasting time walking downstairs to the head, they urinated into an empty Betadine jug.

Chris had thought he was good at focusing until he saw Eng scanning page after page with what looked like superhuman concentration. The skinny black lieutenant didn't move a muscle except when flipping pages, pushing his large red-framed eyeglasses back into place, and scribbling notes now and then.

After two six-hour watches of nonstop research, they knew all about influenza, adenoviruses, syncytial virus, SARS, several kinds of bacterial and fungal pneumonia, and even hantavirus and Legionnaire's disease.

"Have you tested the potable water supply?" Eng asked.

Chris nodded. "All I can test for is fecal coliforms, and I didn't find a single bacterial colony on the culture plates."

"Listen to this quote from the 1918 Spanish flu pandemic," Chris said. " 'They died struggling to clear their airways of a blood-tinged froth that sometimes gushed from their nose and mouth.' Sound familiar?"

Eng nodded. "*Legionella* bacteria can grow in air conditioners or showerheads; anyplace that stays wet. I thought maybe it was growing in the bilges, but the symptoms don't match." He glanced up at the two handwritten lists Chris had taped to the wall:

Case 2 (Maurice Hereford)	All other cases
1. fever	1. fever
2. chills	2. dullness to pulmonary percussion
3. myalgia	3. productive cough
4. weakness	4. malaise
5. acute headache	5. headache
6. delirium	6. bloody sputum
7. seizures	7. purulent sputum
	8. pulmonary edema
NOTE: in all cases, onset is sudden	9. fulminant course leading to dyspnea, stridor, cyanosis, and death within 24 hours after onset

Chris was staring at his computer screen. "According to this database, we've considered every pathogen that has ever been identified in a case of pneumonia in North America."

"And it couldn't be any of them?" Eng asked.

"I've eliminated all but seven," Chris said.

"Do any of those suspects seem likely?"

"No. The problem is Maurice Hereford. None of these bugs are supposed to cause the symptoms he has without affecting the lungs as well."

"Maybe he's infected by a different pathogen after all," Eng said.

Chris shook his head. "I guess it's possible, but it would be a freak coincidence. Six of the seven suspects I've got here are bacterial. Each antibiotic can kill several different families of bacteria, so we shouldn't have to know exactly which species this is to treat it—if we can just narrow down the antibiotics to a few that should work. Goddamn it, I can't believe it's so hard just to figure out what we're up against!"

"*I'm sick*," said a shaky voice behind them.

Chris and Eng both jumped, then spun around.

Tumor staggered into the pharmacy, leaning against the wall. Chris motioned him toward the examination table. With Chris's help, the gangly seaman crawled onto the table and lay on his back, as still as a corpse.

Chapter 25

"Eng," Chris said, "would you go put all the patients on streptomycin instead of chloramphenicol? That's the only change I've identified so far that we ought to make."

"Aye, sir," Eng said with a wry smile.

Chris grinned back at the scrawny officer. It was scary how this crisis had turned the *Vermont*'s command structure upside down, so much so that a corpsman equivalent to a petty officer was now giving orders to a lieutenant.

"God, this rots," Tumor groaned.

Chris looked the anxious country boy over, feeling surprisingly strong pity. Tumor's face was even paler than usual, causing his patchy stubble and acne to stand out under the harsh fluorescent light. His eyes were bloodshot and his big ears were red, but at least he wasn't coughing at the moment.

"Tumor, do you think you can finish building that pressure switch?"

"Huh? I was done with that ages ago. I've been helping the A-gangers with the air ducts. They've almost got them hooked up."

Chris tried to smile. "I guess I owe you ten bucks."

"Keep it," Tumor said. "I won't have much use for it now."

Chris put an electronic thermometer under the homely sailor's tongue. When it beeped, he read the digital display on its handle. "Ninety-eight point one. You're not sick, Tumor."

Tumor glared reproachfully. "I threw up! And I've been having trouble breathing."

The acne-ridden sailor appeared to be on the verge of tears. He was wringing his hands so tightly that their skin had turned red. His trembling lips were surrounded by a pale halo.

"I wish my mom was here," Tumor said. "She always took real good care of me when I was sick. Dang, don't tell anybody I said that."

"Don't worry, I don't blame you."

"Dang it, this stinks," Tumor said in a quavering voice. "I never . . . I wish I had a girlfriend. I'll bet I could have found one if I'd tried."

"You never tried?" Chris asked.

Tumor shook his head. "A man hadn't ought to look for a woman until he can afford a house."

"Tumor, vomiting has not been a common symptom in the other patients. When did you throw up?"

"About fifteen minutes ago."

"How many times?"

"Once."

"Any blood?"

"I didn't look."

"Are you still having trouble breathing?"

"A little."

Chris told Tumor to remove the top of his coveralls and his shirt. He placed the stethoscope on the seaman's pimply back and listened while Tumor breathed deeply.

"I don't hear any congestion."

"Feels more like it's my throat," Tumor said.

"Is it sore?"

"No, just . . . tight."

Chris used a tongue depressor to check Tumor's throat. "Healthy pink," he reported. "Tumor, how scared of this disease would you say you are?"

"I'm not."

"Honestly," Chris said.

Tumor raised his voice. "What's to be scared of now? It's too late for that. I've already got it, and we know it's fatal."

"Do you think it could be just the fear that's making you feel sick?"

Tumor appeared to give the possibility consideration. "Nope."

Chris sighed. "So you're convinced you're going to die."

Tumor nodded, and tears came into his eyes. "I just hope I can hang on long enough to get the next familygram and find out if my mom's going to be okay."

"What's wrong with her?"

"She's having an operation tomorrow. They're putting in an artificial heart valve. She's had a bad heart for a long time."

"I hope she'll be okay. Tumor, I'm sorry, I have to get back to work."

"You're not going to put me in one of the sick bays?"

"Not as a patient. You'd catch the bug from the others."

Tumor looked shocked. "If I stay out here, everyone else will catch it from me!"

"Fine. We still need more volunteers to care for the patients. And you're still able to work, right?"

Tumor nodded. "So far."

"Would you be willing to play nurse?"

"You betcha! I figure I'm probably going to heaven. I've never done anything really bad. This ought to clinch it for me. I'll tend to the guys who are really bad off, since I've got nothing to lose by touching them."

"Okay, thanks." Chris leaned over to look into Tumor's anxious blue eyes. "Look, you do understand that I don't think you're infected, right?"

"You betcha," Tumor said.

Chapter 26

After Tumor left, Chris returned to his research. His stomach felt raw from too much coffee. The lines of text blurred across each other when his concentration lapsed. He had been working nonstop for twenty-one hours, more intensely than he had ever worked in his life, and he'd started the marathon with a palpable sleep deficit.

Not exactly the way to optimize the old immune system.

Throughout this long day, Chris had felt a gnawing déjà vu and a smoldering temptation to panic. Four words kept running through his mind like a whisper from a ghost: *There is no escape.*

After two more hours, he thought he'd figured out a combination of antibiotics that would be safe for the patients and would cover all the possible pathogens, except for the species that weren't susceptible to antibiotics. But he still wasn't confident that it was the best he could do.

What if I misinterpreted something? What if some of this info is out of date? What if there are treatments other than antibiotics that require me to know the exact species of pathogen?

He started deliberately rereading the most critical articles. When the Dialex phone receiver rang, he realized that he'd been reading the same paragraph over and over.

Dreading bad news, he picked up the phone and said, "Pharmacy."

Eng's tired voice said, "Doc, they just finished install-ing the vacuum duct to the wardroom. We're about to turn the system on. You want to come down and check it out?"

"Absolutely!"

When Chris stood up, his legs felt stiff and his head spun for a moment.

He trotted forward and down one level to the ward-room and knocked on the door. Someone ripped the tape off the inside and let him into the sweltering, fetid chamber of horrors.

Three new patients lay on mattresses on the floor. They were all on supplemental oxygen, asleep or preoc-cupied with the effort of breathing. Two were quaking with chills and coughing up blood—Chris could see red spots on the insides of their transparent oxygen masks.

Maurice Hereford was still alive but appeared to be gradually getting worse.

With the door closed, Chris gave Tumor the honor of flipping the toggle switch to turn on the pressure control circuit. The air compressor was too far away for them to hear its motor, but they heard a faint hiss of air being sucked into the new vacuum duct. A few seconds later, Chris felt the growing pressure differential across his eardrums and swallowed to let it equalize.

The hiss of flowing air stopped. "Nine-nine-six milli-bars?" Chris asked. That was the pressure he had re-quested for the sick bays. The *Vermont* was normally kept at one thousand millibars, average atmospheric pressure at sea level.

Eng looked at the handheld digital barometer he had brought in to test the system. "Right on," he said.

Chris flung the door open. A blast of fresh air from the passageway nearly knocked him over.

"Nine-nine-seven," Eng called out, bracing his skeletal frame against the wind. "Rising fast."

The wind immediately began to subside.

"Nine-nine-eight."

Tumor was reaching into the new duct, feeling the air "Hey, it's on!"

"Yes!" Chris yelled, spreading his arms in the open doorway. The breeze was now gentle compared with the initial gust, but it remained strong enough to make his baggy coveralls luff. "Let there be wind!"

"Nine-nine-nine-point-five," Eng said. "Nine-nine-nine-point-seven. Holding steady now at nine-nine-nine-point-seven millibars."

"Did you see that?" Tumor shouted with a maniacal grin. "The compressor came on right at nine-nine-eight. I set it to come on at nine-nine-eight and go off at nine-nine-six so it won't kick on and off all the time."

"Fantastic," Chris said. "You did it." He slapped Tumor on the back.

Eng stepped around him and shut the door. "Let's not waste air."

Chris had been leaning into the wind. When it was cut off, he failed to correct his balance fast enough. He stumbled into Eng, who grabbed his arm to steady him. "Easy there, Doc. If a guy your size fell on one of the patients . . ."

As if on cue, one of the three new victims began to weep. After one long howl, he settled down to alternate sobbing and coughing. The noise woke another one, who started coughing as well. The man jerked his oxygen mask aside and expelled a stream of greenish, blood-streaked phlegm onto the floor.

Tumor grabbed a wad of paper towels. "You guys stand back! I'll get that." He wiped up the mess, then swabbed the floor with Betadine.

Chris palmed his sweaty scalp, allowing his exhausted eyes to unfocus. The patient coughing up bloody phlegm had caused him to flash back for a split second to Kyle Orbison's gruesome death. *I wonder how much more of this I can take.*

When he tried to refocus his eyes, it took so long that he began to worry. The hellish wardroom finally came into focus, but now his head was spinning. He also felt queasy again. *Is it disgust, fear, or hunger? When was the last time I ate?*

"I wonder why we're diving," he said.

Eng's alert eyes scrutinized Chris. "What are you talking about? We're not diving."

"You can't feel the pitch angle?"

Eng glanced at Tumor, then spoke in a suspicious tone. "The trim is dead level, Doc."

"The hell it is! Just look at the deck!" Chris felt a rumble of nascent panic, a killer squall coming over the horizon.

"Turn around," Eng ordered.

"Why?"

"Just turn around."

Chris turned around.

"Which way is the deck tilted now?"

Chris looked down. Now the *Vermont* appeared to be nose-up. "Oh no," he said. "What does that mean?"

"I don't know. You're the doctor."

"I am not a fucking doctor! That's the whole problem! We need a doctor here! I'm just a goddamn sailor with some first aid training, and you expect me to deal with *this*?"

Chris's eyes burned. His throat was tight. He felt like punching a hole in the nearest bulkhead.

He realized Tumor and Eng had both stepped back against adjoining walls like cornered mice.

Chris stooped with his big hands on his knees. He closed his eyes, trying to breathe deeply through his taped-on mask. *I must never lose my temper. Never, never, never!*

Tumor's timid voice said, "It probably just means you need some rack time, Doc."

"Possibly," Eng said.

Chris opened his eyes and saw that Eng was wiping down an electronic oral thermometer with alcohol. When Chris focused on the tiny but powerful instrument, the fear he had held back for three days broke through and flooded his mind. The squall was upon him now, threatening to capsize him. The wardroom tilted even more and began spinning counterclockwise. The bright fluorescent lights grew dim.

Chris sat down on the floor as gracefully as he could. *This is not the way I want to die. A depth charge or torpedo would be so much better. How will Soony take it? What will my parents do? Will the crew be able to stop the outbreak without me?*

"Exhale slowly," Eng said.

Chris complied while Eng pulled back a corner of the tape around his mask and stuck the thermometer into his mouth.

Chris mashed the sticky tape back into place around the thermometer. He waited for the beep, breathing deeply and listening to his own pulse, wondering how many more breaths and heartbeats he would get. It seemed to take forever, but the thermometer finally beeped, blasting him with a nauseating surge of dread.

Eng pulled the thermometer out. He seemed to be moving in slow motion, taking his sweet time. "Nine-eight-point-five."

"What? Say again?"

"Nine-eight-point-five," Eng repeated, "and bedtime, before you do something you'll regret."

Chapter 27

Chris staggered next door to the galley and made himself a ham sandwich with at least a half pound of meat. He'd had no appetite for a while, but he knew it was vital to maintain his strength as best he could.

When he finally landed in his rack, he expected to go to sleep immediately, but he couldn't. He tossed and turned, trying in vain to get comfortable. He had heartburn, his head was still spinning, and something in his abdomen kept twitching.

Random images from the last few watches flashed through his mind. The gruesome memories seemed unusually vivid, as if a projector in his head were beaming them onto the insides of his closed eyelids. He tried to block them out by visualizing Soony's pretty face. To his dismay, he was unable to call up her image.

Since I'm awake, I might as well try to think this through. What haven't I done? What have I done that I shouldn't have? What's going to happen next?

Rigging the sick bays for lowered pressure had been a triumph of teamwork, but he knew it might not stop the outbreak. Germs could still escape on the volunteers or objects they carried. The pathogen might also remain at large among the rest of the crew, jumping from one host to another before they got sick enough for the screenings to catch them.

Chris heard a cough.

He stopped breathing to listen, his heart thumping.

The powerful heartbeats actually hurt. He knew that meant the muscle was exhausted—it had felt that way after his toughest football games. Now his heart was fatigued because too many moments like this one had come and gone since he'd rested adequately.

Several seconds passed with no more coughs. Chris resumed breathing but remained still, listening. The cough had sounded normal, not like the desperate phlegmy hacking of the victims. Still, it could have been the first symptom for an unlucky berth mate.

He returned to sleepless rumination. *Did I make a mistake, enlisting in the Navy?* This was the first time Chris had ever thought the answer to that question might be yes.

Chris opened the wardroom door without knocking. The door was no longer being kept sealed with tape— the vacuum inside ensured that any air leaking around its edges would be directed into the room. He stepped in and leaned against the door to shut it, then looked around.

"Oh, Christ."

The overheated wardroom now contained six patients. There was almost no floor space left to stand on. Despite the recent influx of fresh air, Chris could smell a nauseating blend of purulent sputum, excreta, and sweat.

Maurice Hereford was weakly rubbing his fingers and muttering something about them being numb—one more thing for Chris to add to his list of mysterious symptoms.

Tumor was the only volunteer present. He leaned close to Chris and whispered, "The antibiotics ain't doing squat."

"The patients are all worse?"

Tumor nodded. "One more died while you were racked out."

"What? Why didn't you wake me?"

"Gee whiz, Doc, you've got to sleep sometime. It's not like there's anything you could have done."

Chris sighed and looked away from the patients, who were gazing up at him with pleading eyes, trying to inhale the oxygen flowing into their masks without coughing. "Damn it, we can't start stacking them two deep. Is the torpedo room rigged for vacuum yet?"

"You betcha, but it's full of the guys who just might be sick."

"We'll have to build a third isolation room," Chris said. "Keep giving them all of the antibiotics. Maybe they just haven't had time to work yet. At this point I'll bet it's a virus, though; probably hantavirus or an H5N1 strain of flu like HK97. Do you need me to bring anything down from the pharmacy?"

Tumor looked at the wardroom's log book, which was now a spiral-bound notebook instead of a napkin. "More cipro . . . cipro . . ."

"Ciprofloxacin," Chris said. "Coming right up."

He walked upstairs one level and headed aft through the missile compartment toward the pharmacy. On the way, he ran into Oral, who was wolfing down an enormous cup of chocolate ice cream as if determined to use up the *Vermont*'s supply before the end.

"COB, you got a minute?"

"Sure, I'm off watch. What's on your mind, son?"

"Can you get the A-gangers to start building another low-pressure room?"

"Sure. Where?"

"The officers' study?" Chris suggested.

"Sure, I'll get permission and get right on it."

"Thanks, COB."

In the pharmacy, Chris found the door of the drug cabinet standing open. Several boxes were strewn on the floor, along with one shattered vial in a puddle of clear liquid. Taking care not to get cut, he picked up the remains of the vial by the adhesive label that still held most of the shards together. It was vancomycin, the precious antibiotic of last resort, the only one that almost no bacteria had evolved any resistance to.

Damn it, I should have seen this coming!

He compared the remaining stocks with the pharmacy's inventory. It was apparent that the thief had attempted to take only enough of each antibiotic to last one person for the rest of the run. That suggested a lone perpetrator rather than a conspiracy. Chris wondered whether the thief would have taken more if he hadn't been interrupted by someone.

The puddle of vancomycin was almost dry, so there was no point in looking for the thief nearby. Chris decided to ask Weps to lock up the remaining antibiotics in the small-arms locker, for which only the weapons officer and the chief of the watch had keys.

Eng poked his head into the pharmacy, blinking behind his red-framed eyeglasses and rubbing his shaved temples. "I just woke up with an idea, Doc. You could autopsy one of the dead men."

Chris palmed the top of his head. "Holy shit! I didn't even think of that!"

"You haven't had time," Eng said. "I'll bet you could do it now, though."

"Maybe, Eng, but I'm not a pathologist. I wouldn't know where to begin." Furthermore, the thought of cutting into a cadaver's infected chest cavity made Chris's skin crawl in a hundred directions at once.

"Just pretend you're operating on a live patient."

"Eng, I'm not a surgeon either."

"Don't you have a manual for surgery?"

"Actually, I do, and it may include instructions for autopsies! I think an autopsy requires special tools that we don't have, but we could probably make do with some big knives from the galley."

"You'll need a bone saw for cutting the ribs," Eng said.

"Would a hacksaw do?"

"Probably. They all died of pneumonia, so getting the lungs out is all that matters, right?"

"There might be damage to other organs that would

give us a clue," Chris said. "The problem is, I don't even know what healthy organs are supposed to look like."

"Your manuals are bound to have photographs," Eng said.

Chris paused to think for a moment. Dissecting a man who had died of a respiratory infection might be extremely dangerous. Sawing through bones might fill the air with aerosol particles, and he could picture infectious fluids spilling, squirting, and splattering all over the place. He would have to wear a makeshift biohazard suit and perform the autopsy inside one of the low-pressure rooms.

"We have to have clear objectives, Eng. There's no point in cutting open a corpse if we don't know what we're looking for."

"Some of the articles we found on different diseases contained pictures of the victims' lungs," Eng said. "I'll hunt them down and get the CO's permission while you get started."

"You're not going to help me? I can't do everything by myself—I'll have dead body glop all over my hands!"

Eng looked pained. "Doc, I'm not afraid of the ocean. I'm not afraid of any human enemy. I'm not even afraid of growing old alone—I'm resigned to it. But I've gone about as close as I can make myself go to this kind of evil." The skin-and-bones officer looked and sounded ashamed. "My immune system really is weak, Doc. I almost died of a fever when I was eight years old."

"What kind of fever, sir?"

"I never found out. I was reared by my grandparents in one of the poorest counties in Georgia. They were both illiterate, both true believers, of course. When my fever got really bad, my grandma kept trying to call their preacher to ask him what they should do. I sneaked out and walked to the hospital. Six miles. I was told later that I walked into the emergency room and sat down as if I could wait all day—I've never been able to remember the last half of the trip. I'll help you if you can't get anyone else, but I doubt I'd be the best man for the job."

Chris nodded. "Tumor will help. You just try to find those pictures of diseased and healthy lungs by the time we're ready to start cutting. Okay?"

Eng saluted. "Aye, sir!"

Chris felt his face flush. "Sorry, sir. I didn't mean it to sound like an order."

"Quite all right," Eng said with a smile.

Chapter 28

The officially designated place on a Trident for performing emergency surgery was the table in the officers' wardroom, but Chris knew better than to do the autopsy in front of the patients. The torpedo room was the only other compartment that had been rigged for reduced pressure so far.

Chris and Tumor marched the men with pending cases out of the torpedo room and upstairs to the officers' study, which had been sealed off with tape and caulk by now. The men grumbled about being packed into a smaller space, but they all obeyed Chris's orders. The relocation was swift, and all of the men wore taped masks, so he figured it had not significantly increased the danger to the rest of the crew.

His plan was to use the officers' study as Purgatory from now on. Once they were done with the autopsy, the torpedo room could start taking overflow patients from the crowded wardroom.

Chris and Tumor asked the torpedomen to load a torpedo into tube one so they could use its empty storage rack as a makeshift operating table. Then they spread a sheet of plastic beneath the rack and started surrounding their work area with a levee of rolled towels to prevent body fluids from spilling into the bilges.

"Looks like you guys are expecting a flood."

Chris looked up and saw Freud leaning lazily against

the open door, fingering his gold necklace and grinning
beneath his dark shades.

"We don't know what to expect, sir."

"Would you believe I once got it on with a redhead
down here?" Freud asked.

"No way!" Tumor said.

Chris said nothing. The torpedo room was off-limits
to civilians when it contained tactical nuclear warheads.
He continued rolling towels, squatting on the floor.

"Right here in this corner," Freud said, pointing.
"Doggy style. Seeing all these warshots really got her
going. Damn, she was fine—a senior at Bremerton High,
one of their cheerleaders."

"Dadgone!" Tumor said. "Weren't you afraid of getting caught?"

"Hell, no. I never get caught."

Chris said, "Would you like to help us today, sir?"
He spoke with a gruffer tone than he had intended.

Freud backed out through the door, palms up. "Hey,
I've got duties."

Then go fucking do them, Chris thought.

Tumor said, "I don't blame you for being scared, sir.
I'm doing this because I've already got the bug. It just
ain't getting me down as fast as some of the others."

Freud looked Tumor up and down, grimacing, then
grinned again. "I'm not scared of this crud. Nothing bad
ever happens to me. I've been lucky since the day I
was born."

"Sure sounds like it," Tumor said. "Gee whiz, I wish
I was you."

Chris finished with the towels and stood up. Freud
was gone.

"What do we do now?" Tumor asked.

"We should get everything we might need together,"
Chris said. "We don't want to have to leave in the middle of the procedure to go get something."

"What all do we need?"

"Lots of paper towels, and some buckets. We should

make up a lot of bleach solution for rinsing our hands and the instruments. Let's bring down an assortment of knives from the galley; also some tongs and spatulas."

"What are we going to do with the, uh, the parts when we're finished?"

"We'll need a needle and thread to sew him back up," Chris said. "We can't just leave a bunch of infectious organs lying around."

Eng came by to show them pictures of what they should look for in the cadaver's lungs. He had confirmed that an autopsy might allow them to distinguish among the possible pathogens.

Chris and Tumor went up to the galley to fetch their specimen.

Chris opened the door of the cold storage compartment. The four cadavers were stacked against a pallet of boxed oranges. The *Vermont* had only two black body bags, so Chris had wrapped the other two corpses in thick translucent plastic, sealing it with green EB tape. These two were lying on top of the pile.

He stepped in and squatted beside the cadavers. "I can't tell which one is which," he called back to Tumor.

"What does it matter?" Tumor said.

Chris shook one of the cadavers to clear the condensation droplets on the inside of the plastic. Evidently, the warm bodies had given off a lot of moisture after they were sealed up.

"Gee whiz, just grab one," Tumor said. "You're letting all the cold air out."

Chris rolled one of the cadavers over. The bottom of the body was stuck to the plastic. This victim had landed in the chill box facedown. His left eyelid and the left side of his upper lip had been dragged open by the plastic. Chris could see the white of his eye and two or three upper teeth. The face was bluish gray without a hint of pink, yet the streaks of blood on the plastic near the mouth were still bright red.

Chris moved the plastic-wrapped corpses and selected

one of those in the body bags, which had three handles on each side.

"I don't reckon I've ever known a man who was this limber when he was alive," Tumor said as they carried the heavy bag down the stairs.

"Feels like it's falling apart," Chris said.

"You hear that sloshing sound?" Tumor asked.

They carried the awkward load into a narrow passageway lined with protruding gadgets. "Yeah. Be careful not to snag it."

In the torpedo room, they donned white chemical hazard suits with green rubber boots and gloves. Instead of relying on surgical masks, they each put on an EAB and hooked their stiff, short hoses into the air manifold. The final items they donned were headlamps, which would help them see into the cadaver despite the shadow of the torpedo rack above it.

"I wish you wouldn't make me wear all this hot and heavy crap." Tumor's voice sounded muffled and nasal through his EAB mask. "There's no point, you know."

"You could smell the air in the room if you weren't breathing through an EAB," Chris reminded him.

"Oh, right. Do you think this guy stinks already?"

"Probably. The inside of a human body can't smell good, even one that's alive and healthy."

They unzipped the bag, taking care not to let it spill open. Chris saw the cadaver's pear-shaped figure, close-set eyes, and blond muttonchops, and he knew it was Kyle Orbison.

Orbison's coveralls were soaking wet. Murky liquid had pooled in the bottom of the bag. Tumor reached in with a towel to sop it up. "Gee whiz, what do you reckon all this stuff is?"

"Probably just condensation," Chris said. "He was dry when we bagged him. Maybe his bladder let go afterward."

They removed Orbison's clothing. Most of the body was gray, but broad patches of potato white extended across the chest, the abdomen, and the fronts of the pudgy thighs. The white patches were surrounded by dark purple halos.

"Why is he different colors like that?"

"Hypostasis," Chris said. "He was lying facedown. All this bruising is where gravity caused his blood to pool at the bottom. The skin that was actually touching the floor is white because it was compressed and blood couldn't drain into it."

Chris had taped a page of instructions to the green torpedo on the rack above Orbison. Following a diagram on the page, he picked out a paring knife he'd brought from the galley and started a Y incision. First he made a cut across the bruised chest, from one shoulder to the other, dipping below the collarbones. Then he made a cut extending from the middle of the first cut downward to the groin.

Dark blood, almost black, oozed from the incisions but did not flow freely.

Tumor gasped. "I thought dead people didn't bleed."

"This is the side he was lying on," Chris said. "We didn't give the pooled blood time to drain back out."

Chris wiped away the blood with a paper towel and probed the incisions with his double-gloved fingers. His fingertips went in about an inch, but they wouldn't go through into the abdominal cavity. He pulled the upper edge of the abdominal cut open by tugging on Orbison's flabby sides. Focusing his headlamp with one bloody hand, he peered into the V-shaped fissure. On the sides of the cut, he could make out a stratum of purplish-gray skin with pink fat beneath it. The bottom of the incision ended in the thick fat layer.

"Didn't cut deep enough," he muttered.

The autopsy instructions he'd found had said he should use only one knife per incision. Why, he didn't know, but he doubted it mattered in this case. He selected a long butcher knife and started deepening the cuts.

"Oh," Tumor said.

Chris looked up. Tumor was holding the torpedo rack above his head with one hand, clutching his EAB with the other.

"What's wrong?" Chris asked. "You feel sick?"

"No," Tumor said, weakly.

Chris watched him for a few seconds. Tumor slowly lowered the hand from his EAB but continued holding the rack. "Go ahead, Doc."

Chris resumed cutting. He heard a scraping sound and looked up again as it was followed by a thud.

His assistant was gone.

"Tumor?"

Chris tried to walk around the torpedo rack. He was brought up short by his EAB hose. "Damn it!" He held his breath, unhooked the hose, and stepped around the rack.

Tumor was stretched out on his back.

Chris was still holding his breath and trying to decide what to do when Tumor came around and reached up one arm. Chris helped him to his feet. Tumor wobbled for a few seconds, holding the upper torpedo rack again.

Chris stepped back around the rack and hooked his hose up to the wall manifold. "What happened? Did you faint?"

"I guess so."

"You okay now?"

"Yeah, go ahead."

"You're sure? You don't feel sick?" Chris was concerned that Tumor might pull off his EAB mask if he had to throw up.

"Yeah, go ahead," Tumor said irritably.

Feeling queasy himself, Chris finished the Y incision and peeled back the fatty flesh over Orbison's chest to expose the breastbone and rib cage.

"Oh, fudge."

Tumor hit the floor before Chris could look up.

Chapter 29

Chris rinsed his gloved hands in the bucket of bleach solution, then relocated his EAB hose near the phone and started calling the other compartments, hoping to find a new assistant. Pigpen was racked out after pulling a quadruple shift. No one else would volunteer, except Eng.

Tumor weakly sat up. "I'm sorry, Doc."

"It's okay." Chris helped him to his feet again. "Rinse yourself with Betadine and wait outside to give Eng your protective gear. And please don't look at the body again on your way out."

"Okay. I won't."

While waiting for Eng, Chris went to work on Orbison's exposed rib cage. Now he had to depart from the standard autopsy procedure because he didn't have the proper tools to saw the breastbone in half and spread the sides apart. Instead, he started cutting the ribs at the sides of Orbison's chest with a hacksaw, leaving the breastbone in place. He planned to cut loose the whole front of the rib cage and lift it off in one piece.

The operation did not go as planned. The hacksaw blade refused to stay in one place on the slippery bones, and Chris couldn't find an angle where the long blade would cut into the ribs without hitting other parts of the body that obstructed its motion. Worst of all, the corpse kept wobbling and sliding around.

The instant Eng opened the door, Chris shouted, "Sir, come here and hold this damn thing down for me!" Inside the EAB hood, his own voice sounded muffled but deafening.

Eng was bundled up in the garb Tumor had given him—Chris had convinced him that Tumor was not really infected. He muscled the door shut against the wind, then turned around and froze. "Oh, shit. What are you doing?"

"I can't get the damn bones out of the way!" Chris shouted, holding up a floating rib that he had torn out of Orbison's chest with his hands. He was fighting the urge to throw the rib against the wall and start pounding on the corpse in frustration.

Looking sideways, Eng crept to the torpedo rack and put one gloved hand on Orbison's forehead, the other on his hip. "Please hurry."

In desperation, Chris hacked at the ribs more and more violently.

"Careful there, Doc."

Chris glanced up at Eng. The distraction caused the hacksaw blade to slip and hit one of his hands. "Shit!"

"Oh, shit. Sorry," Eng said at the same time.

Chris stepped back in shock, dropping the bloody saw. It clattered on the deck. He had felt the saw's teeth sting his skin.

After a moment of indecision, he rinsed his hands and inspected his double gloves. It took a while because his hands were trembling. The faceplate of his EAB was fogged, and sweat was running into his eyes.

Finally he held his hand out to Eng, feeling his rapid heart rate subside. "I think it's okay. You want to have a look?"

Eng gently scrutinized the hand, training his headlamp beam on it. "I can't see any holes, Doc. You should fill the inner glove with water and check for leaks."

Chris pulled on a third pair of latex gloves. "Later. I'll die of heat stroke if I stay in this getup much longer.

Would you call someone to bring us a set of bolt cutters?"

Eng obeyed. Chris was glad he didn't say "aye, sir."

They discovered it was easy to snap exposed human ribs with bolt cutters, but the dull edges of the tool would not slice through the tough membranes surrounding the bones. Chris tried twisting and yanking with the large steel cutters. That didn't work, so he resorted to using a scalpel after the bone was broken.

I hope I can get this done before I puke or pass out like Tumor.

After several minutes of breaking and cutting, he removed the front of Orbison's rib cage, then cut loose the lungs and lifted them out of the chest cavity. He dropped the slimy mass onto the sheet of plastic covering the floor and took a break to catch his breath. Squatting beside the bloody pile of infection-ravaged tissue, he closed his eyes and recited prime numbers in his head, beating back the nausea that had been gaining on him throughout the procedure.

Eng had backed away from the cadaver. He was just standing there silently.

Chris scooped up the lungs in a trashcan lid and weighed them on a scale he'd brought down from the galley. They were approximately twice as heavy as they should have been.

He carefully dissected one lung with a scalpel. The alveoli were full of viscous bloody mucus, but there were no other visible abnormalities. The edema and bleeding could have been caused by any of several pathogens. He and Eng concluded that they had found none of the definitive diagnostic evidence they'd hoped for.

Chris could hardly believe they had put themselves through this for nothing. He kept examining the photos of diseased lungs laid out atop a Tomahawk cruise missile, comparing them with the heavy bags of bloody pulp he had lifted out of Orbison. "What's weird is the damage looks bacterial, not viral."

Eng stepped up beside him. "It does."

"So why aren't the antibiotics helping?" Chris asked.

Eng shrugged. "Let's clean up and get out of here."

They were dumping Orbison's lungs back into his rib cage when the door sprang open, admitting a whoosh of air that blew a spatter of blood across Chris's chest. He saw Freud standing in the doorway, staring at the mangled cadaver with wide eyes. The ensign was not wearing his shades at the moment. He was also not wearing a mask.

Chris yelled, "Shut that door, goddamn it!"

Freud jumped back and dragged the door shut, then shouted through it. "You'd better come quick! You've got to see Hereford!"

"What do you mean?" Chris asked.

There was no answer. He could hear Freud running away. "If that's all he had to say, why didn't he just page us?"

Eng was tugging the edges of the body bag up around the mutilated corpse. "He probably wanted an excuse to peek in here."

Chris could hear vague retching noises coming from the direction Freud had run. "He must not have liked what he saw."

Chris hastily zipped up the body bag, using his other hand to shove an errant lobe of inflamed lung tissue out of the way. He'd decided he didn't have either the time or the fortitude to stitch Orbison back together.

Chapter 30

Chris and Eng wiped everything near the cadaver with Betadine solution—the body bag, the floor, each other. Then they headed for the wardroom, peeling off the insufferable EABs and chem-hazard suits on the way.

When he got to the stairs, Chris heard a new sound. He was pretty sure it was a human vocalization, but it was not the now-familiar stridor of a victim drowning in his own body fluids. He had never heard a sound quite like this, but his instinct told him it was a repeating shriek of sheer horror.

He bounded up the stairs.

Eng followed.

They burst through the wardroom door, then closed it against the wind.

Maurice Hereford was sitting up on his mattress. The other patients had crowded against the opposite wall, along with Pigpen. Hereford was the source of the noise. He was screaming with every breath, and there was apparently still nothing wrong with his lungs.

His fingertips were another matter. He was holding them in front of him, palms up, each finger curving inward as if he had just painted his nails and was blowing them dry. The fingers had turned as black as coal up to the middle joint. His nails looked like flakes of obsidian. The boundary between healthy-looking pink skin and

black necrosis was sharp—the only transition was a band
a few millimeters wide that looked like smooth brown
plastic.

"What happened?" Chris shouted over Hereford's
wails.

"He just woke up," Pigpen shouted back. "His
hands . . ."

Hereford's nose was as black as his fingertips. Chris
could also see the screaming victim's naked right foot
sticking out from under his blanket—apparently he'd
pulled his sock off. All of the toes and the front half of
the foot had turned black. Chris couldn't help wondering
what Hereford's penis looked like. He imagined that he
could see the blackness creeping upward from the victim's extremities, turning him inch by inch into a rotten
corpse while he was still alive.

Necrotic extremities were not Hereford's only problem. Chris could also see a large lump on the front of
his exposed right hip. Another huge swelling was visible
beneath his left armpit, and two large oval swellings
bulged from opposite sides of his neck.

A ragged black fissure ran about two inches up and
down the middle of the swelling on the right side of
Hereford's neck. The perforation was surrounded by a
greenish sheen, and it was oozing a steady stream of
bloody gray pus that flowed down into his shirt collar.
Drops and smears of what looked like the same pus
were scattered across Hereford's blanket and on the
floor.

Chris pointed to the grotesque wound. "What happened there?"

"A few minutes ago, that . . . that thing on his neck
just *exploded*," Pigpen said.

Chris turned around, wondering where Eng was. He
saw the stick-figure lieutenant squatting in the corner
behind him. Eng's bony hands were clasped over his
ears, and his eyes were squeezed shut.

Perfect. Pigpen is scared stiff and Eng has gone bye-bye—now it's all up to me.

Chris grabbed a roll of paper towels and cautiously advanced toward Hereford, whose screams had begun to weaken.

"Don't touch him!" Eng shrieked.

Chris froze and looked back at the cringing officer.

Eng had opened his eyes. He was pointing at Hereford and digging at the floor with his heels as if trying to propel his skeletal frame backward through the wall. "Get away from him!"

"Eng, what is your damn problem . . . sir?"

"It's so obvious," Eng wailed. "It's so damn obvious! Why didn't I realize?"

"Realize what?" Chris shouted. He felt like throwing the roll of paper towels at the lieutenant's trembling head.

"I know what it is," Eng groaned.

"You mean the pathogen?"

Eng nodded, emitting a low whine. *"Yersinia pestis,"* he said.

Pigpen seemed to snap out of his trance. "That's the name of the bug? How'd you know that just by looking at him?"

It took Chris a second to connect the modern Latin name of a bacterium with the one deadly disease that had shaped European history more than any other. The revelation left him stunned, but he managed to say, "You're right, Eng. We should have recognized it before."

"Recognized what?" Pigpen shouted, causing his thicket of frizzy blond hair to quiver.

Chris looked around at the other patients, who were now staring at him and Eng instead of Hereford. One of them pulled his oxygen mask aside and coughed out the words, "What . . . is . . . *Yersinia . . . pestis*?"

Chris thought about telling Pigpen in private but decided against it. *These men have a right to know they have a disease that's supposed to be invariably fatal unless antibiotics are started as soon as the symptoms appear.*

Chris allowed his deep voice to broadcast over Hereford's wails, Eng's moaning, and the coughing patients. "Plague," he said.

Chapter 31

"How can you be certain it's plague?"

Lieutenant Commander Kurlgunn was sitting on the edge of his chair, gripping the armrests, regarding Chris suspiciously.

Chris and Eng were reporting their findings in the CPO lounge. Captain Scott and Oral were the only others present.

"The combination of symptoms we've observed in the patients is unique to plague," Eng explained. "*Yersinia pestis* can cause three different syndromes. When it attacks the lungs, the illness is called pneumonic plague. When it invades the bloodstream, it's called septicemic plague. That's what's causing Maurice Hereford's extremities to die and turn black. Along with the dark bruises plague can cause all over the skin, peripheral necrosis is why the plague pandemics that struck Europe in the fourteenth century came to be known as the Black Death. Hereford also has a textbook case of bubonic plague, the third variety. It causes buboes—large swollen lymph glands on the neck, armpits, and groin. Buboes are excruciatingly painful, and they can fill with so many bacteria that they rupture."

Chris was trying to listen, feeling somewhat eclipsed by Eng's extensive knowledge about plague. Three watches had gone by since he'd last had a chance to sit down, and he had just recently cooled off from the sweltering ordeal in the makeshift biohazard suit. What little concentration he could muster was being devoted to not snoring in front of the officers.

It didn't help that Eng was nervously talking even faster than his usual swift speed. He was hunched forward as if he were cold, which didn't surprise Chris, considering the lieutenant's underweight body and the *Vermont*'s powerful air-conditioning. Eng was also making a small rocking motion, forward and back. Since seeing Hereford's full-blown plague symptoms, he'd worn the most haunted expression Chris had ever seen.

Chris gradually became aware of the XO's bullet gray eyes squinting at him again. He jumped a little when Kurlgunn's sharp voice said, "Why didn't you realize it was plague before now, Long?"

"What? Oh . . . I probably should have, sir. If only I had thought to do an autopsy sooner and had looked for swollen lymph nodes. . . . Plague is one of the pathogens we were considering, but the symptoms we'd seen were not conclusive until Hereford developed buboes and acral necrosis all of a sudden. Besides, plague is relatively rare nowadays. When you make a diagnosis, you're not supposed to start guessing exotic causes until you've eliminated the more common ones."

Kurlgunn shifted his tight grip on the armrests. "Is knowing what's causing this scourge going to help you stop it?"

"I hope so, sir. The good news is that plague is treatable with antibiotics. We've already started giving the whole crew a dose of doxycycline during the fever screenings. It's supposed to be the best prophylactic for people who have been exposed to plague but don't seem to have it yet. Hopefully, we can stamp out the epidemic before the doxycycline is used up."

"Do you have the right kind of antibiotics to treat the poor souls who are already sick?" Oral asked.

Chris nodded. "Streptomycin. All of the patients have been getting it for a while already, but we might ought to start practicing triage. If just a few more men get sick, we won't have enough to last through this run."

"Triage?" Kurlgunn said. "Do you mean saving medicine by not giving any to the men who look like they're going to die soon anyway?"

Chris winced. "Yes, sir." He hoped the officers wouldn't be too disgusted with him for suggesting such a callous tactic.

"Good idea," Kurlgunn said. "Get started."

Chris did not feel relieved. "Sir, the problem is, I don't have enough experience to tell which men are beyond help."

"I'm sure you can guess, Long. If you're not up to making those kinds of decisions, bring them to me."

Captain Scott spoke up. "If you don't know for sure which men are doomed, there will be no triage."

"Aye, sir," Chris replied before Kurlgunn could object.

Captain Scott was slumped in his chair, leaning sideways. His bushy red and gray eyebrows were squeezed together, forming a deep frown. At their last meeting, Chris had thought the grief-stricken captain seemed to be in denial about the outbreak. This time his impression was different. The aging officer looked consumed with worry, as if he were privately struggling to make some terrible decision.

"Another problem is that our streptomycin is designed to be given intravenously, and we've already run out of IV bags," Chris said.

"Can't you just refill them?" Kurlgunn asked.

"No, sir. They're disposable. Even if I could mix more saline with the right composition, I couldn't keep it sterile once it cools to room temperature. With your permission, I'll dilute the streptomycin and administer it as frequent intravenous injections. That will be painful for the patients and take a lot of work, but it should come close to the same effect as a continuous drip."

"Very well." Captain Scott sounded as if he had a bad headache. "Can you give us a casualty projection?"

Eng removed his red-rimmed glasses and rubbed his bony temples. "Even with the best antibiotic treatment, primary pneumonic plague has a mortality rate of about forty percent, and it typically kills in one to two days after the first appearance of symptoms. Even in victims who survive, it's totally incapacitating for several days. If we all come down with it, the *Vermont* will be essentially unmanned."

Kurlgunn mulled that over, flexing his jaws and staring at the door. "Why have all the cases except Maurice Hereford taken the pneumonic form?"

"Victims cough out infective droplets, and other people inhale them," Eng explained. "That's usually the only way plague can be transmitted directly from person to person. It causes the pneumonic form because the bacteria begin their invasion in the lungs."

Oral leaned forward with his elbows on the table, glumly resting his jowly cheeks on his palms. "Sounds to me like you couldn't come up with a worse disease to turn loose on a submarine."

Kurlgunn whirled toward the COB. "Do you think this was a deliberate attack?"

"Sort of," Oral said with an enigmatic groan. The overweight COB was glancing around at the others apprehensively. Chris couldn't help noticing that his big, brown, protruding eyes were reminiscent of a cow's.

"There's no way an enemy operative could have gotten onto this boat," Kurlgunn said. "Who do you think did it? How did they release the germs?"

Oral said nothing.

Kurlgunn stood and glowered at Chris and Eng, flexing his striated jaw muscles. "Have you two even considered the possibility that we've been attacked with a biological weapon?"

"It occurred to us, sir," Chris said. "Plague is one of the diseases that the American germ warfare program at Fort Detrick weaponized before it was shut down in 1969. The illegal Soviet program developed an even more sophisticated plague weapon in the eighties. Other nations have undoubtedly worked on plague too. But this looks more like a natural outbreak. And like you said, how could an enemy agent sneak a bioweapon onto a Trident with all of the security at the base? And why would they?"

"Why do you say this looks like a natural outbreak?" asked Captain Scott.

"Release of a bioweapon would have infected all of its victims at once," Chris said. "As far as we can tell, every victim on the *Vermont* caught it from one of the two index cases, Orbison and Hereford, and they both apparently had it before they came aboard."

"Very well. How did they catch it?" Kurlgunn asked.

"Our current theory is that Hereford had it first," Chris said. "He told us he spent the last two weeks before this run on his uncle's farm in California. That's probably where he caught it. He must have given it to Orbison on the night before we left. You know how they pack them in at the Spirit Tender—tighter than we do on the sub. You have to wonder if anyone else caught it at the bar. There may be a plague outbreak back on land too."

"Why do you think Hereford caught it on his uncle's farm?" Kurlgunn asked. "Who would have given it to him?"

"Not who—what," Eng said. "Plague is endemic in the western United States. It's carried by rodents, including prairie dogs and ground squirrels. Plague strikes about eighteen Americans per year on average, more people than rabies. Pet cats are a common intermediary vector. They catch it from rodents they've killed, then pass it on to their owners. Plague is almost unheard of in Washington State, but it's more common in California. Perhaps Hereford contacted some infected farm cats or helped trap some rodent pests while visiting his uncle."

Kurlgunn was staring at the door, flexing his fists. His suspicious squint was even darker than usual. Chris wondered whether some new and unpleasant thought had occurred to him.

"Hereford doesn't have the pneumonic form," Kurlgunn said, "so how did he produce infective particles for Orbison to inhale at the Spirit Tender?"

Eng shrugged. "Perhaps the bacteria were on his skin. Have you noticed the white dust that collects on surfaces inside houses? Most of that dust is dead human skin. We all shed about fifteen million microscopic flakes every day."

After a moment of silence, Kurlgunn said, "Where is Hereford now?"

"Wardroom," Chris said.

"Is he conscious?"

"Yes, sir."

"Good. All of you—go get some sleep. That's an order."

Oral, Chris, and Eng glanced at Captain Scott, who nodded and said, "Dismissed."

Chris left the CPO lounge and trudged toward his berth. His feet were sore. He'd been working nonstop for nineteen hours.

As he crawled into his rack, he wished for the hundredth time that he'd proposed to Soony before the *Vermont* got under way. He also wondered what nightmares he would have tonight.

Chapter 32

As soon as he was alone, Kurlgunn called the wardroom. One of the medical volunteers answered. "I want Maurice Hereford taken to the forward crew's washroom, right now," Kurlgunn said.

"Sir, if we take him outside the—"

"It's only temporary. He doesn't have the pneumonic form of plague, so he won't contaminate the air. I need to ask him some personal questions, and I want to respect his privacy."

"Give us fifteen minutes, sir."

"Very well."

Kurlgunn marched aft to the forward crew's washroom, which was at the front of the missile compartment. On the way, he picked up one of the gas masks designed for defense against nuclear, biological, and chemical weapons.

In the washroom, Kurlgunn checked to make sure the cleaning mop was there. Then he put on the gas mask and waited.

Only the pneumonic form is passed directly from person to person, he reminded himself, *and Hereford doesn't have it. On the other hand, Long and Eng think he somehow caused Orbison to develop the pneumonic form, but that's just their dumb theory. I wonder how the bubonic and septicemic forms are usually transmitted. In contaminated water?*

Two volunteers brought Hereford in on a stretcher.

"Put him down and get out," Kurlgunn ordered.

Hereford's hands and feet were completely black now, shriveled and lifeless. His black nose had fallen flat beneath his filthy surgical mask, and the creeping blackness was beginning to take his ears. Kurlgunn was amazed that the man was still alive.

When the volunteers were gone, Kurlgunn hung a sign on the outside of the door saying that the washroom was closed for cleaning. Then he locked the door, grabbed the mop, and stood over Hereford, trying to look into the victim's eyes without getting close enough for Hereford to reach out and touch him. It wasn't easy—there was barely enough room for Hereford to stretch out on the floor. Kurlgunn would rather not have been confined in such a small space with the plague, but he figured the washroom would be easy to clean up after this session. He also figured its walls were less likely to leak sounds than those of most compartments on the *Vermont*.

"What are . . . what are you doing?" Hereford's voice was weak, slurred, and hoarse.

"Did they give you a painkiller?" Kurlgunn asked.

"Morphine," Hereford croaked.

"We'll just have to work around that," Kurlgunn said. "I'll only ask you this once. Who are you working for?"

"What?" Hereford said.

Kurlgunn edged back between two tiny stainless steel sink basins, maximizing his distance from Hereford. Then he leaned over and shoved the top of the long mop handle against the swollen red bubo on the left side of Hereford's neck, the one that had not yet ruptured.

Hereford shrieked in pain and twisted his head away.

"Shut up!" Kurlgunn whacked him across the mouth with the mop handle.

Hereford cried out again.

Kurlgunn spun the mop around and mashed the dirty bundle of strings against Hereford's face to muffle him. "Are you going to be quiet?"

Hereford nodded.

Kurlgunn withdrew the mop.

Hereford sobbed as quietly as he could.

Keeping his voice down, Kurlgunn said, "You fooled that rookie corpsman. Somehow you even fooled Eng. But you can't fool me. I know what it means when plague breaks out on a warship. It's a biological weapon, isn't it? You carried it on board in your own body to make sure it was undetectable, like a suicide bomber. You and Orbison both. *Didn't you?*"

"No, no, no!" Hereford wept.

Holding his portable respirator in place, Kurlgunn stepped on Hereford's mouth to smother his screams. He jabbed the top of the mop handle into the bloody gauze dressing covering the ruptured bubo on the right side of Hereford's neck. He shoved so hard that the dressing was forced down into the wound. Then he twisted the mop back and forth.

Hereford blacked out.

Kurlgunn stepped back against the door, trying to control his fast breathing and resist the urge to pull off the infuriating gas mask. He caught a glimpse of himself in the mirror above a sink. His tiny, outward-tilted ears had turned red, and his black crew cut was wet with sweat. But his pale gray eyes looked satisfactorily calm, without any traces of fear.

For many years, Kurlgunn had trained himself in various forms of physical self-discipline. Now the investment was paying off by controlling his nerves and the atavistic instinct to pity his victim. But he couldn't stop worrying that someone would knock on the door while he was waiting for Hereford to come around.

Kurlgunn knew he was committing a terrible act if Hereford was innocent. Even if Hereford was guilty, he was sure he could be court-martialed for torturing the pathetic traitor. Convincing Hereford to turn over his handlers could be a major intelligence coup, but Kurlgunn knew better than to expect any thanks, especially if witnesses were listening outside the washroom. At the very least, he'd get a dishonorable discharge, which would be worse in some ways than a firing squad.

If that happens, I will have given my life for my country.

That thought almost made Kurlgunn call off the interrogation. He had no desire to sacrifice himself for Uncle Sam, who had left him in the care of his drug-abusing, mentally ill whore of a mother until he escaped at age thirteen. Kurlgunn had entered the military to get away from the civilian world—its undisciplined squalor, dissipating decadence, ambiguous power structure, and ass-kissing, backstabbing phoniness. He had not joined to do favors for the United States government or to become a martyr.

Hereford was beginning to come to. Kurlgunn watched him weakly squirm and grimace.

Damn it, he's bound to die within another day. If he's guilty, and I fail to get the truth out of him now, the opportunity will be lost forever. So will the opportunity to punish the motherfucker for ruining everything on the eve of my own command.

When Hereford opened his eyes, Kurlgunn brandished the mop handle. Keeping his voice low and menacing, he said, "I want to know who did this, and I want to know why. Why the *Vermont*? Why this run? I know you lied to Eng and Long. If you lie to me, I'll hurt you so badly you'll look back on this part with nostalgia."

Hereford resumed feebly sobbing. Kurlgunn could hardly make out what he said next. It sounded like, "I didn't catch it on purpose."

"How did you catch it, then?"

"I don't know!" Hereford wailed.

Kurlgunn barely resisted the urge to break the mop handle in half. *Goddamn it!* Hereford sounded sincere, and it was hard to imagine a spy resisting torture while dying of bubonic plague. Could an enemy operative have infected Hereford and Orbison without their knowledge? That would be one way for the real perpetrators to make sure their carriers didn't squeal or back out.

"Were you given any injections just before this run?"

"No," Hereford wept.

"Were you pricked or scratched by anything, like an umbrella or a pencil?"

"I don't . . . think so."

"I want to know everywhere you went between the time you got back from California and the time you boarded the *Vermont*."

"I went home to pack. Then to the Spirit . . . Tender."

"Then where?"

Hereford didn't answer.

Kurlgunn brandished the mop handle.

"Okay—don't! I went to the Pine Ridge Motel."

"Why?"

"I was with a girl."

"You're married."

"I know. Please don't tell."

"*Please don't tell?* What do you care? You're dying!"

Kurlgunn despised adulterers. He would have had no qualms about flipping a switch that gassed them all. He was pretty sure his wife cheated on him while he was at sea, although he had never managed to catch her, despite repeated efforts.

"Did you tell the corpsman about your little rendezvous?"

"No."

"You should have. What happened at the motel?"

"We had sex."

Kurlgunn made a mental note to ask Chris and Eng if plague could be transmitted sexually. "Without a condom?" he asked.

"No. I had one with me."

"What happened next?"

"She smoked a cigar."

"Did you have one too?"

"No. I hate cigar smoke."

"Then what?"

"We watched some TV . . . went to sleep."

"What's the name of your mistress?"

"She . . . I don't remember."

Kurlgunn poised the mop handle to stab a bandaged bubo on the front of Hereford's right hip. "Don't you lie to me, sailor!"

"I swear!" Hereford moaned. "I'd just met her."

That fanned the flames of Kurlgunn's suspicion to a new height. "Did she scratch you with her fingernails or do anything else that seemed strange?"

"No. She . . . we started doing it, and there were bugs in the bed. I know she saw them, but she kept going. Most girls can't stand bugs. I guess she was too turned on to care."

"What kind of bugs?"

"I don't know. Little black things. Bedbugs, I guess."

"Did any of them bite you?"

"Yeah," Hereford slurred, "a lot."

Kurlgunn made another mental note to ask if plague could be transmitted by bedbugs. "Was Kyle Orbison at the motel that night, by any chance?"

"Yes," Hereford said. "So was Tumor."

"Did they have sex with the whore too?"

"She was not a whore."

"Did they?"

"Of course not. They had their own girls."

Kurlgunn couldn't think of anything else to ask. The thing to do now was tell Eng and Long about the secret assignations at the Pine Ridge Motel and see what they thought. But how could he do that without revealing the methods he'd used to extract the information from Hereford? He could wait until Hereford died, but what if Long needed to ask him more questions?

Kurlgunn decided to think it over during his daily kung fu workout, which he never skipped for anything, not even the plague. Keeping his voice down, he said,

"We're done here, you stupid little fuck. If you tell anyone about this"—he waved the mop over Hereford's ghastly face—"I'll come back and stab you with it a thousand times. Got it?"

Hereford nodded weakly.

Chapter 33

.

Chris woke to the sensation of a hand grabbing his shoulder. He shot upright, his heart pounding hard. For the second time, his bald head cracked against Cheever's rack. The pain made him see multicolored geometric shapes for a few seconds, but he managed not to yell.

The hand was still gripping his shoulder, its sharp fingers digging into his flesh. Chris jerked open his curtain and saw that the gloved hand belonged to Gene Kurlgunn, who was wearing a gas mask.

"We have to talk," Kurlgunn hissed.

Chris followed the XO to the Goat Locker. It felt as if he had just fallen asleep. Looking at his watch, he saw that the feeling was accurate.

Eng and Captain Scott were there, both looking hungover.

Scott said, "Park your carcass, Doc."

Chris gladly complied. His heart rate was just now returning to normal. He could still feel the impression from Kurlgunn's fingers on his shoulder.

"I'm sorry we had to run you out of your rack so soon," Scott said. "Mr. Kurlgunn thinks the *Vermont* has been attacked with a biological weapon after all."

"*What?*" Chris gasped. *Oh, God, what have I missed? Or is Kurlgunn just being paranoid?*

Kurlgunn took over. "Maurice Hereford just confessed something to me that he wanted to get off his chest before he dies. It made me suspect he and Orbison were deliberately infected by female operatives posing as submariner groupies."

Chris leaned on the table to support his heavy upper body and listened as Kurlgunn repeated what Hereford had told him in the washroom.

When Kurlgunn mentioned the bedbugs, Chris shouted, "Bedbugs! Was Hereford sure they were bedbugs?"

"Don't interrupt me, Long. He said they were little black things."

"Let me guess," Chris said. "They bit him and hopped around a lot."

"He said they bit. How did you know?"

"Because Tumor told me about *his* trip to the motel that night. He didn't tell me Hereford was there, but I think he did mention that Orbison came along. Anyway, Tumor's bed had fleas in it."

"Son of a bitch," Eng whispered.

"What?" Kurlgunn asked.

"Fleas can carry plague," Eng explained. "If a flea sucks the blood of an infected rodent, *Yersinia pestis* will proliferate in the flea's gut until its digestive system is plugged. Then if the flea bites a human and tries to suck blood, it's so full of bacteria that it regurgitates the *Yersinia* cells into the new host's bloodstream. That's how humans actually catch plague from rodents or cats. It's the transmission pathway that leads to the bubonic and septicemic syndromes."

Chris was bent over, squeezing the top of his bruised head with one strong hand. "Shit! Damn it! I can't believe I didn't remember the fleas as soon as we realized it was plague. Tumor told me about them the night I came aboard, but so much happened between then and the first time plague came up, and I've been so damn worn out, I just . . . I'm sure I would have remembered if Tumor had gotten sick along with Orbison and Hereford, or if he'd told me the other beds had fleas in them too, which I'm sure they did. Oh, shit, shit, shit!"

Kurlgunn prodded Chris's shoulder. "Watch your mouth, Long. Whatever you're talking about, the damage is done."

Chris tried to remember how many days into this cursed voyage they were. He couldn't figure it out. He had long ago lost track of which watch it was, much less whether it was day or night on the surface. The back-to-back marathons in the sick bays, these grueling meetings, the irregular meals, the brief, fitful, interrupted naps—it had all blended together by now into a dizzying, numbing, never-ending nightmare.

"Cigar!" Chris shouted. "Damn it!"

"What about a cigar?" Kurlgunn asked.

"Orbison woke up just before he died, and he said one word: *cigar*. Pigpen and I thought he wanted a last cigar, but he must have been trying to tell us how he got infected. He must have figured it out. Hereford said his girl smoked a cigar. So did Tumor. How many women smoke cigars? It can't be a coincidence."

"I thought you said the men caught plague from flea bites," Kurlgunn said. "How could they have caught it because of their whores smoking cigars?"

"Peer pressure," Eng said with a trace of a wry smile. "It's a killer."

Chris tried to laugh and almost coughed. "Tumor told me his girl tried to get him to smoke a cigar, but he wouldn't do it. You said Hereford turned down the cigar too, right?"

"That's what he told me," Kurlgunn said.

Chris was lolling back in his chair now, resting his head on its back. He felt a need to stretch his tense muscles, but the urge to not move at all was even stronger. "Well, I'll bet a whole box of Havana's best that Orbison took the bait, and that's why he came down with the pneumonic form. Hereford probably got the bubonic and septicemic forms because he caught his infection from flea bites instead of a cigar."

"The tobacco leaves were probably coated with a special slurry of *Yersinia* cells," Eng added. "The bacteria could have been aerosolized and drawn into the victim's lungs when he inhaled through the cigar."

Captain Scott had been listening to the speculation with the same expression of tormented indecisiveness he had worn during the previous meeting. He suddenly said, "I've never heard such a load of elephant crap! Enemy operatives attacking with a bioweapon would use a bomb or some kind of sprayer, not trick cigars and trained fleas."

Kurlgunn sighed bitterly. "Actually, it's ingenious."

"I concur with the XO," Eng said. "The enemy must have predicted—correctly—that we would not recognize such unconventional methods of attack in time to abort this run. Or perhaps those were the most effective methods they've developed. *Yersinia pestis* is not easy to disseminate—explosions and sunlight kill the bacteria, even in the freeze-dried form. Dispersing infected fleas is more reliable. The Japanese dropped millions of plague-ridden fleas from airplanes over China during World War II. They managed to infect and kill quite a few Chinese."

"But why use fleas and cigars, both?" Chris asked.

"For the same reason they tried to hit three crewmen instead of just one," Eng said. "Redundancy, in case one method failed. I'll bet the copulation was not just intended to lure the targets into position for the fleas. The women had probably swabbed *Yersinia* into their vaginas."

"Three separate methods used on three different victims," Chris mused. "They must have wanted to make *damn* sure plague would break out on the *Vermont*."

"What about Tumor?" Scott asked. "If he was one of the three targets, why doesn't he have plague?"

"He thinks he does," Chris said, "but that's beside the point. It just means all three inoculation methods failed in his case, and I know why. He said he wouldn't smoke the cigar because he was afraid it would make him sick. He wouldn't have sex because he was afraid the girl had an STD—good call there, eh? And he went out to sleep in the car as soon as he saw the fleas, because he's scared to death of insects."

"I'll be an orangutan's uncle," Scott said.

Kurlgunn raked one hand over his black crew-cut hair and clenched it into a fist. "We have to find out who did this."

Chris was wondering whether the enemy behind this attack was the same as the enemy the *Vermont* had been sent here to possibly wage nuclear war against. "Who would have three female operatives willing to infect themselves with plague? The women could have been vaccinated and taking prophylactic antibiotics, but there would still be some risk of such huge exposures overwhelming those defenses."

"Maybe we should start by asking why, instead of who," said Captain Scott. "Assuming this was an attack and not a natural outbreak—which hasn't been proven, by the way—the fact that they chose to hit this particular run suggests our armed forces have a major intelligence leak."

"Why's that, sir?"

Scott leaned forward and took a deep, weary breath, massaging his chest. "I doubt any group that's organized enough to pull off such a sophisticated attack would waste it on a random target. The turkeys must have known they'd only get one shot, because we'll develop countermeasures against the same kind of attack after this one. And they must have known there will be hell to pay if the U.S. military ever finds out who they are. So whatever their objective was, it must have been terribly important to them. My guess is that they knew the *Vermont*'s secret orders, and their objective was to stop us from carrying them out. If that's the case, who knows what's going to be waiting for us in the Gulf, because they know we're coming."

"We're really going to take a Trident into the Persian

Gulf?'' Chris asked. Normally, Tridents were never driven into hostile waters, and the Gulf was almost too shallow for such a large submarine.

Kurlgunn gave Captain Scott a contemptuous glare.

Scott blushed. "I assume Corpsman Long will keep that tidbit of information to himself."

No wonder it seems like we've been running at flank speed forever, Chris thought. By sea, the Persian Gulf was about the most distant point on Earth from Bangor, Washington. Not only would they have to cross the Pacific and Indian oceans; they would have to dip below the equator almost to Australia to get around the dense islands and shallow seas off Southeast Asia.

Eng said, "Perhaps they just wanted to incapacitate the crew so they could board the *Vermont* and steal some of our technology. Imagine what our sonar suite would be worth to an aspiring sea power."

"Or maybe they want to steal the nuclear warheads," Chris said.

Scott spread his knobby hands on the table. "Gentlemen, I suggest we assume for now that their objective was to stop us from carrying out the present operation, since the implication of a high-level intelligence leak makes that the worst-case scenario."

"So what do we do now?" Chris asked.

All eyes turned toward Captain Scott.

The captain weakly shrugged, smoothing down his thick red mustache. "We carry on as best we can."

Chris sat up straight, crossing his thick arms over his chest. "Sir, shouldn't we at least try to notify STRATCOM so they can start looking for the spy? Who knows what other operations he may have compromised."

Scott's bushy reddish gray eyebrows came together. "For the hundredth time, Long, *we will not break radio silence*! If we don't let the enemy find out whether they managed to infect us or not, it may deter them from trying to finish whatever they started by softening us up with germs."

Kurlgunn unclenched his muscular jaws long enough to add, "They may be out there right now, just waiting for us to expose our position so they can move in for the kill."

"And the mere fact that they've attacked a boomer suggests they intend to do something somewhere that could provoke the launch of our nuclear missiles," Scott said, "so maintaining our launch readiness is more important now than ever."

Chris had thought of an argument that he'd failed to put forth the last time he'd recommended they turn back or call for help. "Captain, if this op is really so crucial, surely the Navy has sent another Trident for redundancy. If we turn back now, the other sub can still carry on."

"There may be a backup," Scott said. "Or we may be the backup. I honestly don't know. But what makes you think the other boomer doesn't have the same situation we do, or worse? If the enemy knew about our orders, they knew about the other sub as well. They probably hit it the same way they hit us."

Chris hadn't thought about that. It made sense. "Sir, we're sitting in the most powerful war machine ever built, and we've been attacked in the most evil, underhanded way imaginable, and you're saying there's absolutely nothing we can do about it?"

Scott stood up with a groan, signaling the end of the meeting. The fifty-one-year-old captain looked as stiff and weary as a centenarian. "That's exactly what I'm saying, Corpsman Long."

Chapter 34

Chris marched into the wardroom to find Tumor. He knew it was possible that Tumor just hadn't thought to mention that Maurice Hereford was one of the three crewmen who'd had a wild time at the Pine Ridge Motel, but he suspected that Hereford had sworn Tumor to secrecy.

He found Tumor sitting on the floor with a large artist's sketch pad propped on his upraised knees. Apparently there were no crises at the moment, so Tumor was occupying himself by drawing while watching over the patients. His concentration was so intense that he didn't seem to notice Chris coming in.

Before he could start interrogating Tumor, Chris saw the drawing, and it took his breath away. It depicted Kyle Orbison's flabby body lying open on a torpedo rack. A hulking figure dressed in makeshift biohazard garb was stooping over the bloody cadaver, aiming his headlamp into the chest cavity. The examiner's eyes appeared to glow with fear and determination.

"Is that me?"

"Of course," Tumor said with sad eyes. "You can't see me in this frame because I'm laid out on the floor."

"Have you done any other drawings?"

Tumor flipped back through several pages that contained poignant renderings of the patients. There were also portraits of arguing officers that captured their desperation. "I'll stop drawing if you think I'm wasting time, Doc."

"No, no. As long as none of the patients need you, keep it up. It's our only visual record of what's happening here."

Cameras were allowed on American subs, as long as no pictures were taken in the secret engineering spaces back aft, but none of the men on this run had happened to bring a camera.

Tumor resumed drawing.

An announcement over the 1MC by Kurlgunn paged Tumor to the CPO lounge. Tumor dashed out of the wardroom before Chris could warn him what he was probably in for.

There was no one else to watch the patients, so Chris stayed in the wardroom. He remained on his sore feet so he wouldn't fall asleep. When that began to fail, he tried standing on one leg at a time, which really made his heels ache.

Tumor finally returned. He looked extra pale and had a greenish halo around his mouth. Without looking at Chris, he picked up his sketch pad and slid to the floor, hugging it. He said, "I'm sorry, Doc," and burst into tears.

"Are you okay to watch the patients?" Chris asked.

Tumor nodded.

Chris fled from the wardroom.

He had almost made it to his beckoning rack when an unusual sound caught his ear. Submariners were trained to listen for any new noises being emitted by their boats that an enemy sonar might be able to detect. At first he thought the source was mechanical. Then he realized it was the sound of a man with congested lungs hyperventilating.

The rhythmic *whoosh-hiss* was not loud, but the cavernous missile compartment was filled with its echoes. Chris tried turning his head from side to side, but he still couldn't discern the direction of its source. Finally he thought he had it, but when he looked behind the missile tube, no one was there.

Am I hearing things? Chris figured he was past the level of exhaustion where that could become a real possibility.

He searched around the thick burnt orange tubes, homing in on the sound by its volume, until he saw a quivering shadow. He crept around a tube to see what was casting the shadow. A small man was huddled on the deck with his back to the tube, hugging his knees. His coveralls were soaked with sweat.

Chris took a step back from the ghastly apparition. The man looked as if he had drowned and come back from the dead. It took Chris several seconds to recognize him.

"Freud?"

The formerly handsome ensign slowly looked up at Chris, still hyperventilating. Sweat was beaded on his face, which had turned from its normal Polynesian bronze to greenish beige. His eyes were bloodshot and swollen. His elaborate coiffure had melted into a hanging mop of sweat-soaked strings.

"I think . . . I think I might be sick," Freud said.

Chris was glad he had not yet removed the mask he'd been wearing in the wardroom. He ran his fingers along its edges, making sure the tape still formed an airtight seal. "Are you able to get up?"

Freud shook his head. "I had . . . an accident . . . in my pants."

"Aside from that, are you able to get up? We have to get you to one of the sick bays."

"No, it's just the crud," Freud moaned.

Chris remembered the extra mask he'd been carrying around in his pocket for this kind of emergency. The memory had been delayed only slightly by his thick fog of fatigue. He pulled out the mask and handed it to Freud. "Here, put—"

"Get away from me!" Freud leaped to his feet and disappeared around the missile tube.

Damn! I thought he was too sick to get up!

Chris ran after Freud, but his worn-out reflexes took more than twice their usual time to kick in. By the time he rounded the tube, Freud was sprinting forward in the central aisle.

He must be spewing out germs by the billions. I can't let him get to the crowded areas in the forward compartment!

Despite his fatigue, Chris launched himself forward with a tremendous burst of power. A subconscious part of his brain took over—not an instinct, but the deepest level of training. The task at hand was so familiar that his body could perform it automatically, regardless of his physical and mental state. All he had to remember was that he wasn't wearing a helmet or shoulder pads.

His thick arms pumped like pistons. His lungs drew in many times their usual volume of breath. His massive legs slammed his feet against the deck so hard that everything in the missile compartment seemed to shake.

Three seconds later, Freud was almost to the doorway but Chris was closing on him, zooming past the big orange missile tubes so fast that they blurred in his vision. Freud was athletic, but he was also sick, and Chris had a much longer stride. Ten feet from the door, Chris executed the final lunge and sailed through the air. He tackled Freud around the shoulders, and they crashed down on the deck together.

When his right side slammed against the steel deck, Chris noticed that it felt rather different from a grassy football field. The pain didn't shock him as much as the noise. He was used to fretting over slammed doors, banging toilet lids, and dropped wrenches, much less a thundering high-speed tackle.

As soon as they landed, he let go of Freud and rolled away. The last thing he wanted to do was hold on to a struggling plague victim. If the diminutive ensign tried to bolt again, Chris figured he could lunge and grab him.

That turned out not to be necessary.

Freud curled into a ball and began coughing uncontrollably, drooling greenish mucus onto the deck. Chris was having trouble getting enough air through his mask to catch his breath, but he managed to scramble away from Freud's face. He stood up, wobbling from a head rush. He grabbed an overhead pipe and held on until he regained his balance.

What do I do now? Try to tie this mask on to him? What if he fights me? What if he tears my mask off or gets phlegm in my eyes? But I can't just let him keep spraying germs into the air!

Chris let go of the pipe and leaned over Freud. "Sir, you have to put this mask on."

"Fuck you!" Freud screamed between coughs.

Chris felt panic counteracting gravity. *Every cough could mean a man's death.* He kicked Freud's left thigh. "Put the mask on, sir!"

Freud rolled over, glaring daggers at Chris. Then he coughed with his mouth closed, his cheeks bulging.

Fresh adrenaline exploded inside Chris as he realized Freud was about to spit on him. He grabbed the back of the ensign's head, curling his gloved fingers in the sweaty hair, and slammed it against the deck.

Freud went limp.

Chris sprang backward, falling on his behind, heaving for breath through his mask.

Freud still wasn't moving. A small puddle of bright red blood was expanding on the deck around his right temple.

Oh, God; he's not dead. He can't be dead!

The sight of another man lying unconscious by the work of his own hands hit Chris like a bullet in the back. It filled him with such intense déjà vu and resurrected self-loathing that his own labored breathing stopped for a moment.

Freud resumed breathing in quick gurgling wheezes, but he did not appear to wake up.

I swore I would never beat anyone up again. How did this happen? Is this what will always happen when my instincts take over?

In the next second, Chris realized that it had been self-defense this time, and that he had stopped as soon as he was out of danger. This time he had done exactly the right thing, by instinct alone. *Yes! Maybe I should start trusting my instincts again!*

"Oh, my Lord! What did you just do to that poor soul?"

Chris whirled around, still sitting on the floor. Oral was standing behind him. The COB's bulging brown eyes were riveted on Freud's motionless form. His thick lips hung open in an expression of shock.

Chris stood up, fighting another head rush.

Oral backed away, his eyes full of fear.

At first Chris assumed Oral was backing away from Freud, who was obviously still spewing germs. Then he realized that the big, ungainly COB was afraid of him, not Freud.

"I saw you smash his head." Oral's voice was tight with apprehension.

"I didn't mean to, COB. He was going to spit on me!"

"That's crazy." Oral backed off some more, then turned and ran, shaking the deck with each step.

Chris thrust his palms up at the overhead and yelled, *"What the hell?"*

He tied the spare mask over Freud's mouth and nose and carried the limp officer down to the torpedo room.

A volunteer named Sean O'Clair bandaged Freud's head. The sick ensign lay faceup, motionless, like a corpse in a casket. His face was completely slack. The bandage covered his right eye, but his left eye was open, apparently staring at the overhead.

"Freud?"

No response.

Chris waved a hand over the open eye. The eye didn't move, but a few seconds later it blinked. Except for the blinking eye, Freud appeared to be in a deep coma.

Chris glanced at his watch. *Damn it, I have to go to sleep.*

As Chris was getting up to leave, Freud spoke in a cold, detached voice. "You should not have brought me in here."

Chapter 35

This time it was Tumor who shook Chris awake. "Sorry, Doc. The captain and XO want to see you in the CPO lounge again."

Chris quietly crawled out and put on his shoes, noticing that Tumor looked beyond exhaustion.

He glanced at his watch. Two hours of sleep. He remembered hearing distant coughing the whole time. He wasn't sure whether he'd been awake or dreaming it.

Chris staggered to the CPO lounge, rubbing his raw eyes.

When he knocked on the open door, Captain Scott said, "Close the door and grab a seat, son." His tone sounded ominous.

Chris obeyed. He stared at Scott's lighthouse mug, trying to focus his eyes and avoid yawning as he waited for the captain or XO to speak. The three of them were alone. Tumor had gone down to tend the patients in the torpedo room.

Please don't let this be about Freud.

Scott leaned toward him with a sad, sympathetic smile. "Chris, I want to apologize for . . . Damn it, I know I haven't been providing as much support as you might have needed. And I know you've been under tremendous stress."

Chris appreciated that, but he worried about what it was leading up to. "Is that all, sir?"

"Not quite," Kurlgunn said. "We'd like you to explain what just happened between you and Freud."

"What did Oral tell you already?"

The officers exchanged a glance. "We'd like to hear your version," Kurlgunn said.

Chris told the truth. He didn't trust these two to judge him fairly, but he had to get this situation resolved so he could get back to sleep for a few hours, then back to work. He just hoped they wouldn't confine him to his rack under guard. That was the standard procedure for incarcerating prisoners on a submarine, since there was no room for a brig.

"So you admit that you slammed Freud's head against the deck hard enough to knock him unconscious?" Scott asked.

"Yes, sir. But I didn't mean to do it so hard."

Scott glanced at Chris's mammoth shoulders, which bulged with muscle even inside his baggy coveralls. "Son, I find it hard to believe that you don't know your own strength."

"Captain, it all happened so fast, *and I'm so damn tired,* and . . . and . . ."

Scott angrily scratched his thick red mustache and rubbed his red stubble, which he hadn't shaved since they'd gotten under way. "What a rat-fucking mess," he muttered.

"Sir, do you think I'll be court-martialed if I get home alive?"

"Of course!" Scott replied.

Chris silently sat hunched over the table, leaning on his arms, which were tightly crossed even though his thick muscles made it uncomfortable.

Scott groaned. "Look, son, for all I know, you deserve a medal. And I know there's a shitload of mitigating circumstances. But the fact remains that you attacked and seriously injured an officer. Do you think he's going to die?"

"Yes, but not from the concussion I gave him! I don't know how he kept the screenings from catching him, but he let his pneumonia go so long that I doubt the antibiotics can reverse it."

"If he dies, his body will be vital evidence at your court-martial," Scott said. "We'll keep it in the chill box until a medical examiner can determine the cause of death. Hopefully that will clear you of a murder charge."

Chris lowered his head until his face was just inches from the tabletop. He supported its weight with one hand while gripping his bare scalp with the other.

Murder?

Scott sighed. "Meanwhile, procedure calls for me to relieve you of all duties until—"

Chris leaped to his feet. "Christ, sir, you can't do that! Your crew is dying! I have to . . ."

Kurlgunn had jumped up to stand between Chris and Scott, reaching his full height at the same time Chris did. Seeing the look in Kurlgunn's lead gray eyes, Chris felt a sudden conviction that if he ever tangled with the XO physically, he would lose, and he might lose more than the fight. Chris hadn't felt that kind of apprehension about a potential adversary since grade school.

Of course, he had no intention of threatening either of these officers in any way, and he hated Kurlgunn for thinking he might.

Scott held up a hand. "Relax, Gene. You too, Chris. As I was about to say, our situation obviously makes it impractical to relieve you of duty, so for now we will assume that what you did to Freud was justified, as you say it was. Just bear in mind that if something similar happens again, it will more than double the odds against you at your court-martial."

Kurlgunn stabbed the air with a forefinger, gesturing for Chris to sit down.

Chris obeyed. "Aye, sir. And what exactly would you prefer me to do if another man goes berserk when he gets sick and tries to run all over the ship?"

Scott thought for a moment. "Do exactly what you say you did with Freud. Just try to minimize the brutality."

Chris closed his eyes and clenched his big fists under the edge of the table.

"Look, I know it's a shitty deal," Scott said. "But somehow we have to balance the victims' rights with everyone else's. And above all, we have to maintain order on this boat."

Chris opened his eyes, trying not to glower. "I also have to keep myself alive as long as possible, sir. Otherwise, who's going to play medic?"

"Eng probably could," Kurlgunn said.

"Eng is still doing some research in the pharmacy, sir, but now that he knows it's plague, he can't even go into the isolation rooms."

Kurlgunn smirked. "What do you mean, 'can't'?"

"I saw him try, twice. He started shaking and ran back out."

"How does knowing that it's plague affect you?" Scott asked.

Chris yawned in spite of everything, then shook his head and bounced his calves up and down a few times. "When we first ID'd it, I was more scared than ever. That's probably everybody's gut reaction to plague. But plague is treatable with antibiotics, and this could have turned out to be a pathogen that wasn't."

"The antibiotics *are* working," Kurlgunn said, "right?"

"Actually, no, but they may have just not kicked in yet. We'll know after a couple more watches."

"Okay," Scott said. "Dismissed."

"Aye, sir."

Practically sleepwalking, Chris went to the pharmacy and let Pigpen screen him. His temperature was ninety-eight point one.

A minute later, he crawled into his rack with a sigh of relief. The thin mattress felt so good, it almost made him smile, in spite of the multiple dooms that seemed in store for him.

An announcement came over the 1MC: "Attention, all hands. This is the XO. It has come to my attention that some men may be tempted to resist going to the sick bays after they have come down with plague. Since any breach of quarantine may threaten our mission, disobeying orders from the corpsman and his volunteers will be prosecuted as treason. The captain has authorized Corpsman Long to use whatever force he deems necessary to quarantine everyone who may be infected. If you have any symptoms, do not jeopardize the lives of your shipmates and your own future freedom by resisting quarantine. That is all."

Hardly aware of his actions, Chris took out Paul Treacle's cigarette lighter and gripped it in his right fist, wrapping his left hand around his right one.

Now I don't just have to pretend I'm a real doctor; I also have to play the enforcer and terrorize the whole crew into submission—then get court-martialed if I hurt anyone.

Chris's primary reason for joining the Silent Service had been to make a few lifelong friends. Now it would be no surprise if what was left of the crew hated him by the end of this cursed run.

Chapter 36

"I'm not asleep," Chris whispered when Tumor pulled back his curtain and shook him again. This time he'd only been in his rack for a few minutes.

"Freud is missing," Tumor whispered. "We're getting the whole dang crew up to look for him."

Chris put his shoes back on, noticing they were still warm. "I left him in the torpedo room. Somebody's always watching the patients in there. He couldn't have just walked out."

"Actually . . . I think he did, Doc."

They were soon walking swiftly forward through the missile compartment. Chris tried not to limp. After spending a few minutes off his feet, he could feel how sore they were.

He glanced at Tumor. The country boy's acne-ridden face was obscured by a mask and the broad green tape surrounding it, but his eyes looked utterly miserable.

Tumor spoke in a low, confessional tone. "I fell asleep, Doc. One of them coughing woke me up, and Freud was gone."

"Did he do or say anything before . . . that might suggest what he's up to?" Chris was having trouble finishing his sentences. *God, I've never been this tired!*

"No. He was writing something; a letter to his wife, I reckon."

"Tumor, I don't think you should worry. About falling

asleep, I mean. You can't be in as much trouble as I'm in."

They ran into Kurlgunn and Eng on the stairs. Kurlgunn was barking orders at a cluster of chiefs who were wearing gas masks, telling them to spread out and search every compartment. As Chris and Tumor approached, Kurlgunn dismissed Tumor with a shooing gesture. "Get lost, sleepy."

Tumor flinched and moped away.

When Tumor was out of earshot, leaving Chris alone with Kurlgunn and Eng, the XO lowered his voice and said, "Freud may be working for *them*."

"Who, sir?"

"Whoever hit us with plague, stupid!"

All Chris cared about was finding Freud so he could get back to bed, but he still noticed Kurlgunn calling him stupid. *If you think I'm stupid now, just wait until I've been kept awake for a few more hours.*

"If any officer in this crew could be turned, it would be Freud," Kurlgunn said.

"Why do you say that, sir?"

The XO grimaced, flexing his ropy neck muscles. "You should see all the expensive junk at his house—swimming pool, two-thousand-dollar barbecue grill. He may have been selling secrets, like the Walkers."

"You know how Freud is always asking personal questions," Eng added. "In my opinion, he just has an insatiable appetite for gossip, but it could be more than that. He does love to court danger. I know he's into gambling and drag racing."

"Sir, Freud didn't believe he had plague when I caught him. Maybe he still doesn't. Maybe he's just hiding out to avoid being kept in a sick bay with the other victims."

Kurlgunn nodded. "Maybe, but we can't afford to take chances with a possible traitor on board."

"What are you afraid he's going to do, sir?"

"I'm not *afraid* of *anything*, Long. He might try to

scram the reactor. I've already posted armed guards to make sure he doesn't get near the RCP." RCP stood for reactor control panel.

"He could blow the main ballast tanks," Eng said.

"That's covered too," Kurlgunn replied.

Chris tried hard to think through the thickening fog of sleep deprivation. "What about the active sonar? He could fire off a ping to tell an enemy where we are."

The Tridents originally had no active sonar, which was useful only when attacking an enemy vessel. Recently, however, several Tridents had been refitted so the fleet could begin adapting to new missions in the post–Cold War world. Some had been converted to carry tactical cruise missiles instead of ICBMs. Others, including the *Vermont,* had been given an active sonar rig.

Kurlgunn stepped forward and grabbed a hand mike from the overhead. "Sonar, XO. Post a guard to keep Freud out of the sonar shack."

Eng was searching the engine room when he caught a whiff of something that smelled like human feces. He knew bad smells had a way of projecting themselves within the confines of a submarine. But he didn't think it could have come from someone passing gas—it was too strong, too acrid, and it wasn't dissipating as recirculated air blew into the room. He also doubted it was from the heads, the sanitary tanks, or any of their piping, which were nowhere nearby.

Eng glanced around at the watchstanders in the large, equipment-packed engine room. None of them seemed to have noticed the foul odor.

Freud could have sneaked through here easily, Eng realized. All of the watchstanders were concentrating on their instruments, and the sound of soft footsteps would have been inaudible beneath the hum of the massive turbine engines and the reactor coolant recirculation pumps. The *Vermont* emitted hardly any interior noise to the ocean, because her internal decks were not directly attached to the hull—they were mounted on sparse, sound-insulating rubber bushings. Within the engineering spaces, however, the machinery noise was always loud.

Eng walked back and forth, sniffing the air. The foul odor was detectable in only one place. That explained why none of the engine room crew seemed to have noticed it.

He looked down. There was nothing obvious beneath the steel mesh deck separating the main and lower engine rooms that could explain the smell.

He looked up. Directly above him was the rear escape trunk, one of the three vertical access shafts designed to be used as airlocks during a deep-sea evacuation if the sub was ever sunk but not flooded. He noticed a narrow gap above the gasket of the heavy round hatch at the base of the shaft.

Eng felt a surge of dread. That hatch should have been securely shut and dogged.

He tiptoed up behind the nearest watchstander and placed his lips close to the man's ear so his whisper could be heard over the machinery. "Dundalk, put your console in a stable mode and leave the engine room quietly."

Looking confused, Dundalk started to say "aye, sir."

Eng shushed him with a bony forefinger held over his own lips, nodding toward the doorway.

Eng repeated the order for every watchstander who could leave his station without endangering the ship. When he got to the last one, he added, "Tell Boyd to come in here quietly. He's one of the men guarding the reactor."

Eng waited, watching the suspicious hatch.

Petty Officer Marc Boyd—a pudgy, brown-haired Utah Mormon—ran into the engine room, looking around. He was holding a short-barreled twelve-gauge shotgun. "Sir?" he whispered.

Eng pointed up at the hatch. "I think he's up there. Cover me while I open it."

Boyd squatted beneath the escape trunk, a little to one side, aiming his weapon upward.

Eng opened the hatch.

A folded piece of paper dropped onto the deck.

The foul odor abruptly grew stronger.

The escape trunk was dark until Eng reached up and flipped the overhead light switch.

The bright white fluorescents illuminated Freud's body. He was hanging from a noose tied to the dogging wheel of the hatch at the top of the shaft. His body was motionless, suspended in the center of the shaft with his back to the ladder. His eyes bulged from his gray face. He had taken off his mask. The tip of his tongue protruded between his blue lips. His bare feet were purple and swollen from blood that had drained into them.

"Jesus!" Boyd jumped up and stepped away from the hatch, covering his mouth and nose with one arm. There was no stench of decay, just the feces Freud's intestines had released at the moment of death.

Eng stooped and picked up the folded piece of paper with a bony, trembling hand.

Chapter 37

Chris woke to the sound submariners dread most: the roar of flooding. At first he thought it was another nightmare. Then he heard other men shouting and jumping out of their racks, and the collision alarm started shrieking.

He pulled on his Velcro-fastened shoes and ran from his berth, following the herd forward toward the flooding roar. "Hey, what's going on?"

"Don't know," Cheever yelled in front of him.

The sound of rushing water stopped, but the collision alarm kept sounding.

Then the alarm stopped.

The men halted and grew quiet, listening. The crowded passageway became eerily silent. Then Chris heard a *whoosh* followed by a faint gurgle.

"That's the escape trunk opening!" said someone behind him.

A few seconds later, Kurlgunn's voice boomed from the 1MC. "All hands, return to your watchstations. The ship is secure. Seaman Apprentice Michael L. Ashby has just cycled out through the forward escape trunk. Apparently he chose to desert his country and this crew by stealing one of the Steinke hoods and exiting the ship. With any luck, he will not reach the surface and give our position away. To ensure that this does not happen again, we will now descend to eight hundred feet and continue on our course."

Chris realized that the flooding sound had been seawater filling the escape trunk, raising its pressure to that of the surrounding ocean so its external hatch could be opened. Presuming submariners could withstand the rapid compression as the trunk flooded, followed by rapid decompression as they shot to the surface, they could theoretically escape from a sunken submarine with the aid of a Steinke hood, a specialized flotation device. Steinke hoods were designed to work in water as deep as three hundred feet, and survival remained a theoretical possibility down to six hundred feet.

Kurlgunn's announcement was almost as chilling to Chris as the news of Freud's suicide. The *Vermont* was making good speed at more than five hundred feet. In all likelihood, Seaman Ashby had been torn apart by the current as soon as the buoyant air inside his Steinke hood had lifted him out of the escape trunk. Even if he had survived the current, he would probably drown before reaching the surface.

As soon as he could get through the crowd, Chris staggered to the head, glancing at his watch. He'd slept for nine hours this time.

After relieving himself, he called all three of the sick bays to make sure there were no crises that needed his immediate attention. There weren't, so he went to the galley and hastily threw together a triple-decker ham and cheese sandwich. He figured there was no need to conserve food, since it looked as if this crew was going to either evacuate or perish long before any provisions except medical supplies began to run low.

It was between mealtimes. When he went to sit down in the mess, only one other man was there: Pigpen.

Chris saw that the crude sonarman was eating something that looked absurdly like a large rectangular block of coal. There were black streaks on his face and collar. His blond bird's nest of a mustache was now half black. There was even a thick black smudge on one of the bottle-bottom lenses in his eyeglasses. Yet he didn't appear to be eating recklessly. He seemed to be savoring each bite, chewing and swallowing with his eyes closed.

Chris went to a table on the opposite side of the mess. Surely Pigpen would not be offended, considering the need to minimize personal contact.

As he sat down, an announcement came over the 1MC: "Attention, all hands. This is the XO. We have just received an emergency action message. As of Zulu eighteen hundred, American cruise missiles and bombing sorties have destroyed every structure in the Islamic Republic of Iran that could have housed the Spear of Allah missiles in an upright, launch-ready position. Our analysts believe that most of the missiles survived and are being stored horizontally within warehouses, barns, bunkers, etcetera. The government of Iran has threatened to strike unspecified American targets if our ground forces invade. In a public broadcast at nineteen hundred, President Davis declared that if Iranian attacks on civilian targets cause mass casualties, the United States may respond with full nuclear retaliation. The armed forces are now at DEFCON 1. An Air Defense Emergency has been declared by the commander in chief, North American Aerospace Defense Command. All fleet ballistic missile submarines, including the *Vermont,* have been ordered to maintain an ultraquiet lineup and remain within ELF reception range. That is all." ELF meant extremely low frequency.

Chris chewed his now tasteless sandwich. As he ate, he couldn't help stealing glances at Pigpen. He'd realized that the disgusting sonarman's mysterious delicacy had to be a dark chocolate cake with dark chocolate icing.

Pigpen's eating gradually slowed until he stopped in midbite. He laid down his fork and pulled a crumpled surgical mask from a pocket, releasing a loud belch. He tied the mask on so tightly that the strings bit into his flabby jaws; then he walked to the garbage can and threw away the leftovers along with his plate and fork. Before leaving, he returned to his table and thoroughly cleaned up his mess with napkins and a bottle of bleach, one of several that Chris had ordered to be kept on the tables at all times.

Chris could contain his curiosity no longer. "Hey, where did you get the cake?"

"I made it."

"Just now?"

Pigpen nodded.

"Why?" Chris asked. He hoped Pigpen wasn't cracking. Despite his hygiene phobia, the music-hating sonarman had been Chris's first and most indefatigable volunteer, screening the entire crew again and again.

"I always wanted to try a cake like that," Pigpen explained. "Five times the normal cocoa."

Chris sat back, blinking. "Was it good?"

"Yes, it was."

If Pigpen had gone off the deep end, Chris needed to know. "Where are you going now? To rack out?"

"No, down to the torpedo room."

"Sean O'Clair has it covered," Chris said. "He doesn't need relief until twenty-two hundred."

Pigpen somberly shook his head. "I'm checking myself in, Doc. My temperature just hit a hundred, and I can feel it in my lungs."

Chris didn't know what to say.

"I guess germs aren't my best friends after all," Pigpen said. "But I gave the little fuckers a run for it, didn't I? Good luck, Doc."

Pigpen turned away and dawdled down the passage out of sight.

Chapter 38

Captain Scott walked into the enlisted mess with a bowl of cold bean sprouts. He sat down across the table from Chris and started pouring black pepper on the sprouts, mechanically pumping the shaker up and down.

Officers normally ate in the wardroom. Now that it was a sick bay, they ate with the crew.

"Morning, Doc."

Chris tried to conceal his anguish over Pigpen falling ill. "Morning, sir. Looks like you're eating healthy stuff."

The usual favorites of submariners were pizza, fried chicken, and sliders—hamburgers with so much grease that they just slid down the throat.

The irony of eating health food at a time like this didn't occur to Chris until after he'd spoken. To his relief, the captain did not appear to think Chris was making fun of him.

"Darlene got me into this wellness crap twenty years ago," Scott mumbled. "I can't stand normal food anymore."

"Sir, do you happen to know how many new cases showed up while I was racked out?"

"Six or seven. Three men died, including Maurice Hereford. How did you sleep?"

"Okay."

"Any nightmares?"

"A few. Captain, we're running out of clean air. We've been maintaining lowered pressure in the sick bays by pumping air from them to some of the compressed-air bottles. Meanwhile, we're bleeding clean air into the people tank from the other bottles to maintain atmospheric pressure in the rest of the sub. If we don't come to periscope depth and snorkel soon, all of our compressed air will have gone through the sick bays."

Scott sighed. "We may run out of sanity before we run out of air, Doc. Morale was on the bottom before Freud hanged himself. Now the men are clawing at the overhead. Just between you and me, I suspect most of them would choose to surface and abandon ship if they could, even knowing they'd be court-martialed for desertion, or eaten by sharks."

"Sir, have any other patients tried to leave the sick bays?"

"No. Gene posted armed guards inside all three of them. But there have been some other incidents. Two torpedomen—Greg Margulis and Bobby Ray Downy—got into a fistfight because Bobby Ray was coughing near Greg. It turned out Bobby Ray wasn't sick; he had just gone back to Shaft Alley and smoked an entire pack of cigarettes. Apparently he wanted to make sure he used up his stash before the end."

Scott did not look or sound sarcastic, only grim. Chris listened as he continued.

"Then Gale Drossi went around telling everybody this is just a drill and all the guys who are supposed to be dead are actually waiting inside the sick bays until it's over. After that, Hal Blevins waylaid Flash McCord over the eighty bucks Flash has owed him for the last two years. Hal got a broken finger and Flash got a sprained ankle."

"Christ, sir! Why didn't somebody wake me up?"

"Because I ordered them not to."

Chris wasn't sure how he should feel about that.

"Now Miguel Cervesu won't get out of his rack," Scott added. "He won't eat or use the head. Oral discovered he'd pissed on his mattress."

"Is he sick?"

"No fever," Scott said. "Oral finally got him talking, and he confessed that he killed his girlfriend about a year ago. She supposedly died in a car wreck; I remember it well. What he just told Oral was that they were having a fight and she fell down the stairs and broke her neck, so he put her body in the car and rammed an overpass piling. He said he'd meant it to be a suicide, but he forgot to take off his seat belt, so all he got was whiplash."

While Scott paused to eat, Chris thought about the significance of the captain telling him all of this, considering the huge difference in their ranks. He imagined this was the kind of conversation a captain would normally have with his XO when they were alone. Chris would have preferred to hear better news, but he enjoyed the captain's attention and implied respect. At the very least, it suggested that Scott trusted him, even after the incident with Freud.

"Did anything else happen while I was asleep that I should know about, sir?"

Scott nodded. "A poker game in the officers' study got out of hand. They started betting their houses. And you might ought to look at Benny Derocher, the jack of the dust." The jack of the dust was the crewman in charge of maintaining the sub's food inventory. "Pigpen found him collapsed, barely breathing, but he has no fever. He was wearing a dish towel over his mouth and nose that reeked of bleach. We figure he soaked the towel in bleach, hoping to kill airborne germs. Then he apparently kept breathing in the bleach until it about burned up his lungs."

My God, they definitely should have woken me for that.

"Sir, do you think anyone might try to sabotage our

propulsion or cause a casualty that will force us to surface and request evacuation?"

Scott glumly stared into his bowl, wiping pepper from his thick red mustache. "If any man in this crew is willing to do something like that for a chance to jump ship, there's probably nothing we can do to stop him."

Chris had finished his sandwich.

Scott wolfed down the last of his bean sprouts and got up. "Oral is arranging a memorial service for the dead. We'll muster in here at twenty-one hundred."

"Why not wait until we get home, sir?"

"Because the men need to start dealing with it now. And we have to get those bodies out of the chill box."

"Why? They can't spread germs in there."

"Some of the men are not so sure of that. And the fridge is filling up."

"What? There's plenty room left. We could fit . . ." Chris had almost said they could fit the whole crew into the large refrigerated compartment.

"Doc, all of the surviving cooks got together this morning and refused to go into the chill box for food unless we clear out the corpses."

"Sir, the bodies will decay really fast if we let them thaw out. In a few days, they'll release enough gas to make the body bags explode."

"We'll get rid of them before then," Scott said.

"How, sir?"

"Old-timey submarine burial—weight the bodies and flush them out a torpedo tube."

"Skipper, the investigators back home will want to do autopsies."

"I doubt there will be a lack of cadavers by the time we get home, Doc."

Scott walked around the table toward the exit. As he passed by, Chris said, "Skipper, some of the guys have said you haven't seemed quite yourself lately—I mean even before the outbreak—and they told me why. I just wanted to let you know, if there's anything I can do . . ."

Scott paused to pat Chris's thick shoulder. "Son, I think you've got enough to keep you busy right now without worrying about the mistakes of an old man."

Chapter 39

Before the memorial service, there were no crises that needed his immediate attention, so Chris took the most overdue shower of his life, feeling thankful that he never had to shave. Afterward he put on his dress uniform. It felt strange wearing white to a memorial service, but his grimy coveralls and dungarees were the only alternatives.

The enlisted mess was packed when Chris arrived. Since he was the tallest man on board, he stood at the back to avoid blocking the view.

He noticed that almost all of the men were wearing some kind of mask. It had occurred to him that gathering this way might increase the spread of germs, but not by much, considering how crowded their conditions were already.

On a table at the front, Oral had lit a row of thirteen tall white taper candles, one for each of the deceased. "Do you know where the candles came from?" Chris whispered to Tumor, who was standing beside him.

"His preacher kit," Tumor replied. "He normally lights a couple of candles at the regular services he gives on Sundays."

Oral had placed the victims' folded uniforms behind the candles. Cards leaning against the uniforms bore their names in black Magic Marker. Seven of the thirteen candles had photographs propped upright against the front of the stainless steel candle holders. Chris presumed that no photos of the other six men had been available.

The candles were pretty, Chris thought, but they seemed like shamefully perfunctory props compared to those at a real funeral. No casket, no flowers, no music— just one burning candle for each extinguished life.

While waiting for Oral to begin, Chris looked at the photographs. Most submariners kept a cherished stash of pictures to remind them of the people, pets, and places they missed during the long months in the deep. The photos in front of the candles had obviously been taken from those collections, because they all included other family members as well as the deceased.

The sailor in the first picture had his arm around a woman in front of a sign that read NIAGARA FALLS. In front of them stood a plump little boy with a gap-toothed smile. The next photo was a husband-and-wife wedding portrait. The third photo showed Maurice Hereford standing in front of a barbecue grill with an elderly man whom Chris guessed was his grandfather.

What brought the sting to Chris's eyes even before the service began was the way the people in the photos were all smiling. He tried, unsuccessfully, not to imagine the expressions on the faces of those proud parents and lonely wives when a Navy casualty assistance officer accompanied by a chaplain walked up to their homes and informed them that the young men they missed so much would never come back.

Until now, Chris had been too caught up in his frantic labor to stop and think about the lives being lost or the many more lives being shattered. He had thought of this outbreak as an emergency, not a tragedy. Now he recognized it as both. He deliberately let in the grief, and it joined his exhaustion, dread, and anger.

This time I'm having to watch my brothers die slowly, one by one. If I manage to save any of them, I just hope they won't hate me for failing to save the rest.

Oral called the group to order. It wasn't hard—there

had been only a few subdued murmurs of conversation in the crowded mess. "We have one hour. If you will, please join me in prayer. We'll read from the Twenty-third Psalm."

After the opening prayer, Oral asked one man to stand up and say a few brief words about each of the dead. In each case, the volunteer was a shipmate who knew the deceased well. Nearly all were weeping or seemed on the verge of tears when they spoke. Chris could feel the anguish in their voices, and it made his own tears flow freely.

He noticed Eng standing in a back corner. Even in this tight crowd, the tall, skinny lieutenant somehow managed to appear aloof. Yet he bowed his head at the appropriate times, and tears were flowing down his bony cheeks.

After Oral's closing prayer, Captain Scott stood up, holding a notebook. The aging officer put on his reading glasses and spoke with a surprisingly loud, firm, commanding voice.

"Gentlemen, we are submariners, the special few who volunteer to dive down into the most dangerous environment on Earth, risking our lives to protect the freedom, safety, and comfort we've left behind.

"Now we must honor and bid farewell to thirteen of our shipmates. These brave young men were submariners, but more importantly, each was a unique individual, with his own hopes, fears, and loves. Each was a husband or a boyfriend, a father or a son. Even if some of them don't have a single soul back on land to mourn their passing, they have us. Gentlemen, we must never forget!

"And what is the most important thing to remember? That these thirteen brave volunteers were snuffed out before their prime by a blow from behind. We don't yet know what evil enemy is responsible for this atrocity, but we do know that this enemy was willing to use a weapon that is indiscriminant, uncontrollable, and as morally repugnant as any means of murder ever devised. As long as they are still out there, no one is safe . . . and our job is not done.

"So don't let these deaths weaken you with grief. Don't let them discourage you into giving up. Let the memory of your murdered shipmates remind you that we must carry on until the world is rid of biological weapons and the kind of human monsters who would design, build, and release them. For now, the *Vermont* has another objective to complete, but America will eventually find out who committed this war crime. To that end, this crew must survive and keep fighting to help find this enemy and show them how the United States deals with murderous barbarians—by taking the war to them, with civilized tactics, minimum collateral damage, and no forgiveness.

"Gentlemen, you have proven your loyalty and bravery in the midst of great suffering. I thank you all. Even in the face of death, we will persevere."

With that, Captain Scott dismissed the crew and marched confidently out of the enlisted mess.

Chapter 40

At Chris's request, Scott and Kurlgunn met with him in the captain's stateroom. Chris was surprised to see that the stateroom was neat and clean. He took it as a sign, along with the speech at the service, that Captain Scott was rising above his personal problems, although the shriveled officer still looked as if he were terminally ill.

When Scott invited him to speak, Chris stood up straight, tightened his hard abdominal muscles, and said, "Captain, Lieutenant Commander, whatever our mission was, it's lost at this point."

Scott nodded and slumped into his desk chair as if he were melting.

Kurlgunn, who had been leaning against the far wall, lurched a few inches toward Chris as if intending to attack him. "How do you know that? You don't even know where we are or why we're here!"

Chris did not respond in any way to Kurlgunn's aggressive body language. "I can guess, sir. Besides, it doesn't matter. The antibiotics are not working."

"What? You said they would!"

"That was before we realized this was a deliberate attack, sir."

"What does that have to do with it?"

"I read once that the Soviets inserted genes for resistance to several antibiotics into the strain of *Yersinia pestis* they weaponized," Chris said.

Kurlgunn returned to leaning on the wall. "You think this is an old Soviet bioweapon?"

"It could be. Or some other nation could have duplicated the Soviet efforts, with or without the help of the microbiologists who scattered all over the world looking for work when the Soviet Union broke up. Until now, I still had some doubt that this was really an attack, but the multiple antibiotic resistance almost proves that we're dealing with a weaponized strain. I've also been wondering why our quarantine measures haven't stopped it from spreading. According to the references Eng and I have found on pneumonic plague, they should have at least slowed it down more. The designers of this bug may have also boosted its contagiousness."

Scott blew his ruddy parrot-beak nose, then wadded up the tissue and sat there holding it, leaning forward with his elbows on his knees. "If this strain is immune to antibiotics, does that mean the whole crew is doomed?"

"I would say so, sir, if we stay on the *Vermont* long enough. It seems we can't stop the germs from spreading, and without the effect of antibiotics, pneumonic plague is supposed to be fatal in virtually one hundred percent of the cases."

Chris handed Captain Scott a sheet of graph paper on which he had plotted several points. "These points show the cumulative number of cases on each day so far. The line I've drawn through them shows that half of the crew will probably be infected about fifteen days into the run, which is only three days from now. Eng told me we need at least half the crew to maintain our launch readiness. Would you agree with that, sir?"

"Yes," said Captain Scott.

Kurlgunn sneered at the graph. "That's just a visual extrapolation. The rate of new infections could change."

Scott preempted Chris's response. "How long until we're completely disabled, Doc?"

"That's harder to say, sir. A while longer. At a bare

minimum, how many men do you think it would take to keep the *Vermont* going?"

Scott thought for a moment. "We could get her home with only ten men, but we couldn't fight her."

Chris said, "I couldn't guess how long it would be until we're down to ten survivors, sir. As the crew is thinned out, the number of new cases presenting each day should decrease, so it might drag out for weeks toward the end . . . if we stay in here that long."

Scott nodded. "So, the bottom line: We have about three days of full operational capability left?"

"Give or take a day," Chris said.

Scott sighed bitterly. "Our orders require us to remain on station for several weeks."

After a pause, Chris said, "What do you want to do, sir?"

Scott mulled Chris's question over for what seemed like more than a minute. For the first time ever, Chris thought Kurlgunn looked apprehensive. Sweat was beaded on the XO's pallid forehead, and he seemed to be breathing a little faster than usual as he watched the captain think.

Kurlgunn caught Chris looking at him and pointed to the door with a venomous glower. "You've made your report, Long. Get out!"

Chris stepped toward the door. "Captain?"

Scott looked up. "Huh? No, stay, Doc. From now on, we'll need you to participate in every decision we make. I know you're not an officer, but given the circumstances, I need you to act like one."

Kurlgunn was obviously not happy with the captain's decision, but he said nothing. With a quick jab like a striking snake, he wiped away the sweat that had begun draining down his forehead from his thick black crew cut.

The captain finally spoke. "Our top priority should be informing STRATCOM of our failure as soon as possible. Unfortunately, we can't do that now, because calling from our present position could still alert enemy forces that Tridents are being deployed to their region, and that could blow the element of surprise for other Trident missions."

"I thought it was too late for another sub to replace the *Vermont*," Chris said.

"It is, unless the timetable of the surface forces has changed. I wasn't just talking about a sub replacing us. As you pointed out, Doc, there could be another boomer out there with the same mission as ours, for redundancy. Furthermore, I know for sure that another Trident has already been on station for a while in our op area."

To Chris's surprise, Kurlgunn said, "So we'll head back to Bangor without calling ahead?" The XO's hands seemed to have a death grip on each other behind his back.

"No," Scott said. "That's not the fastest way to inform STRATCOM without compromising mission security."

"What is the fastest way?" Chris asked.

"We're only four days away from our op area," Scott said. "At this point, it's the closest area to us that's routinely patrolled by American attack submarines. We'll call STRATCOM when we get there. We're supposed to call then anyway, to let them know we're on station. If enemy forces intercept our transmission, it won't tip them off that a Trident is in the area. They can't decode our signals, so they'll have no way of knowing the call didn't come from one of our regular attack subs."

Chris stared at the captain. "So, basically, you're just going to make us carry on with this run, regardless."

Scott frowned. "Not regardless, Long. Informing STRATCOM of this outbreak without endangering other Trident operations is more important than saving our own lives, or even the *Vermont* herself. And if you turn out to be wrong—if we manage to stop the plague by the time we arrive in our op area—we'll still be on schedule."

"Are we going to head home after calling STRATCOM?"

Scott shrugged. "We'll do whatever they order us to do."

The captain stood up, adjourning the meeting. He remained behind but did not close the door of his stateroom.

Walking away, Chris and Kurlgunn heard a thump behind them. Kurlgunn jerked and spun around, crouching in what looked to Chris like some kind of fighting stance. Chris glanced over his shoulder. As he did so, he heard Scott mutter, "Fuck a three-legged razorback! Some of those boys are bound to starve to death."

Chris saw that Scott was leaning his forehead against one side of his doorframe. The thump had apparently been caused by him whacking something in frustration.

Scott looked up, saw Chris and Kurlgunn staring at him, and slammed his door.

After a moment of confusion, Chris realized that the starving boys must be the crew of the *Florida,* the Trident that had been overdue at Bangor when the *Vermont* got under way. *So the* Vermont *is on her way to relieve the* Florida *after all. No wonder Scott has been so adamant about carrying on with this run.*

Chapter 41

Captain Scott slumped in his chair and lifted the half-empty bottle of Scotch whisky from his desk. Alcohol was strictly forbidden on American submarines, unlike on their British counterparts. This was the first time he had ever smuggled booze on board.

He threw his head back and tilted the bottle up, letting a long swig flow down his throat.

Scott had bought this bottle on his honeymoon, intending to open it on his thirtieth anniversary, which would have been only three years away. He had taken loving care of the bottle. Its value—before he'd opened it—was more than five hundred dollars.

His eyes were beginning to lose their ability to focus on the handwritten page at the center of his desktop: Freud's suicide note.

> Skipper, I'm sorry I let you down. Being sick has given me a chance to think. It really changes your perspective. I can't go home, even if I survive the plague. I have too much debt to pay the interest anymore, so I've been borrowing money from a guy in Portland, Gabriel Lambeski. I've also been sleeping with Carol Morganstern, Commodore Morganstern's wife. The thing I was worried about most until now was that Beth would find out and burn all my stuff while I'm at sea. I think what I'm about

to do now is a favor for everyone. Please don't
tell Beth how I died or about Carol, and try to
make sure Lambeski doesn't come after Beth
for . . .

Scott wadded up the note and hurled it at his trash
can. It landed in a corner atop a chair-size pile of paper
wads—discarded drafts of official next-of-kin condo-
lence letters.

Two items remained on his desk. He tried to focus on
one of them. It was the frayed photo of his ex-wife,
which he had just torn into pieces and then taped back
together.

Scott allowed himself to remember the day he had
come home from the run before his previous one. When
he couldn't find Darlene among the crew families waiting at the base, he rushed home to see whether she
was there.

He ran to the kitchen and saw an envelope on the
table with his name on it in her handwriting.

"Like a stray bullet," he muttered, alone in his stateroom. He took another long swig of whisky and laughed
at himself. "No, like a car wreck. No reason, no warning,
no second chance."

In the early years of their marriage, he had been
afraid Darlene would lose patience with his demanding
career, or with his urge to be at sea even between runs,
or with the allergies that made him so miserable on land.
Those fears had worn off over time. Now he couldn't
remember when he had begun taking for granted that
she would always be there.

He felt tears rolling down his stubbly cheeks, which
were almost numb from the whisky. Still holding the
bottle in one hand, he reached past the second item on
his desk—a 9-mm Baretta pistol—and picked up her
photograph.

"I don't know anything about germs," he mumbled at
Darlene's picture, his words now slowed and slurred by

the alcohol. "What good is all my experience against an enemy I can't hear? Can't see it, can't . . . run a torpedo under it, can't run . . . hide. They don't need me now . . . just in the way."

Scott had no idea how the rest of this nightmare run was going to turn out, but it would almost certainly include the worst days of his life if he stuck around. He had begun to fear that he might even break down in front of his crew. As nonfunctional as he'd been on this run and his last one, he had managed to resist that ultimate humiliation. The image of himself groveling for some kind of solace from junior men filled him with far more dread than plague ever could.

Instead of waiting to commit an indulgently eccentric suicide after this run, he would be better off putting a 9-mm slug through the roof of his mouth right now and sparing himself the extra misery. The Navy had standard procedures for coping with a captain's death at sea—the XO would assume all of his responsibilities. And Kurlgunn had already done that, more or less.

Scott put down the picture and the bottle. He lifted the heavy pistol, chambered a round, and leaned back in his chair with the muzzle pointed at his stubbly chin.

Your final analysis was correct, Freud—you were a loser. I know just what it feels like.

Chapter 42

Kurlgunn asked Chris to join him in his stateroom. When they were alone, he said words that Chris would never have expected to hear from him: "I need your help with something, Long."

"Aye, sir."

Kurlgunn stood up, turned away, and let out a sigh that sounded exaggerated to Chris. "As you know, one of the duties of an executive officer is to relieve the captain if his behavior makes it clear that he is unfit to command for medical or mental reasons."

Chris did know that. He'd been afraid since he'd first met Scott and Kurlgunn that it might become pertinent on this run.

"Yes, sir?"

"The captain is drunk."

"*What?* Are you sure?"

Kurlgunn sadly nodded. "I can hear him weeping through the door in the head."

The private staterooms of the captain and XO were separated by a narrow washroom. By stepping through it, they could visit each other without opening their doors to the outer passageway. Chris turned to look and saw that Kurlgunn's door to the head was open. On the other side of the head, Scott's door was closed.

"Go ahead, listen," Kurlgunn said.

Chris stooped to enter the head. *Maybe the skipper is just having a nervous breakdown.* He placed his face close to the captain's door. Sure enough, he could hear Scott sobbing and muttering in the distinctive way of a man who is deranged by overconsumption of alcohol.

Chris ducked back out of the head. "What do you want me to do, sir?"

"Declare him unfit to command, based on your medical judgment."

"Are you sure that's necessary?" Chris asked.

Kurlgunn let out a disgusted snort. "Officially, it should be my call. But this crew worships Barlow Scott, and you've probably heard what most of them think of my higher standards. To take command, I'll need at least one supporter, and you are the only man with the clout to convince the rest of them."

"Sir, I'm only an E-6 corpsman!"

"Yes, and you are also the most influential individual on the *Vermont* right now, regardless of your rank and rate. I know this crew, Long. No matter what Barlow Scott does, most of them would rather die under his command than live under mine. If you don't back me up, his followers will defy my decision to relieve him, but they'll listen to you."

"Sir, most of the men hate me too. They think I promised the antibiotics would work."

"Didn't you?"

"*No!* At least I didn't mean to."

Kurlgunn smirked. "They may hate you, Long, but they also fear you. They perceive you as the bringer of life or death. Frankly, I envy you—their fear gives you more power than you can imagine. That is the key to being a great commander."

Chris's back was suddenly covered with cold sweat. He had thought the keys to great leadership were prudence, courage, and compassion.

"Sir, I meant, are you sure we need to force Captain Scott to step down? It seems like you're practically the acting captain already, and it might not be good for morale."

"Fuck morale! There's no morale on this boat! These men are walking dead and they know it!"

Chris wanted to argue. What Kurlgunn had just said simply wasn't true. The crew was probably working harder now than they ever had before, especially his medical volunteers. Even those who weren't directly helping him fight the outbreak were pulling extra shifts to take over the duties of the volunteers, the patients, and the dead. They were driving themselves to the point of collapse, with few complaints. Chris wondered whether Kurlgunn was just attributing his own feelings to the rest of the crew.

Kurlgunn closed his eyes for a moment, then spoke with what Chris supposed was the gentlest voice he could manage. "Doc, the captain is not just drunk. He is also making a big mistake, taking us into the Gulf. With each passing hour, we're going thirty nautical miles farther from home."

Comprehension dawned on Chris. "You think we should turn back now, sir?"

"Absolutely," Kurlgunn said. "First we'll come to PD and call STRATCOM. I've given our situation very careful—*and sober*—consideration, and I've concluded that that would be the best course of action for all concerned. Of course there will be some risk of enemy forces intercepting our broadcast and figuring out it means an American boomer is here, but that outcome is not certain. If we call now instead of waiting, STRATCOM will find out our status almost four days sooner. Who knows how many lives that may save on the surface by allowing our forces to plan accordingly."

Chris nodded, trying to think through the headache that had just started. "So you believe it's more important to brief STRATCOM immediately than it is to make sure we remain undetected?"

"That is correct. And since there will be no need to continue on to the Gulf if we call now, it will shave almost eight days off our trip back to Bangor. I'll also call COMSUBPAC for a medical evacuation. They may be able to put one together soon enough to rendezvous with us at some secure location that we could get to faster than we could get home."

Chris stared at the pale, lipless, pointy-eared XO in amazement. Kurlgunn's plan was exactly what Chris would have proposed ever since he found out the disease was fatal and spreading among the crew. He had just taken for granted that the captain knew more than he did. "Sir, why do you think Captain Scott didn't order us to do what you're suggesting?"

Kurlgunn shrugged. "Maybe he's obsessed. Maybe he's just too lazy or distracted right now to think it through the way you and I have."

You and I. Chris did not like the sound of that. His headache was worse, and his stomach had clenched into a knot.

At this point, Chris had no idea which plan was better, the captain's or the XO's. Choosing wisely would require strategy that was beyond him, and he wondered whether it wasn't beyond Scott and Kurlgunn as well. All he knew was that hundreds if not millions of lives might hang in the balance, and that he was going to have to take sides.

Kurlgunn spoke with a cajoling tone that didn't suit him at all, in Chris's opinion. "Come on, Doc. Just think; we might get out of here in a couple of days. Isn't that what you've wanted all along?"

Was that what it came down to? Was Kurlgunn trying to take over just so he could get off this plague ship sooner? His argument for calling STRATCOM immediately seemed sensible to Chris, but it could have been a snow job. On the other hand, maybe Kurlgunn hadn't actually let panic affect his judgment—maybe he was just trying to win Chris's support by appealing to his fear.

"If Scott gets his way, we'll be stuck in here for at least another week," Kurlgunn reminded him.

Chris tugged at the collar of his coveralls, which had

egun to itch. He still doubted that he had as much nfluence over the crew as Kurlgunn thought, but as long as the XO believed he did, that gave him influence over Kurlgunn. That alone might cause his decision to ultimately determine which course of action the *Vermont* would take. Since he didn't know which plan was better, all he could do was decide which officer to trust. The outcome of a war could be at stake, so he had to make the right decision. But how could he when he didn't trust either of them?

Chris wondered which option would be most likely to confound the plans of whoever had hit the *Vermont* with a biological weapon.

Kurlgunn was staring at him. "Let's keep it simple, Doc. If we abort the run now, you and I will probably survive. If we carry out the orders of that drunken old fool, we probably won't. What do you say?"

Chris clenched his teeth. His gut instinct told him to defend Captain Scott, but what if that was just because he didn't like Kurlgunn's abrasive personality? On the other hand, what if Kurlgunn's real motive was cowardice? Objectively, the evidence favored Kurlgunn. If Scott really was drunk, it would be hard to justify any action other than supporting the change of command.

Kurlgunn grabbed Chris's left forearm and shook it. "Come on, Long; snap out of it. My men are dying out there. Are you going to help or not?"

"Sir, I need to talk to the captain."

Kurlgunn glowered. His pale irises dilated, and his ropy neck muscles tensed. "What for? You know he's unfit!"

The XO's fingers, still gripping Chris's arm, dug into his flesh painfully.

Chris jerked out of the viselike grasp, stepping back.

The violent motion caused Kurlgunn to totter and take a step forward.

For a second Chris was sure Kurlgunn was going to hit him; then the XO sighed, slumped, and turned his back on Chris, leaning against his stateroom's outer door in a passable impression of the weakened captain.

"Scott obviously wouldn't let you in now, Long, and we don't have time to wait. If anyone asks, you can tell them you examined him, and I'll confirm it. If you back me up, and we succeed in taking over, and we get out of here alive, I can guarantee you'll come out of all this looking like a hero, no matter what else you screw up. I'll make sure you get promoted and recommended for every medal the Navy awards. You have my word of honor."

Chris was sure that promise was meant to make him feel better, but it actually made him feel nauseous. What good was a man's word of honor when he was promising something dishonest, like covering up mistakes?

"Sir, what will you do if I don't support your takeover?"

Kurlgunn shrugged. "I'll relieve Scott anyway, if I can, and I'll make sure you're never allowed on board a U.S. Navy vessel again."

Chris knew Kurlgunn had the power to follow through on such a threat. If they both survived, Kurlgunn could sink his budding Naval career as easily as dropping a diamond in the head and flushing it to the bottom of the ocean.

Chris concentrated on not revealing his rising anger, or letting it spill over from his mind and run down to his fists. He hung his head, feigning defeat. "Okay, sir, that makes it clear what I should do."

"Good," Kurlgunn said. "I'll go tell the other officers. You can return to your duties."

"Aye, sir," Chris mumbled.

Chapter 43

Kurlgunn opened the outer door of his stateroom and marched away. After making sure he was gone, Chris closed the door and lunged into the tiny head separating the XO's stateroom from the captain's. He banged his fist on Scott's door and yelled, "Captain! Captain! Fire in the missile compartment!"

It worked. Scott flung the door open out of trained reflex. Chris shoved him aside, stepped in, and closed the door behind him.

Scott tumbled against his rack and fell onto the deck, then slowly tried to hoist himself back up, wobbling. "Fire . . . ," he muttered.

"Skipper, listen to me. Kurlgunn is going to try to seize control of the *Vermont*. He thinks he needs my backing to convince the rest of the crew to go along with it, but in the state you're in, I seriously doubt that."

Scott managed to drag himself onto his lowered rack, where he sat crookedly and tried to focus on Chris, as if having trouble recognizing him. "Wha—? Fine, let him have it!"

"Sir, he plans to take us up and call STRATCOM now."

Scott continued staring at Chris, swaying a little, his dazed expression growing darker.

Chris looked around the stateroom, which reeked of whisky. He saw the pistol on the captain's desk. With a burst of simultaneous pity and anger, he realized what he must have interrupted.

Scott slammed one fist against the bulkhead behind his rack. "That miserable dog-fucking prick! I could tell he was in it for the wrong reasons, but I never thought he'd do something like this."

"Sir, are you certain he isn't right?" Chris started summarizing Kurlgunn's argument for calling STRATCOM now.

Scott shook his head, slinging sweat. "Doc, there's so much you don't know! The Spear of Allah missiles . . . they have intercontinental range . . . and we know what's in their warheads."

Chris was shocked. "What, sir?"

"*Anthrax,*" Scott spat as if he'd just thrown up. "Enough spores to kill everyone . . . everywhere . . . hundreds of times over."

"Do the warheads actually work?"

Scott nodded. "The Iranians knew we would want to prepare for a fast preemptive strike. They sent the president a secret threat that if they found proof of any American nuclear weapons within one thousand miles of their borders, they would take out an unspecified American city with a population of at least one million."

Chris sucked in his breath, feeling numb. Could Scott be lying? Chris wished he could believe that, but he couldn't imagine what the captain's motive might be, or how the drunken officer could have come up with such a story on the spot.

"Sir, why weren't we told? Why hasn't everyone been told?"

Scott hung his head with a haunted stare. When he spoke, his words were slurred but his diction was as articulate as ever. "The commander in chief wants to avoid a nuclear war, Doc. He's trying to disarm the Iranian psychos the civilized way, with conventional weapons. But if the Iranian threat to strike civilian targets with anthrax was known by certain powerful people—

including the American public, probably—they'd want to launch a nuclear first strike instead. Thanks to a few bloodthirsty nuts in Tehran and some trigger-happy cowards in Washington, the entire ancient culture of Persia would cease to exist in about an hour, along with seventy million innocent civilians and God knows how many other species. There's no question that a conventional invasion is risky, that it could provoke the Iranians to do something they wouldn't have done otherwise. A lot of people wouldn't want to take that chance if they knew how serious the threat really is. And maybe they're right! Who knows? But that's not the president's policy."

Chris was leaning against Scott's gear locker, bowing and palming his bare scalp with one hand. "I assume the *Vermont* is already within the thousand-mile limit?"

"She is," Scott replied.

"So, if we get caught here . . ." Chris couldn't even find words to express the horror of warheads falling from space above Los Angeles or Chicago, silently and invisibly spewing billions of anthrax spores into the wind. Unless the tiny warheads were tracked by radar, America wouldn't even know which city had been hit until people started dying by the thousands a few days later.

Scott pinched his large nose and shook with a drunken sob. "Now you know."

Chris squatted, trying to make eye contact. "Does Kurlgunn know too?"

"He does."

Chris thrust up his big hands. "Well? What are you waiting for, sir? You have to stop him!"

Scott bent over, gripping his sweaty hair. "I can't. It's too late. Look at me. You'll have to convince him not to expose us here."

"Me?" Chris shouted. "How? If ICBMs loaded with anthrax didn't convince him, how could I possibly . . . ?"

Chris had seen the captain nodding toward his desk. He had followed the nod with his eyes until they landed on the 9-mm pistol. He suddenly felt as if his stomach had been pumped full of ice water.

"Oh, God, sir. I . . ." Chris picked up the heavy weapon. He could tell by its weight that it was loaded. "You want me to take him prisoner at gunpoint? Is that it?"

Scott glowered, swaying slightly. "Actually, I suggest you shoot the snake-fucking coward."

"Skipper, I can't do that!"

"Why not? You're in the military, Doc. Please don't tell me you're afraid to use a gun."

That was the last straw. "Sir, *you're* the fucking coward around here! We've needed you on this run more than any crew has ever needed a captain, and you haven't been there for us!"

Chris ejected the pistol's full magazine. He pulled the slide to eject the chambered cartridge, then threw the empty weapon at Scott. It clanged off the wall and landed on the mattress.

Scott belatedly lifted his arms to protect himself, then lowered them, hanging his head and massaging his chest.

"And now you were going to abandon us completely and leave that damn bully in charge! *How could you, sir?*"

Scott wiped a tear from his stubbly cheek and blew his huge nose with his thumb and forefinger, not bothering to use a tissue. He used his sleeve to wipe the residue from his thick red mustache.

"If I murdered Kurlgunn, it would defeat the purpose," Chris said. "The rest of the crew would self-destruct, and the *Vermont* would end up surfacing. Goddamn it, sir, what are we going to do?"

Chris stood there and watched the shriveled captain, feeling sicker and sicker. He couldn't tell whether the drunken officer was thinking or falling asleep.

After several seconds, Scott began breathing deeply, his nostrils flaring. His bloodshot dark blue eyes opened wide, gazing back and forth. He lunged across the stateroom, trembling, and grabbed the 1MC mike from its cradle in the overhead.

"All hands! All hands! This is the captain. There has been a breach of quarantine. A lethal concentration of airborne plague germs is drifting aft from the torpedo room. Chief of the watch, secure all ventilation; secure all atmosphere control equipment. Make your depth one thousand feet and then order all stop. Repeat, dive to one thousand feet and then order all stop. Use ballast to maintain depth. All nonessential personnel make your way aft to the engine room and wait there for further orders. That is all."

Scott turned to Chris with what might have been a weak grin. "Diversion . . . to keep everyone busy until I get up to control."

"You're going up like *that,* sir?"

"Wait here," Scott said. He dashed into the head and shut both doors.

A second later, Chris heard horrible retching noises. He surmised that the captain was trying to clear out any alcohol that remained in his stomach. He wondered why Scott had ordered a dive to one thousand feet followed by a stop, then realized it would significantly delay any attempt to ascend. He also wondered when Scott would turn the air back on. Without ventilation, the electronics would start to fry in about fifteen minutes.

Scott flung open the door and staggered out, wiping his face with a wet washcloth. "Okay, let's go."

A few seconds later, they were marching along the linoleum-tiled passageway. Bringing up the rear, Chris was surprised by how few unnecessary curves there were in Scott's walk. The captain was chewing three pieces of gum at once, chomping down in time to his marching feet.

"Sir, I've been told what a good skipper you can be. I hope you're back to stay."

"Not possible," Scott said. "If I survive this run, they're putting me ashore. You convinced me to do my best until this nightmare is over. After that, I'm going to . . . go sailing."

Chris wondered why the deck still had an even trim. It should have had a down angle by now if the officer of the deck had followed Scott's order to dive.

They strode swiftly into the control room. The helmsman, planesman, and chief of the watch all glanced toward their footsteps. There was no one else in the room.

"Who has the conn?" Scott boomed.

The chief of the watch was holding his gas mask on extra tightly with one hand. His eyes looked terrified. "The XO did, sir, but he left when you announced the germs coming from the torpedo room."

"Captain has the conn!" Scott announced, loudly enough—it seemed to Chris—for everyone on the *Vermont* to hear him.

The captain was obviously taking great pains to enunciate clearly. His speech was still slurred, but only so slightly that someone not listening for the effects of alcohol would not recognize them.

Chris felt twinges of excitement and hope at the tone of apparent confidence in Scott's voice. It was a tone he'd heard only once before—in the captain's rousing speech at the memorial service. He wondered now whether Scott had intended that speech as his parting words to the crew before blowing his brains out.

"Sir, Kurlgunn told us to belay your dive order before he left," said the chief of the watch. "Do you still want to dive?"

"No, John. Maintain your present depth, course, and speed. Resume all ventilation."

Scott took down one of the ubiquitous black microphones and announced, "Attention, all hands. This is the captain. The report of a quarantine breach in the torpedo room was a false alarm caused by a faulty barometer. You may return to your watchstations. That is all."

Scott hung up the mike, leaned on the railing encircling the conn, and closed his eyes for a moment, swaying just perceptibly. Then he sighed and grinned at Chris. "That wasn't so hard."

"I'd say leaving a Trident without an OOD is grounds for dismissing an XO," Chris said, "wouldn't you, sir?"

"Abso-rat-fucking-lutely," Scott replied.

Chapter 44

Chris watched as the control personnel returned from the engine room. Kurlgunn looked appropriately startled, then enraged, when he saw Chris standing on the conn alongside Captain Scott.

The captain took Kurlgunn aside. When they returned, Scott gave the crew explicit orders to stay on course, then announced, "XO has the conn."

Without enthusiasm, Kurlgunn announced, "I have the conn, aye, sir."

Scott took Chris back to his stateroom. The aging captain sat down at his desk, groaning and holding his head.

"Sir, why did you leave Kurlgunn in charge?"

"We can't spare an able-bodied officer. Almost half of them are sick or dead, and it's going to get worse. Besides, I don't trust Gene not to attempt some idiotic reprisal if I leave him with nothing to lose."

"Okay, but I'm sure he still wants to jump ship."

"I think he'll behave," Scott said. "As long as he still has a ray of hope that he'll survive and get to command his own boomer someday, I doubt he'll do anything to jeopardize that chance. I promised him I would forget he deserted the conn if he doesn't try to start a mutiny."

Chris helped himself to a seat on Scott's rack. "Why would he want to be a sub captain so much? I sure wouldn't want to. You don't seem to enjoy it much either."

Scott was still holding his head with his eyes closed.

"I used to. I think Gene wants his own kingdom, Doc. Commanding a missile sub is a dream come true for a wannabe tyrant. During the months when you're maintaining radio silence, the captain's word is law. There is no higher authority. To people like Gene, everyone is either dominated or dominating, and I think he feels like he's been dominated for too long."

Remembering the burn marks on Kurlgunn's back, Chris thought that analysis made sense.

Scott got up and staggered to the head to fill his lighthouse mug with water.

"Thank you for telling me what's really going on, sir."

"Did I have a choice?"

"I had already guessed most of it," Chris said, "but I'm still not perfectly clear on everything. Our orders are to relieve the *Florida,* and she's sitting somewhere off the coast of Iran, prepared to take out their Spear of Allah missiles if they try to use them rather than losing them when our ground forces invade. Right?"

Scott returned to his seat with a groan. "That's correct. None of our conventional forces are fast enough to stop them if they try to launch."

"How will we know if they start preparing their remaining missiles to launch?" Chris asked. "And how much warning would we have?"

"They would have to bring the missiles outside and erect them on launchpads," Scott said. "Our satellites would see them, and we have good intelligence that the preparations would take about half an hour."

"That's why we need a Trident so close to Iran?"

"Exactly. Allowing for time to decode the EAM and carry out the launch order, half an hour should be just enough for a D-5 missile to get to any part of Iran, but only if it's launched from the Gulf on a depressed trajectory. As long as we still have the *Florida* hiding in the Gulf, we figured it was worth taking a chance that the Iranians would catch the *Vermont* on her way in. If they do catch us, and they try to carry out their threat against an American city, the *Florida* will take out the launchpad they're using . . . and everything within a hundred square miles of it."

Chris felt a little relief. "So an American city won't actually get hit with anthrax, even if we get caught here?"

Scott got up and staggered to the head for more water. "Hopefully. Assuming nothing delays our intel and the guys on the *Florida* are still able to pull off a quick launch. But it would still mean a thermonuclear weapon will be used for the first time."

Chris thought about that. Trident D-5 missiles carried an entirely different kind of weapon from the two primitive atomic bombs the United States had dropped on Japan. Comparing a fission-powered A-bomb with a fusion-powered thermonuclear device was like comparing a firecracker with a land mine. So far, the United States was the first and only nation to ever use an atomic bomb. If it also became the first nation to use a thermonuclear weapon, the geopolitical consequences might harm America even more than the Iranians' anthrax would have.

Scott returned from the head. He remained standing this time, contemplatively staring into his mug. "In four days, we'll have two Tridents in the Gulf—one with a crew that's starving to death, the other with a crew that's dying of plague. We just have to hope that at least one of those subs can hold out and remain undetected until a third one can sneak through the Strait of Hormuz."

"Sir, are we still going to call STRATCOM when we arrive on station?"

Scott nodded. "That's part of our orders."

"What do you think they'll tell us to do?"

The weary captain took a long drink, massaging his chest. "They'll probably tell us to sit tight and keep our little outbreak secret at all costs."

Chapter 45

Four days later

Gordon Davis, the president of the United States, was having a pleasant dream about a blond White House intern when the red secure telephone beside his bed started ringing. He was not sorry the dream had been interrupted. Most of his erotic dreams evolved into nightmares nowadays, with flashing news cameras and scathing headlines. Davis felt it was unfair for his subconscious to be so paranoid—he had been in the White House for three years now, and, in spite of the incredible temptations that came with having the highest status of any male on Earth, he had accomplished the nearly unprecedented feat of remaining faithful to his wife.

Davis knew the call was bad news. No one called a president at two in the morning to tell him something he wanted to hear. He groaned and rubbed his eyes as the dream faded and reality sank in. Gordon Davis's reality included an overload of domestic responsibilities, an economy in trouble, and engagement of the United States in multiple major wars.

The caller was Martin Bradshaw, his national security adviser. "Mr. President, I'm sorry to wake you. I just got a call from the duty officer in the Sit Room. They received a FLASH message from the NMCC indicating that the *Vermont* has been attacked with a biological weapon."

The Sit Room, short for Situation Room, was the president's alert center in the West Wing of the White House. The NMCC was the National Military Command Center at the Pentagon.

"Vermont, you say?"

"Not the state, sir, the submarine. She's the missile sub on her way to the Gulf."

Davis preferred his advisers to call him "sir" in private, since it was a hell of a lot shorter than "Mr. President."

Gordon Davis had known that effective bioweapons would be used against American forces sooner or later. But how the hell had someone managed to attack a submarine crew? Weren't they sealed off from the outside environment?

"Convene the NSC principals in the conference room," he said. "I'll be right down."

The president could dress however he pleased for this meeting with the National Security Council, and choose when he arrived. Some of his predecessors would have taken the time to put on a suit and comb their hair. Gordon Davis just threw on his slippers and the gray UK Wildcats sweatpants and sweatshirt that he kept under his bed for emergencies. As he used the bathroom, he didn't even bother to check his jowly face and bushy brown hair in the mirror. There would be no news cameras downstairs at this hour.

He briskly descended the stairs to the aboveground basement of the West Wing.

A few minutes later, the NSC Principals Committee was sequestered in the windowless conference room at the heart of the complex known collectively as the Situation Room. Unlike its usual public perception, the conference room was not a large, darkened operations center filled with expensive electronic displays. Although

soundproofed and shielded against electronic eaves-
dropping devices, the conference room appeared posh
and elegant rather than utilitarian or high-tech. It was
also cramped, a square only eighteen feet wide. The
powerful overhead lights kept the small chamber well
illuminated, despite the dark cherry paneling on the
walls.

Twenty-four seats were available, twelve along the
walls and twelve around the long, heavy, wooden table
in the room's center. Tonight only seven seats were occupied. Aside from the president and his national security adviser, the NSC principals in attendance included
the vice president, the secretary of state, the secretary
of defense, the chairman of the Joint Chiefs of Staff, and
the director of central intelligence. These seven were
the top movers in the current administration's foreign
policy machine.

Besides the NSC principals, there was one other individual in the room: Army Major Jackson Porto, the Situation Room director. Porto was in his early thirties,
skinny and darkly tanned with a cleft chin and a slight
harelip.

The meeting began with the principals reading tran-
scripts of the FLASH message sent from the *Vermont*
to STRATCOM an hour before. While they read, Major
Porto quietly opened a panel on the wall opposite the
president's end of the table, revealing a large TV screen.
The screen displayed a secure videoconference feed
from STRATCOM at Offutt Air Force Base in Nebraska. A baby-faced, white-haired admiral at STRAT-
COM waited silently in the camera's eye to answer
questions from the White House.

"Is a corpsman the ship's doctor?" asked President
Davis.

"Yes, sir," said General Toby Douglas, the chairman
of the Joint Chiefs. Douglas was a bear of a man,
dwarfing the other committee members. He had thick
features, hairy ears, stubby fingers, and a half-bald head

with dark freckles on top. He was wearing his Army green office uniform.

When President Davis finished reading, he motioned Major Porto over and whispered, "I want background dossiers on the captain and the doctor."

Major Porto stepped out to relay the order to the Sit Room staffers.

By the time all of the principals had finished reading the FLASH message, copies of both dossiers had been distributed to them. Gordon Davis never ceased to be amazed by the information-managing powers of the Sit Room staff.

The president's advisers were all looking at him, so he spoke. "I can't believe we have more than a hundred American boys dying of a medieval disease on the opposite side of the world, and they only have one medic, and he's not even a real doctor." Davis held up Christopher Long's dossier. "He's just a twenty-six-year-old kid with one year of medical training. How did we let this happen?"

"Mr. President, the Navy can't afford to send out fully trained physicians on its ships," said the white-haired admiral on the TV monitor. "Even if the *Vermont*'s corpsman were a general practitioner or a surgeon, he wouldn't be qualified to handle this situation. What they need is an infectious disease specialist."

"They requested expert medical advice," Davis said. "How soon can we get it to them?"

"I'll take care of that," said General Douglas. He picked up one of the cordless telephones on the table. He identified himself to the Sit Room operator and said, "I need a secure line to Fort Detrick."

Martin Bradshaw, the president's national security adviser, frantically waved for the general's attention. Bradshaw was a small, frail man with bifocals, combed-over brown hair, parchmentlike skin, and a nervous winking habit.

Scowling, General Douglas held the phone aside and nodded for Bradshaw to speak.

"General, I can't stress enough how vital secrecy is in this situation."

"I'm aware of that, Martin."

"Okay." Bradshaw glanced suspiciously around the room, winking vigorously with both of his rheumy hazel eyes. "We just have to make sure everyone we contact understands the need for secrecy as well as we do, and we should minimize the number of people we bring into this."

General Douglas moved to a corner with the phone and began conversing quietly with the commander of USAMRIID, the United States Army Medical Research Institute of Infectious Diseases, based at Fort Detrick near Frederick, Maryland. USAMRIID had been the research center of America's offensive biological weapons program until it was canceled by President Nixon in 1969. Now its primary mandate was developing defenses against germ warfare and bioterrorism.

Davis was still looking at Christopher Long's background dossier. "This kid made terrible grades in high school, and he got in trouble on his first assignment. It'll be a miracle if any of those men get home alive."

"They're probably doomed, regardless of the medic's ability," said the secretary of defense, a tall, thin man with a boxer's nose and black hair slicked back with Brylcreem.

"The corpsman may have a bad record," said Martin Bradshaw, "but according to the *Vermont*'s captain, he's the one who realized the importance of keeping this attack secret. Clearly that should be our utmost concern."

"Why, Martin?"

"Mr. President, this looks bad, really bad. Let's face it—a Trident submarine is a platform for concealment and delivery of strategic weapons of mass destruction, which is exactly what a weaponized strain of plague is. If news of the outbreak leaks, some people are going to believe this bug is a secret American weapon that was part of the *Vermont*'s armament and somehow got loose on board. The political fallout could destroy us, and I don't mean just your administration—all of modern civilization might be at stake."

Davis scowled at his frail national security adviser, whom he regarded as a consummate strategist but a melodramatic worrywart. "How's that, Martin?"

Blinking rapidly, Martin Bradshaw looked around the cramped chamber where so many world-changing decisions had been made. He said, "The Soviets continued developing and stockpiling biological weapons after they signed the international convention that prohibited them in 1975. By the end of the eighties, their germ warfare program was almost as big as their nuclear program, yet no one in the West knew the extent of it until Kanatjan Alibekov defected in 1992. Now everyone knows the Soviets built enough illegal germ weapons to infect every human being on Earth hundreds of times over . . . anthrax, plague, botulinum, tularemia, smallpox. They even tried a genetic cross between smallpox and Ebola that has the worst properties of both viruses. And everyone knows they managed to keep the program secret for decades, partly because none of us in the West wanted to believe anyone would do something so evil and pointless."

Bradshaw paused for a drink of water.

"I see why other countries might suspect the U.S.," said President Davis. "So what?"

Bradshaw blinked at him. "Sir, the other major powers are already uncertain that we have any moral justification for disarming other nations by force before they commit any aggressive acts. If they start thinking we still have an offensive bioweapons program of our own, they won't turn a blind eye on our preemptive actions anymore. Our so-called allies will build a coalition against us. Then we'll have to lay down our guns and watch while the power-crazed dictators and fanatical religious nuts build enough uncontrollable doomsday weapons to exterminate the human race."

Chapter 46

Soony Ulin Nguyen sped along the dark street in front of Gene Kurlgunn's house in her old blue Honda Accord, exceeding the absurd base speed limit by a factor of three. Seeing an empty space, she slammed on the brakes, screeched to a halt, and backed into it, parking with one rear wheel on the curb. The space was in front of a fire hydrant, but that didn't matter now. Soony jumped out and slammed the door without realizing she'd locked her keys in the car. She finished buttoning up her blouse as she ran up the walk to the elegant front porch.

Her frantic ringing was finally answered by a pretty middle-aged woman with straight blond hair, a green dress, and no makeup or jewelry. The woman's eyes were red, and her face was puffy. She seemed to be peering past Soony into the chilly October night. "Can I help you?" she asked.

"Are you Mrs. Kurlgunn?"

The woman nodded. "Penny. Are you—?"

"Do you know what happened on the *Vermont*?" Soony was trying hard to keep her voice even and look more mature than her twenty-two years.

"No, dear. They're not telling us anything. Are you a family member?" Penny's speech was slow and a little slurred, as if she had just woken up.

Soony tried not to shiver. At almost midnight, it was cold on the Kurlgunns' porch, and she hadn't taken time to dress warmly before leaving her college dormitory. Most of her trembling was not due to the cold, though— it was due to fear for Chris and intimidation at the thought of entering this big strange house full of distraught older women whom she had never met. "I'm . . . I'm Christopher Long's . . ."

"Who?" Penny's reaction appeared sluggish, her expression dampened.

"My name is Soony Nguyen."

Penny stared at her as if searching her memory, or dozing on her feet.

Soony lost the battle with her emotions. Her throat tightened, and tears flooded her eyes. "You just called me! Don't you remember?"

"Oh. I guess you were on the list." Penny's words sounded eerily detached. She took a cautious step backward, as if she were afraid of tripping. "Come in, dear. You're shivering."

Soony stepped in. Her blinking had spattered her eyeglasses with small tear droplets, but not enough to obscure her vision.

Penny disappeared into the kitchen, leaving her standing alone by the door. Soony's drive had taken more than an hour. She needed to use the bathroom desperately but didn't know where it was, and now there was no one to ask.

A tight cluster of women was gathered around a tall man in a Navy officer's uniform by the fireplace at the other end of the room. A couple of the women glanced at her, then returned their attention to the officer. Soony noticed that most of the women were overweight. At least two were pregnant. There were no other Asians, and none of them looked as young as she did.

About half of the women looked frustrated but not distraught. The other half were weeping or looked as if they had been weeping recently. One was scrunched up on the sofa, practically buried in the plush blue cushions, holding a tissue box and crying her eyes out.

The fearful mood of the room was contagious. The sights and sounds of grief and dread caused Soony's eyes to fill with fresh tears, but she managed not to sob.

She dared to step closer to the throng, hoping to hear what the officer was saying.

"—don't know, ma'am. I swear. All they told me was there was some kind of accident, so it may have been a radiation leak, but I honestly don't know."

"You won't tell us how many got killed," said one of the women. "Will you at least tell us how many were hurt?"

"Killed?" Soony said. Her back and thighs suddenly felt weak. When Penny Kurlgunn had called, she'd said something had gone wrong on the *Vermont*. She hadn't said anything about men being killed.

"I can confirm that there have been fatalities, since that has already leaked out." The officer spoke as if he were repeating the sentence for the hundredth time. "But I honestly do not know how many."

The woman who had asked the last question was glaring at Soony for butting in. The officer turned back to her and said, "I also don't know how many were injured, ma'am. I'm sorry."

"How did you find out about the accident?" Soony asked.

A couple of the women sighed impatiently.

"As I mentioned earlier," the officer said, "they sent a satellite radio message at about eighteen hundred this evening."

"Are they coming home now?" asked one of the soon-to-be mothers.

"I don't know, ma'am."

Soony edged between two of the largest women. "Do you know if Chris Long was one of the . . . the . . . ?" Her mouth contorted with a silent sob, refusing to let the words out.

One of the women she was rubbing shoulders with, an African American in a red dress, said, "Honey, if he won't even say how many got killed, he's not going to tell us which ones."

The woman on Soony's other side, a tall blonde with running mascara, looked down at her and said, "We're lucky we even found out there was an accident. He said they wouldn't have told us if somebody hadn't let it leak already."

"That's right," the man said. "And now we need your help to keep this under wraps. This is a serious breach of security. Just keep it within the family, like everything else, and please, please spread the word to all the ladies in the *Vermont* wives club—I know some couldn't make it tonight—that we have to keep this secret until the men come home. Otherwise, they might never come home. Okay?"

There were several murmurs of assent.

"Where are they?" Soony sobbed.

One of the younger women rolled her eyes. "Oh, come on, jeez."

"I'm sorry, ma'am. We never reveal the locations of our submarines when they're at sea."

Soony knew that—she'd had to ask anyway.

She stepped forward into the narrow ring of empty space that had somehow remained around the officer. She grabbed one of his arms with both hands. "You have to tell us who was killed!"

"Hey, chill out, sister." The black woman, who was twice Soony's size, gripped her wrists and tried to pull her loose from the officer, with no luck. A second later, Soony let go voluntarily and hid her face in her hands.

The tall blonde put an arm around her shoulders. "He really doesn't know, sweetie. They wouldn't send a man down here who knew something they didn't want us to find out."

"That's right," the officer said. "I'm sorry, ma'am, I truly am."

Soony backed out of the crowd and fled from the house, still hiding her face. She ran to the car and reached for her keys. They weren't in her pocket. Peering through the window, she saw them in the ignition. She slapped the top of the car and let out a shriek of frustration.

The Kurlgunn family's immaculate yard included an elaborate flowerbed surrounded by stones about the size of cantaloupes. Soony marched into the yard and retrieved one of the heavy stones. She walked back around the car and used both arms to heave the stone through the driver's-side window.

The crash started a dog barking on the other side of the dark street.

She grabbed the keys, flung open the door, and got in, not bothering to sweep the tiny cubes of safety glass off her seat. Sitting still, she leaned her forehead against the steering wheel, allowing herself to weep naturally.

Soony had recently read a book about the tragic sinking of the *Kursk* in August of 2000. She knew that serious submarine accidents were like plane crashes. If anyone on the *Vermont* had been killed, it was likely that the whole crew had perished.

Soony didn't care in the slightest that she had just made a fool of herself in front of the close-knit and undoubtedly gossipy *Vermont* wives. In spite of having juvenile diabetes that severely restricted her diet, she could jog for more than an hour. She could also read almost a thousand words a minute and had a 3.8 average at the University of Washington. And she had Chris. That gave her pride to spare. If he came home, she wouldn't care what anyone else thought of her. If he didn't, she wouldn't care about anything.

"We barely had a chance to get started," she wept. "I don't care how bad you're hurt, I don't care what mistakes you've made, I don't care how long it takes you to get well, *just please please please come home*!"

With the gentle night breeze ruffling her long hair through the broken window, she let herself cry until she started to feel cold again. Then she wiped the tears off

her eyeglasses, started the car, and drove toward her
university campus, reminding herself to call Chris's
adoptive parents as soon as she got to her room.

She dreaded the call. What could she tell them?

Chapter 47

In the White House Situation Room, President Davis was still skeptical that revealing the attack on the *Vermont* could doom America's ongoing mission to rid the world of biological weapons. Wouldn't it have the opposite effect by demonstrating how dangerous bioweapons could be?

Seeing his doubtful squint, the secretary of state spoke up. Her name was Donna Covington. She was a heavyset blonde in her fifties, with thick, short hair, a dark blue suit, and a slight overabundance of makeup for someone in her position.

"This is more than a foreign relations disaster in the making, sir. A lot of our own citizens may start suspecting that the U.S. government is still building bioweapons. Some already do, and not just the crackpots who say AIDS was cooked up at Fort Detrick to control population growth in Africa. This could tear our country apart worse than Vietnam, especially if investigators uncover some real black-ops research that shouldn't be going on."

President Davis tried to mash down his bushy brown hair. He sat back with his arms crossed. "Assuming that doesn't happen, no one's going to find any real evidence against us, right?"

Martin Bradshaw, his national security adviser, was blinking hysterically. "Sir, that doesn't matter! The taint of suspicion would be devastating enough. We could invite international inspections of our most secret labs and pharmaceutical plants, and the skeptics would still say we've just moved the operation and covered our tracks, like the Soviets and the Iraqis did when UN inspectors visited their facilities."

Davis frowned. "Can't we just go after the bastards who did this? Once we've caught them, we can exonerate ourselves by showing the world who's really guilty."

Several heads shook in response to that, causing Gordon Davis to feel hot with embarrassment. He knew good presidents didn't let fear of looking dumb inhibit their questions, at least in private councils, but sometimes his freewheeling style made him feel like a fool in front of career specialists like these.

"We can't go after *anyone* once we've lost so much credibility that the rest of the world won't let us," Bradshaw said.

"Mr. President," said General Douglas, who had returned from his phone call to USAMRIID. "Even if we're lucky enough to figure out who attacked the *Vermont* and then track them down, the odds of collecting enough proof to convict them before a war crimes tribunal are slim. And even if we did *that,* we would be suspected of manufacturing the evidence. We would certainly have an apparent means and motive."

"Are you saying we have to keep what's been done to those boys secret until the end of time?" Davis felt genuinely enraged by the thought that even the victims' families would never be told.

Bradshaw nodded. "For the sake of all humanity, that submarine must never come to the surface unless we can guarantee that no one outside the highest levels of the U.S. government will ever know what happened on it."

That statement sent a chill down the president's sweaty spine. "Martin, what are you suggesting?"

"Just that this attack must be kept secret at all costs, sir."

"That means we can't carry out a medical evacuation

overseas," said the director of central intelligence, a short, chubby man in a brown suit. "They'll have to try to get home on their own. Even if they make it back to Bangor, we can't let them open their hatches until we have a rescue team standing by. The rescuers will have to evacuate them with reliable biohazard protection and total secrecy, then transport them to a secure quarantine facility."

"Do we have a team like that near the Bangor Naval Base?" asked President Davis.

No one answered.

General Douglas finally spoke up. "Sir, to the best of my knowledge, there is no such rescue team anywhere in the world. USAMRIID may have the right gear, and their doctors know how to safely evacuate patients from epidemic hot zones, but they don't have top secret security clearance."

"Then get it for them!" Davis said. "And tell them to start secretly preparing a hospital near the Bangor base. We have to get those boys home."

"Does that mean you want the *Vermont* to turn back now?" the general asked. "That would require us to postpone the invasion of Iran. Remember, sir, we got word yesterday from the *Florida* that her crew can't guarantee a quick launch anymore. They've gone too long without food. If we're not sure we can prevent the Iranians from launching any of their Spear of Allah missiles, we must not provoke them by sending our ground forces in. That's the policy you established two weeks ago."

Although very few people outside this room knew it yet, the clock was ticking down to the commencement of an all-fronts ground invasion in fifty-two hours.

The white-haired admiral at STRATCOM spoke up, his voice projecting clearly from speakers beside the TV. "Mr. President, it will take at least ten days to get another Trident missile submarine to the Gulf, even if we order the closest one to abandon her deterrence targets.

Recalling the *Vermont* now could leave us vulnerable to Iran's ICBMs for that long. That could be dangerous even if our ground forces are holding back—the Iranians might figure out we're just waiting for something and try to launch their missiles while they have a chance."

President Davis pointed to the classified documents in front of him. "The message from the *Vermont* says they will start losing their ability to launch missiles in another day or two as well. Which one of those subs do you think will be able to maintain some launch capability longer?"

After a brief discussion, his advisers returned a unanimous prediction that the *Florida* would outlast the *Vermont.*

"Also, the longer we leave the *Vermont* out there, the more likely it is that she will become totally disabled," Bradshaw said. "If it comes to that, she'll either sink or surface wherever she is. Either way, the plague outbreak would probably come out before we could move in and cover it up."

Davis squeezed his forehead. Waking up in the middle of the night had given him a headache. "Okay, that settles it. Admiral, order the *Vermont* to head home now, without contacting anyone on the way. The ground invasion will have to be postponed until another missile sub can relieve the *Florida.*"

"Aye, sir," said the admiral at STRATCOM.

General Douglas retreated to a corner again. He called USAMRIID and told them to start getting ready for the *Vermont*'s arrival in Bangor.

"Sir, we should prepare for the possibility that the *Vermont*'s crew will disobey your orders," said Martin Bradshaw.

"Why would they?" Davis asked. "Surely they want to come home."

"Picture their situation, sir. If you were trapped on a submarine with a contagious, lethal, untreatable disease, what would you be thinking about?"

Gordon Davis was avoiding the temptation to hold his aching forehead. "Getting out," he said.

"Getting out," Bradshaw repeated, blinking steadily. "Any way you can, as soon as you can. All they would have to do is surface and ask the locals for help. Almost any nation in southern Asia would be willing to treat a few plague cases in exchange for a chance to poke around a Trident and question the crew. The *Vermont* will be steaming right by the tip of India, which has had more experience with plague recently than any other country."

The president grimaced. "What you're talking about would be treason."

Bradshaw nodded. "Try to imagine what those men are going through, sir. I wouldn't be surprised if their sanity has broken down by now, never mind their loyalty."

"God in heaven," Davis muttered. He didn't want to think about a crew of plague-crazed lunatics in charge of a Trident and her 192 thermonuclear warheads, but Bradshaw was right. "How reliable do you think the captain is? I glanced at his dossier. Unlike the corpsman, he seems to have an outstanding record."

"He does, sir," said the admiral from STRATCOM. "We chose the *Vermont* for this vital operation because Barlow Scott is the most experienced and most highly regarded submarine captain in the U.S. Navy. He would never disobey orders to save his own life or his crew."

"That's great as long as he's in control," Bradshaw said, blinking faster. "I don't know about the rest of you, but I can't think of a better reason than this for the crew of a warship to mutiny."

"Well, I don't see what we could do about it if that happens," Davis said.

Bradshaw blinked at the ceiling, holding his breath. Then he sighed deeply, blinking at each of the other principals in turn. "Fine. If nobody else has the guts, I'll say it . . . we could sink the *Vermont*."

President Davis suddenly felt cold and hot at the same time. What his national security adviser had just said was now a part of the Situation Room recordings. If the tape ever leaked to the media, it could cause an uproar that would devastate his administration. He had to choose his next words carefully to put himself on the record as wanting nothing to do with such a proposal. Aside from that, he found the idea of murdering a ship full of sick men too repulsive to contemplate.

"That course of action is not an option," he finally said.

Bradshaw was flushed, sweating, breathing deeply. Blinking at the wall, he said, "Please think about it, Gordon. It's a good idea to have at least one attack sub escort the *Vermont* home anyway, in case she runs into trouble. If the *Vermont*'s crew starts to come up after you've ordered them to stay down, the escort sub would be perfectly justified in firing on her."

Davis got up and stood behind his chair, gripping its plush leather back with his sweaty palms. "Damn it, we will not commit a heinous crime just to cover up a false appearance of guilt!"

Bradshaw swiveled around to face him. "Sir, I'm not talking about committing a crime. I'm talking about pre-empting a serious breach of national security. All of those men have sworn to sacrifice themselves, if necessary, to defend the United States. If you order them to try to get home on their own, that will be a death sentence for most of them anyway."

At that moment, Gordon Davis hated his national security adviser. Part of him could see that Bradshaw was making sense, and he knew he would probably forgive the man later for doing his job so daringly, but right now Davis just wanted to order him out of the room.

"Martin, we are going to try to bring those boys home, and that's that. If it ever came out that we sank one of our own ships with all hands on board, that would convince the world better than any real evidence could that we were guilty of something we wanted to cover up. To make sure no 'accidents' happen, we will not assign any other submarines to 'escort' the *Vermont* on her way home.''

Davis looked at the camera above the TV screen. "Admiral, have I made my intentions clear?''

"Perfectly, Mr. President,'' said the admiral at STRATCOM.

"Good,'' Davis said. "Send the *Vermont*'s captain his new orders.''

Chapter 48

Cho Ling Tso was alone in his damp and minuscule stateroom, brooding over a tepid cup of his favorite drink, Earl Grey tea with honey. Tso was captain of the *Shanxi,* a Chinese attack submarine. He was in his mid-thirties and had a thick shock of black hair. He was both tall and hefty for a Chinese, with tiny ears and deep acne scars on his protuberant cheeks.

Captain Tso was not happy with his orders. For three days now, the *Shanxi* had been stationed just outside the Strait of Hormuz, the narrow mouth of the Persian Gulf. Waiting.

What they were waiting for, no one had explained to him. His commodore at South Sea Fleet Command had said his orders would come by radio when it was time to act. Meanwhile, he was to keep his brand-new Type-093 nuclear-powered attack submarine at the maximum depth where its antennae could reliably receive VLF transmissions, slowly circling like a sleeping shark so the sub's depth could be maintained with her planes.

Tso took a drink of the bittersweet tea and once again asked himself the questions that had plagued him since leaving the naval base on Hianggyi Island at the mouth of the Bassein River in Burma. What kind of mission was so secret that they wouldn't even tell the ship's captain what it was? Was it really something so vital to keep under wraps? Or was it something so stupid or suicidal that they were afraid he would refuse to carry out his orders if they gave him time to make other plans?

At least Tso was probably not the only sub captain conning in the dark. During the last few days, almost every boat in China's small but growing submarine fleet had converged on the Strait of Hormuz, forming the largest submerged wolf pack Tso had ever seen.

The Chinese wolf pack included all four of the new Type-093 attack submarines, which the Westerners had taken to calling the *Yangtze* class. The four *Yangtze*s were the only subs China had that might stand a chance against American or British subs in combat. This monstrous wolf pack also included both of the two obsolete *Han*-class attack subs that were still operational, along with eight new diesel-powered improved *Kilo*-class attack subs. The improved *Kilo*s had been built in Russia, which had exported the modern, high-tech design to several countries in recent years.

Whatever was going on, Captain Tso knew his country was spending a fortune on it.

Another clue was the mysterious group of riders the *Shanxi* was transporting. She had been stripped of armament, provisions, and spare parts to make room for forty-five People's Liberation Army/Navy Special Forces commandos, the closest thing China had to America's Navy SEALs. Tso knew it was not unusual nowadays for Western subs to be used as covert delivery vehicles for Special Forces units, but it was not a common practice in the Chinese navy.

The commandos had brought aboard an arsenal of small arms, mostly submachine guns. They had also brought on four large steel chests that looked expensive and heavy. Tso had no idea what was inside the chests, which the commandos had kept locked and guarded at all times.

All things considered, Captain Tso had a very ominous feeling about this operation.

He was pretty sure that at least one individual on

board the *Shanxi* knew what was going on: Colonel Inzu Sze Ma, the commander of the Special Forces unit. But Colonel Sze Ma had refused to even drop a hint before Tso and his crew.

Like any submarine captain, Tso did not enjoy having a rider on his boat who outranked him. It made him feel as if he were little more than the driver of an expensive nuclear-powered taxi. It didn't help that Colonel Sze Ma seemed to see it that way too.

Just as Tso finished his tea and started to get up, Inzu Sze Ma appeared in his open doorway. Colonel Sze Ma was a small man who always moved quickly. His face was so lean and angular that it almost looked like a death's-head, with deep grooves running down from the corners of his mouth to his chin. His eyes were greenish black. His teeth were small with wide spaces between them.

Captain Tso noticed that Colonel Sze Ma was smiling—for the first time, as far as Tso knew. In an instant, Captain Tso sensed that orders had finally arrived.

With a quick thrust, Inzu Sze Ma placed a few pages on the table in front of Captain Tso. In Chinese, he said, "We have been ordered to dive to a depth of fifty meters and travel in a circle with a radius of ten kilometers around our present location, increasing our speed to full power."

Captain Tso was stunned. What could circling at high speed possibly accomplish, other than filling the strait with their operating noise? "That's it?" he asked. "How long do they want us to keep going in circles?"

"Six hours," Sze Ma said. "Then we will come to periscope depth and call fleet command for further orders. While we're at fifty meters, tell your sonar operators to watch for SSBN-seven-eight-one."

"An American missile sub? Here in the Gulf?" Tso was trying not to let his annoyance and confusion show, but this operation was getting weirder by the second.

"Her name is the *Vermont,* " Sze Ma said. "Approximately three hours from now, she will be leaving the Gulf at about six knots."

Now Captain Tso was doubly shocked. He knew that the operations of the Tridents were among America's most closely guarded military secrets. "How do your commanders know something like that?"

Colonel Sze Ma waved his right hand across his mouth with the first two fingers extended, a gesture Captain Tso had come to loathe. "That you do not need to know, Captain."

Tso frowned. "Colonel, the Tridents—as the Americans call them—were designed in the nineteen-seventies, but they are still the quietest nuclear missile submarines in the world. Also, their sonar is much better than ours. They will surely hear us and divert to avoid us long before we could hear them, especially if we are running at full power."

"You have your orders," Colonel Sze Ma said with a smile. "I know you have questions, Captain Tso. All I can tell you is that your magnificent *Shanxi* is part of a bold and brilliant initiative that has been years in the making and will significantly shift the balance of world power in favor of China. Do not be afraid of the Americans, Captain. There is almost no chance that they will discover what we are doing before our mission is completed successfully."

As he watched Colonel Sze Ma march away, Cho Ling Tso's stomach clenched with the most painful sense of foreboding he had ever felt. The United States and China were not at war—yet. In fact, their trade relations were more cordial now than they had ever been.

Tso felt clammy all over at the thought of what had happened in the past to nations that betrayed the United States by pretending to be neutral or friendly while plotting against it. On December 7, 1941, Japan had wiped out a large fraction of the U.S. Navy's Pacific Fleet in their sneak attack on Pearl Harbor. Less than four years later, the once-mighty Japanese empire was reduced to a smoking wasteland, courtesy of the merciless Americans. Of course, the Americans had then rebuilt Japan in their own image, but that was too late for the thousands who had died in the Pacific War.

The American giant has had no opportunity to sleep since then, Tso thought. *And it is already as angry as it has ever been.*

Before going to the control room to begin the dive, Captain Tso searched his stateroom for antacids, going through his drawers with slightly trembling fingers. Finding none, he dropped by the *Shanxi*'s pharmacy. Normally Tso had no digestive difficulties at all, but the thought that he might have to tangle with an American submarine made him feel as if something he had eaten was still alive.

Chapter 49

The *Vermont* had come to periscope depth in the Persian Gulf a few hours before her clean air reserves would have run out. While they waited for new orders from COMSUBPAC, Chris made sure all of the contaminated air in the compressed reserves was replaced with fresh air drawn in through the snorkel.

After completing the air exchange, he went to the meal known as midrats, short for midnight rations. The selection was corned beef hash. Oral had taken over for the last surviving cook, who had just fallen ill. The COB had mercifully taken time to warm up the salty slop before passing it out.

American submarines normally had the best food in the Armed Forces. It went a long way toward compensating for the misery of living in a can. But the *Vermont*'s crew was now too shorthanded to carry on expendable activities such as cooking.

The enlisted mess was packed, except for Chris's corner table, which he soon had all to himself. A few hours earlier, the distinctive cough caused by the old smoke damage in his lungs had returned, apparently to stay. Now the otherwise harmless cough was causing the rest of the crew to shun him. Some of them were grumbling that he should check himself into Purgatory.

It had been several days since he'd heard a cough from anyone else outside the sick bays. At first that had struck him as odd, since healthy people cough fairly often. Then he'd realized that none of his shipmates *dared* to cough if they could help it—they were afraid he and his germ police would confine them under guard in the sick bays, a sentence that so far seemed equivalent to execution.

Unfortunately, Chris had no control over his chemical-injury cough.

He watched the other men as he ate. A few were dozing over their food, despite being jostled by their neighbors. All the others seemed to have nervous, bloodshot eyes with dark bags under them.

When Oral was finished serving the others, he came into the crowded mess with a heaping bowl of hash. After some hesitation, he sat down across the otherwise empty table from Chris.

Feeling he owed Oral some conversation, Chris said, "What do you plan to do after you quit, COB?" Oral had told Chris that he was going to leave the Navy after this run.

"If I get home alive, I'll know God saved me for a special purpose," Oral said. "I already know what my mission is, and I don't plan to let Him down."

Chris was straining to eat and talk without coughing. "What's your special mission?"

"I'm going to rid the world of nuclear weapons."

"Good luck," Chris said, sincerely.

"I'm going to do it," Oral said. "I'll do whatever it takes."

Something about that statement made Chris uncomfortable.

"Everybody's worried about biological weapons nowadays," Oral continued, "but nukes are still the worst weapons of mass destruction."

Chris made a face that would have included a raised eyebrow if he'd had eyebrows. "I don't know, COB. Why do you think nukes are worse?"

"Because they destroy *everything*, " Oral said. "Infrastructure, works of art, churches, libraries, whole ecosystems . . . everything. They can make huge areas of land uninhabitable for generations. If enough of them are used at the same time, soot from the fires could even cause a nuclear winter that wipes out most species of life on Earth. Germs only kill people—they don't destroy property or nature, and they certainly couldn't disrupt the Earth's climate."

Tumor had just joined them. "I think germs are worse," he said. "Especially the ones that are catching, like plague and smallpox, because they can keep on spreading once you turn them loose. The damage from a nuke may be pretty dadgone horrible, but at least it has a limit."

Oral's bowl was already empty. He excused himself to get more. Eng came over and took his seat, apparently thinking he was gone for good.

Chris was still coughing frequently. He felt grateful that his volunteers were willing to hang around him. "What I want to know is *how the hell did we let it come to this*?"

"What do you mean?" Tumor asked.

"I mean technology has allowed us humans to totally dominate the planet. It's given us great medicine and transportation and entertainment and so forth. But in some ways, we were probably better off living in caves. You can bet cavemen didn't lie awake at night worrying about weapons of mass destruction."

"Yeah, they had cave bears to worry about," Tumor said with a wry chuckle.

Chris frowned. "And now all the bears are dead, almost. We've used our big brains to replace bears with nuclear bombs, lethal microbes, and poison gas. Honestly, which would you rather have to live with? How can we be so smart and so stupid at the same time?"

"That's easy," Eng said with a contemptuous smirk. "Some of us are smart but most are stupid."

"Isn't that a little simplistic, sir?"

"Actually, it's profound," Eng said. "The vast majority of human beings are close to average intelligence. If social and technological advancement were left up to them, we'd still be tribes of naked savages, roving around the savannah scavenging bone marrow from carcasses, but we'd be in no danger of causing our own extinction. Human intelligence has a wider range than most people can imagine. It's the one-in-a-million geniuses—the Einsteins and Edisons—who've given us such great achievements and such terrible danger. Our modern high-tech existence is all thanks to them, and the rest of us are just not equipped to deal with it. We may think we are, but that's one of the many illusions in the fog that average human animals grope through all their lives."

"What's your solution?" Chris asked.

Eng snorted. "I don't have one. If we were all as smart as the rare geniuses, perhaps we could use our technology wisely, but that's not going to happen. In any free society, the geniuses will develop new technology, but the relatively feeble-minded majority will decide how to use it."

"Are you saying freedom is bad?" Tumor asked.

"Of course not. When human societies are not free, the people who rise to power are not the most intelligent individuals—they're the most ruthless, fearless, and power-hungry. The smart ones lie low to avoid stress, alienation, and assassination. Gentlemen, I'm afraid the war between human nature and human survival is here to stay. The only way I can see for us to prevent our own bell curve from wiping us out is better global education and communication. And universal freedom is what paves the way for both of those."

An announcement came over the 1MC. The crew froze like statues, hunched over their bowls with food in their mouths and spoons poised in their hands. They stared up at the speakers with hope and apprehension.

"Attention, all hands. This is the captain. We have received new orders from STRATCOM. We will immediately proceed back to Sub Base Bangor with a patrol quiet lineup, maintaining radio silence and avoiding all contacts. That is all."

There were no whistles or cheers, no high fives or slaps on the back. Chris saw tears streaming down one man's face. Whether they were tears of relief or dread, he couldn't tell. All of these men were bound to be glad they were heading home, but home was literally a world away, and they all knew that many of them would not make it.

Chapter 50

The Strait of Hormuz was a shallow passage shaped like a horseshoe with the bend pointing northward. It connected the Persian Gulf on the west to the Gulf of Oman on the east. The Gulf of Oman opened into the Arabian Sea, a bay of the Indian Ocean between Arabia and India.

Captain Scott took the conn as the *Vermont* approached the Strait of Hormuz on course 045, on her way out of the Persian Gulf. He called the sonar shack on the 8MC, an intercom between the conn and the sonar shack. "Who's out there, chief? There's bound to be a crowd this close to the strait."

The sonar chief replied, "We hold five contacts, sir— four merchies and one warship that we think is an Iranian frigate, but she's too far out to hear us."

A while later, the sonar chief called back. "Conn, sonar, new contact bearing zero-five-one. Designate contact number Sierra Sixteen. Sounds like another warship, sir."

The new contact was in the strait ahead of them. "Give me a blade count," Scott ordered.

After several seconds, the sonar chief reported, "Captain, Sierra Sixteen has seven blades."

Most merchant ship screws had only three blades. Most surface warships had four or five. Seven blades meant the new contact had to be a submarine.

"Captain, Sierra Sixteen's course is three-two-zero."

"Check that course again," Scott ordered. A course of 320 was almost perpendicular to the trend of the strait.

"Captain, Sierra Sixteen's course is now three-one-zero. She's turning toward us, sir!"

Keeping his voice calm, Scott said, "Helm, give me left ten degrees rudder. Make five knots by log." He grabbed the 1MC and announced to the whole crew, "Man battle stations torpedo."

Scott switched to the 7MC, the ship control intercom circuit. "Torpedo room, conn. Load ADCAPs in tubes one and two and make them ready in all respects."

He called the sonar shack again. "I need the range to Sierra Sixteen, sonar."

"We're working on it, sir. Recommend coming left to three-one-five for a TMA leg."

TMA stood for target motion analysis. It was a way of determining a contact's range—its distance—by moving along at least two legs in different directions and measuring the resulting changes in the sound's direction and volume.

The helmsman called out the *Vermont*'s course as she turned to the left. "Passing course zero-four-zero. Passing course zero-three-five."

"Come left to course three-one-five," Scott ordered. Aside from assisting the TMA, a course of 315 should keep the *Vermont* from getting any closer to Sierra Sixteen until they figured out who she was.

By now, there should have been an acknowledgment from the torpedo room that tubes one and two were loaded and ready. Scott called on the 7MC. "Torpedo room, conn; what's the status of those warshots?"

"Getting there, sir," said the familiar deep bass of Christopher Long. "I had to call the torpedomen in here from the passageway. They came in without wearing masks, sir."

"Passing course zero-one-zero," said the helmsman.

"Sonar, is Sierra Sixteen still turning toward?" Scott asked on the 8MC.

"Yes, sir," replied the sonar chief. "Her course is now two-eight-zero. She's making turns for twenty knots."

Scott brooded over the delay in the torpedo room. It was an ominous sign of how much the plague had compromised the *Vermont*'s combat readiness.

The sonar chief called. "Conn, sonar; the computer says Sierra Sixteen is a Chinese Type-093. She has a warped bearing in a reactor coolant pump that identifies her as the *Chop Suey*."

U.S. naval intelligence did not yet know the actual names or hull numbers of the four *Yangtze*-class attack subs that China had recently built, so they had assigned the boats names that were easy for Westerners to remember: *Chop Suey, I Ching, Feng Shui,* and *Kung Fu.* American 688i attack subs had trailed all four *Yangtze*s and had isolated unique tonals—constant machinery noises of a certain frequency—that could be used to identify the *Chop Suey* and the *Kung Fu.*

Scott was relieved that the contact was not an Iranian sub.

"Coming up on course three-one-five," the helmsman said, wiping sweat from his temples.

Chris's deep voice came over the 7MC speaker. "Captain, torpedo room; tubes two and three are loaded and ready in all respects. We couldn't get to tube one, sir—patients in the way."

"Very well," Scott said.

"The *Chop Suey*'s course is now two-one-zero," said the sonar chief.

"She's turned past us?" Scott had done the math in his head almost instantaneously. If the *Chop Suey* was still at a bearing of fifty-one degrees, she would have to be on course 231 to head straight toward the *Vermont*.

"Looks like it, sir," said the sonar chief. "And her turn radius is much larger than it needs to be for a *Yangtze* class, even at that speed."

That meant the *Chop Suey* probably had not detected the *Vermont* after all—in all likelihood, she had just happened to be turning at the time the *Vermont* ran across her.

Scott spoke to the diving officer, his tongue now loosened by relief. "Heath, why the hell is a Chinese nuke out here in the Gulf, burning donuts in the ocean for everyone to hear?"

"Don't know, sir," said Heath Evans, the diving officer. Evans was a Tlingit Indian—short, stocky, and dark with thick black hair and small round eyeglasses.

"Now on steady course three-one-five," said the helmsman.

Scott thought for a moment, then announced to the control personnel, "If they keep turning to the south, we'll go around them on the north."

He turned to the quartermaster at the plotting table aft of the conn. "Gary, plot us a safe course along the northern edge of the strait."

Gary Carachez, the quartermaster, was a short and stocky Hispanic with a wide face, a stubby nose, and a wispy black mustache.

Several minutes later, sonar reported another contact ahead and designated it Sierra Seventeen. Scott almost didn't believe his sonarmen when they identified it as another *Yangtze*-class submarine, also doing twenty knots, also making a wide turn. In all his years of conning subs, Scott had never heard of such maneuvers.

"Sonar, conn. Do you still have the *Chop Suey*?"

"Yes, sir."

"What's she doing?"

"She's still turning, sir. She has gone in a complete circle almost twice."

"Are the circles getting wider?" The only reason Scott could think of for a sub to go in circles was to search for something. If that was what the *Chop Suey* was doing, it would make sense for her to start at the most likely location and spiral outward.

"No, sir. She's following the exact same track around and around."

Scott scratched his thick red mustache and pondered the *Chop Suey*'s strange behavior. If the other *Yangtze* was doing the same thing, it couldn't be due to a rudder problem.

"Sonar, conn; does it look like Sierra Seventeen is going in circles too?"

"Yes, sir. Sierra Sixteen is circling on the southern side of the strait. Sierra Seventeen is circling on the northern side. We now have a good firing solution on both contacts."

Maybe they're searching for something after all, Scott thought. *Our intelligence analysts are going to have a fit over this one.*

He turned to the quartermaster. "Gary, if we assume those two crazy Chinese turkeys keep chasing their tails, can you plot a course that will take us between them without getting close enough for either of them to detect us?"

"I'll check, sir."

The quartermaster communicated with sonar, then plotted the tracks of the Chinese subs on a laminated chart with a grease pencil. "Captain, there's a narrow corridor about two miles wide that would take us between their circular tracks at a safe range, no matter how we time our approach."

Scott took a moment to think and blow his large nose. Leaning against the conn railing, he frowned at the overhead repeater screens showing the two sonar contacts.

Whatever the Chinese are up to, it's no concern of ours. My job now is to get these men home before they all croak.

"Very well," Scott said. "Plot us a course down the middle of that corridor so we can get the hell out of here."

Chapter 51

Ziljai Wang—captain of the brand-new improved *Kilo*-class diesel sub, *Guizhou*—had been watching his broad-band sonar operators for two hours as they listened to the roar of the circling *Yangtze*s. The sonarmen looked as if they might throw down their headphones and run away screaming at any moment. The operators of the sophisticated new narrowband processor did not look so annoyed. They had electronically tuned out the loud noise from the *Yangtze*s in order to listen for other, fainter contacts. Whereas broadband showed the volume and location of a sound source, narrowband split the sound into component frequencies to reveal repeating sounds, called tonals, for contact identification.

The *Guizhou* was positioned at the narrowest point in the Strait of Hormuz, where the shores of Iran and Oman were only fifty-six kilometers apart. She was precisely in the center of the strait, between the two circular tracks of the *Yangtze*s. Her crew was using ballast control to hover at fifty meters depth, about halfway between the surface and the shallow bottom.

The *Guizhou*'s battery-powered motors had been shut down. So had most of her other moving parts. Captain Wang had ordered most of the crew to stay in their racks and not move, speak, or do anything else that might make noise. The watchstanders were tiptoeing around in socks or sitting on bare metal chairs to avoid squeaking seat cushions. With the *Guizhou* hovering motionless and rigged for her quietest possible operation, a sub with the best passive sonar ever built could pass by a few meters from her hull without detecting her.

They were into the third hour of waiting when one of the narrowband operators crooked a finger, motioning for Captain Wang to step closer. Wang cautiously approached, silently cursing the slipperiness of his socks on the tiled deck—it would certainly make an audible thump if he slipped and fell.

Wang leaned close, and the sonarman whispered, "Possible contact bearing two-six-five."

Wang silently nodded.

A minute later, the narrowband operator stood up in his stocking feet. "Sir, it's her!" he whispered.

"Determine her speed and course," Wang ordered.

A while later, "Sir, she's coming right at us! Range two thousand meters."

"Hold steady," Wang whispered.

Although the *Guizhou*'s captain was the picture of composure on the outside, inside he was worried that his sub's extreme stealth might lead to a collision. He tried not to picture the nineteen-thousand-ton behemoth bearing down on them. A direct hit would probably rip the *Guizhou* in half, while only damaging the fiberglass sonar dome of the much larger Trident.

"Range one thousand meters," the sonarman whispered. "Still coming at us, sir!"

Wang resisted the urge to sound the collision alarm. He couldn't even warn his crew to brace for impact. This close, the announcement would undoubtedly carry through the water, giving them away.

All of the sonarmen were tense, unmoving, breathing slowly or holding their breath altogether.

The sonar shack had been silent for several seconds when Wang heard a faint rumble with his bare ears. He assumed it was coming from his own boat, and his heart began to pound. *Oh no, they've probably detected us already!*

The rumble grew louder and resolved into a rhythmic *swish-swish-swish*. Captain Wang's heartbeat shifted up a gear, almost keeping time with the ominous noise permeating the stale air inside his cramped vessel. Now he understood that the sound was coming through the hull from outside.

In the twenty years he had served on submarines, this was the first time Ziljai Wang had heard the propeller noise of another sub without the aid of sonar headphones.

He wondered whether it was the last sound he would ever hear. If the Trident plowed into the *Guizhou,* the sea might rush in so fast that the increased air pressure would implode his skull before the nerve impulses could carry the sound of the collision from his ears to his brain.

The noise stopped getting louder. It droned on, seeming to resonate inside the otherwise silent *Guizhou.* Holding his breath, Wang joined his sonarmen in glancing around at the walls, the deck, the overhead—there was no way to tell which direction the sound was coming from. A trickle of sweat stung his left eye, but he didn't dare blink.

Wang knew all the men in their racks could hear the noise too. He could picture their clenched fists and darting eyes. He prayed that none of them would snap under the strain and start yelling.

The Trident was so close that Wang half expected to be caught, even if there was no collision and the *Guizhou* continued to make no noise. He had heard many legends about the uncanny abilities of American sonarmen. He would not have been too surprised to learn that they could hear his thudding heartbeat.

The propeller noise began to fade.

It kept fading.

A few seconds later, Wang forced himself to take a quiet breath. It wouldn't do to pass out now.

He tapped on a broadband operator's shoulder. The man lurched, startled by the touch, but did not make a noise. He cautiously removed his headphones.

"Keep analyzing their speed and course," Wang whispered in his ear.

The sonarman nodded. After a few minutes of concentrating on his instruments, he waved Captain Wang over and whispered, "Course zero-eight-five, speed eight-point-three knots."

Wang could no longer hear the *Vermont* with his naked ears. "Excellent. Let me know when they are too far away to detect our electric engines."

A broadband operator waved frantically for Wang's attention. Forgetting to whisper, he said, "Sir, they just fired on us!"

"What?" Wang stared at the sonar display in disbelief. "Is there a torpedo in the water?"

"Another tube just fired," said a different broadband operator.

"Negative, sir," said the first sonarman. He sounded surprised. "I can't hear the torpedoes. Maybe they malfunctioned."

American torpedoes malfunctioning? Not very damn likely. Wang thought it more plausible that the U.S. Navy had deployed some secret new torpedo with silencing technology. "Keep listening," he ordered, squeezing the back of the narrowband operator's seat.

"Captain, shouldn't we take evasive maneuvers?"

"No! They would hear our engines. Our orders are clear: *Remain undetected at all costs.*"

"Shouldn't we get a snapshot off at them, sir?" A snapshot was a torpedo fired without taking time to program it with target information.

"Not until we hear their torpedoes, Laotung."

"They just fired two more tubes," Laotung said.

"I still don't hear torpedo engines," said the second broadband operator.

"Two more tubes fired," said Laotung. "Why would they fire so many, sir?"

Captain Wang was pretty sure he understood what was going on now—he was one of the few submarine commanders in the Chinese wolf pack who knew what this operation was really about—but he was not allowed to tell his crew what was probably happening on board the *Vermont*. "I don't think they're firing torpedoes," he said. "They must be . . . practicing." In fact, he suspected they were conducting sea burials.

Several minutes later, Laotung said, "Sir, it should be safe to start the engines now."

Wang walked back to the control room, feeling relief from the near miss but bitter disappointment that the *Vermont*'s course made it impossible at this point to trick her captain into entering Omani waters. That meant the high commanders of this massive operation would resort to the first of several backup plans, and Ziljai Wang would probably not get to participate further in this historic endeavor for the future glory and security of China.

He angrily barked his orders to the officer of the deck. "Take us up to periscope depth at one-third power. We have to report our findings."

Chapter 52

Throughout the six-day voyage southeast across the Indian Ocean, Chris frenetically rotated among the three sick bays, all of which were packed with groaning, coughing, prostrate victims. He stayed long enough in each compartment to deal with the emergencies that his volunteers could not handle without him. As he whirled from patient to patient, he felt a kinship with all of the military medics in history who had been overwhelmed by casualties during battle.

He grabbed naps when he could. They were never more than two hours long.

On the third day, he got an excuse to sit for a few minutes when Pigpen begged him to help write a letter. Halfway through dictating the letter to his parents, Pigpen started coughing up rivers of blood. Within five minutes, he was dead. The sonarman had fought the infection for a week, longer than any other victim so far.

By the fifth day, 71 of the *Vermont*'s 155 men had fallen ill, and 24 of those had died. Of the 47 patients crammed into the sick bays, all but 3 were swiftly deteriorating. The three exceptions seemed to be past the worst and gradually improving. Given the purported one hundred percent lethality of untreated pneumonic plague, the existence of three survivors suggested that the antibiotics were providing some benefit after all.

Captain Scott paged Chris to the conn, then took him

aside. "Doc, we need to discuss something that you are not going to like."

Chris wondered whether it was about his upcoming court-martial, which he feared almost as much as the plague. Sickness could cut his life short and torment him with physical pain, but it could not disgrace him.

"Yes, sir?"

"Son, we can't afford to take any more men off duty as soon as they get sick. I know it might make your quarantine efforts moot, but . . . our procedures are breaking down. Men are operating systems that they haven't been trained on. From now on, let the new victims keep working as long as they can. You can put them in one of the sick bays when they collapse."

The *Vermont* was approaching Indonesia when the sonar chief called on the 8MC. "Conn, sonar; new contact bearing one-two-five, designate Sierra Twenty."

That was dead ahead.

Captain Scott stood up on the conn. "Helm, make your speed five knots by log."

The sonar chief said, "Seven blades, Captain."

"Shit fire and launch into orbit," Scott muttered. He had not expected to encounter so much submarine traffic on the way home. Obviously something unusual was going on out there.

He consulted the current navigation chart to decide which way to go around the obstacle. It appeared that a detour to the south would add less time to their voyage than one to the north, although it would require major replotting of their route.

Indonesia included about twenty thousand islands scattered between Southeast Asia and Australia. Scott had planned to begin his traverse of the complex archipelago by cutting between the large islands of Java and Sumatra. After detouring to the south to avoid the new contact, the sub would make better time running along the southern coast of Java, then cutting north through

the islands east of Bali. Either way, he would still have
to navigate through the Makassar Strait between the islands of Borneo and Sulawesi, then cross the Celebes
Sea south of the Philippines to get to the open Pacific.

"Come right to one-seven-zero," he ordered. "Quartermaster, plot us a new course around Java on the
south."

"Conn, sonar; Sierra Twenty is a *Yangtze* class," the
sonar chief reported. "She's making turns for twenty
knots, just like the ones back in the strait."

"Very well," Scott replied, although he was thinking
no such thing. As far as he knew, China was not pres-
ently engaged in any naval conflicts. He couldn't imagine
why they were carrying on so much submarine activity,
unless they had somehow gotten involved in the war
with Iran. But in that case, what were their subs doing
way down here in waters just north of Australia?

"Captain, you're not going to believe this," the sonar
chief said, departing from the standard jargon. "We're
picking up pump noise tonals that identify Sierra Twenty
as the *Chop Suey*."

The *Chop Suey* was the first sub they had encountered
in the Strait of Hormuz.

Scott gripped the railing around the conn and stared
up at the overhead repeater screen that showed the same
image as the broadband screen in the sonar shack. "Are
you sure, chief? She's not going in circles, is she?"

"Her course appears to be steady at three-one-five,
sir. Range eleven thousand meters. She's still too far out
to hear us, but she's coming our way."

"Let me know if she makes a turn in our direction,"
Scott ordered. "Otherwise, we should miss her with
room to spare on a course of one-seven-zero."

Scott wondered how the *Chop Suey* could be here. He
knew it was not physically impossible. The *Vermont* had
been running at flank speed across most of the Indian
Ocean, but she had slowed to a stealthy six knots near
the beginning and end of the voyage. At flank speed, a

Yangtze was almost as fast as a Trident, so the *Chop Suey* could have gotten ahead. But why would she? It seemed terribly unlikely that the same submarine would show up in their path twice in the same voyage by coincidence. Yet the only other explanation was that the *Chop Suey*'s crew had somehow known where the *Vermont* would be and had deliberately headed her off.

Why the hell would the Chinese be dogging us? And how do they know where we're going?

"Conn, sonar; we hold a new contact bearing one-zero-zero, designated Sierra Twenty-one. She's dead ahead and close aboard, sir. Engine noise indicates an improved *Kilo*-class sub. She started up out of nowhere, right in front of us, cavitating like crazy. Looks like we were about to run her down and she was burning rubber to get out of our way. Please advise."

"Shit!" Scott said. "What the hell is going on out there? Can this run get any more fucked up?"

At that moment, all of the *Vermont*'s sonar screens went dark.

Chapter 53

Tumor inchwormed his way out from under a sonar computer and turned off his headlamp, glaring at the exposed wires in the computer's steel cabinet. "Forget it . . . no way. It's fried."

Captain Scott leaned over him. "Are you sure you can't fix it? I'd rather not bore holes through the ocean with no idea what's in front of us right now. There seems to be an uncanny amount of sub traffic out there."

"Not a chance, sir. I'm sorry. Dang it, I knew we shouldn't have shipped out on this emergency run before the *Vermont*'s refits were finished."

Tumor sighed morosely and started collecting his diagnostic tools. Fixing the sonar would have been a perfect way to start redeeming himself for the three screwups he had somehow managed to pack into this aborted run from hell. Fainting twice at the autopsy had been embarrassing but not so harmful. Falling asleep on watch in the torpedo room was another matter. That had allowed Freud to hang himself.

Before either of those goofs, Tumor had committed the worst blunder of all by keeping his promise to Maurice Hereford to not mention his philandering at the Pine Ridge Motel. That had been mortal sin, since the crew's discovery of the attack had been delayed because of his silence.

"What are we going to do now, sir?"

Scott shrugged. "Steam toward home and hope everyone gets out of our way. Are you absolutely certain there's no chance you can fix the sonar?"

Tumor wiped sweat from his pimply forehead. "Maybe if I had a year and two Tridents' worth of spare parts . . ."

"Then you could fix it?"

"I think so."

"Then you can fix it now. Get started. Could you use any help?"

"Gee whiz, of course, but—"

"I'll order all of the electronics technicians to get up here."

"That won't do any good, sir."

"Why not?"

"Because I'm the only one left."

Scott sighed and massaged his chest.

"I'll do my best, sir."

"Good. That's exactly what I expect, son." Scott patted him on the shoulder and left.

Twelve hours later, on board the *Shanxi*—known to the West as the *Chop Suey*—Captain Cho Ling Tso and Colonel Inzu Sze Ma were facing off on the conn. "Colonel, my sonarmen have located the Trident submarine four thousand yards off our port beam. I still do not understand how your commanders predicted what route she would be taking, but evidently they were correct."

"Is she turning to evade us?" Sze Ma asked.

"No, sir."

"Why not?"

"I have no idea, sir."

"If we can hear them, they should have been able to hear us for a while now. Isn't that so?"

"Yes, sir, but the Trident has given no indication that she has detected us or any of the other subs in our pack, which should all be within her sonar range by now. It's very strange, sir, as if . . . as if the crew is dead and she's running on some kind of autopilot."

"Do American submarines have autopilots?"

"Not that I'm aware of, sir."

Colonel Sze Ma gazed at the sonar displays on the control room's repeater screens. Captain Tso was fairly certain that the colonel had no idea how to read the visual representations of sounds, yet a hint of alarm suddenly came over Inzu Sze Ma's expression. It was followed by a deepening of the vertical creases running down from the corners of his mouth to his sharp chin. Captain Tso couldn't be sure, but the new expression looked to him like bitter disappointment.

"We may be too late," Sze Ma muttered, still grimacing in a way that exposed his small, widely spaced lower teeth.

Too late for what? thought Captain Tso. He still had no clue what Colonel Sze Ma and his forty-four commandos had been sent here to do, although it clearly had something to do with the American missile sub.

Inzu Sze Ma turned a stern gaze on Cho Ling Tso. "We cannot let them get past Indonesia. It's our last chance before they reach the open Pacific. You have to get their attention somehow."

"Shall we ram them, sir?"

The colonel's greenish black eyes narrowed. "This is no time for sarcasm, Tso! Get closer. Try making more noise. Hurry!"

Captain Tso ordered his officers to maneuver the *Shanxi* as close to the Trident as they dared, cavitating all the way. He also announced a shipwide order for every spare hand to grab a wrench, hammer, shoe—whatever they could reach—and start banging on the hull. Then he activated the so-called underwater telephone, which used the sonar sphere in the bow dome to broadcast a human voice into the ocean like a loudspeaker.

A deafening cacophony of bangs, clangs, and thuds began resounding throughout the hull.

Captain Tso handed the microphone to Colonel Sze

Ma. "Would you like to say something, sir? Their sonarmen should be able to hear you plainly."

Sze Ma grabbed the microphone. After a moment of hesitation, he began—to Tso's amazement and chagrin—loudly humming the Chinese national anthem.

On board the *Vermont*, the sonar chief ran into the control room with a stethoscope in his hand. "Captain, you'd better come listen to this."

The *Vermont* was equipped with several stethoscopes. They were normally used to help identify the sources of abnormal noises coming from the pipes and machinery. After the sonar shorted out, Captain Scott had stationed the surviving sonarmen throughout the sub to listen to the hull with stethoscopes. Compared to the *Vermont*'s sonar rig, this tactic was like a blind man who could barely distinguish daylight from darkness, but it was better than nothing.

Scott followed his sonar chief to the nearest accessible area of the hull, already listening with his unaided ears for the telltale buzz of an incoming torpedo.

The chief handed him the stethoscope. "It sounds a little like singing, sir."

"Whales?" Scott asked.

"I don't think so, sir. Could be a sick whale, I guess. I've never heard anything like it."

Scott inserted the stethoscope's earpieces and pressed the chestpiece against the cold two-inch-thick steel of the pressure hull. He could hear a murky wailing that gave him gooseflesh. "Jesus, what a ghastly sound. That can't be man-made, chief. Must be biologics."

There also seemed to be a faint banging in the background. It sounded like metal striking metal, a sure sign of a human presence. Scott concluded that the stethoscope must be playing tricks on him. If another sub were stalking the *Vermont*, there was no way her crew would allow their machinery noise to get loud enough for him to hear it with a stethoscope to the hull.

He was on his way back to the conn when a sharp noise resounded through the control room. It sounded like two large blocks of wood being clapped together. It repeated again and again at irregular intervals. Each time Scott heard it, he physically cringed, not because it was so loud but because he knew what the sound was supposed to mean. So did all of the other personnel in the control room, although they had heard it only in simulations. Their reactions were similar to his: hunched shoulders, crouching posture, wild and incredulous eyes.

The distinctive blocks-of-wood ping was produced by a sophisticated Russian-built active sonar. It was used to obtain an exact range to target in the last few seconds before launching a torpedo. Ordinarily, no submarine would use active sonar except when attacking, since the ping would give away its sender's location.

"All ahead flank! Cavitate!" Scott ordered. "Left ten degrees rudder. Dive at twenty degrees down bubble. Launch acoustical countermeasures. Rig ship for collision."

The officers and chiefs burst into activity, simultaneously relaying his volley of orders down the chain of command. The chief of the watch sounded the general alarm, which made a bonging noise.

Scott scratched his red stubble and gripped the conn railing, waiting for the sonar chief to announce that they could hear a torpedo in the water. He wished there were something useful for him to stare at, anything other than the frightened faces of his crew.

"Sir, why do they keep pinging us?" asked the sweating chief of the watch. "Nobody can fire torpedoes that fast."

"I don't know," Scott replied, hanging on to a periscope stand as the *Vermont* pitched precipitously into the dive he had ordered.

The blocks-of-wood sonar was supposed to need only one or two pings before a torpedo was launched, but this one was pinging continuously.

After counting off fifteen seconds, Scott ordered, "Right full rudder." He had no idea where the hostile sub was, so he was following the standard strategy of zigging and zagging randomly in hopes that the torpedo would go for one of the noisemakers the *Vermont* had left in her wake.

Barlow Scott was trying hard—almost successfully—to appear calm on the outside. Inside, he was praying for the sound of a distant explosion that would mean the enemy torpedo had been detonated by one of his countermeasures. In the days since Christopher Long had jolted him into action, Scott had realized how much he still cared about the surviving remnants of his crew.

Chapter 54

In the sonar shack, Tumor felt the deck begin to pitch. He backed out of the tight space between two computer cabinets, reeling for balance. "What the blasted heck?"

The array of tools and spare parts that he had laid out like surgical instruments began falling off the consoles and sliding across the deck, piling up like driftwood against the forward bulkhead. He caught a flashlight in one hand as it rolled off a chair. With the other hand he reached for a falling magnifying glass but missed. The glass hit the deck and shattered.

The voice of Lieutenant Covers came over the 1MC, sounding frantic. "Rig ship for collision! Repeat, rig ship for collision! There may be a torpedo in the water."

Dang it! So close.

To his surprise, Tumor had made considerable progress on the sonar repairs. The processors of the conformal arrays and the towed array were hopeless, but he'd thought he might be able to restore partial function to the Raytheon BQS-13 spherical array within another hour.

He hunkered against a bulkhead and waited for the explosion with his hands covering his large ears. Tumor knew that a single torpedo hit was usually all it took to sink a submarine.

The pinging stopped. After several minutes had passed with no detonations and no more pings, Captain

Scott called off the evasive maneuvers. Either no one was shooting at them after all, or the torpedoes had all lost their target locks and run out of fuel.

"All stop," he ordered. "Maintain a hovering trim at present depth. Rig ship for ultraquiet. We don't know which way to run, so we'll try to hide until we get the sonar back."

He called the sonar shack. "Tumor, any luck?"

"Yes, sir."

"It's fixed?"

"No, but I'm getting there."

"Anything I can do to help?"

"I don't think so, sir."

Scott reluctantly left Tumor alone. *Nothing to do now but wait.*

On board the *Shanxi,* Captain Cho Ling Tso was still puckered from the near collision that had just taken place. The Americans had responded to the *Shanxi*'s pings by attempting to ram her.

Tso tried a wry smile in spite of his elevated blood pressure. He was critical of Colonel Inzu Sze Ma's singing, but apparently the Americans really detested it.

Captain Tso got an unpleasant report from sonar and relayed it to Sze Ma. "We've lost them, Colonel."

"What? They got away?"

"No, sir. They're still close by . . . somewhere. They've shut down all of their noisy systems and disappeared from our passive sonar."

"Try pinging them again," Sze Ma ordered.

"Sir, the last time we lit them up, they swung around and nearly rammed us. Either their captain is as crazy as a Russian, or they didn't know we were there. If we ping them again . . . it wouldn't be safe."

"Safe?" the colonel shouted. *"Safe?* What kind of warrior expects safety in war?"

"Are we at war, sir?"

"Yes!"

Hating Inzu Sze Ma for not explaining this apparently insane operation, Captain Tso ordered his sonarmen to locate the Trident with more active pings.

When the blocks-of-wood sonar sounded again, Barlow Scott cringed and gripped the conn railing, closing his eyes.

"Sir, are we going to execute evasive maneuvers?" asked Heath Evans, the diving officer.

Scott did not open his eyes. He was listening.

"Captain?"

The blocks-of-wood pinging continued.

"They're right on top of us now," Scott said.

"Captain, what if there's a torpedo . . . ?"

Scott opened his eyes. "There isn't. They're too close for a firing solution."

"Sir, are you sure?"

Scott cocked his head. After the next ping, he said, "Reasonably."

"Okay," Evans said, uncertainly.

Scott tried to think in spite of the loud pinging. "They're not here to sink us, Heath."

"What *are* they doing, sir?"

"I don't have a ferret-fucking clue," Scott confessed. "But if we start another blind torpedo evasion, we're likely to run them over."

Barlow Scott knew that collisions were by far the leading cause of serious submarine accidents, accounting for more than forty-two percent throughout history.

"Well? Where are they?" demanded Colonel Inzu Sze Ma.

"Right in front of us," said Captain Cho Ling Tso.

"What are they doing?"

"Nothing."

"They're not running away?"

"No, sir. They're just hovering. I think something is wrong on that submarine."

"Could be," the colonel said.

"What do you want to do now?" asked Captain Tso.

"Wait. We can wait longer than they can."

"How do you know that, sir?"

"Trust me," said Colonel Sze Ma.

Captain Tso was doing what he considered an admirable job of concealing his frustration that Colonel Sze Ma would not tell him their objective. He was now convinced that this operation was going in circles in more ways than one, probably due to lack of communication. And he was beginning to fear that Sze Ma and his forty-four commandos had been sent to do something terrible, something so terrible that their commanders thought a submarine captain might refuse to take part if he knew what it was.

Tumor held his breath and closed the circuit breaker for the equipment he had just repaired. All he heard was the clap of current flowing through the breaker. There were no flames, no sparks, not even smoke or the telltale buzz of a short. He wanted to yell in exultation, but the *Vermont* was in ultraquiet mode, so he didn't make a sound.

Tumor watched the equipment for a few more seconds, sniffing the exhaust from the computers' cooling fans. There was no smell of burning insulation.

He ran into the control room. "Captain! The spherical array is back on line."

"Excellent!" said Captain Scott. "I knew you could do it, Tumor."

Tumor beamed with pride, but only for a second. "Sir, I had to jury-rig a few things. I wouldn't be surprised if the equipment shuts down without warning . . . or catches fire."

Captain Scott waited while his sonarmen went to work. A few minutes later, he could hear a racket of conversation coming from the crowded sonar shack.

When the suspense became unbearable, he got on the 8MC. "Have you figured out who's lashing us, chief?"

Since restarting, the blocks-of-wood pinging had never let up, although it was hitting them less often now.

"We're working on it, sir."

"You still don't have any contacts?" Scott's heart began to sink. Maybe the sonar wasn't fixed after all. It should have been easy to zero in on the source of the loud pings.

"Captain, we're holding multiple contacts. They're showing up faster than we can log them."

Scott was standing solidly on the conn, and the *Vermont* was not moving, and his three-day hangover was long gone. Nevertheless, the sonar chief's words made his stomach feel disembodied. "How many?" he asked.

"Eleven, so far."

"Any IDs?"

"Not yet, sir."

"Focus on the one that's pinging us. She should be the one that's close aboard."

"Captain, they're *all* close aboard. They appear to have us surrounded."

In all his years in the Silent Service, Barlow Scott had never felt a touch of claustrophobia. Modern subs were bright, clean, and spacious compared to the dismal confines of their prenuclear predecessors. He had always been mystified by sailors who claimed that claustrophobia was still the worst thing about serving on a submarine. Now, for the first time, he felt as if the bulkheads were closing in.

"Try to find us a way out, chief."

Several agonizing minutes later, the sonar chief reported, "Captain, we've stopped seeing new contacts. We hold thirteen. Two are *Yangtze*s. Three are improved *Kilo*s. One is a *Han*. The rest are still unidentified."

Since the diesel-powered *Kilo*s were Russian exports,

they could belong to about anyone, but the nuclear-powered *Han*s and *Yangtze*s could only be Chinese. Scott wondered why the hell the *Vermont* was surrounded by a Chinese wolf pack in international waters between Australia and Indonesia.

"Is there a way out?" he asked.

"Yes, sir. They have us boxed in on the east, west, and south, but if we flank it due north, we should be able to get away before any of them can intercept us."

"Captain, that would take us into the territorial waters of Indonesia," said the quartermaster.

Scott stepped down from the aft edge of the conn and looked at the bathymetric chart on the quartermaster's plotting table.

Indonesia was not one of the countries that had given the U.S. Navy permission to come and go as it pleased. Most nations were especially touchy about missile subs skulking around in their backyards. Aside from the implied threat of nuclear attack, the accidental sinking of a single nuclear-powered vessel could contaminate local waters with enough radioactivity to cause an environmental disaster.

"If we go too far north, we'll risk running aground or being forced to surface in the shallows off Java," the quartermaster added.

Scott could see that. "Gary, it looks like we'll have just enough room to outrun these Chinese assholes. Dive, make your course zero-zero-zero, all ahead flank! We'll head north till we run out of water, then turn east. We should be out of this wolf pack's sonar range by then. The Indonesians have no modern submarines and not much of a surface fleet—they'll never know we were there."

Chapter 55

Half an hour later, the *Vermont* was well inside Indonesian waters, approaching the southern coast of Java.

"Where are those contacts?" Scott asked the sonar chief.

"Way behind us, sir. They're still sitting there where we left them."

Scott mulled that over. It almost made sense. The Chinese and Indonesians were not on especially good terms at the moment. Whatever the Chinese wolf pack wanted, it apparently wasn't worth the risk of causing an incident in Indonesian waters. But if they weren't going to pursue the *Vermont*, why didn't they leave? What were they waiting for? Were they hoping to head the *Vermont* off once they saw which way she was going around the island?

"Are we still within their sonar range?" Scott asked.

"No, sir. We can hear them, but they should not be able to hear us anymore."

If the wolf pack had lost the *Vermont*, they couldn't be sticking around to see which way she would go. Scott glared at the broadband repeater screen. *Why the hell are those cabbage-fuckers loitering back there?*

"Helm, come right to zero-nine-zero before an Indonesian skimmer snaps us up. Make your speed all ahead two-thirds."

"Captain, sonar; new contact bearing zero-eight-five!

Designate Sierra Thirty-five. Sounds like a five-blader, sir."

A warship was in the middle of the *Vermont*'s escape route. Scott wondered yet again how much worse their luck could get. "What's her course, chief?"

After several seconds, the sonar chief replied, "Two-seven-zero, sir. She's headed straight for us. Recommend coming around to two-seven-zero to evade."

"Goddamn it, I don't want to go west!"

"She's definitely a warship, sir. Probably Indonesian."

If the *Vermont* got caught and surfaced by the Indonesian Navy, there was no hope of keeping the plague outbreak secret. Scott gave the order to execute a tight one-eighty and head west.

Halfway through the turn, the sonar chief's excited voice crackled over the 8MC. "Captain, we hold a new contact bearing two-seven-five! Another five-blader. Designate Sierra Thirty-six."

This was the first time in Barlow Scott's long naval career that he'd felt truly confused and afraid. Bad luck could only explain so much. Now he had a sick feeling that he had driven his crew into some kind of trap.

Could the Chinese and Indonesians be working together? Given the current geopolitical climate, that hardly seemed likely.

"Which way is Sierra Thirty-six heading?" Scott asked, afraid he already knew the answer.

"*Our way, sir,*" said the sonar chief.

"I've confirmed that Sierra Thirty-five is an Indonesian naval frigate," said another sonarman.

"Captain, what should we do?" asked Heath Evans, the diving officer.

Scott closed his eyes, trying to think. North was land. South was the Chinese wolf pack. East and west, Indonesian skimmers were closing in. And he couldn't disappear by going deep. They were so close to shore that the depth of the ocean was less than the *Vermont*'s length.

A high-pitched ping rang out in the control room. It

was followed by others at a regular interval. Scott recognized the pinging as that of a basic sonar rig on a sub-hunting skimmer.

"Chief, have they got us?"

"Not yet, sir, but they're closing fast. They'll probably start getting a return in about a minute."

Scott whipped around toward the quartermaster. "Gary, what kind of bottom do we have here?"

"Flat," Gary said, "probably sand or mud."

"Put us on the bottom," Scott ordered.

"Pardon, sir?" said the wide-eyed diving officer.

The pinging was getting louder.

"I said bottom this tub!" Scott commanded. "Make your speed three knots by log. Dive at five degrees down bubble. Gary, get one Fathometer ranging and calculate the bottom depth from our depth, then secure the Fathometer so its pings won't give us away. Heath, pull up just in time to set us down with an even trim. Come on, gentlemen; hustle!"

Gary dashed over to the secure Fathometer on the starboard hull and stared at its digital readout. "Forty-eight fathoms to the bottom. Our depth is four-one-zero feet, so that puts the bottom at . . . six-nine-eight feet, which agrees with the charts."

Heath relayed Scott's orders to the helmsman and sternplanesman, who were already carrying them out.

Captain Scott hoped to get the *Vermont* on the bottom before either of the Indonesian skimmers could detect her with their active sonars. If he succeeded, the Indonesians might not be able to pick her out of the bottom return—the sound waves that were reflected back when a ping struck the seafloor. The *Vermont* was not designed to be bottomed—her lower hull had several fittings that could be damaged. As far as he knew, this risky tactic had never been tried in a massive Trident, but it had worked for a few small diesel subs during the world wars.

"Our depth is now four-five-zero feet," said Heath

Evans. He twisted around in the diving officer's chair to face the conn. "Captain, we could get stuck in the mud, or draw grit into the seawater intakes and silt up the pumps and heat exchangers."

Scott knew all that. He also knew that those exact casualties had nearly destroyed another submarine, USS *Seawolf,* during a clandestine cable-tapping operation on the floor of the Sea of Okhotsk in northeastern Asia.

"If we get stuck, so be it," he said. "The commander in chief has ordered us to keep this outbreak secret at all costs."

"Passing five hundred feet!" Heath called out.

Despite his sweaty palms, this whole situation struck Scott as faintly ridiculous. He was tempted to just ignore the Indonesian skimmers and the Chinese subs. If he bluffed his way back out of Indonesian waters and headed home, what were the odds that any of them would dare to attack an American boomer?

On the other hand, if the Indonesians or Chinese sank the *Vermont,* they could probably get away with it. All the U.S. Navy would know was that the *Vermont* had disappeared somewhere in the Indian or Pacific Ocean.

How did the Indonesians know we were coming? They must be working with the Chinese. But why?

"Passing five-five-zero feet."

Scott grabbed the 1MC mike and announced, "Rig ship for collision."

"Captain, Sierra Thirty-five will be close enough to detect our ping return any second now," the sonar chief reported.

"Passing six hundred feet," Heath said. "Looks like we're going down kind of fast, sir."

"All stop," Scott ordered. "Plane up the bow to a level trim. Chief of the watch, flood the trim tanks and the depth control tank to sink us the rest of the way."

"Six-five-zero feet. Still going down fast."

Scott got on the 1MC again. "All hands brace for collision. We are about to run aground."

The control personnel grabbed railings and pipes and hung on.

"Six-eight-zero feet. Here we go, sir. We're still coasting forward at two knots."

Scott gripped the conn railing and waited for his nineteen-thousand-ton, three-billion-dollar responsibility to bury itself in the mud.

He felt a bump, followed by vibrations. A dull rumble and a gentle hiss filled the control room. He felt a slight forward tug, and the deck began rolling a little. The noise, shaking, and rocking continued for another ten seconds. Then all motion ceased, and the control room was quiet except for the distant pinging.

For several seconds, everyone listened for the roar of flooding. They watched one another without speaking. Then the quartermaster said, unnecessarily, "We're on the bottom, captain."

"Where are the skimmers?" Scott asked.

"They're still converging on us," said the sonar chief.

"Did they get close enough to see us before we touched down?"

"They might have, sir, depending on what kind of sonar rig they have."

The control room fell silent again, except for the pinging. Scott could hear the victims coughing in the sick bays. With the *Vermont* on the bottom, there was nothing for the control personnel to do. They sat or stood by their instruments—wiping sweat, listening, and staring up at the overhead. It had always annoyed Scott when submariners stared at the overhead because a threat was above them. Now he was doing it too.

The sonar chief spoke softly. "It sounds like both skimmers are stopping, sir."

"Where?"

"Directly above us."

Scott smacked the closest periscope stand. There was no point in trying to be quiet now. "Fuck a rabid porcupine! Listen for splashes, chief."

"You think they'd depth charge us, sir?"

"I have no idea what they intend to do! Damn it, those turkeys were going straight for us from the start. There's no way they could have heard us before we heard them, is there?"

"No, sir," said the sonar chief. "I'm sure they never did hear us with their passive rigs."

"Well, that means those Chinese assholes must have come up to PD and told the Indonesians exactly where we were headed. The only question is why."

The pinging stopped.

A few seconds later, the sonar chief spoke, sounding confused. "Sir, you'd better listen to this."

"Put it on the conn speaker," Scott ordered.

The *Vermont*'s hydrophones were picking up a human voice being broadcast into the water. The voice was repeating the same message over and over in heavily accented English: "U.S. Navy submarine, this is Indonesian Navy surface vessel. We are responding to your request for medical evacuation of biological weapon casualties. If you are able to communicate, please acknowledge with sound."

Chapter 56

Captain Scott sat down on the conn, trying to appear calm. That was the one thing a sub skipper could still do when all was lost.

He knew that none of his crew could have sent an SOS to the Indonesians. It was physically impossible. The *Vermont* hadn't been at periscope depth since the Gulf, and none of the sub's transmitters could broadcast radio waves more than a few feet through water.

So who had sent the request for help?

Someone who knew about the outbreak.

Someone who knew the *Vermont*'s position, course, and speed.

"Those pig-fuckers know we're dying of plague!" Scott said.

"The question is who told them," said Heath Evans.

"I'm not talking about the Indonesians," Scott said. "I'm talking about the Chinese. They're the only ones who could have told the Indonesians exactly where to look for us. One of those Chinese subs must have come up and broadcasted a distress call, pretending to be the *Vermont*."

"Does that mean the Chinese are the ones who infected us, sir?"

"Probably," Scott said. "They could have found out about the outbreak from a spy, but then why would they want to get involved? Why would they chase us, surround us, lash us with active sonar, then trick the Indonesians into thinking we called for help? Damned if I know why they've done all that, even if they are the ones who infected us, but it looks like one thing's for certain: China has just picked a war with the United States."

After his brief meeting with Scott, Chris had returned to rotating among the sick bays for the next two watches. He hadn't sat down for more than five minutes, much less taken a nap over the past fifteen hours. Every joint and muscle ached and felt as if it might malfunction at any moment.

How long has it been since I slept?

He couldn't remember.

Chris knew he was more frayed than he had ever been. His feet were swollen and sore. The hip muscles that swung his legs forward when he walked had stopped working hours ago, forcing him to shuffle along with a hobbling gait. Whenever he could, he used his strong arms to help out his legs, but he was usually carrying a patient or a load of supplies. He had ceased to do, say, or think anything that was not necessary to the task at hand.

When he heard a 1MC announcement paging him to control, Chris hobbled upstairs as fast as he could.

Captain Scott took one look at him and got up to offer Chris his seat. Chris had never sat in the thronelike OOD's chair. He plopped down without wasting energy on a thank-you.

"Doc, I need to know if we're going to be able to get back to Bangor on our own."

Chris's response was sluggish and slurred. "You mean, are we going to have enough men?"

Scott nodded.

Chris pulled out his rumpled casualty projection and started trying to figure out how he had done the calculations before.

Scott gently shook his shoulder.

Chris opened his eyes. "Huh?"

"You nodded off, son."

Chris stood up, resting the paper on the back of the chair and leaning on the conn railing. After some arithmetic and a few calls to the sick bays, he leaned close and whispered, "Captain, I have to run back and give an injection. Would you care to walk with me?"

Scott glanced at his expression and nodded. "Dive, you have the conn." He followed Chris out of the control room.

As soon as Chris judged that no one could overhear them, he slumped against a wall. "We're not going to make it home, sir."

"Is that a fact?"

"As close to a fact as a prediction can get, skipper. This Java detour was too long, and the rate of transmission has speeded up by at least a factor of three, now that sick men are staying on watch instead of being quarantined right away. Only forty-six men still have no symptoms, including you and me. Unless a miracle happens, we'll all be dead or too sick to work long before we can cross the Pacific."

Scott closed his eyes and massaged his chest. "What do you think we should do?"

Chris stepped away from the wall. He had fallen asleep again for a second, but he managed to piece together what Scott had just said. *Now the captain is not just asking me about medical stuff; he wants me to help him brainstorm the whole tactical picture. He must have run out of officers.*

"Could we just sneak out of here, sir?"

"Not unless those two skimmers give up and leave before we all croak, and that doesn't seem likely. They could wait indefinitely by handing us off to other ships."

"What other options do we have, sir?"

"We could stay down here forever."

"Do you think we should?" Chris asked with hardly any feeling. His feelings and hopes were all but burned out at this point.

"Personally, I'd prefer to try bluffing our way out," Scott said, "but that would look mighty suspicious to the Indonesians. They think we asked them for help with treating bioweapon casualties, and apparently they are willing to give it. If we run away now, they're bound to think we have something to hide."

Chris sluggishly nodded. "And we should avoid the appearance of a cover-up at all costs, right?"

"Affirmative," Scott said. "That's probably more important at this point than trying to conceal the outbreak, since those Chinese pig-fuckers have already sent an unsecure broadcast announcing to the whole world that a contagious germ weapon is loose on our sub."

"Skipper, I think we need to call COMSUBPAC again."

Scott massaged his hairy chest. "I believe you're right, Doc."

Scott returned to the conn and ordered the ascent, instructing his crew to move far enough laterally to make sure they didn't come up directly beneath one of the skimmers. The *Vermont* had no difficulty lifting off the bottom, which was apparently made of firm sand, but halfway to the surface she started rolling. That meant the weather was bad.

"Rig ship for rough seas," Scott announced.

The rocking grew steadily worse. In the wardroom, two patients were injured by rolling oxygen cylinders before Chris could secure them.

At periscope depth, Scott raised the search scope and slowly rotated it in a full circle, hanging on to its horizontal handles as the deck pitched and swayed. It was supposed to be early afternoon, but the day was almost as dark as night. He could see frequent flashes of lightning. The sound of thunder was diffusing through sixty feet of water and the *Vermont*'s hull as a faint rumble.

He could also hear the muffled smacks and sloshing of crashing waves.

Jesus. An hour on the surface in a tropical blow like this would make us all too seasick to walk.

Underwater, the *Vermont*'s cylindrical hull minimized hydrodynamic drag, but on the surface it was much less stable than the V-shaped hull of a skimmer.

Scott saw a ship off the starboard beam. He could tell it was a small warship, but he couldn't make out what colors it was flying. It appeared to be loitering as close as it safely could in the storm. He surmised that it had followed the *Vermont* during her oblique ascent with its active sonar, which was still pinging away.

Looking astern, he saw that the other skimmer was catching up. Its running lights seemed to wink on a few at a time as it approached through the heavy downpour, pitching and rolling on the waves.

Scott knew a medical evacuation by the Indonesians was probably the last chance for any of his crew to survive, but even if COMSUBPAC allowed it, evacuation in this weather might be physically impossible.

Chapter 57

By the time COMSUBPAC replied to Captain Scott's request for orders, four hours had elapsed, two patients had died, and three new victims had fallen ill. The *Vermont* was still hovering at periscope depth, rocked by the storm waves.

Scott made an announcement over the 1MC: "Attention, all hands. The commander in chief has ordered us to surface and accept the offer of medical assistance from the Indonesian Navy."

He paused, wondering whether there would be any response. There was none. The surviving remnants of his crew knew all too well that abandoning a Trident submarine in foreign waters was a tragic and unprecedented defeat for the U.S. Navy.

Scott continued. "For now, we will leave the *Vermont* at anchor. The Navy is dispatching a large surface fleet along with several six-eighty-eight attack subs from Guam and Diego Garcia to help the Indonesians secure a perimeter around her. To make sure no one suspects the United States of trying to cover up the possession of biological munitions, American forces will not board the *Vermont* until a team of weapons inspectors from the United Nations has arrived to collect evidence. I need two qualified reactor operators to volunteer to stay on board and man the plant until the inspectors get here."

Scott hung up the mike, then sat on the edge of the

conn and hung his head. He could hardly believe his government was so desperate to avoid any appearance of guilt that they would expose the inner workings of America's most potent and secret war machine to foreign nationals. Some if not most of the UN weapons inspectors were bound to be undercover spies working for the intelligence services of their home nations. This could very well be the darkest day for the U.S. Navy since December 7, 1941.

Chris was in the torpedo room when he heard the announcement of surrender. Despite the crushing fatigue and nervous burnout, he had been trying to think about their tactical situation while caring for the dying and disposing of the dead. Now he was afraid COMSUBPAC was making a mistake.

He hobbled to the control room. "Captain, how long will it take our other ships to get here?"

Scott blew his large nose and tossed the tissue over his shoulder. "About three days."

"Well, sir, are you sure two men is enough to leave on the *Vermont* in the meantime? What if the Indonesians decide to board her as soon as they get the rest of us off?"

"They've agreed not to."

"That's great, sir, but two men couldn't stop them."

Scott frowned. "They wouldn't dare."

"Sir, someone dared to attack us with plague. If any of our enemies really believe we're carrying bioweapons, they might bribe the Indonesians to seize the evidence before our own forces could get here and dispose of it."

Scott's expression transformed from despair to anger. "Come to think of it, the devious little turkeys could probably get away with boarding us. We drove into their territorial waters with nukes on board. If that's what they're planning, it could explain why they're so eager to take a chance on catching plague from us."

"My thoughts exactly, sir."

A trace of a grin appeared beneath Scott's thick red mustache. "Here's what we'll do, Doc. In addition to the reactor operators, I'll get enough able-bodied volunteers to secretly stay on this infested pigboat so we can submerge and drive her away if we have to."

"Good luck, sir."

"Oh, I can convince them, Doc. We'll only need about a dozen. I'll stay behind, and I assume you will too."

"Thank you, sir. Of course I'll stay, as long as I'm useful."

Scott nodded toward the sonar shack. "You can operate some of the sonar gear, right? I recall Steve Brady saying you were going to become a sonarman before he booted you for napping on the job."

"Sir, I tried my hand at the broadband stack, but—"

"Good. You'll be useful. Eng has already volunteered to stay in Maneuvering. He can direct the two trainees who volunteered to keep manning the reactor—there are no qualified RO's left. Oral is staying on too, although he's too sick to get up. He said he wants to stay and take his punishment, bless his heart. He seems to think this outbreak is God's wrath for our sin of carrying nuclear weapons. I ought to send him ashore, but he convinced me to promise I wouldn't."

"Tumor will want to stay," Chris said, "but I don't think he's qualified on anything except electronics repair."

Scott nodded. "That's fine. You never know when you'll need a good circuit-head."

"Sir, will keeping a skeleton crew on board violate our orders?"

Scott bobbed his head back and forth. "Maybe a little. We'll tell COMSUBPAC and the Indonesians that the men staying behind are among the dead, which will probably be true soon enough. Meanwhile, anyone who tries to violate our hatches will get a nasty surprise."

Chris nodded. "There's one other thing, sir. I'm not so sure we should take a chance on letting this bug loose on the surface, especially in a crowded third-world country like Indonesia. Remember, this strain can't be stopped with antibiotics, and it seems to sneak through quarantine barriers like a ghost. I'll bet the standard plague vaccine won't work against it either."

Scott hung his head, mashing his eyes and massaging his chest.

In the silence that followed, Chris fell asleep on his feet. He woke up when he started to fall and grabbed the conn railing to steady himself. Scott looked up and saw him swaying but did not comment.

Finally, the aging captain said, "It's out of our hands now, Doc. We've been ordered to surface. I'm sure the top people have considered the possible consequences."

Chris lethargically nodded. That was all he had come to say.

Scott wanted to make the *Vermont* fast to a pier before letting the crew disembark. In rough seas, it could be dangerous or impossible to transfer men from the low topside deck of a submarine to the higher deck of a surface ship. In the past, several submariners had been crushed or drowned during attempted rescues from disabled subs in stormy weather.

Failing that, he begged the rescuers to let him maneuver closer to shore, where the waves wouldn't be so high.

The Indonesians refused both requests. Their strategy for preventing an epidemic on land was to treat the evacuated submariners aboard ships. They planned to keep the ships far out at sea until the survivors could be transferred to American vessels and the Indonesian ships could be certified free of plague by medical experts.

Finally a plan was agreed upon, and Scott ordered the chief of the watch to blow the main ballast tanks. He had considered postponing the rescue until the storm passed, but the Indonesians had assured him that it was a wide tropical depression and would remain over the area for at least a day.

"Attention, all hands. This is the captain. We are about to surface. Wave motion will become extremely violent. Put on your floatation vests and make your way to the muster point beneath the escape trunk for your section. Do not attempt to carry the patients; drag them along the decks. I will not be going with you and will probably never see most of you again. I wish you all a safe passage home and fair sailing for the rest of your days. That is all."

Chapter 58

Chris waited beneath the lower hatch of the forward escape trunk, holding on to the dogging wheel above his head like a grab rail. The *Vermont* was fully surfaced. He could hear dull thunder reverberating through her thick hull, rain pounding on the topside deck, and killer waves crashing against the flat side of the sail.

Chris was surrounded by prostrate plague victims and able-bodied crewmen who were crouching against the bulkheads, hanging on to anything they could reach and grip. It was night outside now. Captain Scott had switched the *Vermont*'s lighting to the red night lights in hopes that the men would be able to see where they were going when they crawled outside. The sweaty faces were covered by masks, respirators, or handkerchiefs, except for those of the men who were vomiting from seasickness, but even in the dim red light, Chris could see the fatigue and defeat in their eyes, as well as fear of the dangerous operation they were about to attempt.

The deck was gyrating in all directions. The apparent weight of Chris's exhausted body alternated between almost light and unbearably heavy as the *Vermont* rose and fell on the waves. The rolling was even more terrifying than the vertical excursions, especially when an extra-large wave made the cylindrical sub feel as if she were going to roll all the way over.

Chris looked over at Gene Kurlgunn, who was sitting in a meditative position with his eyes closed. The would-

be mutineer appeared calm, oblivious to the horrors surrounding him and at ease with the deck's violent motion.
When the deck tilted, he prevented himself from falling
over by gripping a vertical pipe.

Tumor was also waiting nearby. After being seasick
for a while, he looked at Chris with a hint of an encour-
aging smile.

Finally Chris heard banging above his head. That was
the signal. He waited until the deck was somewhat level,
then spun the wheel counterclockwise to undog the
hatch. His worn-out legs responded with unexpected
strength as he raced up the ladder through the escape
trunk.

When he opened the topside hatch, his face was
blasted by cool rain and a downward surge of blessedly
fresh air. Lightning forked across the sky, illuminating
thick clouds and temporarily blinding him.

"Is anybody there?"

He doubted his yell could be heard over the crashing waves.

A vague silhouette appeared, kneeling on the tilted
deck above Chris. A flashlight switched on, and Chris
saw the sidelit face of a young Asian sailor with wet
black hair and a soaked tan uniform. An orange webbing
harness crisscrossed the sailor's torso. One end of a thick
chain was attached to the back of it. Chris couldn't see
the other end of the chain. He assumed it was hooked
to the safety track inset in the *Vermont*'s outer hull.

The sailor was not wearing a mask or gloves. Chris
wondered if he knew his commanders had sent him on
a potentially suicidal mission.

"Take rope!" the sailor yelled, shoving a thick coil of
deck line into the hatch. Before Chris could catch it,
the rope fell down through the tilted shaft, uncoiling as
it went.

The rescuer had disappeared. "Hey, where—?"

An onslaught of seawater poured down over Chris,
drenching his hair and clothing. It tore off his mask and

got into his ears and nose, but he managed to hang on to the ladder. He coughed and spat out the salty water, then looked up again, blinking.

The Indonesian sailor reappeared, dripping and bleeding from a small cut on his right temple. "Hurry fast!" he yelled with an angry expression. "Tie under arms!"

Chris shimmied back down the wet rungs. He stumbled to the nearest patient and dragged him to the base of the ladder. The man was unconscious, so Chris had to prop his upper body against the ladder while looping a slip knot around his chest.

Tumor crawled across the wet deck to help. He and Chris both held on to the ladder with one hand while manipulating the rope with the other, bracing the victim between their knees so the heaving deck couldn't toss him aside.

Three Indonesian sailors were peering down through the hatch now. Chris was about to signal them to hoist the victim up when another wave washed across the topside deck, dumping several hundred gallons of seawater down into the compartment. Chris managed to hang on, but the heavy deluge broke Tumor's hold on the ladder, sweeping him downhill. He collided with the men huddling against the wall. When the deck rolled the other way, Tumor took advantage of the tilt to slide back to the ladder on his belly.

Meanwhile, Chris noticed that the patient wasn't coughing. In fact, he didn't seem be breathing, and his lips were blue. Chris probed his cold neck for a pulse.

"Goddamn it! This one's dead. Tumor, get the rope off him and move him out of the way. I'll go get another one."

A little less than an hour later, all of the men who planned to leave the *Vermont* had disembarked. Chris and Tumor were now alone in the foul, wet compartment. The rest of the skeleton crew was hiding on the lower decks where the Indonesians couldn't see them.

"Do you wish you could leave too?" Tumor asked, blinking and shivering.

"What do you think?" Chris replied.

Tumor nodded. "Yeah, same here."

Chapter 59

Chris gathered the skeleton crew and showed them the proper doses and timing of their antibiotics. He also explained how to use the oxygen respirators, which were sure to become necessary in a matter of hours. Then he searched for a place where he could lie down without being rolled very far by the *Vermont*'s wild rocking.

In the galley, he found a niche about two feet wide and five feet long between an oven and a cutlery locker. After calling to tell Captain Scott where he was, he crawled into the niche, collapsed on his side, and fell asleep with the waves knocking him back and forth against the steel panels.

Chris was wrenched awake by a boom that was so loud it felt as if he had been punched in the chest. He lunged upward, banging his arms and head on the steel walls of his narrow cubbyhole. He'd been sound asleep when the noise entered his ears, but he was certain that it had been an explosion of naval ordnance—nothing else could have been that loud.

He listened for the roar of flooding but heard nothing. The deserted galley seemed eerily silent.

The dim red lighting was still on. Chris took that to mean it was still nighttime, since the main reason for the red lights was to avoid ruining the night vision of personnel who might have to look out through a periscope.

The *Vermont* was still rocking, but much more gently

than she had been when he'd fallen asleep. He was able
to walk without holding on to anything. His stomach
ached from hunger and thirst, but his legs worked a little
better than they had the last time he'd been on them.

He had started running toward control when Captain
Scott's voice blared over the 1MC. "All hands! Man battle stations torpedo! Rig ship for dive!"

Chris raced through control toward the sonar shack,
which was now his designated battle station. He saw that
Scott was tensely staring out through the binocular
search periscope. "Skipper, what's going on?"

"Somebody just blew that Indonesian skimmer to
kingdom come, Doc."

Chris stopped running. *The one with our crew?*

Scott remained glued to the scope. "No, the other one.
The rescue ship is anchored a few miles off. They left
the other ship close by to guard us. Her bow just went
under. Looks like one raft of survivors got off."

"Holy shit," Chris said.

"Doc, get on the sonar and tell me what you see!"

Chris ran into the sonar shack and put on headphones.
He started to sit down but froze halfway to the chair.
He was staring at the waterfall display of the broadband
stack. There were so many leaning white lines on the
background of vertical green streaks that he couldn't
count them at a glance.

He slowly lowered himself into the chair, feeling weak
all over. If he'd been watching the sonar instead of sleeping, he would have seen these contacts coming before
they got within torpedo range. Now they were all so
bright that they had to be close aboard.

Forgetting to use the 8MC intercom, he yelled, "Captain! Contacts all around us!"

"How many?"

Chris counted. "Thirteen, sir."

"I can't see anybody on the surface except the frigate
that took our men off," Scott shouted.

"How's visibility, sir?"

"Unbeatable. Storm's gone. Still getting swells off it, but the air's clear and a full moon is out."

"Sir, these contacts are really close. They've got to be submarines. Maybe we should call the rescue ship and warn them."

"I'm sure they know, Doc. Yeah, it looks like they just hoisted anchor. They're turning away, kicking up a wake. What are those contacts doing?"

"They all seem to be on courses that are roughly perpendicular to their bearing angles."

"They're circling us?"

"Yes, sir. Clockwise."

"All of them?"

"No. One's getting fainter, and its bearing is not changing."

"It's moving straight away from us?"

"That would be my guess, sir. I don't know how to determine a contact's exact course."

Scott's voice became even more urgent. "The one that's leaving! Which way is it going?"

"Its bearing is zero-nine-five, sir."

"Goddamn it!" Scott bellowed. "That's the bearing of the rescue ship! *Get me a firing solution on that target, Doc!*"

Chris heard Scott run into the radio room and yell, "Indonesian surface vessel, this is U.S. Navy submarine. A hostile sub is coming after you from the west, range about one mile. Recommend you launch torpedo countermeasures and take evasive action!"

The reply was a burst of some foreign language that Chris assumed was Indonesian. He couldn't understand a word of it. From the confused tone of the voice, he guessed that the Indonesian radio operator had not understood a word Scott had said either.

Chapter 60

A spike of noise lanced into Chris from his sonar headphones as if he'd been shot through the head with an arrow. He slung off the headphones and jumped up, holding his throbbing ears.

As his hearing returned, Chris looked aft into the control room and saw the diminutive captain hanging from the search scope as if he were about to throw up. His face looked as if it were made of wax.

"Sir, what just happened?" All Chris could see on the waterfall display was that the receding contact between the *Vermont* and the rescue ship appeared to be coming back.

"They killed them all," Scott groaned.

"They hit the rescue ship?"

Scott slowly nodded. "Torpedo under the keel, amidships. Broke her in half. She's going down too fast for anyone to get off."

"Do you think they'll hit us next?"

"No. They would have sunk us already if they were going to."

It occurred to Chris to try calling for help. Even if no help was available, it was essential to report this surprise attack to COMSUBPAC so they would know what had happened. He dived into the radio room and put on headphones. Thirty seconds later, he was trying to convince a three-star admiral that he was in the middle of the first real naval battle ever to involve an American nuclear submarine.

"Try to calm down," the admiral ordered. "Who is attacking?"

"I can't tell for sure, sir. I'm not really qualified on sonar."

"Who would you *guess* is attacking you?"

"They haven't attacked us yet, sir, but they sank both Indonesian skimmers. I'd guess it's the Chinese. They had a wolf pack harassing us before we—"

"They can't be Chinese," the admiral said. "There are no serious conflicts at this time between the U.S. and China, or between China and Indonesia."

The admiral's response brought home to Chris how hopeless this was, trying to explain the situation in the heat of battle. Apparently, this admiral was not one of those Captain Scott had been in touch with since the *Vermont* had ascended.

"Sir, can you get us some air support?"

"You're in about the worst possible place," the admiral said. "A pair of Hornets is taking off now from Diego Garcia, but that's more than two thousand miles west of you. Even when they get there, all fighter planes can do against enemy submarines is discourage them from surfacing. We'll also mobilize our closest ASW assets and ask the Aussies to pitch in, but it sounds like the action is going to be over by the time any P-3 Orions can get to you." ASW stood for antisubmarine warfare.

"Admiral, I need to go."

"Very well. Try to report when you know who's attacking."

Chris dropped his headphones and ran back to the sonar shack to listen for torpedoes.

The instant he pushed the first button on the broadband stack, a sizzling sound came from somewhere inside the console. All of the lighted buttons went dark, and the waterfall displays winked out. A curl of smoke rose from the console in front of him.

"Captain, the sonar's dead!"

Chris hurried out into the control room to await orders.

On the 1MC, Scott said, "Tumor, get up here! We're in a tactical situation, and the sonar just keeled over!"

Tumor had been assigned to help in the engine room.

"Scope's all we've got," Scott muttered as he returned to peering out through the search periscope. He began rotating the scope, then stopped with a lurch. "I don't believe it! I'd trade my dick for a deck gun!"

Chris couldn't resist looking out through the attack scope. As he rotated it toward the bearing Scott was looking at, all he saw at first was crisp moonlight sparkling on almost calm water. Deep but gentle swells were passing by. Then he saw a sinister silhouette off the *Vermont*'s stern. The floating shape was long, low, and smooth, except for a tall black rectangle rising from its back.

A surfaced submarine.

Chris heard a clanking, jangling noise and jerked his head up. It was Tumor speeding around the conn toward the sonar shack, lugging a toolbox.

Scott got on the 1MC. "Weps, have you rigged the ship for dive?"

A distant yell came from somewhere aft. "Getting there, Captain."

Scott glanced at the chronometer. "Damn it, with the whole crew working, we could have been submerged already."

Chris returned his attention to the monocular eyepiece and increased the magnification to 2×. He saw dark figures running around on the other sub's deck. They were getting into an inflatable raft tied alongside. He couldn't be sure of the colors in the moonlight, but the rubber raft appeared to be black. So did the figures' clothing.

Zooming in to 5×, he saw that the figures were wearing helmets with clear visors and toting black submachine guns.

The raft sped away from the surfaced sub. Chris and Scott followed it with their scopes until another inflatable raft appeared in their fields of view. The other raft was larger and bright yellow. It was crowded with men who were frantically slapping at the water with two oars and their bare hands. Chris assumed they were the survivors of the first sunken skimmer.

The ninjalike soldiers in the black raft cut their engine and drifted close to the yellow raft. Three of them lifted their submachine guns. Chris heard a muffled roar of automatic gunfire.

The survivors in the yellow raft jerked a few times, then fell down and disappeared behind the gunwales or lay draped over the sides. One fell overboard. Tiny geysers erupted from the raft where it had been punctured by bullets below the waterline. In the moonlight, the blood running down the sides of the yellow raft looked black.

Chris forced himself to keep watching, feeling sick and numb. He had never witnessed a killing before. Shooting unarmed survivors in the water was about the worst war crime sailors could commit.

"Sir, why are they slaughtering the survivors?"

Scott was still watching too, gripping the scope handles with white knuckles. "Probably so no one will be around to see what they're going to do next."

Chapter 61

"That sub is still spitting up more of those ninja-looking shitheads," said Captain Scott, who was looking through the search scope, massaging his chest with one hand. "Here comes another raft. Jesus, there must be fifty of the little warthog-fuckers, and they've all got machine pistols."

"Sir, the first raft is speeding toward us," Chris reported.

Scott made a growling noise. "Weps, submerge the ship and attempt a hovering trim at periscope depth."

Weps, the long-faced Texan with a handlebar mustache, was now acting as chief of the watch at the ballast control panel. "Sir, the rig for dive is not complete!"

"Take us down!" Scott ordered. "We'll worry about flooding later."

Those were words Chris had never expected to hear on a submarine.

Weps echoed back Scott's command while executing it. Chris heard the geyserlike sound of air and spray venting from the main ballast tanks.

He also heard running boots above his head, then the topside hatch of the forward escape trunk being opened. Apparently the enemy had launched a previous raft of commandos that he and Scott had not seen.

Scott heard the hatch too. He grabbed the 1MC mike. "Enemy soldiers are attempting to board us. All hands, take a position to defend our hatches with small arms. Go! Go! Go!"

Scott dropped the microphone, not bothering to return it to its cradle, and pulled out the 9-mm Baretta holstered on his hip. He had broken out the small arms and distributed them to the secret skeleton crew after the evacuation. "Come on, let's go! Everybody out except Weps. Submerge us as fast as you can, lieutenant. We've got to leave those turkeys swimming before they overrun us."

The boom of a shotgun resounded through the sub. It was followed by a burst of rapid fire from a submachine gun, then more shotgun blasts and pistol shots.

Scott leaped down from the conn and ran toward the aft passageway.

Chris grabbed his shoulder and spun him around. "Captain, wait!"

A deafening blast made them both cringe. Chris knew it must have been some kind of grenade.

"Let go!" Scott snarled. "We have to back the others up!"

"Skipper, it's too late! There are too many of them. They'll kill us all before we can submerge."

Another grenade went off. The sounds of gunfire were multiplying by the second.

Red-faced, Scott yelled up at Chris, trying in vain to pull out of his grasp. "What do you want to do? Surrender? Let go of me, you yellow chickenshit!"

Two other men had run into the control room. They stopped and stared at the midbattle confrontation between their beloved captain and the enlisted newcomer who was disobeying a direct order. One of them raised his pistol, aiming it at Chris. The other one took Chris's pistol out of its hip holster.

Ignoring them, Chris yelled over the echoing gunfire. "Skipper, listen to me! We should all hide. Whatever they want, they're going to get it at this point, whether we fight them or not. We should try to find out what they're after and live to tell STRATCOM about it."

Scott stopped straining against Chris's grip on his coveralls. After a half second of hesitation, he said, "Shit! Okay, let's go!"

Chris released him.

Scott called Maneuvering. He ordered the nukes to abandon the reactor and hide.

Chris sprinted toward the firefight to tell the others his idea. Scott had recruited twenty-four men for his skeleton crew. Surely half that many could hold off the boarders long enough for the other half to scatter and hide.

As he neared the forward escape trunk, a loud burst of automatic fire was accompanied by a line of new bullet holes stitching the beige tile on the floor. Chris dived into a crossing passage just in time.

He heard a shotgun blast followed by a yell and a thud, then more yells and pistol shots. There was no sound of submachine guns, so he assumed the enemy was not returning fire at the moment. He dashed back into the main corridor and lunged against the wall behind two squatting men who were aiming pistols up at the lower escape trunk hatch.

He yelled at them, but they ignored him. He couldn't hear his own voice over the gunfire, so he was sure the other men couldn't hear him either. In desperation, he grabbed one of them and dragged him back into the crossing passage.

"Some of us have to hide! Spread the word!"

The man was sweating profusely, trembling all over, wearing a confused frown. He first shook his head, then nodded.

Chris repeated the maneuver with two more of the hatch defenders before running aft to hide.

Great plan! Now where do I stuff 260 pounds of ex-linebacker to make myself undetectable?

Chapter 62

Chris stood in the central aisle of the missile compartment, catching his breath and trying to think.

The enemy commandos would spread out and search the ship to make sure it was secure, but they might miss some of the hiding men. Even if he got caught, the element of surprise might give him a chance to kill the soldier who found him before the soldier could alert his comrades—but only if Chris could kill without making any noise.

He turned and ran forward toward officer country.

By the time he got to the XO's stateroom, he could still hear guns blazing on the deck above, but the battle seemed to be winding down. That meant most of the hatch defenders were dead. Within seconds, the horde of cutthroats who had murdered every human being within sight of the *Vermont* would pour in all at once like a catastrophic flood.

When Chris lifted Kurlgunn's bunk-pan lid, he saw what he needed. He had hoped to find the XO's butterfly knife, but that was a toy compared to some of the cutlery now laid out before him. The bunk pan was filled with flat Plexiglas cases displaying a collection of exotic-looking knives with Oriental carvings on the handles. The blades came in all shapes and sizes—single-edged, double-edged, straight, curved. One knife had two blades, one on each end of the handle. The various blades gleamed with a dark crimson hue under the stateroom's dim red night light, as if they were already coated with blood.

Chris selected a classic bowie knife for his right hand and a slender dagger for his left.

Along with the knife cases, he saw some of the antibiotics that had been stolen from the pharmacy.

He ran down two levels to the torpedo room. By the time he got there, the sounds of gunfire had ceased. All he could hear was distant shouting in some harsh Asian language.

He opened the breech door on the lower right torpedo tube—number four—and started to crawl into it.

The tube was already occupied.

The sound of running boots came from the upper decks.

Chris stared at the greasy brown hair of the head he could see about two feet inside the tube. His heart was pounding like a jackhammer. Where else could he hide? The three other tubes had torpedoes in them, and he couldn't unload one in time.

"Hey!" he whispered. "Scoot back and make room!"

The man in the tube did not respond. Chris realized he must be dead. He'd probably died just before the evacuation. The volunteers had loaded him into the tube but had never gotten around to flushing him out.

It was too late to jettison the corpse now. The enemy commandos would hear the tube firing.

Chris could hear boots descending the stairs.

There's no other place to hide!

He reached in and grabbed the man's greasy hair, trying to shove him in farther. Three men could lie end to end in one of the long tubes, so surely there was room for both him and the corpse. The stiff neck gave enough for the head to bend inward, but when he let go, it thudded back into its former position.

The boot steps on the stairs were closer.

Chris bit his lip to stop himself from cursing in frustration.

He peered into the tube. Hardly any of the compartment's dim red light reached its interior, but he could see the vague silhouette of a second body behind the first one. Even with his great strength, there was no way Chris could get enough leverage to shove two bodies farther in by himself. He would have to drag the front one out and take its place. But if he left the body on the floor, the invaders would wonder where it had come from.

The boots were marching on the bottom level now. They sounded like a whole army on parade.

Chris got an idea. If it worked and he was fast enough, it was bound to give him the best hiding place on the sub.

He dropped the dagger into a breast pocket of his coveralls and held the bowie knife between his teeth. Bracing his left hand beside the breech door, he reached in with his right hand and yanked the body out of the tube with one mighty pull, catching it in his arms. After gently lowering it to the deck, he got down on all fours and stuck his feet back into the tube. Using his arms to support his upper body, he inched backward with the bowie knife still in his mouth.

The marching boots seemed to be coming toward the torpedo room. Chris could clearly make out the individual voice of an enemy soldier who seemed to be barking orders to the others in their caustic language.

When his shoes collided with the head of the body that was still in the tube, Chris grabbed the torpedo guide rails on the sides and shoved with his feet. To his surprise, the body wouldn't budge. He'd counted on being able to scoot a single body farther into the tube with his legs.

A grunt came from behind him. He felt a hand grab his left ankle. A brief yelp escaped from his own lips before he could stop it.

"Who's there?" Chris whispered.

"Me," replied the man at his feet. After a groan and

a gasp that sounded like a stifled cough, the man added, "Weps and Tumor put me in here. They said not to make any noise."

It was Oral. No wonder Chris hadn't been able to move him. "They're coming, COB! Scoot back!"

Oral was already shuffling backward.

The marching boots sounded as if they were just outside the torpedo room.

Chris reached down from the open breech door and grabbed the dead body by its feet. In such an awkward position, it took all of his strength to drag the body off the floor. He had to shove himself backward with one hand on a guide rail while dragging the body in with the other. It was maddeningly slow going.

He saw movement in the torpedo room and froze. It was too late. The soldiers were streaming in. The first soldier flicked on the bright overhead fluorescents.

These soldiers couldn't be just a team conducting a security sweep—there were too many of them. *Damn it, they must have heard me. Why else would so many come into the torpedo room?*

One of them came around a torpedo rack and stopped in front of the open tube. Chris couldn't see the soldier's head, but he presumed the soldier was looking down at the corpse. Chris had dragged the body into the tube up to its armpits, but its head and arms still dangled outside the open breech door.

Chris spat out the bowie knife. It landed behind the corpse's right shoe with a gentle clunk. The soldier didn't seem to have heard it.

Chris forced his body to go limp, resting his head on the dead man's shoe. He could still see past the body with one eye. A small segment of the brightly lit torpedo room would have been visible outside the open breech door, but now it was mostly blocked by the thighs and torso of the enemy soldier.

Chris could hear Oral breathing. The sick COB was obviously straining not to cough.

The soldier said something to his comrades in their dissonant tongue, then stooped to peer into the dark tube above the corpse. He had taken off his helmet. His face was in shadow, but Chris could see the whites of his Asian eyes. They were staring directly at him. Chris figured he was mostly hidden by the darkness inside the tube, but he still didn't dare breathe or blink.

The soldier pulled out a flashlight and aimed it into the tube. The beam lanced into Chris's right eye. Now the soldier had a clear view of his head.

Chris concentrated on keeping his face slack and his eye open. He held the stinging eyeball as still has he could, looking straight into the light, wondering whether the soldier had seen his pupil contract.

The flashlight beam remained centered on his face. Could the soldier see the sweat oozing from his forehead?

Tears filled his eyes. Chris was sure the soldier could see the pooling liquid if he watched closely enough. If a teardrop fell, the soldier was bound to notice.

Chris had been holding his breath for several seconds now. His face was undoubtedly turning red from the strain. Could the soldier see his color changing? Was that why he was still aiming the light at Chris?

He felt a teardrop spill from his aching eye and roll across his nose. At the same instant, the commando withdrew his flashlight and disappeared from the tube's opening, saying something to his comrades with a nervous laugh.

Chris exhaled slowly, hoping his breath wouldn't whistle in his constricted throat.

His chest felt as if the smoke damage in his lungs was about to make him cough again. If the cough came back now, there was no chance that the enemy commandos would fail to hear it.

Oral seemed to be having more trouble avoiding a cough as well. His breathing was gradually growing louder. It would soon be loud enough to hear outside

the torpedo tube. Considering that Oral was dying of
pneumonic plague, Chris was amazed he hadn't given
- them away with a cough already.

At least a dozen of the commandos were walking
around the torpedo room, all dressed in black wetsuits.
They had removed their black crash helmets and lain
them aside. They seemed to be moving swiftly and pur-
posefully, speaking only to give and acknowledge orders.

Most of the Vermont's *secret technology is in the sonar
shack or the engine room. What the hell are these commandos doing down here?*

Chapter 63

The enemy commandos carried in four heavy stainless steel crates. When they opened one of the crates, Chris could see part of the object inside it, a silver metal cylinder about a foot in diameter. The cylinder was open at one end, and Chris could make out some kind of complex mechanism in its shadowed interior.

A bomb?

It stood to reason that if they wanted to sink the *Vermont* with explosives placed inside her hull, they'd do it in the torpedo room, where the torpedoes could enhance the blast. But why would they have gone to so much trouble when they could have just launched one of their own torpedoes at the *Vermont*?

The commandos shifted the crate a little. Some letters on the sinister-looking cylinder entered his narrow field of view. The letters were "U.S.A."

The soldiers couldn't be Americans. They all had Asian features and spoke in a language that sounded to Chris like Chinese, although he wasn't sure. To his American ears, their tongue sounded harsh and nasal. It had a quick tempo and a staccato abruptness that reminded him of quarreling ducks. He wished he could somehow ask Soony what language it was. She knew both Vietnamese and Mandarin Chinese and could probably recognize several other Asian languages.

Chris's windpipe felt partially clogged. He couldn't tell whether the obstruction was from fear, ordinary mucus, or the first products of pneumonic plague. *If I don't cough soon, I'm going to die in here!*

He tried willing his body to relax, knowing that the tension of hiding could bring on another bout of chemical-burn coughing at any moment.

The enemy soldiers were not the only source of tension. This was by far the closest company he had kept with any of the plague victims. At least the one in front of him was not spewing out infective cough droplets. Somehow, Oral was also restraining himself from coughing. But Chris could tell from the growing stench that the air in the torpedo tube was not circulating much, and he was not wearing a mask—he hadn't had a chance to get another one since his was torn off during the evacuation.

In addition to the four large crates, the commandos brought in some smaller metal cases. From these they removed a variety of tools, everything from ordinary screwdrivers and hacksaws to devices that looked expensive and specialized, probably custom-built. Chris recognized a miniature welding torch, a soldering iron, and a pneumatic rivet driver hooked up to a tank of compressed air.

The Asian commandos moved swiftly and surely, laying out their tools in specific locations around the room. They reminded Chris of a dance troupe, as if their motions had been choreographed and rehearsed many times.

One of them picked up a handheld power saw with a small rotary blade at the tip. He plugged it into a battery in one of the cases and began cutting into the side of a long red Tomahawk cruise missile resting on its rack. First he removed the waterproof launch capsule, then he began slicing into the missile itself. An arc of sparks flew up from the incision, and the room was filled with an ear-splitting whine. Another commando stood with his back to the first one, like a mirror image, and began dissecting another stowed Tomahawk.

Chris suddenly thought he understood. He'd heard that the four Tomahawks on the *Vermont* were armed with tactical nuclear warheads. Apparently the Chinese had carried out this whole elaborate scheme, probably including the plague attack, to get their hands on American nukes. The W88 warheads in the huge D-5 ballistic missiles were not easily accessible, but the smaller W80 warheads in the Tomahawks could be removed and carried off the sub through the crew hatches. If Chris remembered correctly, the W80s were so slender that several had recently been lowered down a borehole and detonated to demolish a natural dam that had caused a dangerous buildup of subglacial meltwater in Antarctica.

It came as a surprise that the enemy's motives apparently had nothing to do with the invasion of Iran. That revelation left Chris wondering why they had picked this run to attack. Perhaps their spies had told them that the *Vermont* would probably not turn back or surface for a medical evacuation until the outbreak had debilitated her crew, leaving them vulnerable to manipulation and assault.

Sure enough, the commandos removed the nuclear warheads, at least from the two Tomahawks Chris could see. Then they started working with the strange cylindrical devices they'd brought on board in the stainless steel crates. They appeared to be installing the devices inside the empty warhead compartments of the Tomahawks.

Chris was bewildered. They had the nuclear warheads. Why didn't they just leave? Were they replacing the stolen warheads with dummies in hopes that no one would realize what they'd taken?

The commandos were now using their specialized instruments to perform intricate reconstructive surgery on the Tomahawks. Chris watched and waited for several eternities, holding his breath whenever one of the soldiers stepped close to his torpedo tube. Maybe it was just his imagination, but the odor given off by the corpse in front of him seemed stronger every time he inhaled.

He ignored the cramps in his legs, the blockage in his throat, and the pain in his hip from lying atop one of the four sharp-edged guide rails.

He heard a low rumble. Apparently the commandos heard it too—they stopped working and listened as the roar grew louder. When it reached a crescendo and began to fade, Chris realized it must be the Navy jets that the admiral at STRATCOM had promised. Eagerly holding his breath, he waited for the thunder of AGM-65 Maverick missiles blasting the surfaced enemy submarine out of the water.

The jet roar faded away.

The commandos went back to work.

Chris felt like crying. The Hornets had been right overhead, no doubt armed to the teeth, and they hadn't fired.

Was it still nighttime? Maybe the pilots couldn't see the two submarine hulls, which were both black and had no running lights. Or maybe the subs were too close together for the planes to bull's-eye the enemy without hitting the *Vermont* as well. Even more likely, the pilots could have blasted the enemy sub but were waiting for orders. Until someone got on a radio and told them, they had no way of knowing for sure that the *Vermont* had been boarded.

Finally the commandos seemed to be finished. They started cleaning up and collecting their tools. The Tomahawk missiles appeared brand new. Chris was sure no one could tell by looking that they had been tampered with. So why had the commandos bothered to insert dummy warheads?

In a breathtaking flash of comprehension, Chris was sure he understood what the commandos were really doing. If he was right, stealing the nuclear warheads was just a sideline. Until now, he would never have guessed how clever, ambitious, daring, and evil their primary objective was.

Chapter 64

The sudden revelation of the enemy's intentions made Chris gasp in a way that he was sure the commandos could have heard. However, at the same time, the sound of running boots approached in the passageway outside, along with the voice of a commando shouting orders in their nasal language.

The troupe's choreographed procedures turned chaotic. They began recklessly throwing tools into their cases and slamming them shut. A minute later, they were gone. The torpedo room looked exactly as it had when they'd entered it.

Chris surmised that the cavalry was coming.

He shoved the corpse out of the tube and crawled out as fast as he could. Chris hoped he and Oral were not the only Americans left alive on the *Vermont*.

His idea of hiding had worked. Now he had another idea, a brilliant one at that, but one that was likely to get him killed.

A choking sound came from the torpedo tube, followed by coughing and spitting. A phlegmy voice said, "What's going on?"

"Stay here, Oral. I'll come back for you."

Chris picked up Kurlgunn's bowie knife and took off his shoes to avoid the squeaking of rubber soles. He could still hear running boots on the upper decks. Limping because his left leg was still half-numb, he ran to catch up with the enemy soldiers before all of them could leave the *Vermont*.

He was passing by the front entrance to the missile compartment when he heard another group of running boots. Two men, maybe three. He could tell by the echoes that they were about to enter the long missile compartment at the other end. He was pretty sure the large team of commandos from the torpedo room was just around the corner ahead of him, so he couldn't run ahead to hide. Turning back the way he had come, he heard running boots in that direction as well—several pairs, judging from the sound.

There were only three ways he could go, and all three led to immediate execution by a firing squad.

He dashed into the missile compartment and hunkered down between the first two tubes on the right. He tried to catch his breath and listen without making noise.

Chris could see only a short segment of the central aisle in front of his hiding place, but he could tell where the commandos were by the sound of their boots. He heard one small group jog into the aft end of the missile compartment. At about the same time, the ones who had been behind him ran past the forward doorway, apparently on their way out of the *Vermont*.

The commandos in the missile compartment were coming closer. It sounded like there were just two of them. Chris wanted to hold his breath, but he didn't. In a few seconds, he was going to need fully oxygenated muscles.

This will be your only chance, Long. Don't screw it up!

He knew his quarry's course but not their speed or position. Those variables he would have to judge with his ears. Timing was going to be everything.

I am a human sonar rig.

He listened and watched the aisle. Everything seemed to be the same crimson color under the dim night lights. The jogging commandos were close now. Chris readied himself, flexing his legs like a hunting cat.

Two Asian commandos entered his field of view.

Now!

Chris sprang from his hiding place and grabbed the closest commando. He wrapped his thick left arm around the man's head, covering his eyes. His captive thrust back an elbow, but the soldier was so much shorter than Chris that his elbow struck him harmlessly on the thigh.

The other commando lifted his black submachine gun.

At the same time, Chris pulled the sharp edge of his bowie knife across the throat of the man in his grasp. The blade cut so deeply that he thought he could feel it scraping against the man's spine. Warm blood sprayed across his hand, the deck, and the face of the other commando, who was dodging to the right, trying to get a clear shot.

The commando Chris was grasping went limp. He held on to the short body, and, lifting it off the deck, he managed to place it between himself and the submachine gun just as the gunner let loose a deafening burst of automatic fire.

Chris felt the slugs slamming into his human shield. He also felt sharp stings on the left side of his chest, hip, and thigh.

Fighting the instinct to lunge away, he stepped toward the gunner, still holding the body up in front of him. He stuck the bowie knife into the body's chest to keep it handy. Then he used his freed hand to grab the short barrel of the submachine gun even as it was firing at him. The smoking barrel seared the flesh of his palm, sending a thunderbolt of pain up his arm that was a thousand times worse than the stings on his side. He jerked the gun out of the commando's hands and hurled it between two of the missile tubes.

The commando ran after it.

Chris dropped his bloody shield, pulling out the bowie knife as the body fell. He tackled the commando, but his grip was slippery with blood. The commando broke free and rolled onto his feet with a military survival knife in his hand.

Chris figured from the commando's first swipe that he was trained in knife fighting. Chris was not, but he had a longer knife and at least eight inches more reach. Going for broke, he pretended to stab at his opponent's face but redirected his blade in midthrust toward the commando's knife hand, a closer target.

The ruse worked. A small stream of blood squirted into the air like water from a drinking fountain. The commando gasped as his knife and his severed right thumb fell onto the deck along with the spattering blood. With wide eyes, he stepped back and drew in a breath, obviously preparing to yell.

Chris punched him in the face as hard as he could. The commando flew backward, slamming into a missile tube. Then he pitched forward and sprawled on the bloody deck, apparently unconscious.

The burn on Chris's right palm was stinging so intensely that he could hardly feel the pains on his side. He knew some of the submachine gun bullets had nailed him. They obviously hadn't hit any bones or arteries, but he wondered how much blood he was losing.

He stooped to check the commando's pulse. It was going strong. Blood was still surging from the stump of the man's right thumb, pooling on the floor.

Chris heard running boots again. This time it sounded like only one man. The sound was approaching the missile compartment from forward.

He dragged his unconscious prisoner into the crimson shadows between two missile tubes. Judging by the sound of the running boots, he didn't have time to do anything with the half-beheaded corpse sprawled in the aisle. He could have tossed it behind a tube, but there would still have been blood all over the deck. Since everything looked red under the dim night lights, the blood was hardly visible, but there was enough of it to fill the air with its sour smell.

Chris compressed himself and his captive into a dark corner between a missile tube and a gray box that seemed just big enough to hide them from anyone passing by in the aisle. The box was a steam generator that ran on rocket fuel. It was designed to instantly boil enough water to launch the adjacent missile from its tube, hurling it up through sixty feet of ocean and into the air, where its own rocket engine would ignite when it began to fall.

Chris peered through a dark, narrow gap between the steam generator and the missile tube. He saw a single commando run in through the forward doorway. The man stopped when he saw his slain comrade. He looked around, crouching tensely and holding up his submachine gun.

The prisoner moaned and began to squirm. Chris clamped a hand over his mouth.

The investigating commando whirled around and fired a few rapid shots between the two missile tubes on the other side of the aisle. He'd heard the prisoner's moan, but the missile compartment's complex echoes had apparently confused him.

Chris didn't have to wonder what would happen if a bullet penetrated one of the D-5 missiles or its attached steam generator, both of which were packed with explosive solid rocket propellant.

Breathing fast, the wary commando turned back toward Chris and his prisoner, squinting into the crimson shadows. He took a slow step toward Chris's hiding place, then another. One more step and he would see Chris on the other side of the steam generator.

Holding his breath, Chris prepared to jump up with the captive held in front of him as a shield. The prisoner was starting to struggle harder now. Chris knew he couldn't keep him quiet much longer without knocking him out again, and that would make an audible thump.

The searching commando stopped. He seemed to have stepped on something. He moved his foot aside, looking down.

Chris cursed himself for not hiding in the same gap

where he had thrown his captive's submachine gun. It was on the other side of the tube his sweaty back was pressed against. If he'd had the gun now, he could have shot the commando while he was looking at the floor.

The commando picked up the object he'd stepped on and examined it with an expression of disgust. It was the severed thumb. He walked back to the body in the aisle. He kicked the body, turning it over. Its arms flopped out, splashing the blood on the deck. When the commando saw that the body was not missing a thumb, he dropped the thumb he'd found and returned to searching the shadows, approaching Chris's hiding place again.

A yell in the harsh Asian language came from somewhere far forward. The commando abandoned his search. He hoisted the blood-soaked corpse up around his shoulders and headed back the way he had come.

Chapter 65

Chris dragged his prisoner along the passageway by the collar of his wetsuit. The commando was conscious but no longer struggling. He groaned with every step Chris took, bleeding from his mouth, his nose, and the stump where his thumb used to be. Chris had used the captive's boot laces to bind his wrists and ankles.

With any luck, the prisoner would yield priceless intelligence on the enemy's motives and whereabouts, and surely no one would doubt who the perpetrators were if the United States had one of them in custody.

"Anybody here?"

Chris could hear the desperation in the metallic echoes of his own voice.

Except for him and his prisoner, the *Vermont* seemed deserted, at least of the living—he could easily imagine ghosts wandering the red-lit passageways, bleeding eternally from battle injuries or dripping spectral pus from weeping buboes.

He noticed that the air seemed to smell like blood in every compartment, even where none had been spilled. He also began to see bloody boot prints. As he slowly made his way forward, the prints became darker and more numerous.

On his way to control, he passed beneath the forward escape trunk. Six of his murdered shipmates were sprawled in the passageway. The Asian commandos had apparently taken all of their own casualties when they left.

Beneath the escape trunk, the deck was awash in blood from wall to wall. There was no way around it. The cold liquid soaked through his socks—he hadn't yet returned to the torpedo room for his shoes. The blood made the deck slippery, but it also made dragging his prisoner easier.

He waded across the crimson lake and staggered on toward the control room.

"Anybody?"

No reply.

The pain in his right palm was unbelievable. He imagined this was what Paul Treacle, his foster brother, had experienced after grabbing the knob of the attic door with fire on the other side. Chris wondered how long the agony would last.

He finally staggered into the control room and dumped the prisoner. The commando fell over on his side, curled up, breathing heavily.

Chris sat on the edge of the conn and removed the top of his coveralls to examine his left side. He found two bullet holes and one long gash where a bullet had grazed the skin. The wounds all looked superficial, and none of them seemed to be bleeding very fast, but they added up. He felt lightheaded, although that could have been due to some effect of combat other than blood loss. This was the first time Chris had experienced real war, so there was no telling how it might affect him.

He'd discovered that the commandos had bulletproof vests under their wetsuits. Chris was sure that was all that had saved him. If it weren't for the vest worn by his human shield, even the relatively slow pistol bullets fired by the submachine gun would have probably passed through the man's body, retaining enough momentum to kill him.

Chris rested for a minute, holding his smooth scalp in

a bloody palm, flexing the other hand into a fist to stop his fingers from trembling.

He got up and wandered into the sonar shack. To his surprise, all of the indicators were lit. Tumor must have restored the system in the few minutes he'd had before the commandos came aboard.

Chris glanced at the broadband stack. Four contacts were visible. After a moment of scrutiny, he concluded that three were moving toward the *Vermont* from the east, west, and north. One was moving away to the south. He stepped to the narrowband console and worked it until he identified the contact heading south. It was the *Chop Suey,* the *Yangtze*-class submarine that they had encountered twice before during their voyage from the Persian Gulf.

It had just occurred to him that full electrical power was still on. That meant the reactor hadn't scrammed, which might mean someone was still alive back in Maneuvering. He snatched down the nearest 1MC mike. "Anybody! If anybody can hear me, please call the sonar shack."

He immediately got a call from Eng. "Doc! You're alive! Are they gone?"

Chris slumped back in relief. "Yeah. Thank God—I thought I was the only one left, except Oral."

"That's what we thought too. Where did you hide?"

"Torpedo tube. How about you?"

"Reactor compartment. We had just enough time to deactivate the alarm and get inside before the bad guys came back here to look around. I could hear their boots the whole time. As soon as they were gone, we came out and hid in the engine room, but we were in the RC long enough to get a pretty bad dose."

Chris knew Eng meant that he and the other nukes had been bombarded by neutrons and gamma rays. Thick shielding around the reactor compartment protected the rest of the ship from radiation emitted by the core, but levels within the reactor compartment were high enough to kill and cook a human in a few minutes.

"Did you radio to request assistance?" Eng asked.

"I think some ships are already coming," Chris said. "Probably more Indonesians. Eng, if enough of us survived to get this heap moving, we've got one more thing to do before we get off. How many of you nukes are there?"

"Five, believe it or not. But we all have burns, and we'll start succumbing to radiation sickness in a few hours."

"Six men are not enough," said Chris. "We need at least ten or twelve. Maybe some more are still hiding. You guys spread out and search the engineering spaces while I—"

"Doc, I hate to remind you, but unless the captain survived, I am the *Vermont*'s commanding officer now."

"Right. Right. Sorry, sir."

"What do you have in mind?" Eng asked.

"I'd like to put the assholes who did this on the bottom, sir."

"So would I," Eng said, "but I think we'd better leave that for—"

"Sir, you don't understand! They didn't just kill two whole ships full of men. I'm pretty sure they're also the ones who infected our crew with plague, and even that's nothing compared to what they're really trying to do." Chris quickly summarized what he'd seen in the torpedo room.

He waited for an answer, panting to catch his breath and holding the gunshot wound under his left armpit, the worst of the three. "Sir, if we don't catch them before they're out of our sonar range, we probably won't get another chance."

Eng finally spoke. His voice seemed to contain an edge of cold rage. "We will determine if anyone else is alive back here. You search the forward compartment. I'll call you back in five minutes."

Chris pumped his throbbing right fist in the air, a small but savage gesture. "Aye, sir!"

He tried to run but ended up walking along the passageways. "The ship is secure!" he yelled.

He got no responses until he passed by the frozen storage compartment, where he heard muffled yelling and banging. To his surprise, the sounds seemed to be coming from the freezer.

When he opened the door, he saw something that made him jump back. On the frosty floor lay a body bag. The body inside it was moving its arms and legs and letting out pitiful moans.

Chris realized what must have happened. He stepped into the freezer and tried to unzip the bag. The zipper was stuck, so he pulled Kurlgunn's slender dagger from his breast pocket and cut the thick plastic.

The man inside thrust his head out, gasping for air.

It was Tumor. His face was bluish. His teeth were chattering. Sweat was frozen in his eyebrows. He threw his arms around Chris and hugged him. "Thank you, Doc. Oh, thank you! I couldn't get out! I thought I was going to die! It was so dark and cold . . . cold and dark. I didn't think anybody else was left. If you hadn't—"

"Tumor, shut up," Chris said. "Help me look for others."

They found no one else alive.

On their way back to control, Chris started feeling like he might faint. The faintness could have been due to either his injuries or disappointment. He doubted the nukes had found any other survivors, and seven men were not quite enough to move a Trident forward and put a warshot on a target.

Chris saw fresh wet footprints on the deck. The liquid looked strangely thin. Peering closer in the dim red light, he saw that it was water, not blood. He grabbed Tumor and motioned him to silence. Together they cautiously followed the tracks into the control room.

Captain Scott was sitting on the edge of the conn with

his head in his hands. Two other officers lay on the conn beside him. All three were soaking wet. They looked almost too exhausted to breathe.

"*Skipper!* Where have you been?"

Scott lurched and looked up, swaying with fatigue. "We grabbed oxygen bottles . . . climbed out through the sail while they were coming down the escape trunks. They had guards all over the deck. We dived over the side before they could nail us. They winged Weps here on the leg—nearly blew his dick off."

While Scott was speaking, Chris noticed that his prisoner's hands were no longer bound with a boot string, yet the man was prone and motionless.

"He was dead when we got here," Scott said. "You captured him?"

Chris nodded, wishing he had the energy to kick himself. "Damn it, he must have gotten loose and taken a suicide pill. I didn't think to search him."

Still shivering, Tumor spoke to the officers. "Gee whiz, didn't they try to shoot y'all in the water?"

"They shot a lead mine at us," Scott said, "but they lost us when we swam underwater far enough to hide on the other side of their own sub. They probably would have seen us in daylight, or our bubble trails at least, but we got to the shadow their hull was casting in the moonlight."

"Sir, I'm sorry," Chris said. "Ten of us survived, five up here and five back in Maneuvering. That's enough to move and shoot. If those killers are still within sonar range, we have to go after them before they get away."

Scott stared at him, massaging his chest. "Doc, are you out of your muscle-bound mind?"

Chris swayed, stumbled, and went down on one knee. Holding his head low, he said, "Sir, please trust me. I'll explain . . . once we're moving."

Chris waited, determined not to faint. He was looking at his own blood-soaked socks, but he could hardly see them because his vision had almost blacked out.

"Very well," Scott said. "Weps, you finish rigging the ship for dive. Tumor, you put the engine order telegraph on all ahead flank. Do you know how?"

The captain's voice sounded like a distant burble to Chris.

"Yes, sir!" Tumor said. "I mean, aye, sir!" He raced to the helmsman's console, reached under it, and rotated the lever to all ahead flank. Chris could barely make out the large needle that indicated the response of the throttleman back in Maneuvering. It swung around to match the order lever as fast as it ever had.

Tumor said, "Maneuvering is answering all ahead flank, sir!"

Chris heard the hum from the power plant increasing in volume and pitch. The deck began to tremble as the twin steam turbines spun up to maximum power, sending sixty thousand horsepower down the shaft to the screw.

I have to get to the sonar shack. Without a sonarman, they can't find the target.

Chris fell on the deck and lost consciousness.

Chapter 66

Chris woke up choking. He coughed and sputtered, then sucked in a breath.

"Sorry, Doc, sorry!"

Tumor was stooping over him with a can of 7-Up.

Chris weakly grabbed the can and took a long drink. His thirst was all-consuming.

"Gee whiz, I thought you were a goner, Doc. You look awfully peaked. I'm glad a little pop brought you to."

Chris drank some more and belched. His head was splitting, his right hand was stinging, the wounds on his left side were aching, and he needed to use the head. "How long . . . ?"

"You were only out for a few minutes. You want some water too?"

Chris nodded and took the canteen Tumor was offering. He could barely hold on to it. "Help me sit up."

Tumor grabbed his burned right hand.

Chris yelped in pain.

."Oh! Sorry, Doc, sorry!"

Chris looked at his hand. The broad palm was covered with long, juicy, red blisters.

Tumor grabbed Chris's coveralls and heaved upward with a grunt. "Dadgone, Doc, you're a heavy son of gun!"

Chris settled for a half-sitting position, leaning back against a bulkhead with his legs stretched out. The compartment he was in was mostly dark, but it was pervaded by a dim green glow. Through the doorway, he could see bright fluorescent lights outside. He finally got his bearings—someone had dragged him into the sonar shack.

Judging by the roar of the turbines and the vibration of the deck, the *Vermont* was making flank speed and then some.

"You okay now? They need me back in the engine room."

Chris nodded. "Thanks, Tumor. Go."

"No problem, Doc. You've taken good care of me through thick and thin."

Tumor ran out of the sonar shack.

Chris felt light-headed and short of breath. His skin was cool and clammy. Between gulps of 7-Up and water, he couldn't stop panting. He was hardly moving a muscle, but his heart seemed to be going as if he had just run an eighty-yard touchdown.

He recognized his symptoms as those of shock due to blood loss. He needed to be rehydrated intravenously, but hopefully the oral fluids would be enough to save him.

Captain Scott was sitting at the sonar console with his back to Chris, drumming one heel up and down on the deck.

"Sir, I can . . . explain now."

Scott replied without turning around. "Just take it easy, Doc. Eng told me what you saw down in the torpedo room. By the way, I'm sorry I called you a chicken-shit. Hiding was a good idea."

Scott jerked down a microphone and spoke on the 1MC circuit. "Weps, Evans, they're going deep. Take us down to eleven hundred feet."

Chris surmised that Weps and Evans were operating the control yokes, and that there was no diving officer to watch the ship's control panel and manage them.

One of them yelled from the control room, apparently

unable to take his hands off the yoke to grab an inter-com mike. "Captain, that's close to test depth, and we're running at all ahead flank!"

Only in a tactical situation would a submarine ever run at top speed near test depth. If the drivers lost control, the sub's forward momentum could cause it to plunge past crush depth faster than the crew could react. Running a sub at test depth, all ahead flank, was like skimming the treetops at supersonic speed in a jet fighter.

"Dive now!" Scott ordered on the 1MC. "Five degrees down bubble. Eng, you have to increase power. We're about to lose them."

The strained voice of the engineer came over the 1MC. "Sir, the maximum speed of the *Yangtze* class is slightly less than that of a *Trident*. Therefore, we must be catching up."

Scott said, "They're heading for blue water, Eng. In about twenty minutes, they'll pass the point where the ocean is too deep for divers to reach the bottom."

"Captain, the reactor is running at one hundred percent," Eng replied, "and the temperature of the turbine bearings is already in the red zone."

"Damn it, Eng, I don't care! Give the engines all the steam you can, and don't worry about overpowering the reactor."

"Aye, sir. Opening steam valves all the way."

The lights dimmed a little as steam was diverted away from the two ship's service turbine generators to the two main engines.

"Pull the control rods out more," Scott ordered.

"That will cause a scram," Eng warned.

"Safety short the reactor first!"

Scott wanted Eng to override the automatic shutdown circuit that would drop control rods into the reactor core if it overheated.

Eng's reply sounded desperate. "Sir, overpowering a

safety-shorted reactor could cause a prompt critical rapid disassembly!"

When too much was asked of a naval nuclear reactor, the result could be spectacularly bad. A prompt critical rapid disassembly was a kind of nuclear explosion that could be caused by water that was too cold entering the reactor core and moderating the neutron flux too well. The slowing of too many neutrons could cause the fission energy output to increase thousands of percent in a few seconds. A prompt critical rapid disassembly was not the same as the chain reaction in a nuclear bomb, but it would cause a steam explosion powerful enough to rip a Trident submarine in half.

Scott shouted into the 1MC mike. "It's worth taking our chances, Eng. Pull those rods as fast as you can, and take all the steam she'll give you."

Chris was sitting all the way up now, but he knew he was not able to stand. Despite his lack of movement, his breaths were still shallow gasps. He wanted another 7-Up, but Scott was busy at the sonar and no one else was around.

A few seconds after the exchange between Scott and Eng, Chris heard the drone of the turbines increase to a muffled but urgent scream. The deck began shaking in a way he had never felt before. He could sense that Eng was now driving the reactor well beyond the maximum power it had been designed to safely produce.

Chapter 67

After the 1MC had been quiet for a minute, Chris was sure they were just waiting to catch the *Chop Suey,* so he worked up the energy to speak again. "Captain, do you think they know we're chasing them?"

Scott was still glued to the sonar console. "I doubt it, Doc. We've been in their baffles since we started. If they suspected a trail, they would have zigged by now. I'd say they're just clearing datum before those three new Indonesian skimmers can snap them up. And I'd say the little monkey-fuckers are in for quite a surprise." Clearing datum meant making a fast escape from the last position known to the enemy.

"Why do we need to sink them in shallow water, sir? I just thought we should make sure they don't get away with our nukes."

Scott kept his back to Chris, watching the waterfall display. "You're bound to be right about the devices they put back in the Tomahawks, Doc. I'd bet my dick those are working biological warheads with the same strain of plague bacteria that wiped out my crew. One of them probably has a crack that could have released the germs by accident."

Chris had reached the same conclusion while hiding in the torpedo tube. He knew that cruise missiles would be an ideal vehicle for stealthy dispersal of an airborne biological weapon upwind of a target area. And, hypothetically, if the United States had developed a version of the Tomahawk for germ warfare, the ideal place to deploy the weapon would have been on Trident submarines.

Scott continued, sounding distracted. "Unless we can prove the Chinese planted the plague warheads, they'll get away with framing the United States for possession of biological weapons. The only proof we have is on the *Chop Suey,* so we have to sink her in water that's shallow enough for divers to recover it."

Chris groaned, looking at the stinging red blisters on his palm. Despite the pain, he strained to speak loudly enough to be heard over the *Vermont*'s roaring engines and coolant pumps. "Don't we have plenty of evidence already? Bullet holes, the bodies of the men they shot to pieces, the DNA in the blood they lost. . . . Their boots left bloody prints everywhere they went. You'd think they were *trying* to leave tracks."

"They were!" Scott said. "Think about it, Doc. If you had to seize a submarine, would you do it the way they did? With machine pistols?"

"No. I'd gas the crew first."

Scott tossed up a hand. "Anybody in their right mind would! And you probably wouldn't have worn heavy combat boots that made you sound like you were stomping ants. But those devious little turkeys were wearing standard-issue Chinese army boots. They also used standard-issue Chinese military weapons, no doubt loaded with standard-issue Chinese ammunition. Makes it so a ten-year-old retard could tell we were boarded by Chinese soldiers, right?"

"Oh hell . . . I think I get it, sir."

Scott stomped the deck in frustration. "We've got *nothing* . . . nothing that the U.S. Navy couldn't have fabricated. Even the soldier you captured—I guarantee he has no identity records. He could have been some bum the Navy shanghaied in Shanghai, or in New York. What we—"

Scott was interrupted by the wailing radiation alarm.

He killed the alarm and grabbed the 1MC mike. "Eng! What's going on back there?"

Eng's voice was so tense it was barely understandable. "Captain! The cladding on a fuel element has ruptured. The radioactivity of the primary coolant loop just jumped to fifty thousand percent of normal, and it's still climbing fast."

"Very well," Scott replied.

After a moment of silence, except for the screaming turbines, Chris said, "What about the sinking of the Indonesian skimmers, sir? Surely that will make it obvious to the world that the *Vermont* really was attacked."

"Doc, you need to save your strength. Has anybody ever told you you ask too many questions?"

"Now and then, sir. Why?"

Scott angrily shook his head. "When UN inspectors find those plague warheads on the *Vermont,* it's going to look like American forces killed their own men and all those Indonesians, then boarded the *Vermont* and planted whatever evidence they could throw together in a hurry to frame the Chinese for the attack. It will look like their objective was to retrieve the plague warheads, but they had to abort when the rest of the Indonesian Navy showed up. That's what the Chinese planned it to look like, anyway. Now that the *Vermont* is flanking it toward international waters, it looks like the American forces decided to snatch the whole sub back rather than aborting the evidence grab."

Chris was barely able to keep up at this point. He felt as if trying to follow the logic of the Chinese scheme would have made his head spin even if he weren't in terrible pain and running a few pints low. "Sir, why don't we just dump the plague warheads overboard? We could say the Chinese stole the nuclear warheads and leave it at that. The plague warheads would never come up."

"Yes they would, Doc. Literally. The Chinese would tip the Indonesians off, and divers would recover the plague warheads from the bottom. Then it would look like we threw the evidence out the window while the cops were chasing us—those three Indonesian skimmers are falling behind, but they're still on our tail. Let's face it—if that Chinese sub gets to deep water, we are screwed three ways at once."

Chris groaned. "I just hope we're interpreting everything correctly. We don't actually know for sure that the warheads they planted contain *Yersinia*."

Eng's strained voice came over the 1MC. He had to yell to make himself audible over the roar that filled the engine room. "Captain, leaking around the shaft seals has doubled."

"Very well," Scott replied, drumming a heel on the floor.

Chris tried closing his right hand, but the palm was too painful and swollen. At least his three gunshot wounds had nearly stopped bleeding. "Skipper, do you think we'll catch them in time?"

"Maybe," Scott said. "If we don't blow a turbine and the reactor doesn't melt down. On their present course, they'll be over the abyssal plain in—let's see—eleven minutes. We'll catch up in about . . . ten. You know, Doc, war didn't used to be like this."

"How's that, sir?"

"It used to be, if somebody snuck in and crapped in your shoes, you could just go after them. You didn't have to justify it to the goddamn United Nations."

"Do you really miss the days of 'might makes right,' sir?"

Scott hesitated. "I guess not."

"Skipper, why would the Chinese want to frame the United States for having biological weapons?"

As Chris spoke, Scott flipped a switch to change the mode being displayed on the sonar console.

With a faint pop, the console went dark.

"Tumor!" Scott yelled.

Chapter 68

Tumor ran into the sonar shack with his toolbox and got to work.

Scott swiveled around in his chair and scrutinized Chris. "Doc, you look like a run-over pile of dog shit."

"Thank you, sir. I wish I felt that good."

Scott pursed his lips so that they disappeared beneath his thick red mustache. "Here's the deal, son. If Tumor gets the sonar back online in the next five minutes, we may still have a shot at sinking those turkeys in time. I was planning to man the fire control console when we attack, but I can't do that and work the sonar at the same time."

Chris nodded. "Help me up, sir?"

Scott stooped and put Chris's right arm over his narrow shoulders, then tried to heave upward. After a second of straining, Chris landed on the chair. His head was spinning so fast he couldn't tell whether he was balanced or falling over.

"Steady, there." Scott nudged his side to help him stay upright. "You going to make it?"

"Yeah," Chris panted, gripping the console. "Let's do this."

"How's it coming, Tumor?" Scott asked.

Tumor was rummaging for something in his toolbox. "Getting there, sir. Just a blown fuse this time."

"Okay, I'll go start up the fire control console."

Scott headed out to the control room. "We're probably within ADCAP range already. We won't have time to do a TMA, so go active as soon as the sonar is back on. I'll be ready to shoot when you give me the range."

"Sir, hitting them with an active ping will tell them exactly where we are. With all their sonar operators working, they're bound to get a firing solution faster than I can by myself. At the very least, they'll launch a torpedo before we can sink them."

"Fine," Scott said. "It won't reach us before we launch the unit with their name on it. Just hang on, son—this melee will be over soon, one way or another."

Scott left the sonar shack to man the fire control console. Chris heard him tell the helmsman, the stern-planesman, and the chief of the watch to keep her steady on the present course and speed.

Chris waited, trying to breathe deeply to stock up on oxygen.

So this is a suicide attack. So be it. We've already lost 145 crewmen, plus hundreds of Indonesians. Ten more won't make that much difference. Besides, if I die today, I won't have to face a court-martial.

Scott yelled from the control room, not bothering with the intercom. "I've programmed units one, two, and three with approximate transit parameters. If those turkeys haven't changed course, we should be getting very close now."

Tumor twisted himself out from under a computer cabinet. "Here we go!"

The sonar console lit up.

A bright white line stared back at Chris from the waterfall display.

"Captain, sonar contact bearing one-seven-five, dead ahead! We're right on her tail, sir!" He half expected to feel the *Chop Suey*'s spinning propeller cutting into the fiberglass sonar dome that formed the bow of the *Vermont*.

"All back full," Scott ordered. It was necessary to slow down before firing torpedoes.

The throttleman back aft spun the forward throttle wheel to its stop position. At the same time, he spun the reverse wheel to wide open. The hull shook and the lights flickered as the steam surging through the massive pipes of the secondary coolant loop was diverted to rotate the screw in the opposite direction. In the sonar shack, Chris could actually feel the sub's deceleration this time.

"Light her up!" Scott yelled.

Chris was already reaching for the active sonar controls. He unleashed a single ping. The sound wave was reflected back almost immediately, giving him the range to the *Chop Suey*. *"One-one-five-zero yards,"* he yelled.

Now it was out of his battered hands.

He listened intently to the diverse noises of two racing submarines, waiting for a whoosh followed by a telltale buzz. A few seconds later, the sinister sounds he anticipated came through his headphones. "Captain! Torpedoes in the water!"

"Hold your course and speed," Scott ordered the three men steering the *Vermont*. "No evasive maneuvers. How many did they launch, Doc?"

"Two, I think."

Chris curled his right hand into a fist, despite the painful blisters. *Come on, skipper; shoot!*

He listened for the familiar sound of the *Vermont* launching torpedoes. How long could it take to program the expected target range into an ADCAP? Chris didn't know. He did know it would take only a few minutes for the two enemy torpedoes to speed back to the *Vermont*. He also knew that Scott had to not make any mistakes. They wouldn't get a second chance. Even if they had time to shoot another salvo before an enemy torpedo struck, there was only one survivor stationed in the torpedo room, and he couldn't reload the tubes by himself.

"Firing point procedures, tubes one, two, and three,"

Scott announced. A few seconds later, he said, "Firing units one, two, and three!"

Chris heard three loud whooshes in rapid succession, then the fading buzz of the small external combustion engines that drove the ADCAPS. "Units one, two, and three running hot, straight, and normal!" he reported.

"O'Clair, cut the wires and close the muzzle doors," Scott ordered. He was speaking to Sean O'Clair, the one man in the torpedo room.

Mark 48 ADCAP torpedoes unreeled a thin wire behind them so they could communicate with the sub during their runs. But this shot was short and straight, and the expensive drones had their own active sonars with almost foolproof homing algorithms, so they shouldn't need guidance from the *Vermont*'s computers.

"Execute evasive maneuvers," Scott ordered. "Helm, give me left full rudder, all ahead flank. Ten degrees rise on the fairwater planes. All remaining countermeasures are away. Let's clear datum and pray those three units do their job."

By now Chris had tuned the broadband processor in to the enemy torpedoes, which were moving at about forty knots. They had traveled far enough from the *Chop Suey* to show up as separate sound sources on the waterfall display.

"Estimate three minutes to impact of enemy torpedoes," he yelled. "Four minutes to impact of our own units."

"What's our course?" Scott asked.

"Passing one-one-zero," the helmsman said.

"Keep coming left to steady course zero-eight-zero," Scott ordered. "Level out at six hundred feet."

Chris wiped sweat from his forehead and left his hand poised by his headphones, ready to yank them off before the incoming torpedoes reached the position where Scott had launched the countermeasures. "Estimate two minutes to impact of torpedoes," he called as the deck tilted upward, forcing him to hang on to the console.

When the moment came, he pulled off his headphones and shouted, "Torpedoes have reached the position of our—"

Chris was interrupted by a jarring boom. He waited for another one, holding his breath. He exchanged a pleading glance with Tumor, who was crouching on the deck, bowing his head and muttering.

One of the two white lines representing the enemy torpedoes had winked out. The other line was still burning, brighter than ever. Chris put his headphones back on. "One torpedo detonated by countermeasures, one torpedo still closing. I think it's locked on, Captain. Estimate one minute to impact."

"Right full rudder," Scott ordered. "Full rise on the fairwater planes. Emergency blow the forward group. Maybe it will lose us if we get above the layer." The layer was the depth where warm, mixed surface water abruptly gave way to cold deep water. This boundary tended to act like a sonic mirror, reflecting back sound waves that attempted to penetrate it from above or below.

Chris heard the loud rush of compressed air blowing into the forward main ballast tank, forcing seawater out the vents at the bottom. The deck angle pitched upward even more. Steeper, steeper, steeper—he lost his grip on the sonar console, and his chair slid backward against the wall behind him. Or below him, depending on how he looked at it.

The torpedo was so close now that he could hear its chemical engine running in his headphones. "Captain, impact is imminent!"

Chris didn't bother removing his headphones again. This time he figured it didn't matter.

A concussion slammed him back against the wall and the overhead above his chair. He slid down the inclined wall to the deck, gripping his ears and groaning in agony. It felt as if his head had been smashed between two sledgehammers. All he could hear was a warbling high-pitched tone, like a scream of terror caught at the high note and replayed indefinitely. He knew it couldn't be a real sound.

Feeling wetness on his left hand, he looked at it. His palm was bloody. *Shrapnel? Scalp laceration?* No, he realized, the explosion had ruptured his left eardrum. Probably the right one as well.

Without intact eardrums, Chris could not hear the roar of flooding. Nor could he sense the increase in air pressure as water rushed in and displaced the sub's atmosphere.

That must have been a direct hit. We must be flooding fast. But where?

Chris tried to listen for flooding or the blare of 1MC announcements. All he could hear was the piercing warble.

The *Vermont*'s pitch angle was still nose up by at least thirty degrees, maybe forty. Chris expected the angle to get even steeper as floodwater poured into the stern. By the time she sank past crush depth, she would probably be standing on her tail.

The lights went out, and red emergency lighting came on.

Someone grabbed his right wrist and started dragging him across the steep deck. He looked up. It was Tumor.

Chris pulled free of the seaman's grip and tried to stand but collapsed on the deck, which now seemed to be spinning like a carnival ride. He had no idea whether the wild spin was a real gyration of the sinking sub or just his own vertigo. He rolled over and tried to crawl, but his arms gave out and he fell on his side, sliding downhill to the wall.

Tumor resumed dragging him. This time he did not resist.

Chapter 69

Ninety nautical miles south of Java, the ocean was calm and the sky was clear. Sunlight sparkled on gentle waves. There were no ships and no land within sight. The tranquillity of the infinite sea revealed no hint of the battle raging in the dark depths below.

The flat ocean surface suddenly bulged upward. A split second later, an enormous bullet-shaped object erupted from the water. The black object was the bow of a submarine. It continued to ascend until the fairwater emerged. Then the steel leviathan crashed down like a breaching humpback whale, sending out a loud boom and high plumes of white spray.

Within a few seconds, most of the waves had dissipated and the long steel cylinder had stopped bobbing. It floated like a black iceberg, mostly beneath the surface with only its long sleek back exposed to the equatorial sun.

An hour later, Chris lay on his back, stretched out on the hard rubber anechoic tiles at the edge of the *Vermont*'s topside deck. His whole body ached, but a dose of ibuprofen had dulled the pain, especially in the miserable burn on his right palm.

Tropical sunlight was beating down on his hairless chest and face. The unfamiliar brightness of the sun hurt his eyes, but he didn't care. He concentrated indulgently on the salty fresh air, savoring each breath.

Apparently his eardrums had not been completely destroyed—he could vaguely hear waves lapping against the hull beside him. It sounded as if his ears were full of cotton, but he could also hear the other survivors talking, and the flapping of the American flag they had hoisted atop the towering black sail.

Turning his head toward the sound of raised voices, he saw that Eng and Oral were lying about ten feet apart, also stretched out on their backs, apparently unable to get up. They seemed to be exchanging harsh words about whether their survival had been a product of divine intervention.

The Chinese torpedo's proximity fuse had detonated behind the *Vermont*'s screw. The entire propeller had been blasted off, but the shaft had fractured aft of its pressure seals, so the sub had not flooded. They had continued their emergency ascent to the surface, driven only by the buoyancy of the blown ballast tanks. Now the *Vermont* was a gently rocking derelict, seaworthy but without propulsion.

Chris languidly watched an object floating by. When he realized it was a boot, he turned his head away in case it still contained a foot.

He heard a distant rumble to starboard. It swiftly grew louder. Shielding his eyes with a hand, he peered into the bright blue sky and saw two faint dots just above the horizon. A few seconds later, the dots became gray Navy jets. They were F/A-18 Hornets, with two outward-tilting tail fins and twin engines in the stern of the broad airframe. The Hornets zoomed across the *Vermont*, flying so low that Chris caught a glimpse of one pilot waving. He was momentarily deafened again by their thunder.

"Nice of them to fly over and say hi," Tumor said.

Tumor was squatting beside him with a full canteen. He helped Chris lift his head enough to drink. Still weak, Chris trembled, causing him to spill water on his chest. Tumor mopped it up with a sleeve before it could soak the bandages he and Captain Scott had put on the superficial gunshot wounds.

"Thank you," Chris said.

"Do you want anything else, Doc?"

"Dark shades," Chris replied, "and a Cadillac margarita with salt."

As Tumor walked away, Chris glanced at the sketch pad he'd left lying on the sun-drenched deck. Tumor had been drawing a picture of a country cottage with a chimney and hedges and a pretty lady in a dress on the front porch swing.

Tumor brought him sunglasses, a can of Pringles, and a cup of bug juice.

The Tennessee country boy sat cross-legged and picked up his sketch pad with a frustrated sigh. "Dadgone it, Doc, are you *sure* you didn't hear our own units detonate?"

Chris shook his head. "But that doesn't mean we didn't get them, Tumor. We'll probably never know unless divers find the *Chop Suey* on the bottom. Hey, how are the other guys doing?"

"Oral actually seems to be getting better," Tumor said. "Eng got knocked around by the torpedo blast, but I think he'll be okay. The rest of us are doing fine. You know what? I'm beginning to think I might not have caught the plague after all."

In spite of his multitude of aches, Chris grinned.

Tumor smiled back. "Guess what the captain did a minute ago, Doc. When he radioed COMSUBPAC to tell them where we are, he had them call my mom's hospital. They said she came through her heart operation just fine. That's the kind of thing Captain Scott is famous for."

"I'm glad she's okay," Chris groaned.

"I bet all ten of us that are left will make it from here," Tumor said.

Glancing at the sail, Chris saw that Captain Scott was

sitting alone on top of it, staring off at the horizon. "I sure hope so, Tumor. I sure hope so."

A Navy skimmer took the survivors to Pearl Harbor. There they were kept in quarantine for three weeks. Doctors wearing biohazard suits treated their various afflictions.

While quarantined in Hawaii, Lieutenant Matthew Covers—Weps—developed pneumonic plague and died. Oral continued to recover, becoming the strain's only confirmed survivor. The wounds Chris had sustained began to heal, and his hearing returned to almost normal. Eng and the other nukes suffered diarrhea, malaise, and anemia from their brief exposure to radiation in the reactor compartment, but all of them recovered with a few burn scars.

The U.S. government seemed determined to allay international suspicion by being unusually open to the media about the attacks on the *Vermont*. When Chris was not being debriefed by government officials or interviewed by reporters, he spent most of his time watching and reading the news. He was a star player in much of it. The media had seized upon his distinctive, brawny, bald-headed appearance and turned his image into an icon of the American warrior.

Chris and Tumor were watching the news and eating a pepperoni pizza in their sterile white isolation ward when Tumor said, "How does it feel to be a living legend, Doc?"

"I don't know about the legend part, but the living part feels pretty damn good, even in this jail."

"Say, you and I probably had more exposure to plague than anybody," Tumor said. "Why do you reckon we never caught it?"

"We don't know yet that we didn't," Chris said, "but through it all, I was careful to protect myself however I could."

"What about me?" Tumor asked. "I wasn't careful."

"I know. I guess you're just lucky, Tumor."

"Dadgone, I sure hope it lasts," Tumor said.

When they had moved on from the pizza to ice cream, Tumor said, "I can't believe the Chinese thought they could get away with framing the United States."

"They might get away with it yet, Tumor. They only made one mistake."

"What mistake?"

"They didn't think any of us would have the balls to stay on that death ship a second longer than we had to."

United Nations weapons inspectors collected evidence from the *Vermont* before a team from USAMRIID came aboard to sterilize her interior. The inspectors found that the Tomahawk warheads contained viable powdered *Yersinia pestis* of the strain that had infected the crew. They also discovered that one of the warheads was leaking. The United Nations Security Council reported that no definite conclusions could be drawn from the evidence unless divers found wreckage of the Chinese submarine purported to have attacked the *Vermont*.

A massive international search effort was laid on to determine whether the Chinese sub had been sunk. The United States paid for the search but did not participate. Each day that passed by with no results from the search made the world more skeptical of the survivors' farfetched claim that Chinese commandos had planted the *Vermont*'s biological warheads.

Chapter 70

After three weeks of tests to make sure none of them were infected, the nine survivors were flown home in a business jet. Chris was listening to Soony's reading of *The Three Musketeers* for the third time when the snowcapped peak of Mount Rainier came into view. It was lit by the pale orange glow of sunset. The majestic volcanic dome was the only land protruding above the blanket of clouds that obscured the coast of Washington State.

With a zing of anticipation and a grin so big it hurt, he thought, *She's down there somewhere*!

Barlow Scott was sitting beside him. Chris took off his headphones and said, "Sir, why do you think the Chinese want to frame us for having biological weapons? What did we ever do to them?"

Scott sighed. "It's not what we've done, Doc. It's what we were going to do. Those plague warheads are bound to be fully functional. If they weren't top-of-the-line technology, the UN inspectors would know they are not American made. That probably means China has the most massive and sophisticated bioweapons program in history, and they've kept it hidden all this time. They probably figured we were about to catch on to them, and this was their way of heading us off. Now we know their secret a little sooner than we would have, but we can't do a damn thing about it if the rest of the world thinks America is the country with a clandestine bioweapons program."

Chris lowered his voice. "Skipper, after all that's happened, and considering Freud's suicide, am I still going to have to face a court-martial for knocking him out?"

Scott gravely nodded. "It may not seem fair, Doc, but there can be no exceptions in the code of military justice."

A few minutes later, they were on the ground. The copilot finally opened the door, then dodged in the nick of time as Chris bolted from the cabin.

The passengers had to cross a hundred feet of tarmac to get to the terminal. When Chris saw the crowd of reporters, family, and publicity-hungry officials staring out through the windows, he slowed down and tried to look dignified.

"Dadgone, look at that!" Tumor said behind him. "Maybe we should get back on the plane, Doc."

Chris was searching the faces in the windows. He couldn't see her. After four or five steps, his dignity gave out and he ran the rest of the way, ignoring the pain it caused in his healing wounds.

When he stepped inside, the throng converged, forming a barricade around him. He stood on his tiptoes, peering over the forest of cameras and microphone booms.

"Mr. Long, does the United States have a biological weapons program?"

"No."

"How does it feel to be home?"

"Great."

"Have you suffered any symptoms of post-traumatic stress disorder?"

"A few."

"Are you going to stay in the Navy?"

"You bet. Excuse me." He reached out his massive arms and gently parted the paparazzi as if they were bushes in a jungle. He'd seen something bobbing up and down way back in the crowd. It looked like the top of someone's head, someone who was short and had straight black hair.

"Chris!"

"Soony!"

He was careful not to trample any of the gawkers who were separating them. Most of the people in his way saw the look in his eyes and hastily stepped aside.

She leaped into his arms.

He swung her around, squeezing her as tightly as he thought was safe. "Thank you for being here," he whispered in her ear.

"Thank you for coming back," she wept. "I love you, Chris."

He continued holding her, closing his eyes as the cameramen caught up and began flashing away.

When he finally put her down, he saw his parents standing there, patiently waiting and smiling shyly for the cameras. He hugged them both.

It took another three hours to get Soony alone. They were in her car, and she was driving. They had just dropped off his parents in front of their motel.

"Soony, stop the car."

She hit the brake. "What's wrong?"

"Nothing. I have something to give you."

"Chris, I'm blocking traffic."

"That's okay. This can't wait."

He pulled out the somewhat worn velvet box and opened it so she could see the small diamond engagement ring. "Soony, will you marry me?"

A driver behind them honked, then sped around, gunning his engine.

She shifted to park and threw her arms around his neck. "Yes!"

"Tomorrow?" he asked.

"Tonight!" she replied.

Chris grinned. "Will tomorrow do? I don't think I could get the guys together tonight."

They found out that Washington State required a three-day waiting period after obtaining a marriage license before the ceremony could be performed. That gave them some time to prepare. The day of the wedding was the happiest day of Christopher Long's life, so far. The weather was fair, so he and Soony chose to be united under a towering hemlock in the backyard of Captain Scott's house. All of his eight surviving shipmates attended the simple ceremony. Some of them brought lavish wedding gifts, which he had not expected on such short notice. Their opinion of him now was clearly different from the blame and mistrust he had endured in the final days of the outbreak.

On their way to the car, the newlyweds were caught by another gang of reporters. Katie Onnopah, a tall and very thin African American representing Fox News, begged for a brief interview. Standing in Scott's driveway, she smiled into her cameraman's lens and began with an announcement of breaking news.

"About an hour ago, at approximately the same time Christopher Long and his bride were saying 'I do,' the Pentagon announced that the British research submersible, *Merganser*, has located wreckage on the seafloor off the southern coast of Java. The shipwreck is approximately five miles south of the location where the USS *Vermont* was hit by a torpedo on October fourteenth. According to Brian "Batty" O'Connor, the *Merganser*'s captain, the wreck looks like a military submarine. He said its appearance was, quote, 'fresh, no sediment on top, and whatever hit her blew her to smithereens.'"

Katie Onnopah explained some background for her viewers, then held her microphone in front of Barlow Scott. "Captain, do you think this wreck is the submarine you tried to hit?"

"I certainly hope so, Katie. I hope divers can get into the wreck soon."

She turned to Chris and the shipmates surrounding him. "This must be the news you gentlemen have been waiting for. Would any of you care to share your personal reactions?"

"It's the best news I've ever heard in my life," Chris said.

"I think we will all sleep more satisfactorily tonight," Eng said.

"Hallelujah," said Oral.

Chris noticed an unfamiliar gleam in Eng's lonely eyes. It appeared that Katie Onnopah had captured the gaunt engineer's attention with more than her microphone. He seemed to be peering at her hands, which bore no rings.

After the reporters broke up, Chris and Soony walked to her car. She got in and said, "Come on!"

"Just a sec." Chris was watching Eng, who was standing like a statue in the middle of the road, staring at the rear end of a blue Caprice Classic that was parked against the far curb. Katie Onnopah was standing beside the car, apparently waiting for another passenger. Chris could see three bumper stickers on the car. One said, IF YOU THINK EDUCATION IS EXPENSIVE, TRY IGNORANCE. Another said, RELIGION STOPS A THINKING MIND. The third said, IF YOU THINK PRAYER WORKS, PRAY FOR SOME COMMON SENSE.

Eng finally stopped staring and walked over to the blue car, stopping about ten feet from Katie. "Your car?" he asked.

She nodded and smiled.

"Nice car," he said, adjusting his enormous red-rimmed eyeglasses.

"Thank you," she replied.

Eng took a step closer, blocking a white van that had started to pull away from the curb. "Would you like a . . . uh . . . wedding cake?"

"Excuse me?"

"I mean a piece! Would you like a piece of wedding cake? I think there's some left, over on the, uh . . ."

Chris could stand no more. He squeezed himself into Soony's small Honda, reclining his seat so his bald head wouldn't rub the roof. Soony drove them toward their short and affordable honeymoon—a camping trip in Olympic National Park.

After the wedding, Tumor had an appointment with a man from New York. The man had said he wanted to look at the forty-seven drawings the young seaman from Tennessee had completed during his ordeal on the *Vermont* and his subsequent quarantine. They met in the drab white bachelor housing complex where Tumor lived. It was across a spruce-lined street from the identical building that Chris lived in. The visitor had said his name was Bernie Goldberg. He represented a consortium of art galleries.

Mr. Goldberg turned out to be short, fat, and about seventy years old. He was wearing an olive green suit.

Tumor laid out his drawings on the kitchen table and counter.

Mr. Goldberg paced back and forth in front of them for a while. "Very disturbing," he said. "Exquisite . . . unique . . . delightfully disturbing. How much are you asking?"

"I thought you just wanted to look at them," Tumor said. "That's what you said on the phone."

Bernie Goldberg laughed. "Good one, sonny. How much?"

"I'm sorry, Mr. Goldberg. They're not really for sale. I think these are probably the best pictures I've ever drawn."

Mr. Goldberg glanced at his watch. "I have to get back to the airport in an hour, sonny. If I were you, I'd close the deal today while this exhibit is still tied in to the news. Publicity depreciates fast."

The pressure made Tumor angry, so he threw out a ridiculous figure. "Fine! A million bucks!"

Mr. Goldberg glanced at the ceiling. "That's absurd. I could never get approval for more than two hundred."

"Two hundred dollars? No way!"

Mr. Goldberg laughed again. "Sonny, you've got a great sense of humor, considering what you've been through. Okay, I might be able to squeeze out two hundred twenty thousand."

"Oh!" Tumor said. "Oh, gee whiz . . ."

He made it to the carpeted living room before he fainted on the floor.

Chapter 71

Two weeks later, the *Vermont* survivors gathered at the Bremerton Yacht Club to wish Barlow Scott farewell. It was a sunny day, unusually warm for late autumn in the Seattle area. Scott had announced that he planned to make a solo voyage across the Pacific Ocean on the *Coral Sky,* his thirty-nine-foot cruising yacht. He had already resigned his Navy commission and put his house up for sale.

Chris was worried that Scott did not intend to ever return to land. He hadn't yet decided whether to tell any of the others about his concern.

The sailboat's open cockpit barely had room for nine men, but these nine were all accustomed to close quarters.

Standing down in the cabin beneath the helm, Scott handed up a can of peanuts and passed out bottles of beer from the built-in icebox. Chris noticed that the captain was clean-shaven except for his neatly trimmed red mustache. His horseshoe of reddish gray hair was freshly cut.

After everyone had a beer, Scott passed around a box of cigars. They all laughed at the sign he had taped on the lid: CERTIFIED FREE OF PLAGUE. Soon the crowded cockpit must have looked from a distance as if it were on fire. Chris leaned over the side to breathe.

"A toast," Scott said, raising his beer. "To the *Vermont* survivors!"

Chris clanked his bottle against Tumor's. "To brotherhood!"

The diminutive captain stood on the stairs to address his crew over the binnacle. "Gentlemen, the nightmare we lived through left us with something special, something no one can ever take away."

"Yeah, scars," Eng said around a mouthful of peanuts.

Instead of passing it on, the skinny engineer was holding the peanut can between his knees, gulping down its contents. Chris had noticed that Eng looked as self-absorbed as ever, but his expression now suggested dreamy enthusiasm rather than bitter resignation.

Scott sneezed several times. When he recovered, he said, "In all seriousness, I propose a pledge to maintain the solidarity of this group until the last of us passes on. What do you say?"

"Aye, sir!" Chris replied, and the others followed suit.

"The men who were killed defending our hatches are the real heroes," Oral said. "I recommend we make taking care of their graves and families the top priorities of this little club."

They all agreed.

"Now I have an announcement to make," Scott said. "Keep this to yourselves until it's officially released. We are off the meat hook and the Chinese are on it!"

"Yeha!" Tumor cheered.

"All right!" Chris said. "Divers got into the wreck?"

Scott nodded. "They found our tactical nuclear warheads; also, the custom-built tools those turkeys used to make the switch. Another thing they discovered was kind of strange—the Chinese army colonel who was leading the commandos had a bullet lodged in his skull. The sub's captain was lying right beside him with a pistol in his hand. You have to wonder what happened on that boat in the final seconds before our units homed in on it."

Scott passed out another round of beers. "Now, what's

this I hear about you reenlisting, Doc?" He was scowling disapprovingly at Chris.

"You think I shouldn't, sir?"

"Damn right, I think you shouldn't. You should get commissioned through the Seaman to Admiral program and go to the best college you can get into. I know your grades in high school weren't up to muster, but—trust me—you won't have any problem becoming an officer."

"How do you know that, sir?"

Scott grinned. "Consider it a token of my appreciation for saving my ship and my life."

"Sir, I appreciate it, but I believe the drawbacks of command outweigh its advantages."

"You may be right, Doc. But if you truly want to serve your country, you'll do what you do best. All of us here have seen your ability to take the initiative and lead other men. That talent will not be fully utilized if you don't go for a commission."

There were nods and murmurs of agreement.

"You would be several years behind most ensigns, but you would also be one of the few who already have combat experience," Eng added.

"By the way," Scott said, "the University of Washington football coach called me to chat last night, and your name seemed to keep coming up."

Trying not to squirm, Chris said, "Do you guys really think it would be the best way for me to serve?"

"We do," Eng said, chewing the last of the peanuts.

The others all agreed.

Chris shook his head. "Okay, then, I'll do it."

"Excellent," Scott said. "Now, who wants to come down and help me make burgers?"

Chris volunteered. He climbed around the helm and stepped down the marine ladder, an acrobatic stunt for a man his size.

Stooping beneath the low overhead, he glanced around the cabin. He noticed that it seemed to be provisioned for a very long voyage. He also saw that the bookshelf atop the short sofa across from the stove was packed with heavy reading, mostly maritime history. The narrow windows between the books and the overhead were lined with tins of ginseng tea.

Chris was looking for a missing bottle of Tabasco sauce when he opened an unlabeled drawer and could hardly believe what he saw: packs of new condoms, at least a hundred of them.

Scott saw him staring and blushed. "Hey, get out of there! You don't need those anymore."

Chris continued looking for the hot sauce, turning away so Scott couldn't see his grin. "Where exactly did you say you're going, sir?"

Scott glanced up at the others in the cockpit. They were busy advising Tumor on how to shop for a house. The captain lowered his voice to make sure they couldn't hear him over their own conversation.

"I was faithful to Darlene all those years, Doc. But whenever I had fantasies, I was always with some exotic beauty on one of those South Pacific islands, you know? You only live once, and I've got nothing to lose. I'm going to sail down there and try my luck."

Chris was still grinning. "Hey, go for it, skipper. Just go for it."

Epilogue

At his court-martial for assaulting an officer, Christopher Long was acquitted on the basis of testimony by eight witnesses to his character and to the character of his alleged victim.

Eight months after the tragedy on board the *Vermont,* the FBI's foreign counterintelligence division arrested Fingshan Wu, a cryptographer at STRATCOM headquarters in Nebraska. A year later, Wu was convicted of espionage for selling copies of secret U.S. communications to Chinese intelligence officers. He was sentenced to life in prison.

On the eve of the planned American invasion, the Iranian military surrendered unconditionally. Weapons inspectors from the United Nations searched the country and concluded that Iran had no facilities capable of manufacturing the sophisticated anthrax weapon contained in the warheads of their Spear of Allah missiles. Under international pressure to reveal the source of the warheads, the Iranians admitted that they had secretly purchased them several years before from a covert program sponsored by the People's Liberation Army/Navy of China.

THIS MARINE UNIT IS FIGHTING A
VERY DIFFERENT KIND OF COLD WAR...

DEEP
CURRENT

by
Benjamin E. Miller

A marine unit, accompanied by a science
team, is deployed to investigate an iceberg
larger than Manhattan that poses a threat
of incalculable scope as it flows against
the current, leaving a path of destruction
in its wake.
And it's heading—*aiming*—for Hawaii.

Their mission: land on the floe, itself, and
do whatever it takes to disable the threat.

0-451-41129-3

Available wherever books are sold or at
penguin.com

S825

ZERØ

A NOVEL OF TECHNOLOGY V. NATURE

HOUR

THE

COUNTDOWN

BEGINS.

ONYX

BENJAMIN
E. MILLER

AVAILABLE IN PAPERBACK FROM ONYX
0-451-41000-9

ONYX

CHRISTOPHER HYDE

The first conspiracy of World War II begins with

THE SECOND ASSASSIN
A Novel

The year: 1939—and the world readies itself for a war that is sure to come.
The conspirators: A group of powerful men who want to keep America out of the approaching conflict—at all costs.
The plan: Assassinate the King and Queen of England on American soil, destroying any hope of an alliance between Great Britain and the United States—and ensuring victory for the Nazis in World War II.

0-451-41030-0

And don't miss
THE HOUSE OF
SPECIAL PURPOSE

0-451-41108-0

Available wherever books are sold or at
penguin.com

S630

ONYX

**"A master storyteller...the finest
adventure writer on the scene today."
—Clive Cussler**

JACK Du BRUL

The Medusa Stone   0-451-40922-1
Ten years ago, the spy satellite *Medusa* burned up upon
reentry—but not before its sensors revealed a secret buried
deep in the earth, hidden for thousands of years from the
eyes of humanity. A priceless discovery that some would
die to find—and kill to possess.

Pandora's Curse   0-451-40963-9
During World War II, in a secret Nazi submarine base,
boxes made from looted wartime gold were hidden away.
These "Pandora's boxes" contained an artifact so lethal that
whoever possessed them held the power to unleash hell
upon the Earth.

River of Ruin   0-451-41054-8
At a Paris auction house, geologist Philip Mercer's bid for a
rare diary makes him the target of three ruthless assassins.
Why? The answer is in the diary.

Deep Fire Rising   0-451-41118-8
Philip Mercer finds himself drilling straight into the epicen-
ter of an age-old conspiracy when a reclusive order of
monks predicts the end of the world.

Available wherever books are sold or at
penguin.com

S541

ONYX   (0451)

USA TODAY Bestselling Author
MICHAEL DIMERCURIO

"A master rivaling Tom Clancy."

—*Publishers Weekly*

Terminal Run   410467
The new techno-thriller featuring the dramatic,
final undersea showdown between Admiral
Michael Pacino and his most hated nemesis,
Alexi Novskoyy.

Threat Vector   409086
Submarine commander Alexi Novskoyy has
been sprung from prison by a multi-billion-dollar
organization with a special agenda: wreak
havoc on international trade...

Also Available:

Voyage of the Devilfish   410122

Barracuda: Final Bearing   407423

Attack of the Sea Wolf   180518

Available wherever books are sold or at
penguin.com

S539

Penguin Group (USA) Online

What will you be reading tomorrow?

Tom Clancy, Patricia Cornwell, W.E.B. Griffin,
Nora Roberts, William Gibson, Robin Cook,
Brian Jacques, Catherine Coulter, Stephen King,
Dean Koontz, Ken Follett, Clive Cussler,
Eric Jerome Dickey, John Sandford,
Terry McMillan…

You'll find them all at
penguin.com

*Read excerpts and newsletters,
find tour schedules and reading group guides,
and enter contests.*

Subscribe to Penguin Group (USA) newsletters
and get an exclusive inside look
at exciting new titles and the authors you love
long before everyone else does.

PENGUIN GROUP (USA)
penguin.com/news